T 8349

Donated
by
Kathy Babst

p 273
True
Detective

Books by Jonathan Kellerman

FICTION

ALEX DELAWARE NOVELS

Bones (2008)
Compulsion (2008)
Obsession (2007)
Gone (2006)
Rage (2005)
Therapy (2004)
A Cold Heart (2003)
The Murder Book (2002)
Flesh and Blood (2001)
Dr. Death (2000)
Monster (1999)
Survival of the Fittest (1997)
The Clinic (1997)
The Web (1996)
Self-Defense (1995)
Bad Love (1994)
Devil's Waltz (1993)
Private Eyes (1992)
Time Bomb (1990)
Silent Partner (1989)
Over the Edge (1987)
Blood Test (1986)
When the Bough Breaks (1985)

OTHER NOVELS

True Detectives (2009)
Capital Crimes (with Faye Kellerman, 2006)
Twisted (2004)
Double Homicide (with Faye
Kellerman, 2004)
The Conspiracy Club (2003)
Billy Straight (1998)
The Butcher's Theater (1988)

NONFICTION

*With Strings Attached: The Art and Beauty
of Vintage Guitars* (2008)
*Savage Spawn: Reflections on Violent
Children* (1999)
Helping the Fearful Child (1981)
*Psychological Aspects of Childhood
Cancer* (1980)

FOR CHILDREN, WRITTEN AND ILLUSTRATED

*Jonathan Kellerman's ABC of Weird
Creatures* (1995)
*Daddy, Daddy, Can You Touch
the Sky?* (1994)

TRUE DETECTIVES

JONATHAN KELLERMAN

TRUE DETECTIVES

A NOVEL

**Doubleday Large Print
Home Library Edition**

BALLANTINE BOOKS

NEW YORK

This Large Print Edition, prepared especially for Doubleday Large Print Home Library, contains the complete, unabridged text of the original Publisher's Edition.

Copyright © 2009 by Jonathan Kellerman

Published in the United States by Ballantine Books, an imprint of The Random House Publishing Group, a division of Random House, Inc., New York.

BALLANTINE and colophon are registered trademarks of Random House, Inc.

ISBN 978-1-60751-681-1

Printed in the United States of America on acid-free paper

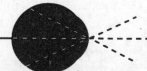

**This Large Print Book carries the
Seal of Approval of N.A.V.H.**

In memory of
Marcia Biloon

TRUE DETECTIVES

1

August 9, 1979

Alleged air-conditioning," said Darius Fox. "What's your take, John Jasper? Motor pool morons set us on bake or broil?"

Jack Reed laughed and used a meaty, freckled forearm to clear sweat from his face. Scanning the night-darkened dumpsters and butt-sides of shuttered, low-rent businesses that lined the alley, he sucked on his Parliament and blew smoke out the cruiser's window as Darius kept the car moving forward at ten mph.

Ten years ago, to the day, the Manson Family had butchered Sharon Tate and a whole bunch of other people. If either Fox or Reed was aware of the anniversary, neither thought it worth mentioning.

Crazy Charlie's crimes might as well have been on another planet; big-ticket outrage on high-end real estate. Fox and Reed's Southwest Division shifts were filled with nonstop penny-ante crap that sometimes blossomed into stomach-churning violence. Reality that never made the papers because, as far as they could see, the papers were works of fiction.

Fox said, "Man, it's a steam bath."

Reed said, "Alleged, as in this is a motor vehicle. More like a shopping cart with a cherry on top."

Fox had prepped for driving the way he usually did, hand-vacuuming the driver's portion of the bench seat, then wiping the steering wheel down with his private bottle of Purell. Now it was his own sweat coating the plastic. "Hand me a tissue, J.J."

Reed complied and his partner rubbed the wheel till it squeaked.

Both men continued to study the alley as they crawled. Nothing. Good. One half of the shift had passed.

Jack Reed said, "Alleged, as in Jimmy Carter's a commander in chief."

"Now you're getting unpleasantly political."

"That's a problem?"

"Night like this it is."

"Truth is truth, Darius. It was Peanut Boy helped that loony towel-head back into Eye-Ran and look at all the crap that brought down."

"No debate on Farmer Bucktooth being a nitwit, John Jasper. I just don't want to pollute our precious time together with small things like international affairs."

Reed thought about that. "Fair enough."

"I'm known for my fairness."

Slow shift; the usual drunk and disorderlies at Mexican dance halls on Vermont, a couple of false-alarm burglary calls, an assortment of miscreants warned and released because none of them was worth the paperwork.

The last call they'd fielded before embarking on alley-duty was yet another noise complaint at a USC fraternity, already taken care of by the campus rent-a-cops by the time Fox and Reed arrived. Rich, confident college boys saying yessir and nossir, scooping up beer bottles from the lawn, hurrying inside to continue the merriment. Wink wink wink.

Reed smoked his Parliament down to a shred, pinched it cold between his fingers, flicked the remnant out the window. He was a ruddy, blond fireplug, five nine on a good day, two hundred muscled pounds, thirty but looking older, with skin leathered by the sun and a nose flattened by high school football. A hay-colored crewcut topped his bullet skull. A naturally grainy voice was coarsened further by two packs a day.

Three years out of the service, all his time spent running an armory in Germany.

He said, "Tell you what *alleged* is, Darius: L.A. nights cooling off. Night like this, might as well have stayed in Bull Shoals."

"And missed the opportunity to ride with me?"

Reed grinned. "Perish the thought."

"Damn heat," said Fox, dabbing sweat from his straight-edge mustache. He was a tall, rangy black man, thirty-one years old, a former air force mechanic who'd been told by many people that he was handsome enough to act.

Jack Reed, a small-town Arkansas boy,

was comfortable with black people in a way northerners could never be. He found L.A. scary. Everyone pretending to love everyone else but the streets hummed with anger.

Working with a black man—sitting side by side, eating, talking, trusting your life to a black man—was a whole different level of comfort for a transplanted southerner, and he was surprised how fast he'd gotten used to riding with Darius.

Knowing what Darius was thinking without Darius having to put it into words.

He could only imagine what his cousins would say if he bothered to talk to them anymore, which he didn't. All that ignorance and stupidity was history.

He contemplated another cigarette as Darius exited the alley, drove a block, entered a neighboring back lane. More garbage and accordion-grated rear doors.

Same old same old; both patrolmen were bored and crazy-hot.

Darius used his forearm to wipe sweat off his chin. Shiny nails flashed. Jack resisted the urge to kid his partner about the weekly manicures. Night like this, no sense being tiresome.

Jack had been to Darius's neat little bungalow in Crenshaw for barbecues and the like, played with Darius's little boy, made chitchat with the woman Darius was supposed to be committed to till death do us.

Madeleine Fox was a small-waisted, curvy, strong-featured white girl who thought she was an artist but had no talent anyone else could perceive. Great teeth and hair, even better body. Those big soft . . . Jack imagined Darius getting close to her. Sliding down the bed and putting his manicured hands on . . . Jack's own face and body and hands transferred to the scene.

Feeling like a shit, he shut down the movie, lit up another Parliament.

"You okay?" said Darius.

"Yeah."

"You got fidgety. Pumping those knees, like you do."

"I'm fine."

"Okay."

"Okay, what?"

"You fidget when something's bugging you."

"Nothing's bugging me."

"Okay."

Jack said, "All that intuition, apply for detective."

"Big fun," said Darius. "Sitting on my ass all day typing, no more stimulating conversation with you? Not to mention fringe benefits?"

Jack had been riding with Darius for thirteen months, knew the perks his partner was talking about.

Comped meals, "donations" of merchandise by grateful civilians.

Last week, both he and Darius had gotten brand-new pocket calculators from an Arab with a store on Hoover after they'd busted two kids trying to shoplift cassette tapes.

Darius's favorite perk had nothing to do with tangible goods.

Police groupies. Hit the right cop bar at the right time and they swarmed like ants on molasses.

Sad girls, for the most part, not Jack's thing. But he didn't judge.

Sometimes he wondered, though. Darius married to a good-looking, downright sexy girl like Maddy, nice backyard, cute little Aaron.

Jack ever got married, he was pretty sure he'd never step out.

Sometimes he thought about Maddy, those teeth. The rest of the package. Sometimes that brought on headaches and long, itchy thoughts. Mostly when his crappy little single in Inglewood got real quiet and *Penthouse* wasn't gonna cut it.

Darius said, "Wind blows the heat in, then the heat just sits down and stays until another wind finally decides to kick its ass out of town."

Jack said, "Tonight's weather report is brought to you by Cal Worthington Dodge. Now for the latest on them Dodgers."

Darius laughed. "Nasty night like this, almost a full moon on top of the heat, you'd think we'd be having more fun."

"People carving each other up," said Jack.

"People shooting each other full of holes," said Darius.

"People stomping each other till the brains ooze out of their cracked skulls."

"People strangling each other till the tongues are sticking out like limp . . . salamis."

"For a moment I thought you were

gonna say something else—hey, look at the land-yacht."

Pointing up the alley to a big white car idling, maybe ten yards up, pulled to the left. Lights off but the security bulb of a neighboring building cast an oblique band of yellow across the vehicle's rear end.

Darius said, "Caddy, looks pretty new. How come it's smoking worse than you?"

He rolled closer and each of them made out the model.

Big white Fleetwood, matching vinyl top, fake wire wheels. Tinted windows shut tight.

Someone's A.C. wasn't alleged.

Darius rolled close enough to read the tags. Jack called in the numbers.

One-year-old Caddy, registered to Arpad Avakian, address on Edgemont Street, no wants or warrants.

Darius said, "East Hollywood Armenian. Bit of a drive to Southwest."

Jack said, "Maybe something worth driving for."

"*Real* worth driving for."

Both of them thinking the same thing without having to say it: no logical reason for Arpad Armenian or whoever was using

his wheels to be in this crap-dump neighborhood in a newish luxury boat unless
someone had a serious *jones.*

Dope or sex.

Or both.

Guy with a fresh Caddy had the potential to be a fun bust, bit of diversion from
the brain-dead locals they usually dealt
with.

If Arpad was polite, they might even let
him go with a warning. Some of those Hollywood Armenians owned stereo stores
and the like. Nothing wrong with chalking
up another grateful civilian.

Darius got closer, put the cruiser in
Park. Got out of the car before Jack could
place his hand on the door handle.

Jack watched his partner hitch up his
trousers, approach the Caddy with the cop
swagger that originated when you learned
to walk with all that heavy gear on your belt.
Like making your way on the rolling deck
of a boat; eventually, you came to like it.

Darius walked right up next to the Caddy,
shined his flashlight at the driver's window,
holding it high, the way they were trained, to
prevent it being grabbed. His free hand hovered near his holstered .38, and Jack felt

his own paw settling on his weapon. Nowadays everything had to be logged, so he called in the stop, caught a bad connection on the radio, tried twice more before reaching Dispatch.

Meanwhile, Darius was rapping on the window.

Tinted almost black. It stayed closed.

"Police, open up."

The Caddy sat there, smoking away.

Maybe suicide? Or a carbon mono accident? Normally, you had to be in an indoor situation to asphyxiate yourself with exhaust, but Jack had heard about venting gone bad.

"Open up *now.*" Darius put that menacing edge in his voice. You'd never know this was a guy who loved his weekly salon manicure.

The Caddy's window remained shut.

As Darius repeated the command, he reached to unsnap his holster and Jack moved for his own gun and opened the cruiser's passenger door.

Just as he got to his feet, the window slid down silently.

Whatever Darius saw relaxed him. He dropped his gun arm. Smiled.

Jack relaxed, too.

"License and reg—"

The night cracked.

Three shots in rapid succession. Each hit Darius square in the chest. Each caused him to buck.

He didn't fall back the way they did in the movies. He sank down into a sitting position, hands flat on the asphalt, as the Caddy lurched into gear and shot forward.

At first glance, just a guy resting.

Crazily, Jack thought: He's okay.

Then Darius pivoted, half faced Jack. What looked like motor oil leaked through Darius's tailored navy shirt. His face was that of a stranger.

Jack screamed and fired at the fleeing car. Emptying his revolver as he ran to Darius.

"Oh man, oh Jesus, oh man, Lord Jesus . . ."

Later, he'd learn that one of his bullets had pierced the Caddy's rear window, but that hadn't slowed the big car down.

Darius continued to sit there. Three wet holes in his chest.

Jack cradled him, put pressure on the

wounds. "Hold on, Dar, you're gonna be fine, just hold on hold on hold on."

Darius stared at the sky with dull, sightless eyes.

His mouth gaped.

Jack felt for a pulse. Gimme something, c'mon, c'mon, gimme . . .

Darius's skin turned to ice.

Jack began CPR, covering Darius's cold mouth with his own.

Like breathing into an empty cave.

Darius lay there.

Still as the heat that had blown in from the desert and decided to stay.

2

By now, Aaron Fox understood Mr. Dmitri.

Once a level of trust had developed, he'd stay out of your face.

Aaron's favorite type of client.

Real deep pockets made Mr. Dmitri the *perfect* client.

Before his first meeting with the guy, Aaron had done his usual research. Googling *Leonid Davidovitch Dmitri* and coming up with two dozen hits, the most informative a rags-to-riches tale in a business journal: Moscow born, trained as an electrical engineer, Dmitri had been stuck for fifteen years in a dead-end Communist job measuring noise levels at restaurants and filing reports that never got read. At the age of thirty-seven, he'd emigrated to Israel, then the U.S., taught night school math and physics to other Russians, tinkered in his kitchen, inventing numerous objects of dubious value.

Ten years ago, he'd patented a tiny, wafer-thin stereo speaker that produced outsized sound and was perfect for cars—especially high-end sports models with their limited cabin space.

Aaron's Porsche had been outfitted with Dmitri's gizmo when he'd had it customized and the fidelity was kick-ass.

The article estimated Mr. Dmitri's net worth at a couple hundred million, and Aaron was expecting to meet some tycoon sitting behind an acre of desk in an over-the-top inner sanctum crammed with imitation Fabergé and God knew what else.

What he encountered was a short, bald, stubby-limbed, bullnecked man in his late fifties with a pie-tin face blued by stubble, sitting behind a plywood desk in a no-window hole at a factory in a Sylmar industrial park.

Dmitri was maybe five five, at least two hundred, lots of that muscle, but also some fat. Dark brown laser-sharp eyes never stopped moving.

Two hundred biggies, but the guy wasn't spending it on wardrobe. Short-sleeved pale blue shirt, baggy gray pleated pants, gray New Balances. Aaron came to learn that it was Dmitri's uniform.

Cheap digital watch.

Fake-o tongue-and-groove covered all four walls of the office. Same for the door, giving the place a claustrophobic feel.

That first meeting, he'd played it safe clothes-wise, not knowing what kind of rapport he'd have to develop with the client.

That kind of individual attention was one of the many keys to Aaron's success.

Variety was what he liked about the job. One day you might be meeting at Koi with a pathetically tucked, youth-chasing record producer still thinking he could pull off hip-hop. Chopsticking miso black cod and waiting as the client struggled for nonchalance, inside he's rotting from insecurity as he fumbles to explain his reason for hiring a detective.

Finally the confession: He needs to

know, is his twenty-seven-year-old fourth wife blowing the good-looking guy someone saw her with at Fred Segal, or is Darrett really a gay hairdresser she took along as a shopping buddy?

Situation like that, you don't dress down to the client's level but you don't wear a suit. Aaron met the poor fool wearing indigo Diesel jeans, a slate-colored, retro Egyptian cotton T-shirt from VagueLine, unstructured black linen jacket, perforated black Santoni driving shoes.

The following day, he was at a downtown law firm, corporate client talking through a six-hundred-dollar-an-hour mouthpiece, needing someone to check out the goings-on at a Temple Street construction site where tools and building materials were disappearing at an alarming rate. For that one, Aaron chose a navy pin-striped Paul Smith made-to-measure, pearl-gray Ferré shirt, maroon Sego tie, blue pocket square, brown kidskin Magli loafers.

Enjoying the feeling of good threads because tomorrow, he'd be made up like a skuzzy, psycho homeless bum, wheeling a shopping cart past the excavation.

For Aaron's first meeting with Mr. Dmitri,

he selected an olive Zegna Soft three-button he'd found at the outlet in Cabazon, maize button-collar shirt and brown linen tie from Barneys, bittersweet chocolate Allen-Edmonds wingtips.

For all Mr. Dmitri noticed, Aaron could've pranced in wearing leotards and a codpiece.

Guy was ready to offer him the job, knew Aaron's rates, including the premium expense allowance, had a big fat retainer check faceup on the desk.

Big fat retainer.

"May I ask who referred you, sir?"

Dmitri picked up something that resembled a Rubik's Cube but had about twenty surfaces to it and squares embossed with Greek letters. Without glancing at the numbers, he whirled rapidly, checked out the result, put it back down.

"Certainly, you may ask." Foghorn voice. Dmitri's accent turned it into *Syertenly you mayyesk.*

Smiling.

"Who referred you, sir?"

Dmitri said, "Serinus Canaria."

Another foreign guy? Didn't ring a bell. "I'm sorry, sir, but that doesn't—"

Dmitri said, "Common canary."

Aaron stared.

"Little bird," said Dmitri. No more smile. "You want the job or no?"

Aaron glanced around the office for signs of some special interest in ornithology. Nothing on the hideous paneling except curling posters of Mr. Dmitri's patented SoundMyte speaker in "new-age designer colors."

Aaron said, "Tell me about the job."

"Good answer, Mr. Fox."

The first assignment had been shockingly simple—pilfering from Dmitri's shipping bay. The culprit had to be one of six clerks, and within thirty-six hours Aaron had the idiot on hidden cam slipping speakers into four backpacks, stashing one after the other into the trunk of his Camry.

Slam-dunk, three-thousand-dollar tab. Aaron wondered why a man of Mr. Dmitri's technical abilities had bothered to hire out.

Testing Aaron?

If so, he'd passed, because the second gig arrived two months later and it was anything but simple.

One of Dmitri's secretaries was concerned that her seventeen-year-old honor-student daughter was "fooling around" with a gangbanger named Hector George Morales.

"Find out, Mr. Fox. I'll take it from there."

"Nice of you to do that for an employee, sir."

"Here's the check."

Morales turned out to be a serious badass, third-generation Mexican Mafia, with a five-page juvey sheet Aaron cadged out of an LAPD records clerk using a hundred-dollar bribe. Ten additional pages recounted a pattern of adult felonies. Morales was suspected of several murders but had only been convicted of a single ADW, serving half of a ten-year sentence at Chino. Thirty-three years old, the fool hung out with extremely bad guys in clear violation of his parole.

Aaron caught him and honor-student-but-not-so-smart Valerie Santenegro on video emerging from an East L.A. motel near the county coroner's office, reported to Mr. Dmitri, and offered to use his LAPD contacts to get Hector busted.

"Good idea, Mr. Fox."

Hector got sent back up for another ten and Valerie was shipped to Dallas to live with her married sister's family.

Mr. Dmitri said, "Good," and peeled off a wad of bills.

Ten extra hundreds. "What's this, sir?"

"Appreciation, Mr. Fox. Go buy more fancy shirts."

Over the past six months, Aaron had handled two additional assignments for the Russian: industrial espionage involving a competitor that took him to Eugene, Oregon, for three weeks of serious high-tech observation, and another in-house theft at the Sylmar factory, this one involving truck drivers.

Every suspect turned up guilty, which was no big surprise. Guy like Dmitri didn't hire you unless he had a pretty good idea what was going on. Aaron's business, in general, posed few whodunits, lots of prove-its.

The fifth case was different.

Dmitri played with his mega-Rubik's. "You are well, Mr. Fox?"

"Great."

"I'm thinking, perhaps I should call you Aaron."

"That would be fine, sir."

"You may call me Mr. Dmitri."

Aaron laughed.

"Yes, it was a joke." An edge to the Russian's voice said, Don't even think about getting familiar.

"Aaron," said Dmitri, as if testing out the sound. "From the Bible. Your parents are religious?"

"Not really, sir."

"Moses's brother."

"Yes, sir." *If you only knew.*

"This new one," said Dmitri, "maybe we won't learn the truth. One of my bookkeepers is Maitland Frostig. Master's degree in mathematics but he prefers to work with addition and subtraction. Mr. Frostig always looks sad. More recently, he is apparently sadder. I say apparently because I don't get involved with emotions. This year, the Christmas party, my wife said, 'That man is extremely depressed. Like we used to be in Moscow.' I looked at Maitland Frostig with . . . new eyes and agreed. But I forgot about him."

Dmitri ran a hand over his shiny dome. "My wife did not forget. She is a psychiatrist. In Soviet Union they tried to make her inject dissidents with drugs. She refused and was sent to gulag. We never had children."

"I'm sorry, sir."

"Regina talks, I listen. I called in Maitland Frostig for a meeting, he says everything is okay. I tell him no it isn't." Small smile. "I say it with confidence because my wife is never wrong."

"In general, sir, that's a good philosophy of life."

"You are not married." Statement, not a question. Aaron was certain Dmitri had hired someone to check him out before writing that first check. Maybe one day he'd find out who.

"Haven't found the right woman."

"Maybe," said Dmitri said. "Anyway, I tell Maitland Frostig something is wrong and he tells me the story. He lives alone, a widower since his daughter is four. Now the daughter is twenty and she is missing. Caitlin Frostig. For fifteen months she is missing, the police do nothing."

"Someone that age," said Aaron, "no sign of foul play, they'll file it as a missing person and put it aside."

"I made some calls, got the file sent to Homicide detectives. Nothing."

"Which division?"

"I don't know."

"Where was the girl last seen?"

"Maitland's house is in Venice."

"Twenty and still living at home."

"Yes."

"Venice is Pacific Division."

Shrug. *Don't bother me with details.* "Police do nothing. My call was before I know you. Now I know you."

3

Forget yesterday. What have you done for me today?

Moe Reed—scarlet-faced, panting, biceps swelling to their full nineteen inches, put down the curl-bar and tried to catch his breath.

His arms pounded. *All* of him pounded.

Hundred forty pounds on the bar, four sets of fifteen reps each.

No doubt some felonious scumbag in a prison yard was outlifting him at this very moment, but for one of the good guys, Moe figured he was doing okay.

Job-wise was another story.

Leaving the spare bedroom he'd set up as a home gym, he walked to the bathroom dripping sweat on the carpet, toweled off, stripped down, stepped into a cold shower.

After as much of that as he felt like enduring, he cranked up the hot water and shampooed his wheat-colored crew cut. Soaped up the rest of his thick, iron-hard body and dried off.

The soap part used to take longer. His own hands no longer aroused him. Not since Liz.

He thought about calling her, just to hear her voice, remembered she'd just gotten back from that bone conference in Brussels, would be suffering through her usual jet lag, better to give her some time.

By seven a.m. he was dressed in the usual blue blazer, khakis, white shirt and striped tie and black oxfords. Breakfast was hot tea, three bowls of Special K, and nonfat milk chased with a boneless chicken breast. By half past seven he was climbing into his latest heap, a rust-scarred Dodge. The drive from North Hollywood to West L.A. could be brutal and he wanted to be at his desk early, even if the detectives figured him for a hot dog who needed to prove himself.

Forget yesterday. What have you done . . .

He'd been part of the team that closed the marsh murders, high-profile, great P.R. for the department. Success had earned him a nod from Deputy Chief Weinberg and quick approval of his transfer from Pacific to West L.A. Division.

Since arriving at his new desk, the only attention he'd received from downtown were memos on the case he thought he was leaving behind.

In Re: Caitlin Frostig.

Nice girl, Caitlin. From all he'd gathered.

For the last eight months she'd been nothing but a thorn in his butt.

He'd made it to Pacific Homicide a year ago, not bad for twenty-eight, got assigned to a no-brainer gang shooting that he closed in seventy-four hours.

His second case was Caitlin Frostig, already missing for half a year by the time her file got transferred from the unsolveds of an old D who dropped dead of a heart attack.

Not a homicide case, strictly speaking. But someone with pull—Moe never found out who—wanted the case prioritized.

He started the way you're supposed to, with family. In Caitlin's case that boiled down to a mumbly-nerd father who'd raised her alone since she was little but didn't seem to know much about her beyond the obvious. The other man in her life was a boyfriend named Rory Stoltz who came across so wholesome that he set off Moe's antennae.

Also, nine times out of ten it's Romeo who kills Juliet.

This Romeo turned out to be alibied for the night Caitlin walked out of the Riptide. Moe dug into Stoltz's background anyway, turned up nothing but All-American Lad, basically Caitlin's male counterpart. Still living at home, waiting tables at the same place, studying hard. Both of them A students at Pepperdine, Malibu.

Rory's eyes got misty when he recounted meeting Caitlin in a philosophy class.

Moe questioned him to the nth, nothing there.

Caitlin's dad let Moe search her room. No sign of foul play—none anywhere in the little frame house on Rialto, south side of Venice. Hipness encroached all around the neighborhood but Maitland Frostig hadn't changed a doily since his wife's death sixteen years before.

Real quiet, real depressed guy. Moe got permission to trace Caitlin's Discover card. No recent activity.

No California Jane Doe DBs matched the missing girl and from what Moe could gather, she'd led an exceptionally boring life: studying hard, working at night, no social life other than Rory Stoltz. Moe rechecked Stoltz, came up empty. Turned to missing persons databases, working his way east until he'd covered the entire country. He even tried police departments in Mexico, for what that was worth.

Last step was dealing with Canada, which was no easy feat, place was huge and the cops were cautious. Still, he managed to cover Our Northern Neighbor.

Zilch. As Milo Sturgis would say.

He talked to Sturgis about Caitlin, because the lieutenant had been his guru on the marsh murders.

Be honest, Moses, Sturgis solved the marsh murders and you tailed along.

Talk about continuing education; working with someone that seasoned was a semester at Homicide Harvard. Wanting to learn more from the lieutenant was the reason he'd requested transfer to West L.A.

If he lost Caitlin Frostig along the way because her file bore a Pacific Division number, all the better.

Once news of his request got out, the wisecracks from the other Pacific D's were a pain in the butt.

Changing your sexual orientation, Detective Reed?

Is that eye shadow? Or just too much Ecstasy at that Boystown dance club, what's it called, oh yeah, Do Me Bob.

Don't ask, don't tell. Most of all, please don't swell.

Moe ignored them. When he'd started with Sturgis, to be honest, there was that initial discomfort.

Hard to believe a big, gruff guy like that

was . . . who cared what people did in private, the thing was the job and Sturgis *did* the job.

Some years—lots of years—the lieutenant ended up with the best close record in the department.

Moe let the jokes sail past. If the transfer didn't come through, staying here would be hell.

It came through.

The Frostig file traveled with him.

Second day at his new desk, he left the big detective room and knocked on the doorjamb of the tiny office set well away from the big detective room.

Sturgis was in there, unlit cigar in his mouth, big feet on his desk, reviewing what looked to be cold cases.

"What?"

Moe told him.

Sturgis said, "Sounds like you've done everything."

"That's what I thought, but any suggestions, Loo?"

"Not from what you've told me."

"Okay, thanks."

"You might wanna check with Dr. Delaware."

"This is a psycho case?" said Moe. "You're assuming she's dead?"

Sturgis stretched, played with the cigar. "Kiddo, everything's psychological, but that doesn't mean we need shrinks for it. Mostly, it's a matter of connecting dots. But this kind of thing . . . sometimes he comes up with an idea out of left field— didja happen to notice the coffee situation out in Times Square?"

"Still hot," said Moe. "I'll get you a cup."

"Cream, two sugars."

Delaware was friendly enough, but no wisdom there, either, and Moe figured this was one that wouldn't close unless some bones turned up somewhere.

If she *was* dead. Boring life like hers, maybe she'd gotten an itch for more.

Last week, he'd made his way through the maze that was Federal Records for the second time. As far as anyone could tell, no one had commandeered Caitlin's Social Security number, no other signs of identity theft.

The unused credit card did make him wonder. If the girl was alive, what was she doing for dough?

Maybe working in a small town where the locals weren't nosy. Or she'd joined a cult. Run away with the circus.

Met a rich guy and got swept off her feet.

Any of that was true, she wouldn't *want* to be found.

He thought about that pretty face, the slender body, the cloud of blond hair. Six feet under or discarded with haphazard brutality in some remote gully.

Or weighed down and dumped in deep water, psycho killer watching her fade from view . . .

Time and bacteria doing their inevitable thing.

Death one, Moses zero.

CHAPTER

4

Aaron met with Maitland Frostig at the man's crummy little house.

He'd already introduced himself to Frostig at work, entering Frostig's cubicle in the accounting bay of Mr. Dmitri's factory, letting him know he'd be taking on Caitlin's case.

Expecting some sort of grateful reaction, but Frostig just nodded and kept staring at his computer screen.

Aaron glanced at the screen. Columns of numbers. Frostig's fingers rested on the keyboard, poised to resume typing. Skinny, white-haired guy, saggy skin, sun-spotted hands. Looking a lot older than the forty-seven listed in his personnel file.

Finally, he said, "Thank you, Mr. Fox."

Aaron suggested tomorrow night, eight p.m., Frostig's residence.

Frostig said, "Sure." His fingers started moving. Numbers shifted.

Frostig's employment record was spotless. Ten years at Lockheed, eight at Amgen, the rest at SoundMyte Inc.

M.A. in math and certified as a CPA before starting at the aerospace giant, which meant passing rigorous tests. But he'd settled for bookkeeper, with a much lower pay scale.

Someone who didn't like to be challenged?

Or losing his wife had knocked him low?

Maybe grief was why Frostig looked so old. Now his only kid was gone, poor guy.

Still, there were all kinds of ways to cope and if Aaron found himself in that situation, he'd be up on his feet, feisty and furious, sparring with Bad God. Transforming righteous anger into constructive energy.

That wasn't theory; he knew about loss.

◆

Doorbell rings early one summer morning. Mom trudges over to see what's up, still in her pajamas, those blearily gorgeous blue morning eyes of hers.

Aaron tails her, like he always does, earning his nickname. My little Puppy Dog. Wearing his Batman p.j.'s, the taste of Froot Loops sweet and slick in his mouth, cartoons playing on the tube, just another morning.

Except it isn't.

Mom opens the door.

Big, unhappy men stand there and look nervous and start to talk.

Mom loses her balance, falls to the floor.

Aaron rushes forward but the big men are handling the situation. One of them glances at him and the guy's lip trembles and he's a tough-looking man, the kind who wouldn't be bothered by anything small, and that's when Aaron knows something terrible has happened.

We bear our own crosses.

Still, Aaron couldn't help the small bit of contempt that he felt facing Frostig in his crappy little living room, the guy hunched,

all weighed down, unfocused, advertising the fact that life's been beating him up at regular intervals.

Might as well wear a *Kick Me* sign.

The best revenge was living well. Cold-cock Bad God and move on.

He said, "I know this is tough, sir."

"Yes."

The room was cramped, dim, crowded with cheap furniture, anything not peach or green was fake pecan. Not a stick of upgrade since the eighties and the TV was one of those old heaps with the puffy gray screen.

No cable or satellite box.

Was Frostig one of those guys whose lips curled at the idea of entertainment?

A single photo of Caitlin stood on an otherwise empty coffee table.

High school graduation picture, the inevitable *Can-I-finally-unlock-my-face?* grin.

Pretty girl, tan, some freckles peeking through. Lots of nice, thick, straight blond hair, intelligent brown eyes under carefully crafted brows.

No mom in her life but she knew how to be feminine.

Definitely nice enough for guys to notice; maybe the wrong guy had noticed.

Maitland Frostig continued to sit there, looking as if he were dreading a prostate exam. Aaron said, "Appreciate your meeting with me, sir."

Even though it should've been just the opposite.

"What would you like me to tell you, Mr. Fox?"

"Anything, sir."

"Anything," said Frostig, as if the word were foreign. "That's pretty broad."

"You know her better than anyone," said Aaron.

Frostig blinked. "She's a good girl. Let me show you her room."

A short walk past a kitchen that appeared unused, took them to a ten-by-twelve space. Pink walls, a single high window, beige drapes that managed to clash.

Beige bedspread on a twin-sized mattress.

A cheap desk took up half of one wall. The dresser across the room was similar: boxy, no style, five drawers. The only decorative touches were three framed prints

of flowers that looked as if they'd been cut from an old book.

No posters, no cute girlie touches, no mementos of adolescence.

"Have you changed anything?"

The suggestion seemed to offend Frostig. "Of course not."

"Caitlin's a serious girl."

"Pardon?"

"This seems like the room of a mature, serious person." More like a jail cell.

Frostig said, "Caitlin's extremely serious." Backed into a corner as Aaron checked out the closet, pawed through drawers.

White cotton underwear and bras, Levi's, two pairs of black slacks, an assortment of Made-in-China tops. The overall feel: budget-conscious, leaning toward conservative.

Pepperdine was a Baptist school.

"Is Caitlin religious?"

"We're not churchgoers."

Aaron went through the closet again. The girl seemed to have no outside interests. "Is anything missing, sir?"

"No one goes in here. I vacuum the rug, that's all."

"There don't seem to be many personal items, Mr. Frostig."

"Caitlin keeps cosmetics in the bathroom. The upper shelf in the medicine cabinet is hers."

Is this guy thick? "I was referring to yearbooks, diaries, that kind of thing."

"If you haven't found them, they're not here," said Frostig. "Caitlin's not sentimental."

"Philosophy major," said Aaron, tossing in one of those irrelevancies that sometimes shake people up so they say something impulsive.

"Yes," Frostig.

Fun dad.

Aaron had entered the case figuring a voluntary rabbit was unlikely. Now he wondered. How long could any sane person live here?

"Okay," he said. "Let's sit back down and you can tell me about the last time you saw your daughter."

"The last time was that morning," said Frostig. "Seven forty a.m. I leave the house at seven forty-five to be at work by nine. Sometimes I arrive early and get an early jump. Caitlin wakes up at seven and has breakfast while I'm having coffee. She leaves for Pepperdine at different times, depending on when her first class is. Generally, we see each other at night, except when Caitlin's working late, in which case I'm asleep by the time she arrives home. But I hear her come in. It's not a mansion."

"The last time anyone saw her was leaving the Riptide just before two a.m. Tell me about her job there."

"Riptide," said Frostig. "No *the.* They probably think that's avant-garde." His mouth turned down. "She worked there for four months prior to disappearing."

"I'm sensing you didn't approve."

"It's a bar. They might call it something else, but it's a bar and that means people drinking too much."

"You're wondering if that had something to do with her disappearance."

"I felt Caitlin could do better than work in a bar. Caitlin's opinion was that the location—on the way home from Pepperdine—made it convenient. I suppose that's true, strictly speaking, but there are other restaurants she could have chosen."

"Why'd she choose Riptide?"

"Her boyfriend worked there."

"Rory Stoltz."

Nod.

"Tell me about him," said Aaron.

"Nice boy. From what I saw. The police talked to him. He has nothing to offer."

"You don't suspect him."

"Why would I?"

"Often people are . . . harmed by those they know."

Frostig blinked. "Everyone says he's a nice boy. Caitlin says he's a nice boy."

"She talked to you about him."

Frostig scratched his chin. "Caitlin isn't one for discussion. She told me she was dating him. She didn't ask my permission. Do you have children, Mr. Fox?"

"No, sir."

"If you ever do, you'll see that higher education can cause a certain . . . confidence to set in."

"Thinking she's grown up and maybe she isn't," said Aaron.

Frostig's eyebrows rose. "She's grown up. Always has been. College made her think that was sufficient."

"For—"

"Making important decisions."

"As in—"

"Working at Riptide. I went over there, Mr. Fox. It was my first stop when Caitlin didn't return home. The second was Pepperdine, which was useless because Caitlin commuted, wasn't considered part of 'campus life.'"

"What'd you learn at Riptide?"

"What you'll learn if you waste your time there. They looked at me as if I was a nuisance."

"They weren't helpful."

"Not in the least." Frostig's voice tightened. His eyes were scalpel-cuts. "Caitlin worked her usual shift, nothing unusual happened. I've learned from Web-surfing that the clientele is a mixture: locals who like to drink and so-called celebrities."

"Such as?"

"People I've never heard of. The management claimed no one had an altercation with Caitlin, no one followed her out. The police claim they followed up on that. *They* even suggested that she ran away voluntarily, which is utter garbage. She's never used her credit card and her car hasn't turned up. This is California. Where's someone going to go without a car?"

Guy was unwilling to imagine his daughter beyond the borders of the Golden State. Seeking her own truths out in the big, bad universe.

Aaron said, "Good point."

"I'm glad you see it that way, Mr. Fox. The police certainly didn't."

"Fifteen months and they don't see it as a suspicious disappearance?"

"He doesn't," said Frostig. "One detective, and obviously not very experienced. I haven't talked to him recently because what's the point?"

"When's the last time you did talk to him?"

"Eight months ago. It was obvious further contact with him wouldn't be useful. I phoned his superiors but those calls were never returned."

"Frustrating."

Frostig's look said, *What else is new?*

"What have you done personally to look for Caitlin?"

"I haven't hired any other detectives, if that's what you mean."

"I mean anything."

"The Web," said Frostig. "I'm on it constantly. Plugging in Caitlin's name, checking missing persons sites. I've logged onto philosophy chat rooms, because Caitlin was interested in philosophy."

"People talking about the meaning of life?"

"People will talk about anything, Mr. Fox. The computer grants permission."

"To . . . ?"

"Communicate."

"Was Caitlin into cyberspace?"

"She didn't have her own computer," said Frostig. "We share."

Talk about lack of privacy. A voluntary rabbit was looking more and more feasible.

Aaron said, "What'd you guys do, divide up the time?"

"We guys," said Frostig, frowning. "Caitlin used the computer for academic purposes."

"Homework."

"Term papers. But feel free to examine the computer. I was just offering an example of the lengths to which I go to find Caitlin."

"What else can you tell me about Caitlin, sir?"

"About Caitlin," said Frostig, as if redigesting the concept.

What an oddball. Half an hour in this place and Aaron felt ready to molt his skin. Voluntary rabbit was climbing toward Probability.

Maitland Frostig said, "She's a good girl with a good brain. She's neat and diligent and reliable."

Sounded more like a Boy Scout than a daughter.

"I don't want to think," said Frostig.

"About?"

"Where she could be after all this time."

"What was the name of the police detective you spoke to?"

"The police," said Frostig, "are utterly useless."

"Even so, sir."

"You're going to waste time going over old ground. On Mr. Dmitri's dollar."

Aaron forced himself to smile. "Generous man, your boss."

Frostig turned his back, headed to the living room. Walked through the room and positioned himself by the front door.

Aaron said, "Is there some reason you're uncomfortable with my taking on your daughter's case?"

"Because you're black? Absolutely not."

Race hadn't entered Aaron's head. Frostig had seen nothing but the color of Aaron's skin.

"It's not you, Mr. Fox. I'm not hopeful, that's all. Fifteen months and no one's given me the time of day."

"Now that's changed, Mr. Frostig."

"I suppose it has." Frostig's smile was unsettling. "I apologize if I've been rude. I certainly haven't intended any rudeness."

"None observed."

"Well that's polite of you, Mr. Fox. I'm sure you'll do your best."

Aaron opened the door and let in a sliver of evening. He said, "The name of that police detective, sir."

"Reed," said Frostig. "Moses Reed. You're wasting your time."

Aaron walked to his car, head spinning in a whole new direction.

5

The big detective room echoed.

Just Moe Reed at his desk and D-3 Delano Hardy in a far corner, on the phone, talking to someone about a court appearance.

Hardy had as many years on the job as Sturgis—had partnered with Sturgis back when the lieutenant still did that. Moe, still feeling like a trainee, had made it his business to eavesdrop when the older detectives talked.

Delano's case sounded like a gang shooting, bad guy nabbed early, easy confession. Routine, nothing to learn. Moe was just about to pay attention to his own work when tension snaked into Hardy's voice and his volume rose.

Turned out this bad guy was a fifteen-year-old girl and her lawyers were pushing a child abuse/diminished capacity defense. On top of that, she was Hispanic and Hardy was black, so the race card was going to be used to sully the confession.

Hardy grunted, drank coffee, grunted.

Sturgis made those same sounds when he was pissed. Maybe that was the mark of decades on the job. Or getting old. Moe wondered if someday he'd end up sounding like a wounded steer.

He tasted his own coffee, long cold. Drinking out of one of those body-outline mugs from the coroner's gift shop. Present from Liz. Cute, but it didn't improve the taste of D-room swill.

Flipping through the Frostig file, he found Rory Stoltz's cell number, phoned, got voice mail. Rory sounding cheerful and confident. Whatever grief he'd mustered was long gone.

At the landline, Rory's mother answered and as Moe identified himself he searched the file for her name. *Martha.* Work number, the Peninsula in Beverly Hills where she was a room-service coordinator.

"Have you found Caitlin?" she said.

"Unfortunately not, ma'am. I'm trying to reach Rory."

"Why?"

"Doing follow-up."

"Rory's busy at school."

"Any idea when he'll be free?"

"He's an adult," said Martha Stoltz. "I don't keep tabs on him."

"Does he still live at home?"

Silence. *It's not a trick question.*

"Ma'am—"

"I don't understand why you're calling, Detective Reed. You talked to Rory, what, three, four times? Asking the same questions over and over. It was very upsetting to Rory. He felt you were trying to trip him up."

"I wasn't, ma'am," Moe lied. "Sometimes we need to do that just to be thorough."

"It really bothered him, that you could suspect him. Rory was so fond of Caitlin. No one was more upset when she disappeared."

"I hear you, ma'am, but sometimes we need to reinterview."

"Well, Rory's in plain sight, living his life."

Before Moe could respond, she hung up.

Why all the anger? Maybe she'd had a bad day. Or she really was fed up with her only child being drawn into a murder investigation.

He called Pepperdine administration, tried to wangle Rory's class schedule out of a perky secretary, then her supervisor.

No go. Maybe someone with more experience could've pulled it off, maybe not.

At ten a.m. he took a walk, the way he'd seen Sturgis do, covering half a mile of the working-class residential neighborhood that surrounded the station.

No slam-bam insights. He phoned Liz. She answered, sounding groggy, but when she said, "It's you," her voice lightened, and she appended, "Sweetie."

"Did I wake you?"

"No, I'm just lying here with a monster headache and thinking about everything that's piled up while I was gone."

"Poor baby."

"What bugs me, Moses, is I know the physiology of jet lag, did everything I could to hydrate. But no matter how much water I pump, my eyes are gritty and my skin feels like crepe paper."

Moe imagined that. Chocolate-brown paper, smoothing under his touch. "You'll be fine before you know it. How was the flight?"

"The usual delays and they ran out of beverages, except for booze, talk about dehydration." She laughed. "The guy next to me was about a thousand pounds. He popped two Ambiens and snored like a choo-choo the entire flight. Try climbing Mount Fleshy to get to the john."

Moe laughed along with her. "Well, now you're back and I'll take care of you."

"Good, I could use some care, Moses. When do you want to hang?"

"Unless something breaks, I'll be free at four, five."

"Caitlin?"

"Yup."

"You transfer and they send it along," said Liz. "Totally unjust."

"It'll work itself out. You shutting in all day?"

"I was planning to go to the lab to clear my desk. But I'm feeling so punk I think I'll pass. So anytime. Want me to order something in?"

"Whatever you want. See you at five, with bells."

"Bells, huh? Plan on sliding down the chimney?"

"Oh, man," he said. "Symbolism this early in the day."

Liz cracked up. "You bring it out in me, Moses. That's why we're going steady."

Feeling better, he turned back, detoured for a maple bear claw from a coffee shop on Santa Monica, ate it on the way, and reapproached the Frostig file with elevated blood sugar.

Concentrating on the interviews with Rory Stoltz, trying to tease out anything he might've missed.

Across the room, Del Hardy said, "Well, look who the smog blew in."

Chortles and palm-smacking high-fives made Moe glance over.

Del was on his feet, grinning.

At Aaron.

Aaron pretended to ignore Moe, kept shooting the breeze with the older detective. Not deferential to Hardy. Relaxed, a peer.

Moe pretended to ignore Aaron back. Aaron said something to Hardy in a low voice and Hardy laughed again.

Something to do with Del's case? Had Aaron been hired by the fifteen-year-old hit-vixen's lawyers to stir up trouble?

But if Del saw Aaron as the enemy, you couldn't tell from his posture. Just the opposite, two guys, shooting the breeze.

Two black guys. They could've been a rumpled dad and his much cooler son.

Moe the invisible man. He buried his face in the file.

"Moses!"

Aaron was standing over him, grinning. As if he hadn't just shined Moe on. Moe couldn't care less about clothes, thought his blazers and khakis were just fine for the job. But sometimes, when he saw how Aaron put himself together, he felt underdressed.

Today's haute-whatever was a slim-fit black suit, white shirt, orange tie as bright as a Caltrans cone, worn with one of those oversized knots that took up a whole bunch of space and screamed *Serious GQ.*

Moe's knot was always slipping. It felt

loose, right now, but he resisted the urge to yank.

Now Del Hardy was staring at *him,* perplexed by Moe's unresponsiveness.

Moe said, "Hey."

"Morning, bro. Busy?"

"Yup."

"Busy on Caitlin Frostig?"

Moe's chest tightened. "Why?"

"She's mine now," said Aaron. "In addition to being yours."

Moe shut the file. "What are you talking about?"

"I'm talking about free enterprise, Moses."

"Who hired you?"

"Mr. Frostig's boss."

"Why not Frostig himself?"

"Bookkeeper's salary affording my daily? I think not. We need to chat, bro."

"Nothing to chat about."

Aaron placed a hand on Moe's shoulder. Moe removed it.

"It's going to be *that* way, Moses?"

"There's nothing to talk about. The case is nowhere."

"Maybe I can find a somewhere."

"Miracle worker."

Aaron grinned. "It's been known to happen."

Moe turned away.

"Moses, on those marsh murders. I don't think I'd be exaggerating if I said I played somewhat of a role."

"This is different."

"How about a look at the file?"

"Nothing worth looking at."

"C'mon, Moe."

"Forget it."

Aaron shrugged. "From what Mr. Frostig said, I guess I shouldn't be surprised."

"About what?"

"His feeling is you never considered Caitlin worth your time."

Moe's face got hot. He knew he'd turned beet red. Something Aaron could always avoid.

"He can feel what he wants. Not going to change the facts."

"I agree," said Aaron.

"With what?"

"Frostig's opinion not being worth much. He's a weirdo, strange affect—that's shrink-talk for off-kilter emotional responses. Who knows, he could be one of those

Asperbergers—that's an autism-spectrum disorder—"

"I know what it is."

"Been reading up on psychology?"

Actually, Moe had. Going through a pile of books Dr. Delaware had suggested. Interesting stuff, but none of it relevant to Caitlin Frostig.

Moe smiled. His face continued to flame.

Aaron said, "Maitland doesn't bother you?"

"Do I see him as a suspect? Nothing points that way."

"Not a suspect, Moses. A factor—a contributing factor. As in Caitlin's got one parent and unfortunately that one parent is a weirdo and she finally has enough of living with him and decides to book."

"A rabbit," said Moe. "You've got evidence of that?"

"I've got nothing except a big fat retainer that I'd like to deserve. That's why I'm here instead of taking the C4S around the track at Laguna Seca. Which is what I'd planned to do before Mr. Dmitri—Frostig's boss—called me in."

"Vacation time."

"Well earned, Moses."

"No one forced you to take the case."

"Mr. Dmitri's an important client. He beckons, I come."

"That makes you sound like a dog."

Aaron laughed. "We're all dogs, bro. Only question is, are we going to eat quality chow or scrounge in the trash? Come on, give me a look at the file. I'll take you out to lunch and we can brainstorm—I pay."

"Dmitri pays."

"Either way, you don't. How about the Peninsula?"

Martha Stoltz's workplace.

Moe said, "Why there?"

"I like the menu."

"That's the only reason?"

Aaron laughed. "What other reason would there be? C'mon, let's do it."

Over the black silk of Aaron's broad shoulders, Moe spotted Delano Hardy's eyes.

Watching, taking it all in.

Moe thought of the jovial exchange between Hardy and Aaron.

Aaron said, "Be flexible, bro."

Moe stood. Placed the file in a drawer and locked it.

"Okay, I get it, bro," said Aaron.

"Get what?"

"You're the man, I'm hired help."

"Peninsula's fine," said Moe.

"*Great* menu," said Aaron. "I hear the room service is pretty good, too."

CHAPTER

6

November 11, 1980

Maddy watched the baby sleep.

The chair by the crib was a City of Hope thrift-shop find: salmon silk tulip seat with a grimy Sloan label underneath and only a few stains.

Maddy'd paid thirty bucks, considered it the find of the century.

She'd placed it in the living room, dragging it from the van by herself. Arranged it next to the fireplace with a cute little table that held a vase of silk flowers. Just like they did in *House & Garden.*

The day she set it up, she poured herself an unfiltered apple juice, waited for Darius to come home.

He arrived two hours late, reeking of beer and other women. Gaped at what Maddy had done and burst into laughter and pronounced the new addition "beaucoup faggy." Hoisting the chair easily, he carried it to the garage.

Later, when Darius was sleeping, Maddy went out there, draped the silk with a clean white sheet, and sat. Filling her nose with garage dust, motor oil, old cardboard, the metallic perfume of Darius's half-restored Harley.

Sometimes she still went out there and sniffed the air. Very little had changed, but the tulip chair's honor had been restored.

No one to complain when she moved it into the baby's room. From time to time Darius's voice rang in her head. *Pink for a boy? Jesus, girl, you are going to turn him into a first-class swish and if you think that means he'll grow up polite and artistic, think again. I've seen what those guys do to each other when they get all pissed off and namby-jealous . . .*

Maddy's eyes puffed.

The baby stirred.

She hoisted herself up, tiptoed to the crib, stared down at the pink, smooth face, round as a dinner plate. Blue-eyed little angel, like one of those Renaissance paintings.

Angelic disposition, too. As if he knew enough not to upset the applecart.

Five months old and already, the freckles. He'd need protection from the sun. And God knew what else . . .

She touched his soft little tummy, feeling the swell of ample nourishment through terry cloth.

Blue jammy. Darius would approve.

The baby smiled in his sleep.

Maddy said, "Angel. You have no idea."

A slamming door whisked her out of her reverie and she hurried out of the room, shut the door softly, continued into the kitchen.

Ready to shush the obvious culprit. How many times had she *told* him?

Aaron was a smart boy, maybe he did it on purpose.

One thing for sure, he knew what was coming because he shouted, "Mommy!" as if they'd been apart for months and flashed a thousand-watt smile.

That smile. She couldn't help but spread her arms as he ran toward her.

Aaron's little head made contact with her belly. He nuzzled her. She got down on one knee and held him tight. Taking in that little-boy smell.

School clothes grimy with dust, he still managed to look more put-together than any other four-year-old on the face of the planet.

"Good to see you, Mommy! How was your day?"

"Oh, you charmer."

Maddy hugged him harder. Aaron squirmed away. "I must have *Froot* Loops! *Please!*"

"Baby, it's too—"

"*Pleeeeeze.* It's *important*! Oh, my belly *needs* Froot Loops, needs it so *bad*!"

Dancing around the kitchen, not even pretending to take himself seriously. Sometimes she thought he was forty, not four.

He swayed, eyes as big as the universe. "I'm so *hungry,* Mommy!"

Little con man; Maddy fought not to laugh.

The preschool teacher had been more diplomatic.

"Aaron is a charming boy, but sometimes he relies on social skills a little too much."

Blood ran thicker than . . .

"Froot Loops! I will fall over tired, Mommy, on my face, without *Froot* Loops!"

"Shh. Baby Moe's sleeping."

"Baby Moe," said Aaron, turning pensive. "He is my brother and I love him," he stage-whispered. "He wants me to have Froot Loops, without Froot Loops everyone will be sad and Baby Moe will cry—"

"Shh, Aaron. Please."

Aaron turned instantly silent. Stood at attention. Saluted.

Maddy said, "Wash your hands, mister, then go sit at the table like a civilized person and I'll fix you a nice snack."

"Froot Loops is a nice snack," said Aaron. "With chocolate milk. Real dark."

"That's way too much sugar, honey."

"Just a *little* dark."

"Even a little is too much sugar—"

"Puhleeeeeeze?"

"Shh."

"Mommy, I can't be quiet unless my head is happy. What makes me happy on today is—"

"Froot Loops," said Maddy. "With regular milk."

"A *leeetle* chocolate?"

"Fine."

"A leetle more than a leeetle?"

"Don't push your luck, Handsome Boy."

Aaron grinned. "Or it could be Smirnoff."

Maddy froze. "What do you know about Smirnoff."

"Jack likes it. There's a bottle in your room."

Maddy placed her hands on his shoulders. The boy's eyes didn't waver. "Aaron Fox, have you been rummaging in other people's personal belongings?"

"I saw it when I came in to kiss you, Mommy. You weren't there. You were with the washing machine, but I saw it."

"Where was this bottle?"

Aaron didn't answer.

"I need to know, sweetheart."

"Jack did a bad?"

Maddy sighed. "No, Jack didn't do a bad. Tell me where—"

"On the table next to the bed. On Jack's side."

She said, "Sweetheart, Smirnoff's for grown-ups."

Aaron smiled wider. Knowing he'd boxed her into a corner, the little devil.

"Exactly, Mommy, and chocolate milk's for kids. A *leeetle* more dark. Please?"

"Two teaspoons of Nestlé's and that's it."

"Three."

"Two and that's final."

Then it hit her. Aaron had come in by himself.

Her heart began to pound. "Where *is* Jack?"

"Sitting in the car," said Aaron.

"Why?"

Shrug.

"Is he okay?"

Shrug.

"He did pick you up from school?"

"Uh-huh. Can I have my Froot—"

Rushing to the front of the little house, Maddy flung the door open.

The van was parked in the driveway. Jack sat behind the wheel.

Staring at nothing.

She went over to him and he let out one of his crooked smiles.

This was her life. Staring at male teeth. "What are you doing, Jack?"

His hair, beginning to gray, was wind-blown. His eyelids drooped. "Hey, gorgeous."

Reeking of booze.

"You *drank* before you picked him up?"

"Hours ago, gorgeous—"

"I can smell it on you, don't *gorgeous* me!"

Jack didn't answer.

"Are you out of your *mind*?"

"Maddy," said Jack, "you're blowing this way up."

"I'm talking about my child—"

"I love him like he's—"

"So you say—"

"I love him to *pieces,* Maddy." Tears filled Jack's eyes. "Love him maybe not like you do, but he's . . . I love him, honey, he's a great kid, you know I'd never hurt him, honey, you know that, you know that, right? All I want to do is take care of my family . . ."

"Then how could you—"

"It was hours ago," Jack insisted.

"At the Drop Inn."

"Couple of beer-and-shots is all." Jack reached out to touch her arm. She avoided him. "Aw, c'mon, hon. I'da used vodka, you'da never known."

Maddy turned to leave.

Jack got out of the van and hurried to her side.

He did seem to be walking okay.

"I'll call the station, get 'em to bring a Breathalyzer, okay?"

Maddy said, "It's not funny."

"I'm not trying to be funny," Jack lied.

Bad liars were the worst. At least with the good ones you could fantasize they were sincere. Jack's inability to dissemble had caused her to lose respect within weeks of their marriage.

She said, "Don't do it again. Aaron should never smell that on you."

"I'm sorry, honey."

"Forget it."

"Love you, honey."

Maddy didn't answer.

"Either way," said Jack.

By the time they returned to the kitchen, Aaron was at the table snarfing from a huge bowl of Froot Loops. His free hand grazed a glass of milk so saturated with chocolate that undissolved clumps floated on the surface like water lilies.

Cereal speckled the floor. Not too big of

CHAPTER

7

Instead of heading for the parking lot, Moe began walking toward Santa Monica Boulevard.

Aaron said, "We're hiking to the Peninsula?"

"Forget the Peninsula."

"Too rich for your blood?"

Moe picked up his pace.

"Okay, I bite. Where we going?"

"Suzy Q's."

"That dump?"

"Too cop for your blood?" said Moe.

"Bacon on sausage on lard on trans fat

a mess, considering. The boy had always been coordinated.

He'd climbed up to the cereal cupboard, taken the time to close the door, move the chair back into place.

When he saw her, he opened a mouth full of Technicolor mush and said, "Yum!"

Jack winked and said, "Hey, that looks good."

From down the hall came the chuffing of Baby Moe's initial wake-up cries.

Time for *his* snack.

Maddy left the kitchen, freeing her left breast.

with a side of LDL cholesterol? Suit yourself, bro."

A flush spread from Moe's pecs up to
his face. His father—the man whose name
Aaron had never taken—had dropped
dead of a heart attack at thirty-nine. Last
year, Moe had finally dug up the death
report.

The deceased had fallen off a bar stool,
probably cold before he hit the floor.

Moe ate a lot of skinless chicken breasts.

"Suzy's too much for you to handle?
Let's do Indian."

Aaron said, "That place where they
worship Sturgis?"

"That a problem for you?"

"Life is beautiful, I've got no problems."
Four steps later: "You like working with
Sturgis?"

"Why wouldn't I?"

"No reason. So tell me what you've
done on Frostig."

Moe sped up to a near jog.

Aaron said, "Aerobics and chutney in
the a.m. I'm always open to new experi-
ences."

◆

The bespectacled woman who ran Café Moghul recognized Aaron the moment he pushed the door open. She flashed him a neon smile, brighter than her aqua-blue sari.

Moe thought: A whole different greeting from the first time. Aaron had walked in on a marsh-murder sitdown and the woman had reacted to a black face with instinctive anxiety. Despite Aaron's custom suit, the easygoing grin, the deliberately unthreatening posture.

All those strategies his brother used to put people at ease.

Moe had his feelings about Aaron and they made empathy a huge nuisance. But once in a while he let himself imagine what it would be like to *be* Aaron, always having to *present* yourself . . .

"Sir." The woman gave a little flourish and bow. "Please, anywhere you like."

That day, Aaron had eaten nothing, drunk half a glass of clove tea. But picking up everyone's tab and tipping big had bought him some social status.

As they settled at a corner table, the woman said, "Is the lieutenant coming as well?"

"No, ma'am," said Moe.

She appeared to notice him for the first time. Turned back to Aaron: "He is okay?"

Moe said, "He's fine, ma'am."

"I haven't seen him in a few days."

The storefront café was Sturgis's secondary office. The woman viewed the Loo as a human guard dog, a role he'd earned by ejecting a few homeless whacks and just being big and mean looking.

Moe said, "I'll send him your best."

"We have fresh lamb in a very nice curry."

Aaron's hand slipped down toward his flat abdomen and Moe figured he'd give some excuse and order tea.

Aaron said, "Sure. And bring healthy vegetables for Detective Reed."

While they waited for the food, Aaron checked his BlackBerry.

Moe said, "People to do, things to see."

Aaron clicked off. "The Peninsula's where Rory Stoltz's mama works. You changed your mind because you don't want to make it easy for me."

"Whatever you want to do on Caitlin, I can't stop you unless you cross the line. In terms of what I can give you, like I said there's nothing. And Martha Stoltz is a waste of time. I spoke to her this morning. She had nothing to say."

"So you're actively working the case."

"So they tell me."

The food arrived. Heaps of lamb stew for both of them, bowls of every veg the kitchen could offer.

The bespectacled woman said, "Tell the lieutenant how good everything is."

When she left, Aaron looked at the banquet and shook his head.

"Not up to it?" said Moe.

"A little early in the day, no?"

Moe began eating with simulated gusto. Undigested breakfast sat in his gut but damned if he'd wimp out. Maybe lamb was better than beef, cholesterol-wise. Another hour of lifting and a run would keep him virtuous. Tonight, after seeing Liz. *If* he went home.

Aaron said, "Tell me about Rory Stoltz."

"I interviewed him four times, he's alibied for at least one hour after Caitlin left the Riptide. Stayed on to clean up. After that, he went home where Mommy claims he stayed."

"Claims?"

"She's his mother."

"You pick something up hinky about her, Moses?"

"You didn't hear me the first time? She's useless."

Aaron's clean jawline rippled. He took a breath. "Mo—"

"Maybe I fucked up somewhere along the line, but if I did, Sturgis doesn't think so. I went over the murder book with him and he said nothing was missing. Same for Delaware."

"You went to see Delaware because . . ."

"At Sturgis's suggestion."

"Sturgis sees Caitlin as a psycho case?"

"Sturgis doesn't know what she is. No one does. *Including* Delaware. But a girl driving alone, late at night? There are all sorts of possibilities."

"Bad guy on the road," said Aaron. "Except her car hasn't been found."

"So the psycho collects wheels as trophies. Or he dumped it somewhere."

"Psycho garage," said Aaron. "Here's an image for you: rows of vics' vehicles, each one with a skeleton propped behind the wheel."

"You've been Hollywooding too long."

"Little brother, you are right about that. But maybe that'll work to my advantage."

"Why?"

"Maitland Frostig said Riptide gets celebs."

"I was there," said Moe. "All I saw were juiceheads and old surfers."

"Maybe you hit an off night. Stoltz still work there?"

"Don't know."

"I'll find out when I talk to him. Unless that's a problem."

"Talk to him all you want. Kid's not going to give up anything because if he does have something to hide, he's had fifteen months to live with it and get his story straight."

"Nothing hinky about him," said Aaron, "but still you wonder."

Moe glared at him.

"What?"

"You're sounding like a shrink. Bouncing back what I say."

"Bro—"

"I've got nothing on Stoltz except that he was the boyfriend."

"Was," said Aaron. "So you definitely see her as dead."

"Hey," said Moe, "maybe she's partying in Dubai, or whatever."

"White slavery." Aaron grinned. "Always loved that phrase. As opposed to normal slavery."

The racial allusion surprised Moe. He said, "You *don't* see her as dead?"

"Yeah, I probably do. Except for what I said before, she might've wanted to get away from Daddy. She didn't even have her own computer, they shared. What college student doesn't have a laptop? So Maitland could be one of those controlling types. And girls do wanna have fu-uhn."

"She was a virgin," said Moe. "Supposedly."

Aaron's brows arched. "Daddy told you that?"

"Martha Stoltz did."

"How'd it come up?"

"She was talking about what a perfect couple Caitland and Rory were. All-American. Both virgins."

"What was her point in telling you?"

Moe shrugged. "I'm just quoting."

"It wasn't weird?" said Aaron. "Middle of an interview and she volunteers about their sex life?"

"Lack of sex life. I figured she wanted me to see Rory as a choirboy."

"Because he isn't?"

"If he's got a secret life, it's stayed secret from me," said Moe. "What're you gonna do, high-tech-bug his bedroom?"

Aaron smoothed his tie, tugged the big knot tighter. "They're both virgins . . . like Mama's in the backseat with them?"

"Hey," said Moe, "I'm open to anything. You find out Rory's chapter president of the Ted Bundy Fan Club, I'll get interested. But I talked to him four times and he came across exactly what he claimed to be."

"Which is?"

"Clean-cut Pepperdine student."

"That's a Baptist school. We talking Holy Roller?"

"Normal, clean-cut kid," said Moe. "Seemed genuinely torn up about Caitlin. But not over-the-top emotional, like he was trying to prove something."

"Virgins," said Aaron. "Wonder if he's still that way fifteen months later. You planning a fifth chat?"

"The case is still open."

Aaron drank water.

Moe said, "I don't want you stepping on my toes."

"Last thing on my mind, bro."

"But if I tell you to hold off, you're not going to listen." Gas or acid or whatever was rising up his food tube. His belt cut like dental floss. From what, three pieces of lamb and some eggplant? What did they put in this stuff?

"Moses, can't we just put it aside?"

"Put what aside?"

"SOS. Same old shit." Aaron laughed. "Remember when I told that idiot counselor he was just digging up SOS and he near about fell off his shrink chair?"

Moe stayed silent.

"You don't remember, bro?"

"Dr. Gibson," said Moe. As if called upon to recite.

"*Mr.* Gibson," said Aaron. "Had a master's." He shook his head. "Working for the school system filing paper, at night he moonlights, pretends he's an analyst."

"Didn't stop Mom from liking him."

"Mom," said Aaron. "She also liked that massage therapist with the bad breath and the huge mole on her chin and that Polish N.D. we all thought was an M.D.— Kussorsky, Master Naturopath. Guy's doling out little vials of water with invisible ingredients and Mom's telling us we have to take it for our allergies. Meanwhile, she takes in two cats."

He laughed again. "SOS."

Moe thought about fake-shrink Gibson and couldn't muster up any glee.

He'd been fourteen, Aaron eighteen. The two of them going at each other constantly, sometimes it got physical. Mom having no idea.

My father was a hero.

So was my father. What? You're saying he wasn't? You're saying that?

All I'm saying, little bro, is—

Fuck you.

Fuck you.

A whirlwind of scuffle, fists flying, Mom hurrying in, trying to break it up.

The next day, she announced everyone was going to "family therapy."

She'd met Quentin Gibson, M.A., at yoga class.

Guy makes house calls, wimpy, skinny, ponytailed, British tool. *Let's-everyone-*

express-their-feelings. Useful as a tissue-paper condom.

Moe felt himself smile, put a brake on his lips.

Aaron leaned in closer. "I promise not to step on your feet."

"That assumes we're dancing."

"So nothing I'm going to say is going to work."

"Nothing has to work. Do what you want."

"Even if that was my style, I wouldn't handle it that way, bro."

"Stop doing that."

"Doing what?"

"Bro."

Aaron's caramel eyes widened. "I've been doing that your whole life."

"Exactly."

Aaron ran a long, graceful finger along his hairline. "Ok-ay. Detective Reed."

Moe's colon churned. He fought to conceal another belch.

Aaron exhaled slowly. "This is what I am going to do." Lapsing into that school-teacher tone Moe hated. "I will check with you before I interview Stoltz, his mommy, or anyone else you deem important. If I learn anything relevant, you'll be the first to know."

Moe forked food around his plate.

"Detective Brother Reed, *is* there anyone else you deem important?"

"Just Caitlin," said Moe. "If you run across her, tell her to give me a ring."

The bespectacled woman came over, looked at Aaron's untouched plate.

Not a trace of irritation as she said, "May I wrap that for you to go, sir?"

CHAPTER

8

Aaron watched the little pink house.

It was just after ten p.m. For three hours, he'd done nothing *but* watch.

Nice night in the Valley, more than a few stars peeking through a charcoal felt sky, the street lined with neat domiciles, quiet and peaceful.

He sat low in the seat of the Opel, drank green tea, ate the second half of a pastrami sandwich, listened to Anita Baker on his iPod.

Moe had walked out of the restaurant committing to nothing. Aaron tipped the Indian woman generously, then drove to

Heinz the Mechanic's place on Pico, where he garaged the C4S and picked up the Opel.

Deceptive little thing, with its dinged-up body and flat brown paint. The engine was a rebuilt BMW 325i enhanced by Heinz's magical hands. The best of several loaners the German kept around while he worked on Carreras and Ferraris and such. Fifty bucks bought Aaron twenty-four hours. Smoked windows were perfect for the job at hand.

He logged the expenditure into his BlackBerry.

Driving home, he cell-phoned a source at the county assessor's office, learned that Rory Stoltz owned no real estate but Martha Greta Stoltz paid property taxes on a single-family residence on Emelita Street in North Hollywood.

"Thanks, Henry. I owe you."

Laughter. "You sure do."

"Check's in the mail."

"It sure is."

The call was a luxury. Property rolls were public records but saving time was a bargain, in the long run, for Mr. Dmitri.

Henry's fifty got logged.

Aaron could've stretched that but, deep pockets like Mr. Dmitri's, you had to be careful not to get piggy.

Address in hand, he GPS'd the precise location as he drove home to his place on San Vicente off Wilshire. Speed-dialing continuously, using red lights to work the BlackBerry.

His building was a deco-flavored duplex built in the twenties, one of the final reminders that the area had once been residential. Aaron's neighbors were low-rise office structures. Skyscrapers on Wilshire cast long shadows across his roof.

He'd picked up the property at a foreclosure auction for a ridiculous price, spent the next five years remodeling, doing a lot of the work himself. Last year, he'd billed two hundred ninety-six thousand dollars in fees, collected nearly all of that, and this year was looking at least as good. But without the bargain purchase, he'd still be living in a condo.

He unlocked the gate around the small front yard, disabled the security lock, released both bolts in the door, removed his snail mail from the internal slot. The first floor was Work Land, all-black wood floor where it wasn't Berber carpeting, gray suede walls, chrome and leather and glass furniture. Sheets of Lexan were bolted to the inner surfaces of conspicuous windows. Invisible, unless you knew to look.

The décor expressed all the high-tech efficiency clients craved.

This afternoon, Work Land was silent, every message and e-mail cleared during the drive. He loved operating as a solo act.

Checking one of three fax machines, he was pleased to find a fresh clear copy of Rory Stoltz's driver's license, courtesy an illegal search by a source at DMV.

Hundred bucks. Ka-*ching*.

Folding the page neatly, to keep from creasing the subject's face, he headed upstairs to Play Land, worked out in his gym, showered, whirlpool-bathed, shaved.

Feeling loose and confident, he sauntered, stark-naked and swinging a key ring, down a subtly lit, plum-carpeted hallway toward what had once been a rear bedroom.

The space was guarded by a security-hinged door of fiery teak. An ebony silhouette of a top-hatted boulevardier graced the center of the wood. Aaron unlocked and stepped in.

The same teak covered the walls and the coffered ceilings. Recessed lighting set off billiard-table-green carpeting. The twenty-by-eighteen room was sectioned by double-height, industrial-quality, stainless-steel racks he'd snagged at a bargain price from Carlyle and Tout when the Brentwood haberdasher went under.

The left side was devoted to suits, sport coats paired with harmonizing slacks, and topcoats he rarely used. Though his favorite, a charcoal-brown, cashmere/mink-blend Arnold Brant by Columbo, some-times got put to work when he lowered the Porsche's top on windy winter nights.

On the right hung sport shirts and casual jackets arranged by hue, forty-two pairs of neatly pressed jeans with an emphasis on Zegna, a dozen Fila velour workout suits—no, thirteen.

The rear wall was mostly dress shirts. Lots of Borelli, but some Brioni, Ricci, Charvet, Turnbull, Armani Black Label. Flanking hooks held belts and ties, each cravat paired with a harmonious pocket silk. Ringing the entire room above the racks was teak shelving bearing clear plastic boxes containing sweaters and shoes, the latter identified precisely.

Magli Olive Suede Wingtips. Paciotti Black Buckle Loafers. Edmonds Cordovans.

About half of the clothing still bore tags.

Aaron walked among his treasures, fingertips grazing silk, Sea Island cotton, merino, cashmere, alpaca.

He stopped at the Columbo. Cashmere and mink, nothing like it. He loved that coat.

Ten minutes later, he'd made his pick for tonight.

What the well-dressed man dons when sitting on his ass for protracted periods of tedium came down to a loose brown linen shirt-jacket with four flap pockets, tailored to conceal his 9mm, beige cargo pants of the same carefully rumpled fabric that provided another quartet of compartments, cream silk socks, butter-soft pigskin Santoni driving shoes.

By four p.m., he was back in West L.A., sitting in the girlie-cute front room of Liana Parlat's girlie-cute condo off Overland.

Liana, always friendly, seemed especially happy to see him, and he wondered if some of her gigs had dried up due to the writers' strike.

She served him coffee and home-baked white-chocolate chip cookies and offered him a share of the Lean Cuisine lasagna she was just about to nuke. Aaron declined the food but finished three cups of Liana's always excellent Kenyan. She put dinner on hold and sat opposite him, perched like the lingerie model she'd once been, on the edge of a Louis XIV repro chair done up in puce brocade.

Still gorgeous at forty-one, the mop of black hair glossy and carefully layered, the flawless ivory skin allowing her to pass for late twenties, Liana had the charisma and talent to be a movie star. After fifteen years of failure, she'd settled for the anonymity and respectable income of commercial voice-overs.

Freelancing for Aaron supplemented her retirement fund.

They'd begun as lovers, continued as friends and occasional business associates. Once-in-a-while booty-bumps did no damage; Aaron was proud of his ability to maintain complex relationships.

The exception being Moe . . .

Liana said, "For this one, I was thinking perky, slightly nasal, wholesome."

"Go for it."

He gave her the unlisted number he'd obtained from a source at the phone company, sat by as she punched numbers. Ever the Method actress, she cocked her head, altered her posture, squinted somewhat stupidly.

Transforming into a Valley Girl.

"Hi, is Rory there?" Putting a little more headcold into it. "Oh . . . oh, okay, I'm in one of his classes and was wondering . . . no, it's not that important, I'll try later. Thank you *so* much."

Click. "Mommy expects him home by six thirty."

"Thank you, baby. Now for the fun part."

He gave her Riptide's address on Ocean Avenue, two blocks south of Colorado. Partially gentrified stretch, with that giant Loews Hotel pulling in respectable folks. But dingy motels and cheap apartments persisted, as did low-rent bars, and last year there'd been a hostage situation, a captain from West Valley named Decker whom Aaron knew casually ending up a big-time hero.

Aaron said, "Caitlin's father said she considered the location convenient since she went to Pepperdine."

"That's twenty miles from Pepperdine," said Liana.

"But on the way home to Venice."

"Ah . . . drive most of the way home so you don't have much to go when you're really tired. I guess it makes sense."

"I drove by the place at one thirty a.m. last night—around the time Caitlin was last seen. It's pretty spooky, Lee. Park as close as you can—use the hotel, go valet if you want."

Liana smiled. "And be sure to bring back the receipt."

"That would be nice."

"Mr. All Business."

"Aw, you know that's not true, sweetheart. You're hearing the message, right? Personal safety is all."

"We're not exactly talking mean streets, darling. Ivy at the Shore is what, three blocks up?"

"A block can make a difference, Lee.

Last night there were bums pushing shopping carts and lowlifes hanging near a
couple of motels. If something feels even
a little off, don't get brave."

"Fine," she said. "But I've been to Industry parties at Loews."

"Terrific. Charm the valet and maybe
he'll let you park free."

Liana laughed and nibbled an eighth of
a cookie. "This girl—Caitlin. How long did
she work there?"

"Four months."

"You're wondering if she ran into some
psycho, either there, or nearby."

"I don't know enough to wonder anything, Lee. Go in there, order a drink—soft,
if you think hard will impede you. Don't feel
pressured to come up with anything huge.
Just check the place out, get a feel for the
ambience."

"What's my motivation, Mr. De Mille?"

"Two hundred for the first four hours,
forty for each additional hour."

"Ooh," she said. "Generous client,
huh?" Rhetorical, because she knew better than to press for details. "They serve
food at this gin joint?"

"Probably bar food, at least."

"I'll stick with my Lean Quee. Just ambience, huh?"

"If anything specific to Caitlin comes up, that's a bonus, but I don't expect it. After fifteen months, there's no reason for anyone to talk about her."

"But if someone does, that would be significant."

"Don't bring her up in conversation."

Liana's liquid blue eyes flashed. "Now I'm insulted."

"Sorry," said Aaron. "I just want you safe. Paddle out slowly and watch for sharks."

"Didn't know you surfed."

Aaron had, years ago, working his way up to the active waters of County Line Beach.

He said, "I don't. I'm just good at metaphors." He handed her Rory Stoltz's DMV photo, then a copy of the snapshot of Caitlin he'd gotten from Maitland Frostig.

"Cute couple."

"Virgins," said Aaron. "According to Rory's mother."

Liana crossed sleek legs. "You find that unbelievable."

"Don't you?"

"Well," she said. "I was once a virgin." Blinking. "Until I wasn't."

At 10:05 p.m., the little pink house's front windows went dark.

Early to bed for the All-American kid? Aaron could live with a dead end first night. He'd give it another hour.

Nine minutes later, the front door swung open and Rory Stoltz, wearing a dark shirt untucked over black jeans, his pale hair mussed with great intention, ambled to his Hyundai and backed out of the driveway.

Forgetting to switch his headlights on until he was halfway up the block.

Aaron waited until Stoltz reached the corner, kept his own beams off and trailed from a distance. When Stoltz turned south on Lankershim, Aaron illuminated and joined the traffic flow. Keeping three car lengths back in a neighboring lane, he managed a clear view of the Hyundai.

Rory Stoltz turned right on Ventura, then left on Laurel Canyon, continued south toward the city. Aaron let a Mercedes and a Range Rover get in front of him before joining the convoy.

Stoltz drove slowly and cautiously. Braked too early around curves and held up progress until the Mercedes grew impatient and started tailgating.

The Hyundai pulled aside and let the Benz and the Rover pass.

Aaron got in front, too, hoping Rory wouldn't turn off on some side lane.

He didn't, staying on the canyon all the way to Sunset.

Switching on his left turn signal well before the intersection.

Both cars headed east on the boulevard. Three blocks later, Rory slowed just west of ColdSnake's black stucco and red lava-rock façade. The usual fools were lined up behind a black velvet rope. A Samoan doorman in a white leather jumpsuit and a too-small bowler scowled just to keep in practice. His bulk obscured the entrance.

Stoltz's Hyundai had the nerve to pull behind a ruby stretch Hummer and a lime-green Lamborghini Gallardo. The little car looked like a wart on the Hummer's ass. Aaron waited for Mr. Derby to wave the kid out of there.

Instead, the Samoan allowed the

Hyundai to stay. Seconds later, Rory got waved in, fools craning to see who'd earned the privilege.

Mr. All-American Kid had VIP status at one of the hottest clubs in town.

Virgin, indeed.

Moe Reed drove to the Peninsula Hotel.

Noon was approaching, and he figured he had a decent chance at catching Martha Stoltz on her lunch break.

The hotel parking valet regarded his unmarked as if it carried disease.

Moe handed him the keys. "Keep it safe, it's scheduled for the lead position at Daytona."

The valet pretended deafness.

Inside, the lobby was full of high-end tourists and Industry types. It took Moe twenty minutes of wangling his way up the managerial command to locate Martha in an empty banquet room conferring with half a dozen room-service waiters. She spotted Moe and her lips folded inward, as if she'd just downed a laundry-soap martini.

She was a tall leathery woman with efficient copper hair, a strong chin, and downslanted eyes. She resumed talking. Some of the waiters watched Moe.

His phone vibrated in his pocket. Liz saying hi. He texted back. *tied up, 1 hr ok big m*

As he clicked off, Martha Stoltz adjourned the meeting and the waiters dispersed.

"Afternoon, Mrs. Stoltz."

"Has something come up since we talked this morning?"

"If only," said Moe.

Tension around the downslanted eyes pulled them level. Deep green with amber flecks. "Then I don't understand."

"Like I told you, ma'am, I'm updating, ma'am. How's Rory, what he's doing, where can I reach him."

"We already covered that."

"We really didn't, ma'am. You told me I shouldn't be talking to him."

"You're making it sound like I'm being . . . like I'm hindering you. I'm not, Detective Reed. I just don't want Rory subjected to any more stress."

"Being questioned was that stressful for him?"

"Honest people aren't used to dealing with the police, Detective. Being asked the same questions, over and over? Wouldn't that bother you? And now you show up, unannounced, in the middle of a workday, simply because I'm his mother? That stresses *me.*"

"I'm truly sorry, ma'am. I figured I might catch you on break."

Martha Stoltz's laughter was brittle. "Break? What's that?"

"Busy day, huh?"

"Busy *life,* Detective Reed. This place is a small city, I can't afford to be distracted. Please don't take this the wrong way but I find it extremely off-putting having my son harassed."

"I'm not aware of any harassment, ma'am."

The clipboard shifted from one hand to the other. "I've watched enough of those police shows to know the attention always falls on someone the victim knew. But you've already covered everything with Rory."

Moe rocked on his heels. "If it was my kid, I'd feel the same way, ma'am. Unfortunately, the case is being reopened comprehensively." Waiting for her reaction.

None.

"If Rory doesn't want to talk to me, that's his prerogative."

"But that would make you *more* suspicious," she said. "It's a Catch-22."

"Is he still at Pepperdine?"

"Junior year—oh, no, don't humiliate him by coming onto campus."

"Humiliate him?"

"The police showing up in front of his peers? How would you like that?"

Moe thought she was overreacting, and heck if that *didn't* make him wonder.

"Fair enough," he said. "Where else can I reach him?"

"He still lives at home, but I can't give you an exact schedule. He's an adult, Detective. Comes and goes as he pleases."

Moe said, "Does he still work at the Riptide?"

"Riptide," said Martha Stoltz. "There's no

the." Her knowing look said he'd just failed a vital exam. "And no, he doesn't work there. Shortly after Caitlin went missing, he had to leave."

"Had to?"

"Anything that reminded Rory of Caitlin was difficult. He grieved, Detective."

"Where does he work now?"

The clipboard pressed against her chest. "He registered with a temp agency. Wanted to concentrate on his studies and not be tied down to a rigid schedule."

"Is he temping for anyone currently?"

Hesitation.

"Mrs. Stoltz?"

"I don't want to put Rory's job in jeopardy."

"By telling me who he works for?"

"If you come looking for him while he's on the job, he'll be finished. He loves this job, Detective. The pay's excellent and we have two more years of tuition, then law school if he chooses to go that way."

"Ma'am, I can call every agency in town until I find out what I need. Why don't we just keep it simple and—"

"Mason Book. Okay? He works for Mason Book as a *personal* assistant."

Delivering the news with resentment, but also some pride.

"The actor," said Moe, instantly aware of how stupid that sounded. *No, the podiatrist.*

Martha Stoltz said, "Now you see why discretion is so important. Part of Rory's job is shielding Mason from unwanted publicity."

Calling the star by his first name. Meaning Rory probably did. Good old L.A. informality. Or Martha Stoltz had been reading too many stupid tabloids, thought celebs were her buddies.

They're just like us.

No, they're not.

He said, "Is Mason doing okay?"

"With what?"

"From what I understand, he's had personal problems." Kind of an understatement, given the actor's drug issues and well-publicized suicide attempt last year.

"They all have personal problems." Martha's eyes circled the banquet hall. "From the A list on down to the D's, they're—working here for fifteen years, I could tell you stories." She stiffened. "But I won't. And neither will Rory."

"Ma'am," said Moe, "I couldn't care less if Mason Book grows two additional heads or turns purple when he drinks. Same for any lister from A through Z. I'm here to find out what happened to a nice young woman named Caitlin Frostig."

Tough-guy bravado in his voice. *Now who's acting?*

"I know that man is suffering. Caitlin's father. I phoned him shortly after Caitlin vanished. To offer support, one parent to the other. He thanked me and hung up and I realized I'd been stupid. Presuming I had something to offer him. Empathy's damn weak tea, Detective."

Her eyes drooped. "I lost a child myself. Seventeen months before Rory was born. Her name was Sarah, she had the most gorgeous brown eyes you've ever seen and she was three months old when I found her in her crib not breathing."

"I'm sor—"

"When Rory was nine, his father passed. So I figured I could offer Mr. Frostig something by way of understanding. But no one can ever really know how anyone feels, that's just pop-psych nonsense. We're put on this planet for a few years, just us and our shadows, Detective Reed. Maybe there's someone up there, pulling the strings, I don't know. Anyone who tells you he does know wants your money or is trying to get elected to something."

"Ma'am—"

"Rory's a good boy, please don't put his job at risk. It's perfect for him, gives him a toehold in the Industry."

"Rory wants to act?"

"Rory wants to be an entertainment lawyer, or maybe an agent. It's all about connections, he was so lucky to connect right at the top. Mason may have had personal issues but he treats Rory well and Rory loves working for him." Softening her voice. "He's really a nice young man. Mason, I mean. Rory brought him here for breakfast and I served him personally and he couldn't have been more gracious."

"Great," said Moe.

"What is?"

"Success hasn't made him obnoxious."

"Yes," she said. "That *is* nice, isn't it?"

10

Riptide was ripe with the odors of tequila, aftershave, and slightly rancid cooking oil.

Liana Parlat took a stool at the far end of the spar-varnished bar, aware of male eyes shifting as she crossed the length of the room.

Long, dark room, kind of tunnel-like. Off to one side, a double-width doorway led to a small dining area. No one in there she could see.

The action was at Cocktail Central. A few couples in their thirties, the rest men batching it. Beach Boys on soundtrack.

"Don't Worry Baby." Her favorite. Made it easy to smile.

The smile snagged the ponytailed bartender's attention and she ordered a Grey Goose Greyhound, rocks, twist. "Pink grapefruit juice, if you have it."

Ponytail grinned. "Sorry, just regular."

"That's fine."

"I can splash in a little cranberry, if you'd like. For color."

"You know," said Liana, "maybe I would rather have a Seabreeze."

"Good choice." The guy got to work and seconds later, the extra-large cocktail was set down in front of her. Orange slice, which she liked. Maraschino, which was all wrong.

"Yum," she said.

"Enjoy."

Sipping slowly, she took in the flavor of the place. "Good Vibrations" came on. Nice, but earlier stuff—the surf songs— would've fit better with the décor.

She figured it was mostly original: rough plank cedar walls, lacquered coils of hemp rope, ship's lamps, circular glass balls, a couple of buoys. At least two captain's wheels she could spot and she bet there were more in the dining room.

All of it probably a throwback to the bar's previous life as a working-class drinkery.

Before arriving, she'd revved up the old Mac and read up on the place, found a three-year-old gushing travel piece from the *Times* that emphasized a "festive Jimmy Buffett ambience" and the occasional "spontaneous" appearance of celebs.

Britney, Paris, Brangelina, Mel, Mason, even the Governator. Supposedly, they favored the Meyer Rum Tsunami. As if anything those people did was spontaneous. Inane, but what else could you expect from a paper where half the entertainment "articles" were press releases fed by studio publicists?

Obsolete, too, because Liana found no recent name-drops, so any star appeal was history.

Celebs, like sharks, needed to keep moving to breathe.

Not that she needed the Internet to know that; when she'd walked over from Loews there wasn't a pappo or limo in sight.

A few homeless guys, though, Aaron

had been right about that. One of them gave her the willies as his watery eyes followed her twenty-yard traipse and she imagined him snagging Caitlin and dragging her into an alley.

Rather than ignore him, she stopped and stared him down.

Chancy move, but she had to follow her instincts.

The bum shrank back, resumed pushing his cart up Ocean, clattering and bumping on sidewalks long in need of repair.

Too bad those guys didn't have to hang special license plates from their carts. *I M CRAY ZEE.*

She sipped and used her eyes discreetly. Someone at the other end of the bar laughed. The track switched to Jan and Dean. "Dead Man's Curve," eerily prophetic of Jan's auto crash.

Happy song about tragedy . . . at least the floors were clean oak, no sawdust cliché.

Liana knew all about clichés. She trucked in them for a living—using her voice to sell feminine hygiene products, grocery specials, whatever.

Using her looks and her brains to gig for Aaron.

Not exactly what she'd dreamed about back in South Dakota, but at her stage in life, any role came up, you took it.

Tonight she'd gone for sultry but subdued: black V-neck sweater with a triangle of white cammie hiding some but not all of her cleaves, snug gray wool/Lycra slacks that hugged her like a lover.

The absence of panty line suggested bare skin underneath, but her entire lower body was sheathed in support hose.

Everyone said she looked young for her age, but Liana prided herself on self-awareness, so no sense pretending butt and belly were the way they'd been when she auditioned for *Playboy.*

Twenty years ago.

A starlet's entire lifetime; sometimes it seemed like yesterday.

She'd walked out of the *Playboy* session beaming at the photo editor's praise. Two days later, he called to let her down gently. Twenty-four hours after that, he phoned to ask her out.

The perfect retort had jumped into her head.

Sorry, but I limit my social life to men with normal penises.

She'd said, "Sorry, Luigi, but I'm involved with someone."

Twenty—twenty-*one* years ago.

Gawd!

A baritone voice said, "Come here often?"

Just loud enough to rise above the music. Liana glanced to her right.

The nervously smiling face she encountered belonged to a slightly overweight but decent-looking guy around her own age working a beer mug. Sandy hair, five o'clock shadow, nice masculine features; he'd probably been hot ten years ago.

Dark suit, pale blue dress shirt open at the collar, sensible shoes.

"What's a nice girl like you doing in a place like this?" he said. "Glad I worked out this morning 'cause I can tell you're no easy pickup. Your mother must have been a sculptor 'cause you're in great shape. I thought perfection was an ideal until about a second ago."

Liana stared.

He shrugged, smiled.

Despite herself, Liana's lips curved in imitation.

The guy said, "Now that I've used up all the fresh material, I'd better lug out the hackneyed stuff."

"You write for Leno?"

"If I did, he wouldn't be beating out Letterman." He extended a hand. "Steve Rau."

In lieu of pressing flesh, Liana gave a small salute and returned to facing forward. Her top had ridden up, exposing an inch of back. She tugged it down, moved her head in time with the music.

"Ouch," said Rau. But good-naturedly. Liana's peripheral vision spotted motion. His hand gesturing for another beer.

As it arrived, Liana managed another of her famous sidelongs and took in the cut of his suit. Decent, but nothing custom or exceptional. The shirt was pinpoint oxford cloth, eighty bucks, give or take. The shoes were nondescript black loafers but they did look like calfskin. Bottom line: solid, not junk, not haute. Maybe Nordstrom.

Working for Aaron, she'd picked up a few things.

Steve Rau said, "I'd offer to buy you

another, but you haven't made much headway on the first and you might go military on me again." Aping the salute.

Liana chuckled.

The bartender said, "Some nuts or shrimp, Steve?"

"No, thanks, Gus."

You come here often?

Aaron just wanted her to soak up the atmosphere, but here was an opportunity.

She rehearsed an entry line, discarded it, searched for another. Rau made it easy for her by saying, "This is my second beer and my last. For the record."

Liana swiveled gracefully, gifted him with more face and body. The warm, sincere smile. "You are nothing if not temperate."

"Temperate, sane, dependable. Gus can vouch for me."

"Is Gus called upon to do that regularly?"

Rau got flustered. Laughed. "Only for the last three months."

He showed her his left hand. Pale circle of skin on the ring finger. "As they say, an amicable split."

Liana said, "Didn't know that was possible."

"It's not."

"Oops."

"Don't worry," said Rau. "I'm not going to get all maudlin and mawkish."

"A dual guarantee, huh?"

The music veered back to the Beach Boys. "Little Deuce Coupe." The two of them sipped in silence. Liana working slowly because that was her style even when she wasn't on the job. A man needed to be kept slightly off balance.

She said, "Seeing as you're a regular, you know I'm not."

"Visiting L.A.? I ask because sometimes women come over from the hotel."

"No, I'm a native." If you didn't count military bases in six other states.

"Rara avis," said Rau. "Rare bird."

"Quo vadis," said Liana. "Non sequitur, ipso facto. So, Steve, what do you do other than drink Heineken and indulge yourself in Latin?"

Rau motioned to the bartender. "Gus, what do I do when I'm not hunched over in self-pity?"

Gus said, "You're a spy."

"Double-O something, huh?"

Rau said, "Gus is embroidering. I work

at RAND—the think tank, we're not far from here, on Main."

"You get paid to think."

"The official title is security analyst."

"As in stocks and bonds?"

"As in shoe bombers and suicide belt morons." Some edge had crept into the mellow baritone. "But I'm not going to insult your intelligence by making it out as some covert, civilian contractor deal. My degree's in economics. I play with statistics, try to spot trends. Lately, I have been doing more financial analysis than security. It's about as exciting as watching beard stubble sprout."

"Still," said Liana, "at least you know you're doing something important. How many people can say that?"

"On some lofty theoretical plane, I guess that's true. But half my time is filling out grant applications and going to meetings. I used to do something even more blood-stirring. Want to guess?"

"College professor."

Rau stared. "It's that obvious?"

"You've got a Ph.D."

"I said I had a degree."

"I extrapolated."

Rau laughed.

Liana said, "Stanford?"

"Chicago."

"Where'd you teach?"

"Community college. All that came up were nontenured positions, so I switched gears. I was really committed to teaching, figured RAND would be temporary. It's been twelve years, so much for spotting trends."

Liana smiled.

Silence settled between them for several moments before Rau spoke up. "So what do you do—fill in name here."

"Laura," she said. Fishing out the alias she'd used for the *Playboy* shoot because it didn't sound that different from her real name.

Laura Layne. Sometimes she carried pink satin business cards in her purse . . . had she brought any tonight?

Twenty-one years ago.

Rau said, "Same question, Laura. What occupies your days?"

"I'm in between obligations," she said. "My c.v. includes teaching preschool, executive assisting, interior designing, house-sitting, and, before all that, wait-ressing, big surprise."

"Ah," said Rau. "How many pilots have you been in?"

"It's that obvious?"

"RAND doesn't pay me for not reading big print."

"Well," said Liana, "RAND wouldn't have gotten their money's worth this time. Acting's not my thing. Like I said, I'm a California native, not some kid off the bus from Iowa."

"Sorry," said Rau. "For assuming. May I dig myself out by suggesting you take it as a compliment, as in 'looks like an actress'?"

Liana swiveled on her stool and offered him a full view of the goods. "I get that all the time and, yes, I do take it as a compli-ment."

Rau mimed wiping his brow. "Phew—so . . . I ask this at great risk—of all the gin joints . . ."

"I was at Loews, having dinner with friends. It broke up early—they're all mar-ried with kids and needed to return to their mundane lives. I wasn't quite ready for a quiet night with Kurt Vonnegut."

"Slaughterhouse-Five?"

"Welcome to the Monkey House."

"Never read that one . . . I met Joseph Heller, once. *Catch-22*?"

"Did you?"

"Yup," said Rau. "I was in fifth grade and he gave a speech at the U. and my dad was on faculty there—in the med school— and he insisted on taking me. Wanting me to soak up some antiwar fervor. At ten, I was pretty apolitical."

"Dad wasn't."

"Dad was a *highly* principled man." Putting rough emphasis on the word and for a second, Rau's face toughened up.

Anger turned him appealingly masculine.

Liana said, "So he dragged you along."

"He dragged me and after the speech, he insisted we both go up to Heller, going on about how the guy's a genius, meanwhile I'd daydreamed through the whole thing. Dad pumps Heller's hand, makes sure I shake, too, then he goes off on this big oration about *Catch-22* being the ultimate antiwar masterpiece. Heller looks at him and says, 'It's not about war, it's about bureaucracy.'"

"Poor Dad."

"It fazed him, but only temporarily. During the ride home, he informed me authors sometimes didn't understand their own motivation."

"Motivation," said Liana. "A med school prof. I'm putting money on psychiatrist."

Rau's smile was wide, warm. Nice teeth. "You should think about RAND."

"Like they'd take me."

"You'd be surprised."

"I sure would."

Several beats.

"So you're in between obligations," said Rau. "Sounds nice."

"It can be."

Rau scratched his temple. "Laura, I'm not good at this, but . . . since you've already had dinner I know suggesting we shift to the dining area is out of the question. So is, I imagine, *blowing* this gin joint."

"I didn't hear a question in there, Steve. But yes, I think I'll stay put."

Rau beat his breast, bowed his head. "Aargh. Hopes dashed asunder."

Liana touched his jacket sleeve. Smooth fabric, maybe better than she'd initially appraised. "Steve, I wouldn't be a very smart girl if I waltzed off with someone I just met."

"Of course . . . would it be totally out of line asking you for your number?"

Poor guy was blushing.

"Why don't you give me yours?"

Liana expected another burst of self-deprecation but he seemed pleased, as he fished into his pocket, drew out a battered wallet, then a RAND business card.

On the surface, everything looked kosher. Easy enough to verify.

She slipped the card into her purse. This one might come in handy.

Steve Rau said, "Anyway . . . like I said, I'm really not good at this."

"Practice, practice, practice," said Liana, giving him another arm pat. "How long has Riptide been around?"

The change of subject relaxed Rau. "As Riptide? Maybe five years. It got that name when some movie honchos bought it. No one famous—producers and the like. Before that it was a neighborhood bar called Smiley's, before that it was *The* Riptide. I don't know exactly how old it is, but probably at least forty years."

Making that sound antique. Liana suppressed a flinch.

"No more *the*," she said. "Industry honchos thought it was hipper."

"No, they were cheap. A storm knocked down part of the sign. They stuck on that neon martini glass instead."

"Subtle," said Liana.

Rau chuckled. "This is tragic, Laura."

"What is?"

"I meet a highly intelligent woman who looks like a movie star and she's smart enough not to be impulsive."

Liana smiled.

"I guess if you did agree to go off with me, I'd wonder about your judgment." He shrugged. "Story of my life. Ambivalence and second-guessing. My ex said it drove her crazy. My lack of quote unquote 'constructive recklessness.' Why it took eleven years and division of assets for her to reach that insight, she couldn't explain." Deep blush. "Sorry, that was stunningly awkward and inappropriate."

"Hey," said Liana, "you've been through it. Three months is pretty fresh."

"Papers came through three months ago. We've been separated for three years."

His look said it had taken him a long time to give up hope.

"Steve, I, for one, appreciate that you understand about the need for caution. A girl can't be too careful. Even in a nice place like this."

Rau didn't answer.

"It is a nice place?" she asked.

"Never seen a brawl," said Rau. "And Gus keeps his eye on the inebriation level. Yeah, it's nice. Back when the celebs used to show up—two, three years ago—it could get . . . a little different."

"Different, how?"

"Long stays in the bathroom." He touched his nose. "Obviously underage girls, fake I.D.'s. People getting up and dirty-dancing when the music didn't call for it."

"Sounds like fun."

"Gobs, Laura. I stopped coming for a while. Things are a lot quieter now, and I'm sure the owners are feeling it in the pocketbook but I, for one—and I'll bet I speak for all the regulars—don't miss those days."

"Celebs," said Liana. "They do get entitled."

Rau got more aggressive with his beer,

taking two deep gulps. He dribbled a tad and wiped his lips with his napkin.

"How come the egomaniacs don't come here anymore, Steve?"

"They moved on, Laura. That's what they do, it's all about the Next Big Thing."

"Ah," she said.

Rau emptied his mug. Looked over at the bartender but when Gus pointed to the tap, he shook his head.

Liana said, "So two years since it's been celebbed up."

"Two, three. Here's the irony, Laura: Back then, with all the bodyguards and drivers and such hanging around, you'd think it would've been safer than milk. But that's when there were some problems."

He wrapped both hands around the empty mug. The music had switched to Brian Wilson singing about the wonders of his room.

"What kind of problems, Steve?"

"Forget it," said Rau. "Last thing I want to do is spook you. Because I *do* want you to come back."

Staring at her. Soft brown eyes.

Liana said, "I'm a big girl."

"Not important—ancient history."

"Come on, Steve. I don't spook easily."

Rau knuckled his forehead. "Brilliant, Rau."

"What happened?"

"I'm not saying it had anything to do with this place. I'm sure it didn't, because it happened outside . . . oh Lord, I'm *bad* at being single."

Liana wet her lips with Seabreeze. She'd taken in maybe a quarter ounce, felt sharp and on her game as she waited the guy out.

He said, "You really want to know?"

"I do."

"A girl who worked here—in the dining room, as a hostess—back then they served more food—she left after her shift was over and was never seen again. But nothing happened to her here—we're talking a year and a half ago, something like that . . . so I guess some celebs were still here. At least that's the way I remember it. The irony, like I said. Then something else happened shortly after. A couple, tourists staying at Loews, dropped in for a few drinks and also vanished. That I heard on the news. They mentioned Riptide as the last place the couple was seen. After that, I stayed away."

"I can see why you were spooked."

"Not spooked, just . . . Maria had broken off marriage counseling, I was by myself . . . I'm sorry. Now you'll never come back."

"Steve, I do not allow myself to be ruled by the misfortunes of others."

"Laura, all I *do,* day in and day out, is *immerse* myself in the misfortunes of others. This afternoon it was devising algorithms to predict the correlation between economic downturns and the rise of insurgency in Malaysia."

"How's it looking for Malaysia?"

"You don't want to know." Suddenly he stood.

Taller than she'd thought and really not that heavy. Hint of a soft little gut, but broad, square shoulders and long, strong-looking legs.

Tossing bills on the bar, he held out his hand. "Great to meet you, Laura. I mean that."

This time Liana pressed flesh. His was cool, dry, smooth.

"If for some reason you do come back, I hope it's a night that I'm here."

Sighing, he pressed his lips to her fingers. Dropped her hand quickly and shook his head and muttered, "Dork."

Before she could reassure him, he was gone.

"Poor Steve," said someone up the bar. "That wife of his really racked him up."

11

Half the cookie," said Liz Wilkinson.

Moe Reed said, "Pardon?"

"As in Oreo. We are fifty percent of a cookie, baby. Or maybe seventy, seeing as all the crème's *here.*"

Reaching under his butt, she squeezed. Her smooth brown body rested atop the hard bunches and swells of his pale, freckled musculature.

Hips touching. Everything glued together. They'd finally stopped kissing.

He said, "Didn't Oreo used to be a dis? Black on the outside, white on the inside?"

"I'm adapting it for my own purposes."

"Creative."

"I'm glad you agree." She laughed. He loved that sound.

Moments later: "Liz, with an Oreo, the dark part's all crusty and the crème is soft. Isn't this more like a reverse Oreo?"

She propped herself up, looked into his eyes. "Now you're a philosopher."

He craned to kiss her. When their lips parted, he pressed his mouth to her long, smooth neck. She lowered her weight back onto him.

"Mr. Literal."

"I'm with a trained scientist, I want to be accurate." He rubbed her back. "Trained scientist, natural *gorgeous*."

Liz smiled to herself, felt the sting of bone against bone and shifted her pelvis. The movement, an innocent attempt at comfort, produced a *new* swell below. "I can tell you're sincere, Detective Reed, because the forensic evidence is in plain sight."

She sat herself up, ran her hands over those slab-like pectorals. Knowing what human skeletal muscles looked like, beneath the sliver that was skin. Visualizing Moe's striated sheath.

The boy was solid, rock-hard.

Everywhere.

She touched him. Stroked him. He looked up at her, wide-eyed. Guiding him back in, she rocked slowly. Doing it, at first, for his sake, because boys behaved better when they were satisfied to the point of stupor. But soon they were fitting so perfectly and moving so perfectly, Liz's eyes closed and her head began swaying, flaps of her long hair grazing Moe's chest.

She straightened her locks religiously, but some texture remained and he said he liked that. Now the ends tickled his nipples and he turned his head to one side.

"Oh, man." Shifting his hands to her breasts.

She said, "Exactly."

Twenty minutes later, they sat at the breakfast room table of her condo on Fuller Avenue off Melrose, drinking peach Fresca and eating take-out deli sandwiches. The neighborhood was Intensely Ironic Postmodern Hipster but Liz had no interest in any of that. For all the time she spent at home, a motel would've served just as well.

Mother and Father had chipped in for the down payment, tossed in some extra for furniture. One day, she'd have to buy something nicer than the foldable card table at which they were eating, IKEA cases to hold all her books, the mattress on her bedroom floor.

Meanwhile, the simple life served quite nicely, thank you. Moe sure didn't care about interior decorating; his own place in the Valley was neat and clean but except for that gym, it looked like a college dorm room.

Lots of books there, too. Pleasant surprise.

She watched him chomp his sandwich. Skinless turkey breast, because of the cholesterol issue. Liz had ordered the same, even though she preferred beef.

Love, Mother had always preached, was all about compromise.

If only Mother knew . . .

One month out of a Stanford Ph.D. in physical anthro, Liz's dissertation on microchanges in humidity and visceral muscle decomposition had landed her a postdoc with Eleanor Hargrove at the LAPD-affiliated bone lab. The following year, funding came up for a real job at the lab and Liz snagged it. The position meant long hours spent with mummified skin, studying the finer points of rot and shred, the awful detritus that came with finality.

Lots of travel to conferences, because Eleanor wanted the lab to get exposure. All of which Liz had expected and generally relished.

What *hadn't* been in the game plan was hooking up with a guy, let alone one whose formal education had ended with a criminal justice B.A. from Cal State Northridge.

Liz's parents were full professors with Yale degrees. Poli sci at Howard for Mother, sociology at GW for Father. She still hadn't told them about Moe.

The first time she and Moe met, she was waist-deep in marsh muck, pulling up frags of human skeleton. Moe, the first D at the scene, had stood on the banks, conferred with Hargrove, not noticing Liz at all.

Then he'd spotted her, and darn if he didn't take a second look.

Long second look.

She'd been intrigued by him from the

beginning. So young and intense—that earnest boyishness you didn't see much anymore.

Cute, too.

In a Celtic way.

When he asked her out, she accepted without hesitation, despite the fact that Moe wasn't her type.

Light-years from her type. Her upbringing in the rarefied world of black academia had funneled her dating contacts to articulate men with advanced degrees and accomplishments to match.

Men whose skin tone matched hers.

Half a cookie . . .

Moe reached over and touched her hand in that gentle way she adored. The athletics of the previous hour had rubbed him pink in spots and the blotches hadn't faded.

Delicate boy, he never tanned. Strawberry yogurt was the last thing Liz had figured she'd ever find attractive.

Go know. She kissed his knuckles.

He said, "You are unbe*liev*able."

"Keep thinking that, Moses."

"I always will," he assured her. Like a six-year-old promising to be good. Not a *trace* of postmodern irony. *That* was a novelty.

She'd rehearsed her little speech a hundred times. *He's highly intelligent, Mother. Intuitive. Anything* but *simple.*

All of it true, but it rang hollow. Trying too hard.

She was twenty-nine and Moe was barely that. Both of them paying their own bills, they didn't have to answer to anyone.

Right.

He finished his sandwich. She pushed half hers toward him. "I'm full, finish it."

"Thanks." Five bites did the trick. Hungry boy—sometimes, Liz couldn't help but think in kid terms when she was with him.

She adored the way he held on to the guileless part of himself, despite the job. Wondered how the job would play at the Georgetown *salons* Mother favored.

No, she didn't. She knew how he'd be treated.

He got up and cleared the table. Rolled his neck.

Liz said, "Got a crick?"

"Not really."

She stepped behind him and massaged that incredibly dense hunk of neck.

"Oh, wow, that's great."

"Any reason for all these knots, Detective Reed?"

"Not really." Two beats later: "I'm back full-time on Caitlin. Pressure from above."

"That'll screw up the trapezius, all right."

"Hey," he said, "no big deal. I'll work it."

"I know you will. But sorry for the hassle, baby."

"Anything interesting at the lab?"

"No new cases," she said. "Catching up on grant applications."

He turned to face her, slipped his arm around her waist. "Want your own massage?"

"No, thanks, you've loosened me up quite well, sir."

He smiled. A flicker of anxiety sprinted across his eyes. Split-second storm, then it was gone.

"What?" she said.

"It's a loser, Liz."

"You can't create facts on the ground, baby."

"I know . . . it sticks me with a crappy close rate, right at the outset."

"You closed the marsh murders, Moses."

"Sturgis really did that."

"Now, that I won't listen to, Moses. You and Sturgis. It's not like he didn't give you credit."

"He's a gentleman."

"Maybe so," said Liz, "but he was only doing what was right."

"Yeah . . . Aaron's on Caitlin, too."

That caught her off balance. "How'd that happen?"

"Caitlin's father's boss is footing his bill. Aaron thinks all he needs to do is chew through enough billable hours and he'll close it."

"Oh, sure."

"Maybe he's right, Liz."

"At this stage, how would he know if it's closable or not?" she said.

Moe didn't answer.

She massaged him some more. "C'mon, let's get mindless and watch some tube."

"Sure," said Moe. But the evening had changed.

During the months Liz and Moe had dated, she'd met Aaron Fox exactly once.

Six, seven weeks ago, while walking up the leafy pathway to Moe's mom's house, meeting Maddy for the first time—an experience in itself.

Halfway up, a black man appeared around a bend.

Moe tensed up and for a second Liz wondered if the guy posed some sort of threat.

A brief handshake and Moe's curt introductions dispelled all that, but the entire time, Moe never relaxed.

Aaron, on the other hand, had been nothing *but* mellow. One of those people who make you feel you've been friends for years.

Growing up in D.C. she'd seen that brand of charisma in politicians and financial types, distrusted it instinctively.

As Moe and Aaron made small talk on the pathway, Liz tried to figure out how Moe knew him.

Maybe another cop? Then what was he doing visiting Moe's mom?

Sensing a long story, she bided her time.

A personal trainer?

No, something more, he definitely had made her baby tense.

Maybe Mom's young black *boyfriend*?

Aware that she categorized people too quickly, she still couldn't stop herself.

Good looking, but spends way too much time at the mirror.

Great clothes, same issue.

He'd been nothing but polite, with polished diction and intelligent eyes, but way too smooth. What Liz termed Upper Division Player.

Not all that different from the guys she'd dated prior to Moe, minus the Ivy League Polish.

What did he do for a living?

A lawyer making a house call? Possibly.

Or something in show business—an agent? Moe said Maddy had once aspired to stage and screen, never got very far.

Or an acting *coach.* Guy was handsome enough and the clothes and that snappy little Porsche out by the curb said he was doing just fine. Or pretending, this was L.A.

Maybe that's why he came across as Instant Friend—expecting to be recognized.

Liz couldn't recall ever seeing him on anything.

By the time he'd walked off, she'd com-
piled a dossier. Moe watched the Porsche
speed away, a brow-wrinkling frown imply-
ing disapproval.

Conspicuous consumption wasn't Moe's
game. Something else he and Liz had in
common.

**Elizabeth Mae, you really need to
make more of the looks God gave you.**

The sports car was long gone but Moe
continued to stare down the street.

Liz took hold of his tree-trunk arm.
"C'mon, I want to meet the woman who
gifted you to the world."

They resumed their walk.

Liz couldn't control herself. "Does Aaron
work with your mother?"

"He's my brother."

"As in, he ain't heavy?"

"As in sibling."

"No really, baby, seriously."

"I wish I was kidding."

Over the next few weeks, Liz teased out
details of the brothers' upbringing.

Both of their fathers had been cops, both
were deceased.

Maybe *that* was the issue: one dad

stepping in for another, all that blended-family tension. If so, Mama had made her sons' lives even more complicated.

An apparent serial marrier, Madeleine Fox Reed Guistone Entley ("but we don't talk about Entley, dear") had buried her third husband fifteen years ago. A wealthy orthodontist and "visionary entrepreneur," Stan Guistone had invested in enough real estate to ensure his widow a lovely lifestyle. Two years after his death, she'd tried yet again, divorced "Shiftless Bum Entley" within months.

The woman kept framed photo portraits of hubbies one, two, and three propped on her bedroom dresser, a fact that Liz had gleaned during that same Sunday visit, after ducking into Maddy's private bathroom because the main one was occupied by Moe.

Two cops in uniform and a squat, beetle-browed, white-haired man in a wide-lapeled suit.

Aaron was a clone of his father.

Moe was built heavier and thicker than his father, and his fine, symmetrical features were Maddy's. But the coloring was there . . . maybe something around the eyes. The ears, too.

Officer Darius Fox, RIP.

Officer John Jasper Reed, RIP.

Dr. Stanley Edgar Guistone, D.D.S., M.P.H., M.B.A., ditto.

The woman was bad news for the morbidity/mortality stats.

Three husbands, two kids. If she'd had a child with Dr. G, the poor thing might've ended up looking like a depressed raccoon.

Now curiosity about Moe's family history was nibbling her brain even harder, but she resolved to take it slow. Pushing issues didn't work with most men and it sure wouldn't work with Moe.

Between her travel and the open-ended schedule of a homicide detective, the two of them needed to use their time together wisely. No sense dashing good times with the emotional ice resulting from mention of Aaron's name.

Still, that level of sibling hostility did intrigue her. She had two brothers and adored them both. Sean and Jay had suffered through some friction but they got along great now. Played golf together, for God's sake.

Moses and Aaron, on the other hand . . . a stupid person might assume race was the problem, because stupid people always jumped on "the obvious solution" to explain complex problems.

The Little-Person Fallacy, she called it, in honor of a case during her internship. The corpse of a three-foot-eight woman had been found moldering in a Menlo Park apartment, too decayed for an obvious COD. Post-autopsy, Dr. Lieber, the medical examiner, had asked everyone to guess. Those brave enough to venture opted for spondyloepiphyseal dwarfism and the health issues that went along with that.

Truth was, the woman had smoked three packs a day and died of throat cancer.

Liz had spent enough time with Moe to know that he really was that rare color-blind American. And now maybe, she understood why.

Whatever her effect upon male longevity, Maddy must have been an independent thinker, marrying a black man back when that was still a big deal.

Then a white man from the Deep South . . .

Maybe growing up with Aaron had made Moe comfortable enough to *resent* Aaron with no fear of the R word coming up.

But still not comfortable enough with Liz to talk about why he couldn't stand his brother.

Maddy's house up in the hills teemed with ghosts, but as far as Liz could see, the woman didn't feel haunted.

Unlike her younger son.

One day, Liz would figure it out.

12

Twenty minutes after Aaron found a watch spot across the street from Cold-Snake, Rory Stoltz was still in the club.

The line in front hadn't moved much though desperate types clung to false hope behind the black rope. The white-suited ape in the bowler did his best to pretend they didn't exist.

Not a paparazzo in sight, but that didn't account for Stoltz being allowed to park up front and saunter past the bouncer.

Kid was obviously meeting someone inside, but a *Hyundai*?

Aaron checked his cell for messages. A

couple of trash calls and a text from Liana.

back home safe call tmrw

Motion in front of the club. Rory Stoltz emerged.

All by himself.

Keeping his eyes on the Hyundai, Aaron pulled away from the curb.

Stoltz drove east to Highland Avenue, traveled south to Santa Monica Boulevard, where he headed west.

Making a big loop that seemed pointless . . . unless he was interested in cruising the heart of the gay hooker stroll.

So maybe this had something to do with alternative lifestyle. But what did that have to do with nearly half an hour in a hetero dive like ColdSnake?

Aaron followed Stoltz as the Hyundai sailed by languid young men and he-she's in various states of camouflage. Stoltz never even slowed to look at the goods, just kept driving all the way to La Cienega, where he hooked north and got back on Sunset. The Hyundai continued until it was one block east of ColdSnake, then turned left.

One big useless circuit.

This time Stoltz bypassed the scene out front and parked just shy of the alley that ran behind the club. Switching off his lights, but keeping his engine running.

Kid's playing *some* kind of game.

The logical guess was dope: Rory's initial stop had been meeting with customers, taking orders. Problem was, the kid had just driven around, not stopping to pick anything up. So maybe the goods had been in the car all the time and Stoltz had spun a yarn about taking a special trip to pick up premium product. Which, of *course,* would cost a wee bit more . . .

Was All-American boy that clever of a marketing consultant?

Whatever the details, he wasn't what he seemed.

Moe had missed the boat completely by dismissing the kid so quickly.

Aaron drove two blocks past the Hyundai, circled back with his own lights off. Positioning the Opel in a cozy spot three houses north, he waited for Stoltz to get out of the car.

Kid just sat there.

Five minutes, ten, fifteen.

At seventeen, two figures emerged from the alley and made their way toward the Hyundai.

Two men, tallish. From the shaggy out-line of their breeze-blown hair, and the way they walked, white guys.

As they got closer, Aaron saw that one was real skinny, the other beefy. The heav-ier one seemed to be propping up Slim Jim. Midway to the Hyundai, he paused to look around.

Checking for the cops? Stoltz's clients came to him?

Easier to rabbit if things got compli-cated.

Virgin, indeed.

Aaron bounced his eyes between the Hyundai and the two men. Ten feet from the car, Skinny went loose and Beefy's knees bent as he worked at keeping his pal upright.

Looks like someone doesn't need any more controlled substance . . . as the men approached, the Hyundai's lights switched on and the brights flashed. Twice.

The signal for *Come and get it, pathetic addicts.*

Beefy walked Skinny straight to the

Hyundai, keeping one hand on Skinny's arm, the other on the passenger door.

It took a while to tuck Skinny's long frame in the back of the car.

Put your hand on his head and press down, dude. That's how we do it on the job.

Used to do it . . .

Once Beefy had Skinny inside, he straightened, looked to be conversing with Stoltz. Then he slid into the front passenger seat and shut the door.

On-site smoke-up?

Nope, Stoltz drove away.

This time the Hyundai sped north into the heart of Hollywood, turned left on Selma.

Another gay pickup zone. So maybe this *was* a sex thing. Rory with two guys still pretending they were straight?

Aaron's head spun with possibilities as, once again, Stoltz bypassed corner loiterers, drove to Laurel Canyon, hooked right at the first opportunity, up a narrow, winding side road.

Once the Opel turned onto the quiet street, Aaron squelched his lights. Hoping some random Hollywood Division cruiser wasn't out trolling for traffic money.

The road turned steep and the Hyundai stressed its four cylinders climbing, zipping around curves, making frequent turns, chugging up brief, obscure lanes lined with darkened hillside houses. No streetlamps; all Aaron needed was a head-on with some idiot on a cell phone descending obliviously.

Rory Stoltz knew exactly where he was going, putting on maximum speed as he spurted along a series of skinny black ribbons of asphalt.

Swinging abruptly onto what at first appeared to be a driveway but turned out to be Swallowsong Lane.

A yellow sign warned *No Outlet.*

Aaron parked just short of Swallowsong's mouth, cut his engine, jumped out quickly, continued on foot.

Even steeper; it paid to stay in shape.

Big houses here, lots of foliage, high hedges, sports cars under tarps. Night-blooming jasmine sweetened the air. Nocturnal smog wafting up from Hollywood fought that.

Aaron made it to the top just in time to see the Hyundai pass through electric gates.

Iron gates supported by stone posts, lots of Baroque scrolls, medallions, whatever. Aaron peeked through, saw a curving driveway lined with Italian cypress, winding out of view.

Address numerals on the left column. *1001.* He copied down the numerals, returned to the Opel and sat.

Endured two hours of nothing before concluding All-American Boy was unlikely to show himself.

Not a dope deal? Some kind of party?

He drove back home, flipped the lights on at Work Land, looked up the address on his reverse directory, got a phone number.

He'd wait until morning to call Assistant Technical Manager Henry Q. Stokes at the assessor's office.

Then he remembered that Henry sometimes took work home.

Was the guy an early-to-bed type? If he was, too damned bad. He tried Henry's apartment in West Covina.

Seven rings before Henry's voice came through on the other end, thick with fatigue and irritation.

"It's me."

"What the—"

"This'll be more than a Ulysses," said Aaron. "Two Benjamins, so don't go bitching."

"What time is it—oh, shit, it's two twenty, man. Top of that, you screwed up a dream about Paris Hilton *and* her mom."

"One oh oh one Swallowsong Lane, Hollywood Hills."

Henry breathed hoarsely.

Aaron said, "Did you get that?"

"It can't wait?"

"Two Dr. Franklins sound like it can?"

"You could drive down tomorrow, check it out yourself—"

"That's always true, and yet I call you, Henry. We're talking exigent circumstances."

"More like an exigent expense account."

"Yours is not to question why, Mr. Stokes." Aaron repeated the address.

Henry said, "Two twenty for that—are you taping this?"

"Why would I be, Henry?"

"'Cause that's what P.I.'s do. It's one thing at work, I use an extension open to everyone. This is my friggin' home line."

"I don't tape."

"That guy with the Mafia connections, he probably said the same thing."

"Mafia bullshit," said Aaron. "Mario Fortuno, he's a wannabe, Henry. Not to mention a resident of the federal penitentiary at—"

"Exactly," said Stokes. "Because he taped."

"I don't tape my friends, Henry. And what's the big deal—you're accessing public records for a small fee. Free enterprise."

"I'm so reassured."

"Why would I want *myself* on tape?" said Aaron.

No answer.

"Henry, have we ever had anything but cordial business relat—"

"Yeah, yeah . . . which is why calling at two thirty in the morning isn't exactly friendly. I was sleeping, man. That dream . . ."

"Two hundred's worth waking up for, my friend."

"Two plus an additional fifty for fantasy theft."

"Not a chance."

"You had to be there, man," said Stokes. "You think Paris is hot, you should see her—"

"Fine," said Aaron. "Two Bens and a General Grant."

Stokes sighed. "I'll never get the moment back. Hold on."

Ninety seconds later, he returned to the line, voice clearer. "You're getting a bargain, dude. And I don't want to be associated with any part of this. No matter how many dead prezzes show up for the party."

"Who owns the house?" said Aaron.

"You don't know?"

"If I knew, why would I be calling *you*?"

"Verification," said Henry.

"I can't verify something I don't know, Hank. And as you always remind me, I can always drive down to that moldy archive you guys keep and find out myself—"

"Not exactly," said Henry. "This case, you drive down and paw through the ledgers what you're gonna learn is that the deed is owned by a holding company called Malibu Sunset Trust. And that's *all* you're gonna learn."

"You, on the other hand, know that . . ."

"Aaron, you really need to promise me this isn't going to go anywhere public. And that you *don't* tape."

"I promise," said Aaron.

"I mean it, dude."

"I *promise.*"

Henry said, "The tax trail leads from this Malibu Sunset outfit to Vision Associates, Inc., of Beverly Hills to Newport Management Trust, then clear out of state. Seven Stars Management, Las Vegas."

"Your basic paper chain," said Aaron. "Now give me a person."

Henry breathed hard.

"Vegas," said Aaron. "You're worried about some mob thing? Don't sweat it, the place is all corporate now. People in stretch pants and Bermuda shorts lining up at the buffet."

Henry said, "Lem Dement."

Aaron checked his own surprise. His mind swelled and pulsed and raced.

Henry said, "Now'm going back to sleep, maybe if I really behave, Paris and Kathy will show up again. Hey, maybe the sister, whatshername, will also put her little—"

Aaron hung up and switched off the voice-activated tape recorder.

The Internet could be Aaron's best friend, but with someone like Lem Dement, overkill could render his computer useless.

A single jab at the *Enter* button flushed out page after page of blogo-crap.

He started with Wikipedia and fanned out.

Lemuel Houston Dement, born in Flint, Michigan, fifty-four years ago, had been raised by a UAW organizer and a Ford Motor secretary, both admirers of Trotsky. Houston and Althea Dement despised capitalism on general principles, loathed their respective jobs in specific, raised their only child with a borderline-paranoid worldview.

Taught that school was just another bourgeois trap, young Lem obliged with chronic misbehavior and rotten grades that belied his IQ. A month after high school graduation he was riveting axle bolts on the Ford assembly line. Ten months of that lit up the *Exit* sign in his head and he gave community college a try. Decent grades enabled a transfer to Wayne State, studying sociology for three years, then transferring to U. Mich–Ann Arbor, where he talked his way into the film school. Once in, he chased women, smoked dope and dropped acid, did minimal work, barely passed.

Cursed with a sluggish metabolism that heaped on pounds, and a face reminiscent of a boiled potato, Dement was compensated with a sour yet strangely appealing charisma that made him moderately successful with women, a gift for dialogue and the ready quip, and, most important, an innate understanding of how to lie with a camera. Nearly thirty and broke, he slept with the right woman and lucked into a gig directing industrial safety training loops.

By day, he shot his close-ups of snarling machinery spliced with stock footage of mangled limbs. Nights were spent on his art: pseudo-documentaries starring friends and neighbors that highlighted the malevolence of Every Corporation.

In a *New York Times* interview, years later, Dement described those days: "I never spent a second in therapy but I sure understood my true motivation: My parents thought what I did was fascist-lackey garbage and I wanted to redeem myself in their eyes. Then they died in a house fire, I was a basketcase for a long time. But in the end, being orphaned freed me."

Twenty-two months after learning his parents had left more debt than estate, Dement wrote, directed, filmed, and exhibited a docudrama about pollution in Lake Erie at the Ann Arbor Film Festival. Maybe it was the deliberately grainy use of black and white, maybe he was just ahead of his time; no one paid much attention to *Brown Water.*

Next came an exposé of an alleged cabal among GM, the Catholic Church, and the Zionist Organization of America.

Half of Dement's crew quit over that one.

Several lean years followed, during which Dement, pushing forty, married to a former dancer and saddled with a slew of kids, worked as a truck driver and a drywall installer. Then a populist assembly candidate from Flint named Eddie Fixland needed someone to produce campaign commercials on a shoestring budge. Dement got the job by working for free, Fixland won his seat in the House, and though two years of scandal got in the way of reelection, his campaign's class-warfare ads featuring long shots of dying rust-belt towns and sunken-cheeked retirees living in trailers caught everyone's attention.

Dement became the go-to guy when you wanted hard-edged *cinéma-politique.* He grew prosperous, moved to a big house in Birmingham, rewrote and reshot his Lake Erie film using a bigger budget: full color, megadoses of the innuendo and hyperbole he'd perfected working for Fixland.

Brown Water, version II, was nominated for an Oscar. Won a statuette. Lem made a brief, nasty speech, moved to L.A., took meetings, fielded offers. Using other people's money, he shot an exposé of emergency room practices spiced with gobbets of gore inspired by his factory-accident flicks.

Red Rooms was nominated for an Oscar and might've won if a heartrending portrayal of a nine-year-old, blind poet prodigy hadn't surfaced just before the submission deadline.

Upon hearing the verdict, Lem was reputed to have fidgeted in his seat at the Kodak Theatre and murmured, "How can you beat a fucking walleyed Helen Keller incarnation?"

He denied the quote.

The next two years saw Dement's fortunes dip as he tried his hand at "serious cinema." A tale of Shakespearean lust garnered more plagiarism suits than profit. A historical action film depicting both sides in the Civil War as slavering, self-serving barbarians went straight to video, as did a "postmodern shake-up" of *Othello* that recast the tragedy as a metaphor for the Arab–Israeli impasse, with a villain named Iago Bernstein.

Lem Dement's name faded from the buzzosphere, as did tabloid shots of the now three-hundred-pound artiste at The Right Parties, bursting out of a custom tuxedo, his trademark limp-brimmed fishing hat studded with lures perched jauntily on a massive, grizzled head.

Dement went "into seclusion to center

myself." Emerged three years later with a four-hour, unspeakably violent depiction of the earliest days of Christianity, shot during a thirty-two-month stay in Turkey.

Given its creator's sensibilities, everyone expected *Saul to Paul: The Moment* to be an indictment of organized religion. What they got, instead, was a paean to the severest aspects of fundamentalist dogma that trumpeted the virtues of forced conversion and portrayed Arabs, Phoenicians, Mesopotamians, and Jews as hook-nosed heretics.

In a full-page *Variety* ad, Lem Dement announced, "I've been born again in the truest sense. My art and my heart are now focused upon sacraments of truth, purity and redemption."

Quickly condemned as racist agitprop by the Hollywood establishment and the mainstream press, and protested serially by Muslim and Jewish civil rights groups, the film enjoyed a limited release in leased art houses and church auditoriums. Word of mouth grew. Theater chains signed on. Within three months, *Saul to Paul* had taken in four hundred million dollars. Foreign revenues added another hundred fifty.

Lem Dement announced his "retirement to a life of contemplation" and moved to a "multiacre estate" in Malibu.

Same city where Rory Stoltz went to school. Honing his Industry ambitions.

Where Caitlin Frostig had gotten straight A's.

Aaron pushed back from the screen. Paced his office.

Malibu was more a concept than a locale, stretching thirty miles up the coast. But the Pepperdine–Caitlin–Rory link couldn't be ignored.

Aaron considered waking Henry again, to find out if Lem Dement's spread was anywhere near the sprawling campus. Decided against it. If Henry had managed to revisit his dream, busting his fantasy a second time would breed too much ill will.

Plus, at the early stages of the investigation, he needed to be careful about tunnel vision.

Caitlin goes to school in 90265, ditto Rory.

Rory has the gate clicker to a Hollywood Hills house owned by Dement, whose main crib is in 90265.

He flashed back to the house on Swallowsong. The winding driveway implied a big-view lot. High-priced real estate . . . maybe the place housed one of the stoners Rory had chauffeured.

In a Hyundai?

Had to be camouflage. So did leaving the club through the back—that was celeb behavior.

Was one—or both—of the stoners a VIP? That synced with Rory waltzing into ColdSnake.

Aaron returned to the keyboard, paired *Rory Stoltz* with *Lem Dement,* and Googled.

Did you mean demented roar?

No, I didn't, Meddling Cyber-Wienie.

He sat there for a long time, feeling his brain turn to sludge.

Three ten a.m. What he *craved* was sinking his teeth into the case, ripping and shredding like a rabid dog until the facts bled.

What he *did* was slog upstairs to Play Land, undress, fold his clothes neatly over the brass-and-teak valet, slip naked between Frette sheets.

Guessing Caitlin's face would appear in his dreams. He hoped she would.

Back when he'd been on the job, he'd embraced the classic Homicide D's self-congratulation.

We talk for the dead.

And sometimes, the dead talk to us.

CHAPTER

13

Moe arrived at his desk at eight a.m., thinking about the Rory Stoltz–Mason Book connection.

Two messages from Aaron sat next to his computer. Crumpling and lobbing easy two-pointers into a nearby wastebasket, he Googled the actor.

Nearly four million hits. Midway down the second page were accounts of Book's early-morning suicide attempt by wrist-slash.

Paramedics responding to a 911 call at the Hollywood Hills house of heartthrob . . .

Facts were in short supply, but no short-age of lurid rehash: anonymous sources claimed Mason Book was addicted to every drug known to humankind, the hush-hush VIP admission to Cedars-Sinai had cost a heavy six figures for a one-week stay . . .

Moe found a couple of grainy, dark infrared shots of a guy who might've been Book being ushered into a black SUV at a hospital service door. Another hit quoted a plea by Book's unnamed mouthpiece to "respect Mason's privacy during this diffi-cult period. Mason needs to concentrate all his energies on getting well. He thanks everyone for their support."

Moe was about to log off when he noticed the date of Book's wrist-slash.

Printing the citation, he left the D room, turned around a sharp corner, hustled over to the familiar unmarked door, and knocked.

"Yeah?"

"It's Moe, Loo."

" 'S not locked."

The room was so small that opening the door brought Sturgis's rhino frame into immediate close-up. Almost like being charged by a bull, and after all these months still kind of jarring to Moe.

The lieutenant had squeezed his bulk into a wheely-chair, long legs propped on his flimsy desk. Additional cold cases were stacked to the left of a cold computer screen. Sturgis's heavy jaw flexed.

"Got a second, Loo?"

Sturgis removed the cigar and rolled it from finger to finger, like a carny doing a trick. He pointed to a chair in the corner.

Moe didn't consider himself claustrophobic but he didn't like to be hemmed in. He remained standing in the doorway and told the Loo about Rory Stoltz working for Mason Book, Riptide's past life as a Hollywood hangout, saving the best for last: Book had slit his wrists exactly one week after Caitlin's disappearance.

Sturgis said, "You're wondering if he did something to her and felt guilty?"

"I know it's remote, Loo, but right now it's all I've got."

"Remorse as a motive is predicated on Book having a conscience. Does he?"

"Don't know."

Sturgis laughed—that vaguely threatening, phlegmy chuckle of his. "He's an *actor,* Moses. A dope-fiend actor, which is maybe repetitive. But sure, check it out, why not. Pick up any new cases?"

"Nope," said Reed.

"Me neither. Damn slow."

For a second, Moe thought Sturgis might offer to work Caitlin. But the Loo just cursed and rubbed his face. "If the citizens know what's good for them, they'll start killing other citizens so we can earn our pay. For all the service we're offering, we might as well be goldbrick politicians—not that I'm demeaning all your good work on poor Caitlin."

"*I'm* demeaning it, Loo. Haven't learned squat."

"Some cases are like that." Sturgis jammed the cigar back in his mouth, picked up a file, flipped through it, shook his head. "Like this one. So cold I could use it to ice my knee. Sayonara, lad."

Moe said, "One more thing. Book was admitted to Cedars. Your . . . partner is in charge of the E.R. there, right?"

Sturgis shut the file. "Moses, there's something called doctor-patient confidentiality."

"I know, sir. I was just wondering if

perhaps he could direct me to . . . some kind of source."

"Go ask him. Richard Silverman, M.D. He's listed in the Cedars registry."

"That's okay with you?"

"I'm not his parent, Moses. I'm his"— unfathomable smile—"partner."

During Moe's brief absence, Aaron had called a third time. Moe's fist closed around the slip with sudden, crushing force that surprised him. Rather than go for the easy layup, he aimed at a can fifteen feet across the room.

Swish. Three points.

Perversely self-satisfied, he got Dr. Richard Silverman's number and called. Silverman sounded busy—harried, even— and Moe dropped the Loo's name before introducing himself.

"What can I do for you, Detective?" Kind of frosty; no *Oh, yeah, he's mentioned you.*

No *reason* for Sturgis to mention him.

He asked if the doc could direct him to someone with information about Mason Book's hospitalization.

Silverman said, "I assume you don't mean our official spokespeople."

"That's correct, Doctor."

"Book wasn't my patient, but I still can't talk to you. Not that I would, if I could. Apart from legal issues, there are general ethical principles."

"I understand that, Doctor, but—"

"You were hoping that because of Milo, I might relax my standards."

Moe didn't answer.

Silverman said, "I'm not trying to give you a hard time. It's simply something I can't do."

"I understand, Doctor. It's just that this is a murder investigation and a really tough one." He summarized Caitlin's disappearance, making her out to be a saint, pumping more pathos by describing her father as a withering, tragic figure.

Silverman said, "Poor girl."

"Her mom died when she was young, she was all her father had," said Moe.

"And Mason Book's relevant to this because . . ."

"Honestly, Doc, he might not be, but I need to follow up on any lead I get. Turns out Caitlin's ex-boyfriend works for Book, which in and of itself doesn't mean much. But then I learned that Book's suicide attempt happened one week after Caitlin disappeared and I felt I had no choice but to—"

"A week?" said Silverman. "I'm not getting the point."

"It'll probably turn out to be nothing, Doc, but what if the boyfriend did collude with Book on some terrible deed and Book felt guilty and that's why he cut his wrists?"

"Do you suspect the boyfriend?"

"Not yet, sir."

"Then I still don't understand."

"Sorry for bothering you, Doc."

Silverman said, "Book never went through the E.R., got sent straight to Special Imp. You could try someone there but I doubt you'll be successful."

"What's Special Imp?"

"As in 'important.' VIP inpatient ward. If you like living dangerously, ask Milo. I got him placed there last year. When he got shot."

"What's dangerous about asking him?" said Moe.

"He's not into all that *share-the-feelings* stuff."

"So you got the Loo VIP'd—"

"But that doesn't mean I have a pipeline to anyone at Special Imp. Good luck, Detective Reed."

The unspoken line: *You'll need it.*

One hour into a more detailed computer search for articles about Mason Book's suicide attempt, Moe's phone rang. "Homicide, Detective Reed."

"Three hundred North Corsair Lane, Detective Reed's proud mother."

"Hi, Mom."

"How are you, darling?"

"Fine."

"You don't sound fine, darling."

"I don't?"

"You've got that pressure thing in your voice—constriction of the larynx due to stress. You've been affected that way since you were teeny."

"Affected," said Moe.

"Your voice, darling," said Maddy. "It's like a peek into your emotional state."

"Gee, I learn something new every day."

"I miss you, Mosey. When's the last time we had brunch?"

"Hmm," said Moe. "I guess it was . . ."

"I don't guess, I *know.* Eight weeks ago,

as of last Sunday. You and enchanting Elizabeth—you *are* still together."

"We are, Mom."

"Phew," said Maddy. "No faux pas. She's so good for you, Mosey."

"Too good for me," Moe blurted. His face went hot.

"Now, why in the world would you say that, sweetheart?"

Moe didn't answer.

Maddy said, "I'll wait for the blush to fade. Then I'll tell you no one's too good for you, my precious baby boy."

"What makes you think I'm blushing?"

"Am I wrong?"

Silence.

"Just say, 'Thanks for the emotional support, Mom.'"

"Thanks."

"Oh, Mosey, I didn't mean to upset you, I'm just teasing. Though the truth is, if you don't want to be teased, you need to learn not to be so reactive, darling. So anyway, I'd really love to see you. Eight weeks is way too long not to see my baby boy's Adonis face. I've been painting up a storm and I crave your judgment."

"I'm sure it's great, Mom."

"I'm sure it's not, Mosey."

"All of a sudden someone's got a self-esteem problem?" said Moe.

Maddy laughed—that deep, almost mannish burst of glee so at odds with her appearance. Moe had seen people thrown by it. Sometimes, *he* was still thrown by it.

"Self-esteem issues?" she said. "Not me, darling. I'm just a factual appraiser and I'm well aware of the fact that I have absolutely no talent. Zero. A great, yawning void of no talent. Heck, Mosey, my easel *shudders* as I approach. But that's the strength of my character: I don't give a fig. I paint because I love it and anyone who disapproves can go straight to Pasadena. In that sense, we're diametrical opposites, Mosey. You *have* tremendous talent for what you do, but are so displeased with yourself."

"Mom, I'm not displeased—"

"So I'm wrong again," said Maddy. "No problem, I'm totally comfortable being in error because I'm aware of my infinitesimal place in the cosmos. So when are you coming? How about tonight? I'll cook my famous lentil soup—don't worry, I've stocked up on Beano."

"Mom!"

From across the room, a D-2 named Gil Southfork looked up from his desk and Moe knew his voice had risen. Cupping his hand over the phone, he whispered, "Let me call you later, Mom."

"Don't bother," said Maddy. "Just come see me. Tonight."

"What's the urgen—"

"I miss you, darling. Eight weeks."

"Let me see how my day goes and—"

"Six p.m., I'll make those sausages you like—chicken-cilantro, turkey-apple. You'll be off by six, darling?"

"That's the point, Mom, it's hard to pin down a time," said Moe. "I'm on a case and there's no way—"

"Bring Elizabeth if she's free—why aren't you seeing her tonight? You need a social life to balance out your work life."

"She's busy, too, Mom." A semi-lie; Liz would be free by eight, the two of them had left the evening open.

"Too bad, I really like that girl," said Maddy. "See you at six."

When Liana showed up at Work Land at ten a.m., Aaron had her check ready.

She made a show of tucking the paper slowly between her cleavage.

"I'm jealous," he said.

Laughing, she removed it, dropped it daintily into her Kate Spade. Resumed sipping from the demitasse of espresso Aaron had brewed in that cute, copper Italian machine he kept in the kitchenette next to his office.

"Yum, Mr. Fox. You are one class act."

Aaron fooled with a piece of lemon rind.

"Nice shirt," said Liana. "New?"

"Nope."

"Never seen it before."

"Never got around to wearing it before." *Been hanging in the home haberdashery for eleven months.* "Tell me about this RAND guy."

"Don't worry, he's for real, Aaron. First thing I did when I got home last night was look him up on their website. He's there, picture and all. Does exactly what he said he did."

"Chasing terrorists."

"Playing with numbers," she said. "Government contracts."

Aaron said, "Doesn't mean he's not whack."

"He's not, don't be paranoid."

"Talking to strangers, Lee." Aaron tsk-tsked.

"I thought that was the point of last night."

"The point was soaking up ambience, getting a feel for the place."

"It's not the décor you care about, it's the clientele. Kind of hard to tease that out without talking to strangers," said Liana.

"And no doubt, Dr. Rau doesn't look like a leprous summer squash."

Liana stared at him. "You're not serious."

"I care about you, Lee. Just because you meet a cute guy—"

"Stop right there, Mr. Fox." Graceful, slim fingers tightened around the demitasse handle. "Though, if I had to rely on you for nurturance, where would I be, Aaron?"

Aaron slapped his chest. "I am mortally wounded." Doing it with levity. Unlike Steve, whose chest-pound last night had been an outward jest but laced with serious regret.

Liana leaned across the glass slab that formed the top of Aaron's desk. "What *we* have, *mon amour,* is a form of aerobics. Healthy, strenuous, satisfying for what it is, and altogether transitory."

"As opposed to Mr. RAND, who's a deeply spiritual guy, just brimming with empathy and sensitivity. All of which you know from a one-hour bar schmooze."

"This is ridiculous," she said. "You gave me an assignment, I did it A-plus."

"Exactly, Lee. You're valuable, I want you around for a long time."

"Oh, for God's sake, it's not like I'm dating him."

"But you've considered it."

Liana smiled. "You're jealous."

"No, I'm protective."

"Thank you, but I'm quite capable of taking care of myself." Liana put her cup down. "What's gotten into you?"

"I just don't like the notion of mixing business with pleasure."

Liana's eyes slitted. "I'll remember that the next time someone booty-calls me at three a.m."

She sprang up, tossed her hair, turned heel.

"Wait," said Aaron. "Sorry, yeah, I'm being stupid. You mean a lot to me—as a friend, as a freelance." Grin. "As the sexiest, firmest—"

"Stop."

"Okay, okay. Sit down. Please."

Liana exhaled a couple of times.

"Please, Lee."

She returned to her chair, crossed her legs, let the jersey skirt ride up all the way to sleek white thigh. Commandment One: Make 'em suffer.

Aaron said, "I was out of line. My excuse is this case, I can't put my finger on it but there's a certain . . . I don't know, a dark aura circulating around it. I know that sounds hokey and I can't give you a rational reason, but there's something beneath the surface—something *psychy* going on."

"As in paranormal?"

"No, no, none of that crap. As in creepy and sleazy and warped. If you tell me there's nothing weird about Mr. RAND, I'll go with that. But don't you think it's strange that he mentioned Caitlin right off the bat."

"Dr. RAND," said Liana. "He's got a Ph.D. And it wasn't off the bat, there was context—talking about the bar's celeb days, the irony of something happening when there were bodyguards all over the place. And he didn't mention Caitlin by name, just by incident. Plus, he told me about the Rensselaers and they turned out to be a dead end. So it's not like he's fixated."

"The Rensselaers," said Aaron. Glancing at the Internet printout Liana had brought. She'd used *couple vanishes riptide santa monica* as the search heading, reproduced an article from the Rensselaers' hometown of Buckeye Bridge, Pennsylvania.

Ivan and Bettina, formerly owners of an

antiques store, had cut town to escape a big-time eBay bad-check mess, used their ill-gotten gain to finance a West Coast vacation. The FBI had traced the couple to L.A., then lost the scent and gotten sneaky: filing a false missing persons report with several SoCal police agencies and convincing local stations to give the disappearance airplay.

Two days after the broadcast, an alert West Hollywood sheriff had spotted Ivan and Bettina leaving Dan Tana after a huge Italian dinner. The *Buckeye Bridge Beacon* reported "tomato sauce stains on Ivan Rensselaer's brand-new white silk shirt purchased on Rodeo Drive."

Aaron said, "So *Doctor* Rau knew about their disappearance but not their being found."

"As I said, he's not fixated."

"Gets paid to think, huh?"

"Aaron, what is it about him that's wedging itself in your butt-crack?"

"Bringing Caitlin up the first time he meets you. To me that's just off, Lee. Dude's out to pick up a beautiful girl, why set the mood with creepy crime—especially a crime against a female. It just doesn't fit."

"It doesn't fit because he's not a player, Aaron." Unlike someone else we know. "He's kind of a nerd, actually. Not physically—oh, what's the diff, I'll never see him again. Never intended to. Happy?"

"If you mean it . . . one thing that does come out of it are those bodyguards and limos. Be harder for a whack to abduct Caitlin right outside the bar . . . though she left after her shift, so maybe that means nothing . . . still, her car was never found, so it's likely she drove somewhere and got snagged, could be anywhere from Santa Monica to Venice."

"Or beyond," said Liana, "if she got jacked. Meaning, focusing on Riptide could be a waste."

"Rau mention any celebs by name?"

Liana shook her head. "Only names were the ones I showed you from the *Times.*"

"A name not on that list just came up, Lee. Lem Dement."

"That asshole," Liana hissed. "Be nice if he *did* have something to do with it."

Her intensity surprised Aaron. "You don't approve of his religious views?"

"I don't approve of him. Because I once

caught an up-close look at him and his
psyche."

"Where and when?"

"Shortly after that biblical splatter flick of
his opened. San Marino, someone's gigantic house near Caltech, not the usual
Industry types. Church folk, captains of
industry, grace before the canapés, cruci-
fixes on every table. Back then, I didn't
know you, used to pass trays for a caterer
to pay bills. It was summer, the party was
outdoors, everyone was dressed for the
heat, except Mrs. Dement—Gemma. She's
wearing a long-sleeved black sweater over
a Chanel frock and way too much makeup.
What caught my eye was the look in *her*
eyes—something I recognized right away
because my older sister hooked up with a
guy who beat the crap out of her. It was
years before *that* bastard had the courtesy
to die, I could never convince Sybil to leave
him."

"Gemma looked like an abused
woman," said Aaron.

"Not just looked, Aaron. *Was*," said
Liana. Fury had deepened the blue of her
eyes. "Hollow, haunted, there's no mistak-

ing it when you see it. Because of my
experience with Sybil, I'm primed. So while
I served shrimp on toast, I kept sneaking
glances at the two of them. Didn't take long
for me to catch it: squeezing her arm just a
little too tight as he propelled her around
the room. Treating her like a prop, never
talking to her. Once, when he thought no
one was looking, he flicked the back of her
neck with his fingernail, had to sting."

"How'd she react?"

"She didn't, that's the point. Numb and
compliant, a good little robot. No one
except me seemed to notice, because
everyone was focused on Dement, all
the money he was raking in, the fat pig.
That stupid hat, he had *fish*hooks in his
hat. With a tux, no less. No one said a
word."

"A few hundred million'll do that," said
Aaron. "Were there any other—"

"But wait, folks, there's more!" Liana
held up a finger. "A while later, I go to the
ladies' room—this mansion has a giant
powder room–makeup area for guests—
and Gemma's there and she's got her
sweater off but when she sees me, she

snaps it back on. But not quickly enough to hide the bruises all up and down her arm. I'm talking livid, Aaron, like she'd been put through a compressor. I pretend not to stare while she pretends to be apathetic, fixes her hair, lays on even more pancake. But I'm getting a close-up look and it's obvious why she's plastering the stuff on. She's got *more* bruises on her neck and shoulders. Plus a definite swelling behind her ear. This is a woman who gets used regularly as a punching bag."

She clenched a fist. "Hypocritical asshole. *Please* tell me he's involved."

Aaron said, "It might shake out that way, but all I've got right now is a real estate link."

"To who?"

He told her about Rory Stoltz's early-morning adventure on the Strip, the gated estate on Swallowsong.

Liana said, "Sneaking a couple of celebs out the back way? No idea who?"

"Too dark, too quick, too far away," said Aaron. "One guy was skinny, the other more of a football type. Neither of them was Dement. Younger, thinner."

"Aaron, Dement beats his wife, who knows what he does to other women? Please please tell me you're going to follow up on him."

"Of course."

"How old were the two guys Stoltz drove home?"

"I can't be sure, Lee. Could be twenties, thirties."

"Dement has a whole bunch of kids— six, seven. He's in his fifties, so he could easily have spawn in that range."

"Junior living in a house Daddy owns? Maybe, but that still says nothing about Caitlin. The link I'm following is Rory."

Liana grew silent.

Aaron said, "I'll follow up on Dement, Lee."

"I know I'm being emotional. You can't imagine the hell my sister went through. And my parents. And the rest of us. We're a close-knit family, Gordon made all of us bleed."

Aaron had never seen her like this. Family made things complicated. "I'll bloodhound Dement."

"Maybe the police have something— domestic violence calls covered up."

Aaron stood, walked from behind his desk, paced.

Liana said, "What's wrong?"

"Working with the police on this one. It's complicated."

15

Madeleine Fox Reed Guistone was a woman of serene temperament.

The shifting hues of her Tuscan-inspired house on half an acre of Beverly Hills POB hillside suggested otherwise.

Which just went to prove the classic detective caution, thought Moe: *Assume means make an ass out of u and me.*

As he pushed his unmarked up the juniper-shrouded lane that led to Mom's manse, his memory dredged up mocha to salmon to sage green to coral to the eye-searing sienna-orange mottle he'd seen eight weeks ago. But he might've missed a few stages.

He reached the top expecting something even more outrageous.

Nope, still "flame-rust villa de Borghese," the pigment-infused plaster slapped on so thickly the house appeared lumpy. Random patches of phony exposed brick completed the picture: typical pathetic, totally *L.A.* grab for a reality that had never existed in the first place. First time he'd seen it, he'd muttered, "Disneyland," but told Mom it was gorgeous. This evening, parking in the circular motor court next to his mother's red Mercedes convertible, the theme park crept back into his consciousness.

And *that* brought back memories.

Moe, plagued with ear infections and motion sickness as a young boy, had always despised the Anaheim ode to corny.

Heaving his cookies after a single spin on the teacups.

Meanwhile, Aaron's leaping into a Matterhorn car. Conquering the "Alps" over and over again. Maddy and Moe waiting until he finally got his fill. Moe clutching his stomach just *thinking* about the Matterhorn.

Contempt on Aaron's ten-year-old face as he points out a crumb of vomit on Moe's T-shirt . . .

A guy who called his office space Work Land; some people never got real.

Moe walked past the Florentine fountain, murky and leaf-strewn as usual, dribbling happily under a gently setting sun. That, Mom hadn't painted, maybe in deference to Dr. Stan Guistone's memory.

Stan had lived in the house on North Corsair for four decades before marrying Mom and until he'd died, she'd changed nothing, including the photos of his deceased first wife set up like icons on an altar table in the cavernous entry hall.

During her years with Stan, Mom had Windexed Miriam Guistone's portraits religiously, pooh-poohed his offer to redecorate, held on to every stick of Miriam's clumsy Victorian Revival furniture.

She'd put up with the original gray-beige exterior that even Stan thought was dreary.

Dr. Stan was a good man. He deserved that level of consideration.

One week after he was laid into emerald-green Forest Lawn turf, the painters showed up at the house, as did the trucks from Goodwill. Bye-bye Agatha Christie, hello Georgia O'Keeffe: delivery vans bearing rooms full of the blocky, serape-draped "Southwest Revival motif" Mom had come to love during her yearly "centering" trips to Santa Fe.

Moe crossed the courtyard to the house. The front door opened and Mom trotted out in ballet slippers.

Her painting smock was a rainbow riot. Paint-pollocked turquoise leggings.

Still channeling Georgia with carefully tinted and highlighted chrome-white hair worn waist-length and French-braided, makeup calculated to look invisible, chunky silver and turquoise glinting from fingers, wrists, neck, ears.

Wind-seamed and thirty soft pounds heavier than her prime, Maddy looked ten years younger than her sixty-three. Or so she said everyone said.

Her own mother had been hale at ninety-one when she'd died in a car crash.

Genetics and lifestyle. One out of two isn't bad, boys.

She ran up to Moe, threw her arms around his waist, and hugged him hard. Stood back and touched his face, as if appraising a sculpture.

"You look great, Mosey. Vital and fit and purposeful. Despite the stress."

Moe kissed her cheek. "You can tell all that in two seconds."

"A mother knows." Taking his hand, she guided him through the manse's big, vaulted rooms, into the kitchen that looked out over sycamore-studded canyons and the roofs of those less fortunate in the real estate game. Moe noticed another redo since his last visit: some of the cabinetry had been painted turquoise and drawers bore cutouts of eagle heads.

"Like it, Mosey?"

"Very appropriate."

"Use it or lose it," said Maddy. "I'm referring to creativity and change—shaking up the vitals. Coffee, tea, Postum, vodka, or Red Bull?"

"You've got Red Bull?"

"No, but I can have Pink Dot deliver." She laughed. "You still take me seriously, God bless you. So what'll it be?"

"How about some water?"

"Ice or room, bubbly or flat?"

"Ice flat is fine."

"My health-conscious baby . . . here you go, a nice chilled bottle of Evian. Which is *naïve* spelled backward, in case you haven't noticed."

Moe sat and drank. Maddy lingered near the eight-burner Wolf range where a single pot simmered. "What are you working on art-wise, Mom?"

"Coloring within the lines." She lifted the lid, peered inside. "Rabbinic cuisine is nearly ready."

"Still on the kosher kick, huh?" said Moe. "Ready to convert?"

"If the sausages are an indicator, maybe I should look into it." She straightened her braid, peered out the kitchen window at her palm garden, offering a profile to Moe. He saw new wrinkles, loosening around the jaw.

Time did its thing, no matter what.

She said, "No, darling, as you well know, nothing organized is for me, including religion. I've decided the most tactful approach is to embrace everyone's deity but not too seriously—think of it as constructive idolatry."

"Last time you called it theologic diversity."

"That, too, Mosey." She sniffed the pot. "Ah, the sausages. Talk about something to pray for."

Maddy, ever at war with conventional wisdom, lost no time telling anyone who listened how deeply she adored L.A. ("Time to stick it to all those pasty-faced New Yorkers who bash us for a hobby.") As if proving her point, she'd set out, last year, to visit every ethnic enclave in the county, sampling food, dry goods, religious gewgaws, DVDs and CDs. Over a twenty-month period, she worked her way through Little Tokyo, Little Saigon, Little India, the Cuban enclave on Venice Boulevard in Culver City, Armenian outposts in East Hollywood and Glendale, the heart of the Orthodox Jewish community in Pico-Robertson. It was on Pico that queues of people trailing to the sidewalk led her to the kosher sausage place. Spontaneous discussion with a yeshiva student waiting for a veal brat comprised her Semitic education.

"Boys, did you know that kosher basically means legit? Not only does the

animal need to be killed quickly—we're long past the vegan thing, right?—but a qualified rabbi needs to inspect the lungs. Which in these days of global warming and smutty air seems pretty darn appropriate to me."

The religiously sanctioned wursts quickly became "those sausages you and your brother like so much, Mosey." Even though Maddy generally devoured three at a sitting and neither brother had ever expressed an opinion, one way or the other. The sausages were tasty enough, but at this point in Moe's life, food wasn't important.

He got up, peered into the pot. A dozen links simmered.

"Planning a banquet?"

Maddy blinked. "Just in case you're hungry. You do look a bit thin. Are you eating right, darling?"

"I've actually gained a couple of pounds and I'm fine."

"All muscle, I'm sure. What's your approach? Three squares, or fast all day and feast at night—like the Muslims do on Ramadan."

"There's no pattern, Mom. I try to be moderate."

Maddy beamed up at him. "My gorgeous husky little one. So. Tell me about your life."

"Not much to tell. I'm working."

"Like a demon, I'm sure."

"Just doing the job, Mom."

"Mosey," she said. "You'd never be satisfied with *just* doing anything. From first grade on, you were a little waterwheel, churning away. I've never told you about the time your preschool teacher called me in . . . that church school, the one I sent you to because they gave scholarships, what was the teacher's name . . . Mrs. . . . whatever. Anyway, the class had just learned about the Israelites slaving away in Egypt and Mrs. . . . whatever, thought you looked confused so she talked to you afterward and asked you if you were okay and you gave her the gravest look and said, '*I* could be a good slave. I *like* to work hard.'"

Maddy touched his cheek again. "So adorably earnest. Mrs. . . . Southwick, that's it . . . Helen Southwick was concerned that you were 'overly mature.' Whatever the heck that means."

Moe had heard the story a hundred times, minimum. He smiled.

Maddy said, "Tell me about your life."

◆

They sat at the table where Moe finished his Evian and Maddy sipped from an oversized mug of Postum gooped with honey.

"Everything's really routine, Mom."

"What cases are you working on?"

"Nothing special."

"Hush-hush confidential?" said Maddy. "Even for close blood relatives?"

"Naw, just nothing special."

"Oh, well, I suppose it all boils down to one person killing another. Do you think you'll stick with Homicide?"

"Why wouldn't I?"

"People change, darling. People *yearn* for change."

"I'm fine."

Several moments passed. Maddy looked at her watch. Generally, time meant nothing to her.

Moe said, "Got something scheduled?"

"I just want to make sure those sausages don't get too puckery."

Springing up, she returned to the stove. "A few more minutes. Another Evian, darling?"

Before Moe could answer, the thud of a

door closing echoed from the front of the manse.

Footsteps grew louder. No surprise on Mom's face. She forked a sausage. Hummed.

Before Moe could speak, Aaron was in the kitchen.

Maddy's older son received the same kisses, hugs, and praise she'd bestowed on Moe.

Unlike Moe, Aaron turned the love-fest into a duet.

"You look absolutely gorgeous, Mom. Hair's great that way, you should keep it long, you've got the mien for that—cool necklace, look at that stone. Arizona turquoise, right? Great specimen, looks like a . . . cat in the natural grain."

"Exactly. What an eye."

"Hopi?"

"Tewa."

"Outstanding." Aaron peered into the pot. "Mosaic wursts, let's hear it for cultural diversity. Any Cajun in there?"

"Two," said Maddy. "Just like you asked for."

Moe left the kitchen.

◆

Aaron caught up with him at the fountain. "C'mon, you can't be *that* touchy."

Moe race-walked to his car.

Aaron kept pace. "You're that much of a diva that you're willing to hurt her because you're feeling all pissy? After all she's been through?"

"What's she been through?"

"Life." Aaron touched Moe's sleeve. Moe grabbed his brother's hand and flung it off, hard enough to throw Aaron off balance. Aaron stumbled back, caught himself. Brushed nonexistent dirt off his gray silk trousers. "Fine, be an asshole."

"I learned from the best."

"You learned nothing from me, that's your problem."

Moe felt his face turn to oak. "Didn't. Know. I. Had. A. Problem."

Aaron mimed a bell-press. "Mr. Reed? FedEx delivery. Carton full of insight being delivered to your door."

Moe groped for his car key.

"You are an utter and complete *baby*," said Aaron. "Talk about arrested development and dogmatic dysfunctional syndrome."

"Now you're a shrink?"

"Don't have to be to know your rigidity is getting in the way of the job. I called you four times today, what else could I—"

"So you collude with Mom?"

"I didn't collude, I—"

"Boys!"

Both men swiveled to see Maddy, standing in the doorway, holding two plates heaped with sausage.

"Dinner's *served*! Come and *get* it!"

"Moe's not hungry," said Aaron. "I'll stay."

Moe muttered, "Oh, sure, and make me the bad guy—fuck off. One second, Mom, I just had to get something from the car."

"Look, let's forget the personal shit. I'm here because of the job. As in, I might have a lead for you."

Maddy called out, "Hurry, boys! I bought ice cream for dessert."

"What kind of lead?" said Moe.

"Later," said Aaron. "And for the record, I *didn't* collude. Mom called me and suggested we all get together soon. It made her happy to think about. She said it's been two months since she's seen you, so I figured—"

"When's the last time you were here?"

Aaron didn't answer.

"Need a calendar?" said Moe.

"Boys?" Maddy walked toward them, balancing the plates with aplomb. All those hard-times waitress shifts at Du-par's not wasted.

"The food's getting cold, boys. The rabbis wouldn't approve."

Dinner was brief, but seemed long. Maddy faked ebullience—or maybe she really was that self-centered—doling out affection to each son with obsessive equality.

As if love, like any other medicine, could be calibrated in doses.

It was the same blithe, painfully fair approach she'd taken when they were young. Seemingly oblivious to her losses, the money problems that forced her to double-shift. The acid stares and mutterings of neighbors each time she moved her curious multiracial family into a newly rented dump.

When they lived in Crenshaw, it was the black folks who derided. In the Valley, the Puritans changed skin tone but not intent.

Maddy had been raised by racist hypocrites, knew all about mindless resentment. She went about her business, wrapped in an imaginary blanket of righteousness and self-determination. That worked, but it took its toll. So did constant laying on the love to her two little hooligans.

If Aaron and Moses had been able to crawl into her head, they'd have found a surprising, *alarming* place crammed with dark corners, shadows, dead ends. The decaying memorabilia of a lifetime of adventure and misadventure that had tapered to boredom.

Now she was set up financially, with the house, the travel, the hobbies du jour.

Empty space in the king-size bed.

Could she take twenty, thirty more years of this torpor? No challenges, nothing to rebel against?

Two kids who looked like men but had never grown up?

Was the psychic abyss dividing them somehow her fault? She didn't think so, she'd always been so—

Stop. No way would she introspect and get all dopey-mopey about *their* issues. She deserved better than that.

Her therapist agreed with her.

She said, "Ready for dessert, boys?

Vanilla cherry for Aaron, chocolate ripple for Mosey. You two are nothing if not ironic."

When the table was clear, she took them to her second-story studio and showed them the huge, bicolor canvases she'd been working on. Variations of light/dark. If either of them got the joke, they didn't let on.

Mosey said, "Nice, Mom."

Aaron said, "Really nice, Mom."

Maddy noticed a thin spot on the edge of one of the paintings. Squeezing pigment onto her palette, she sat at her easel, began filling in.

The boys stood around as she daubed, stood back to gauge, painted some more. The paint was not sitting right, bad-quality acrylics, she'd noticed a definite change in the last few batches . . .

Squeeze, moisten, lift brush, lay it down . . .

When she looked up, half an hour had passed and the house was blessedly silent.

16

Moe said, "So what's this big-time lead?"

The sun was down and the courtyard cobbles were a strange, deep purple. A sad color. Moe wanted out of there.

Aaron kept his reflexive reply to himself. *What's this big-time attitude?* He recounted Rory Stoltz's Hyundai adventures.

Moe said, "So?"

Aaron tamped down frustration by touching the fabric of his sport coat. Super 200s from Milan, silky-smooth, nothing better. He'd bought the jacket in three shades.

"You looked at Stoltz early on, but he came across clean—"

"He didn't come across, he had an alibi."

"Stayed behind at Riptide even after Caitlin left. But that doesn't mean he couldn't have met up with her later. But he's not top of my list. I hear Riptide catered to celebs back then. I don't know who got Rory into ColdSnake but it had to be a VIP, I'm still working on that. That means Rory has an attraction to that world. What if some famous type did Caitlin and Rory protected him?"

Moe thought: *Mason Book was skinny, made perfect sense.* "Rory allegedly loves this girl but he allows her killer to go free so he can run dope errands?"

"Dope errands and maybe more, Moses. He was still in that house until well after three. Maybe sleeping in. That says he's wormed his way into a higher income bracket."

"As a gofer." *Who wants to be an entertainment lawyer or an agent. Makes perfect sense.*

Aaron said, "He thinks it's a start."

Moe said nothing.

"You're not impressed by any of this."

"You saw Stoltz chauffeur two club-rats. We don't know if they're in the Industry."

"How about this, then? The house he drove them to belongs to Lem Dement."

Moe's arms folded across his chest. "You're letting info out in dribs and drabs?"

"I need you to be interested before I waste my time, Moses."

"I'm busy. Spit it all out."

Aaron forced himself calm. "One: Dement owns the place. Two: I have a source says Dement beats his wife. Neither of the two guys was Dement, but he does have a slew of kids. Seven to be exact, and five are sons. Boys learn how to treat women from their daddies." Or from having no daddy. "I worked the Web, found photos of three junior Dements. The two oldest fit the build of the heavier guy I saw."

Moe pulled out his pad. "Names?"

"Japhet and Ahab." Aaron grinned. "Japhet is twenty-five and Ahab's twenty-eight. Ahab used to be a heavy-metal dude, goes by Ax. If you find a criminal history on either of them, I'd appreciate hearing about it."

"Meaning you didn't turn up anything."

"If they're bad boys, they've avoided the press. All I found were a couple of party photos with Ax trying to get his face in the shots."

"Where were the parties?"

"Not at Riptide, if that's what you mean. I'm talking Oscars week, the Grammys, the usual post-ceremony crap—the Standard, the Design Center, Skybar, everyone stoned, pretending they want privacy but they're really out to make the tabs."

"Any genuine celebs in the shots?" said Moe.

"You better believe it. Tom, Julia, Sean, George, the old see-and-be-seen. In one picture, Ax was trying to make it look like he was a pal of Mason Book."

"Trying how?"

"Book's all snuggly with a hollow-cheeked supermodel and Ax is leaning in between them, a fifth wheel—what?"

Moe said, "What do you mean, what?"

"Your eyes just dropped like lead sinkers."

"I was just thinking. Book's tall and skinny. Maybe he's the other guy you saw."

"Sure, but there are tons of skinny guys in L.A." Aaron stood back. "Why am I getting that Book interests you?"

"Because Rory works for Book. As a P.A."

Aaron's jaw grew rigid. "Now who's dribbing and drabbing?"

"I just found out."

"When? How?"

"I don't need to explain my methods."

"Your methods . . ." Aaron's smile was unsettling. "You change your mind about the Peninsula then the moment I'm gone you probably went over and reinterviewed Rory's mommy. Fine, you're the man and I'm hired help grateful to be clutching your coattails. But keep with that attitude and good luck closing Caitlin."

Swinging his car keys violently, he headed for the Porsche.

Moe said, "Thanks for the vote of confidence."

Aaron stopped, turned. "The point you seem to be missing is I *do* have confidence in you, Moses. If I didn't, I wouldn't waste time sharing info and believe me there's plenty of brain-dead morons with gold shields I *wouldn't* give the time of day. Caitlin's iced over, bro. You've got parts of the puzzle, I've got others. The smart thing would be to cooperate. Like that damned song you always listened to on *Sesame Street.*"

"I hated *Sesame Street.* That was you."

"No, no, no, Moses. *Electric Company* was my thing. Morgan Freeman at his best."

"So we play share-zies," said Moe. "Maybe I get my clearance up, either way you rake in nice dough."

"Like that's a felony?"

"You play too loose it could be felonious. I can't afford to jeopardize the investigation."

"Like I'm going to *infect* you with something? Give me a break, Moses. I worked the job, I know the drill. And the hard truth is, either way, I'm going to keep digging. As in, looking into Mason Book the moment my ass hits my desk chair. Because there's more to him than you're telling me. He bugs you and I'm going to find out why."

"The timing is what bugs me," said Moe. "Book's suicide attempt was exactly one week after Caitlin disappeared."

"Really . . . what, a guilt reaction?"

"It's a possibility. Book's an actor and probably a long-term dope fiend, so he'd have plenty of reasons to be messed up mentally."

"Oh, man," said Aaron. "I've had a bad

feeling about Caitlin almost from the beginning—something psycho. Now I'm visualizing big-time ugly."

"As in?"

"As in one of those vicious gangbangs—something that went too far for them to let her leave alive. As in Book and some buddies, maybe one or more of the Dement boys, because they'd know firsthand about abusing women. Maybe Rory himself, for that matter."

"They killed her to keep her quiet," said Moe, "or even uglier, she died in the process."

"Let's say Book's high when it happens, a few days later his head clears, he realizes what he's done and cuts his wrists . . . of course that means the guy's capable of feeling remorse."

Same thing Sturgis had said.

Moe said, "His name pulls up four million Google hits. I spent hours, couldn't find a single useful factoid on the suicide attempt other than he was at Cedars for a week on the VIP ward."

"Special Imp," said Aaron.

"You've been there?"

Big smile. "Not as a patient, but I've

visited. Top floor, city view, nice carpets, private security out in the hall. Not that it means better medical care. In fact, I hear sometimes you don't want to be a celeb in a hospital."

"Why not?"

"People like that, never hear the word *no,* everyone's afraid of them. Normal patient squawks about getting woken up middle of the night to check vitals, staff says, 'Roll over anyway.' VIP patient squawks, staff backs off. The case I was involved in was two years ago, grandson of a gazillionaire goes in for minor knee surgery, ends up with no legs. I'm not going to tell you it was Cedars or any other place in specific. But trust me, special treatment runs both ways."

"Who's your contact at Special Imp?"

Aaron shook his head. "Don't have one, they're tighter than the Pentagon. But this is good, something's shaping up." Risking a hand on his brother's shoulder. "Co-op-er-a-tion, Big Bird would be proud."

Moe twitched but didn't yank the hand off. "What we've got is mutual interest. Now tell me everything you know."

"What makes you think I haven't?"

Moe's turn to smile.

"Fine," said Aaron, "but I really did give you the crux. Don't waste your time searching for other disapperances of Riptide clients because there aren't any. There was a couple named Rensselaer, shortly after Caitlin dropped off the earth. Turns out they were on a fugitive run from a check-kite thing, got found. The only other tidbit that could possibly interest you is Lem Dement's got a big spread in Malibu, sixty-plus acres, used to be a summer camp. Rumor has it he's building his own church there."

"How close to Pepperdine?"

"Ten miles north, which would put it farther from Riptide, so I don't see anything profound there."

"With a big spread, be easy to hide a body."

Aaron nodded. *How did I miss that? Must be sleep deprivation.*

"What else?" said Moe.

"That's it, cross my heart. How about we continue to do our separate things, either of us gets something interesting, we confer."

"I'll do the calling," said Moses. "From my personal cell."

Aaron smiled. "Got a phobia of cooties?"

"Got a phobia of being associated with something that could go extralegal."

"I already told you—"

"You going back inside to be with Mom?"

"Just to say good-bye."

"Say it for me." Moe strode to his unmarked, got in, drove out of the courtyard.

When he was gone, Aaron felt like the only man in the universe.

CHAPTER

17

Instead of driving to Liz's place, Moe sped east on Sunset through the Strip, aiming his GPS at the Hollywood Hills.

His quest took him up into a pretty neighborhood, dark and secluded, lots of gated properties, not much visible from the street. Exactly what a celeb would want. Especially one with a guilty conscience.

After months of nothing, he was getting hyped up about Caitlin. Rory Stoltz gofering for Mason Book didn't mean much by itself, and, when you got down to it, neither did the timing of Book's wrist-slash. But toss it together . . .

Aaron thought it worth pursuing . . .

The GPS lady offered a soothing welcome as he reached the mouth of Swallowsong Lane. Moe's unmarked Crown Vic was conspicuous up here. The *No Outlet* sign clinched it: Park below and continue on foot.

As he climbed Swallowsong, the air felt crackly—coppery, electric, like something was ready to ignite. From somewhere higher in the hills, a coyote screamed.

Something was getting killed. Welcome to real life.

He found the property soon enough. Big gates, fancy metalwork. Darkness beyond, no indication anyone lived there.

Maybe no one did and it was just one of those party houses, used for dope-raves, porn shoots, that whole lifestyle.

He lingered, imagining Caitlin stepping into a humongous-view house, maybe a bit scared, but awestruck. Drinking more than she was used to. Or worse. Before she knows it, her soft, tan body is stretched out on a strange bed and . . . Moe cut his inner movie and began the downward climb.

◆

It was nine eleven, over an hour past the time he'd told Liz he'd drop by. He phoned her from the car.

She said, "So sorry, honey."

"For what?"

"Being late. I just got home. Meetings out in La Puente, construction dig for a shopping center unearthed some remains, they needed to make sure it's not an Indian burial site. I figured I'd get back on time but a big rig rolled over on the freeway. I tried to reach you but my battery went dead. Were you waiting long?"

"Not a sec, I'm just on my way now," he said. "My own excavation."

"Oh . . . that makes me feel better."

She sounded tired. Moe said, "Still up for hanging out?"

"As in chips and dip?" She laughed. "Yeah, I think I can muster energy for hanging out."

She greeted him wearing a baggy red tee and sweats, hair pinned up carelessly, no makeup, a can of Coke Zero in one hand. Kissing him quick and hard, she fetched him a beer. "This is a test. Seeing me at my worst."

"Not much of a challenge."

They sat on the couch. "Um, one more thing, Moses. It's that time of the month. Came on a little early."

"Hey," he said, "we can drink white wine, watch *Oprah* reruns, talk about our feelings."

"Or shoes."

"Don't push it."

They drank beer, talked about nothing, watched a *Project Runway* rerun because Liz liked the show and Moe found it hilarious.

After five minutes, some guy bitching about not enough time to stitch an A-line, whatever that was, Moe felt himself nodding off. Before he could shake himself awake, Liz's head grew heavy on his chest. Seconds later she was sleeping.

He switched off the tube, managed to dislodge her without disrupting her dreams, covered her with a throw, and walked silently into her bedroom, where he activated her laptop.

An hour of Web-surfing produced consensus: Mason Book had been plagued by drug problems since his adolescence in Nebraska.

The former Michael Lee Buchalter was a self-admitted "crappy student" and high school dropout who'd done pills, weed, paint, whatever, to get through night shifts at a fetid meatpacking plant outside Omaha.

Driving to L.A. on a whim, Buchalter worked a series of dead-end jobs until a female studio head, watching him hose her Benz at a WeHo car wash, was struck by the lanky, tousle-haired midwesterner's "aw-shucks star quality. I thought finally, someone both men and women could relate to, a Jimmy Stewart for our time."

If Jimmy had snorted heroin.

Cleaned up and renamed by his patron, tutored by acting coaches, Book demonstrated a surprising ability to don the identities of others, was a star within eighteen months. His affair with the studio head lasted another half a year, at which time she found someone younger.

No sign that being dumped had affected Book; he'd gone on to headline a series of madcap box-office smashes, always emitting low-key, self-effacing aplomb.

Then came the wrist-slash.

Moe probed for details beyond tabloid

basics, got nothing. The Internet was nothing more than a grindstone, sucking up kernels of data and reprocessing until any substance was gone.

He switched his search to *lem dement,* hoping for a direct link to the house on Swallowsong, came up empty. *mason book lem dement* was just as useless. He paired the house's address and the suicide try. Zip. Book had been EMT'd, variously, from his "Hollywood Hills lair," "view crib above Sunset," or "bachelor pad overlooking the Strip."

An image search produced page after page of red-carpet photo-op thumbnails starring Book and a slew of actresses. Moe found surprisingly few candid paparazzi shots and every portrait was complimentary, playing on the actor's lean body, aquiline, slightly oversized features, amiable slouch, heavy mop of too-yellow hair.

Book's smile was custom-made for the camera. Even a couple of photos taken *after* the wrist-slash were kind. The guy actually looked pretty happy.

Near-miraculous recovery?

Soft treatment from the photo corps meant the candid shots were anything but and Moe was pretty sure he knew why. Book, like the smartest celebs, had worked out an arrangement with the digital leeches: *When you catch me, I oblige with a couple of money poses. In return, you don't make me look like a strung-out hype.*

On the other hand, Book's ability to sneak out of ColdSnake—if he was the skinny guy Aaron had seen—said he wasn't being pap-stalked.

Maybe the guy was old news and no one cared. Guy hadn't made a movie in how long . . . Moe clicked keys.

Three years. In Industry terms, that could be Jurassic.

He returned to the image gallery, checked out the kind of woman Book favored in public.

A whole *lot* of women, with some variation in hair color and skin tone, but the dominant arm-candy flavor was leggy and blond. No rarity in L.A., but both criteria fit Caitlin Frostig.

Picking up the hostess? Why not? Book was thirty-three, had never been married, and one tab termed him "still on the prowl." Had the actor taken that literally?

Nice story line, but no facts to back it

up, and Moe started to wonder if a few suggestions by Aaron had launched him on a massive wrong turn.

Aaron had leeway, but *his* options were limited to butt-numbing scut and reinterviews of witnesses.

He needed to get out on the street and *do* something.

He peeked into the living room. Liz had stretched herself out on the sofa, her face mostly covered by the throw.

Moe sat back down, faced the flat black window that gazed into cyberspace.

lem dement children produced references to the director's "huge brood," "slew of kids," "clear slap in the face of overpopulation," "religious fanatical tribe." Moe was about to try something else when he turned to the thirtieth page of citations and came across a one-year-old *Malibu Sunrise* article about Dement's plan to build a replica of a wooden church in Krakow, Poland, that had been destroyed during World War II.

The reporter had some trouble grasping why anyone would want to construct a personal house of worship, but the tone was gushing: Hollywood biggie creates One Big Happy Family.

Lem Dement's new fundamentalist leanings might be at odds with Westside sensibilities, but rich and famous trumped everything.

The puff piece was illustrated by a photo of the entire clan posed in front of a log-sided building. Dement looked relaxed, wearing his fishhook hat and a plaid shirt. Wife Gemma, a fair-haired stick-figure whose pretty-but-pinched features contrasted with Dement's ruddy, porcine mug, looked stiff and uncomfortable.

The two of them flanked the kids, standing as far from each other as possible.

The three youngest kids were tow-headed, bronzed, and prepubescent, with that easy smile that came from being brought up soft.

Ambrose, Faustina, and Marguerite *glowed* with optimism.

Not so Mary Giles and Paul Miki, the skinny, sullen teenagers posed behind them.

At the back, scowling, were a pair of

long-haired, bearded hulks in black T-shirts. Pug-pusses and barrel torsos shouted *No paternity test required.*

Japhet and Ahab Dement could've been twins. Moe would've cast them as *evil twins*—hillbilly pig-farming mutants lurching down from the hills in one of those family-gets-lost-in-the-hinterland splatter flicks.

Japhet waving a chain saw, Ahab swinging grappling hooks. You wouldn't even need to change their names.

Moe clicked for a long time before finding the picture of Ax that Aaron had described. Yup, *Ahab "Ax" Dement, son of director Lem* did appear to be horning in on Mason Book's body contact with a tall, starved blond beauty.

Another half an hour produced something that had eluded Aaron: Mason Book had been spotted by one of the free weeklies in a club named Ant during a gig by Ax's band, Demented. The actor's presence was deemed the most memorable aspect of a "drearily predictable, Prozac-inducing, thrilling-as-lettuce attempt to meld the least redeemable aspects of Metal and Emo."

The date was three weeks prior to Caitlin's disappearance. Moe searched for info on the band. Nothing. Same for the club.

Logging onto the LAPD search engine, he entered his password, got okayed, asked DOJ, NCIC, and every other satellite of the Big Cop in the Sky what they knew about Ahab Dement.

DMV reported the guy's middle name—Petrarch—as well as a couple of speeding tickets and six parkers issued to a Dodge Ram pickup registered at a Solar Canyon address in Malibu.

If Ax was a felonious bad boy, he'd gotten away with it.

The letdown brought on a wave of fatigue. Moe checked on Liz again, saw scurrying motion beneath her eyelids, a faint smile on her lips. Dreaming away at warp speed. Maybe even about him.

Settling on the floor, he watched her for a while. Then, thinking about chain saws and grappling hooks, he covered her feet, dimmed the lights, let himself out.

Mr. Dmitri folded his reading glasses, slipped them into his shirt pocket along with Aaron's expense accounting. Taking a bite out of his kebab pita, he studied Aaron.

"Wish there was more to report, sir, but these things take time."

"Russian trains take time, Mr. Fox. Sometimes they don't arrive."

"This train will arrive."

Dmitri sipped orange soda through a straw.

Aaron eyed his own lunch. Billed as a burger, looked like a burger, how could you go wrong? But the seasoning was weird, cumin or something, smelled like an old person's closet.

Dmitri's secretary had woken him at seven a.m., calling for a lunch appointment with the boss. Some place called Ivan's, Burbank Boulevard, North Hollywood.

Aaron put on a good suit for what he expected to be some Russian hangout, thick-necked guys in black leather jackets listening to balalaika music, feasting on blinis, caviar, whatever those types liked.

Ivan's turned out to be a take-out falafel joint with two outdoor benches for seating and now Aaron was looking out to a pigeon-specked parking lot as clunkers drove in and out. The air was hot and noxious, reeked like a snot-clogged nose.

The good old Valley. He wondered if Moe ever ate here. Nah, not healthy enough.

Dmitri said, "You think this actor could be involved."

"It's worth pursuing."

"Because there is nothing else."

"The timing of the suicide attempt and the fact that the boyfriend now works for Book is suggestive."

"Maybe the actor and *maybe* Dement's

son. *Maybe* the son is a nasty bigot like his father."

"Wouldn't surprise me," said Aaron.

"But that is maybe not relevant, the girl was white."

"At this point it's hard to say what's relevant and what isn't."

Dmitri chomped, got hummus on his meaty chin, swiped himself clean. "Five hundred dollars for 'special communications.'"

The bribe for that weasel O'Geara at the cell phone company. Two-year relationship and the lowlife ups his rate fifty percent.

The excuse: Mario Fortuno's bust had "kicked up the danger level."

Aaron said, "I don't think you want to know the details."

Dmitri was amused. "You are engaging in KGB tactics?"

Aaron laughed. Dmitri's pudgy forefinger nudged the waxed paper beneath Aaron's burger. "You don't like All-American food?"

"It's great." Aaron bit down to demonstrate, earned himself a moldy-laundry tongue. "Sir, has Mr. Frostig talked to you since I started on the case?"

"No. Why?"

"For the time being, I'd keep him out of the loop—not give him any details."

Dmitri's brow furrowed. "You suspect him of something?"

"No, sir, I just want to be careful—truth is, when I talked to him he seemed . . . almost ambivalent. Like he wasn't sure how he felt about reopening the investigation. In my experience, that's an unusual response."

Dmitri tented his fingers. "Okay, we will keep him out of the loop." Tiny smile. "Perhaps the loop will turn into a parabola. Or a hyperbola. Or a Fibonacci series." Rising to his feet, Dmitri waddled to his Volvo, drove away fast.

Leaving Aaron to clean up.

Merry Ginzburg had told Aaron to meet her at a place on Hillhurst, near her office at the ABC studio on Prospect. He got there on time. Fifteen minutes later, she still hadn't shown.

The ambience at Food Tube made up for all the self-conscious I'm-so-hip vibe Ivan's had lacked. Lime-green walls inlaid with glass tiles listed at weird angles. The ceiling was crimson vinyl, the floor was chartreuse cement. Aaron felt trapped in the guts of some giant reptile.

Gaunt, black-clad servers huddled in a corner, trying to avoid three middle-aged women tackling food that looked as if it had been reclaimed from a compost heap. Aaron and the trio made up the lunch crowd.

No one had offered to seat him, so he picked a corner table, waited a good five minutes until a six-two redheaded girl deigned to come over. His mint tea order made her grimace.

"Something wrong?"

"I just hate all kinds of that stuff."

"Tea," he said.

"Yeah."

He sat there for another seven before the mug of hot dishwater arrived. Not his day for cuisine. Boredom was cramping his head.

When out to pick up women, he played coy if they asked what he did for a living, then dropped the truth strategically. What he *never* let them know was how much of the job was phoning and schmoozing and waiting around.

He wanted to get out there and *do* something.

Maybe he'd call someone tonight, go out for a decent meal.

He was still trying to figure out who the lucky girl would be when Barret O'Geara phoned from a number Aaron didn't recognize.

"Prepaid, what do you think? I'm gonna leave a trail?"

"What did you learn?"

"That maybe Mason Book's got social problems."

"What kind of problems?"

"Stud like that," said O'Geara, "you'd think he'd be texting, getting texted nonstop by chicks, the studios, producers, whatever. What I got for the last ninety days is he calls Movie Line, Blockbuster, Beverage Warehouse. And, oh yeah, he does communicate with Dement's kid's cell. Ax, huh? Chop chop. Ax calls for lots of takeout, likes Italian and Thai. Book's only other high-frequency contact is someone named Rory Stoltz who I first thought was a chick but then I looked him up because he's also got an account with us—paid for by Book's business manager, as a matter of fact, and the middle name listed on the account is Jeremy. So that's three guys yapping. We talking gay?"

Aaron said, "How often do Book and Stoltz talk?"

"Once, twice a day, sometimes as much as six. Sometimes late, like three, four a.m. Let me in on it, Foxy, we talking Queerios in a bowl with milk and sugar?"

"What else you learn, Barret?"

"Holding back, huh? Meaning Book really does bat for the other team, all that studly stuff is pure bullshit? Oh, man, there's nothing to believe in anymore."

"You're way off."

"Then what's the deal?"

"You don't want to know. Look up Rory Stoltz for the last year and get back to me A-sap."

"Whoa whoa whoa," said O'Geara. "First of all, you know I never trace past ninety days because after ninety everything's encrypted and sent to a separate data bank at our headquarters so the Feds can snoop on anyone they damn well please. Second, another romp is gonna cost you another five C."

"Cut the comedy," said Aaron. "It's all part of the same assignment."

"Who's joking? Everything's recorded here, man, it's worse than the CIA. Each time I log in, I'm putting my job in jeopardy. Not to mention my nonfelony status and subsequent ability to vote in national elections for the sleazeball of my choice."

"It's the same gig, O'Geara."

"Says you."

"A hundred more, period."

"Five brings it alive."

"Hundred fifty," said Aaron. "You jerk me around, we're through."

"Hear that sound?" said O'Geara. "It ain't rain, it's my tears."

"Suit yourself," said Aaron, clicking off.

Three minutes later, Merry still hadn't shown up when O'Geara called from a different number. "Two seventy-five or it's splitsville and I demand alimony."

"Two even and get back to me yesterday."

"Two twenty-five and would you settle for right now?"

"You've already got it?"

"Two twenty-five says I might—"

"Spit it out, Barret."

"I managed to go back four months, don't ask how, but the picture doesn't change much. Back then Book's still getting a few calls from CAA, but then the agent yak dies. Stoltz and Book keep chatting regularly and, guess what, Stoltz sometimes calls Ahab Dement, I knew this was some faggot thing. Because the only other high-freq number for Stoltz is at the Peninsula Hotel in B.H., the three of them are obviously surfing the chocolate pipeline in some fancy suite, right? Am I gonna read this on Drudge tomorrow, meanwhile you sell the info and get a Ferrari?"

"No and no," said Aaron. "Do one more thing, no charge."

"Oh, sure—"

"Look at it this way, Barret: seven fifty in cash is coming your way unless something goes wrong with the mail."

"You're threatening me? I did the match, you owe the scratch."

"Bye, Barry."

"Getting overly familiar," said O'Geara. "Why do I sense you're intending to screw me over?"

"There's no reason for conflict, Barry,

just do something simple. Seeing as you work so fast, I'll stay on the line."

He spelled out the assignment. Cursing, O'Geara relented. Just as the info came back, Merry Ginzburg stepped into the restaurant, saw Aaron, waved.

Aaron said, "Check's in the mail," cut the connection, switched off his cell. When Merry reached his table, he got up, did the double-cheek-peck bit.

Merry was thirty-seven, short and curvy and pretty with luxuriant auburn hair and the saddest blue eyes Aaron had ever seen. Once a Calendar reporter for the *Times,* she'd been hired by the network affiliate to cover the Industry, delivered occasional gossip bits at the tail end of slow-day news broadcasts. Budget cuts had led to a buyout of her contract in eight months. She hadn't been on camera in ages.

Which explained the pink Juicy Couture sweats, no makeup, hair tied up with a scrunchy.

"Sorry, handsome. Sudden meeting with suits."

"Back in business?" said Aaron.

Merry's headshake was long and mournful. "Just the opposite, they're trying to whittle down my buyout. You believe that? Three months of negotiations just to get to the current state of being reamed and now they want to start all over again."

"Bastards," said Aaron.

"What is it about the Industry that attracts sociopaths? I know why they're doing it. They figure I'll have to hire a lawyer, which will chew up most of the money, so I'll cave." Jabbing a middle finger in the air, she said, "Think again, corporate assholes."

The redheaded stick ambled over. "Everything okay, Ms. Ginzburg?"

"Everything sucks. Bring me the albacore on sprouts, medium rare, on a multigrain roll, no mayo, no mustard, no any other crap. But I do want a ramekin of blackened tempeh bits and some soy sauce on the side."

The redhead pouted. "I'll have to get my pad."

When she was gone, Merry said, "Like that's so hard to remember? We should've gone to Mickey D. So what's up—hold on, Ectomorpha's returning."

Red said, "Okay."

Merry repeated the order. "And throw in some avocado."

When they were alone again, Aaron said, "Ax Dement."

"Probably an utter shithole like his daddy."

"Probably?"

"He's not even Z list, Aaron. He's a waiter so why would I care?"

Aaron said, "Which restaurant?"

Merry cracked up. "Not as in wannabe actor, darling. As in waiting for Daddy to die. Trust-fund baby?"

"Big trust fund?"

"I don't know, dear, I'm theorizing. Daddy pulled in half a bill on that blind-faith abomination. Unless he hates his kids, why wouldn't he dribble a little into their grubby little waiter palms?" She looked over at the klatch of idle servers. "Hey skinny folk—yeah, you. Can a person get some *water*?"

Puzzled stares. No one moved.

"*Wa*-ter? H-3-0? Oh, Jesus." She got up, filled a glass from a pitcher.

Whispers among the cabal. When Red emerged from the kitchen, they said something to her and Red frowned and approached the table.

"Still or sparkling, Ms. Ginzburg?"

"Tap. And more hot water for Denzel Washington."

The cabal began buzzing, as if plugged into a socket.

Red stared at Aaron. Aaron grinned. "She's kidding."

Red's frown said she wasn't sure who to believe.

Merry said, "Hot? Wa-wa?"

When the fluids arrived, Aaron said, "What do you know about Dement Senior?"

"He's richer than God because of that holy-roller crapathon, but no one will work with him."

"Because of the anti-Semitism?"

"You know, honey," said Merry, "Hollywood wasn't started by the Irish. That said, if the upside was big enough, Dement could be Hermann Göring and someone would rationalize a reason to finance his next flick. Lem's problem is he considers himself an *artiste.* Now that he's rolling in dough, he wants to be *creative.*"

"Uncommercial projects."

"Wacky projects, from what I hear. As

in a Druid musical. Or more pseudo-documentaries on sexy topics like colitis—I'm kidding about that, but the Druid thing could be true. Bottom line, if Dement had come up with anything marketable in the last three years, he'd be shooting right now."

Merry's sandwich came, arranged sloppily on a plain beige plate. Redhead turned to leave. Merry barked: "More water."

The girl whined something inaudible.

Aaron said, "H-3-O?"

"In-joke, dear. Heavy water, they use it in nuclear reactors. The implication being I'm going to blow this place up unless someone leases a working brain."

"I'm impressed."

"I was a chem major, premed at Duquesne, for about three days. Decided honest labor wasn't my thing. Everyone said I'd have a shot at national anchor. Now the suits are dumping me and I've got as many prospects as Lem Dement at Wilshire Temple."

"Sorry," said Aaron.

"Maybe I'll go back to Pittsburgh, live with real folk."

"Don't, I'll miss you."

"Sure you will."

"Anything else you can tell me about the Dements?"

"Don't know the kids but I'll bet they're a nasty bunch. Just look at that movie. Violence for its own bloody sake couched in piety. Bad role-modeling, too. Talk is Lem pounds on the little woman."

"Really."

"Can I prove it?" she said. "But she's got that look, you know? Long-suffering? And a friend of mine did some camera work on the Jesus flick swears the one time she showed up on the set, he saw bruises on her neck. He was thinking I could use that, but *A,* all they let me do was happy news and *B,* without something close to proof they'd never run it."

"Domestic violence," said Aaron. "Interesting."

"I hate that term, sounds like the house is punching you. He's a wife-beater, Aaron."

"She bore him seven kids."

"Talk about insane." She nibbled her sandwich.

Aaron said, "Mason Book."

Merry stopped chewing. "Now, sir, you've piqued my interest."

"Why?"

"Book's a screwed-up junkie but he's still got potential to relist himself with the A's. All that charisma, and he can actually act. What's going on, Aaron? Some crazy thing between him and Dement's kid? Something hot I could use to springboard myself back into un-civilization?"

"Not yet, Mer."

She put the sandwich down. "Aaron, this is a real bad time for me. I'm being treated like a thimbleful of spit, my retirement fund's not what it should be because I thought the good times would never end, and I haven't been laid in so long I might as well stitch up the honey pot. My parents would love me back in Pittsburgh so they can *I-told-you-so* forever. If you've got something big brewing, you *have* to cue me in."

Aaron stirred his tea. "There's nothing to tell."

"But there could be."

"It's possible."

She grabbed his sleeve. "Oh, Lord, give me a clue. You know I'm discreet."

Aaron had tested Merry's ability to keep

a secret three times by feeding her fake leaks. Twice she'd passed, one time she'd failed.

"There's really nothing, way too early. If something does develop, you'll be first. I swear."

Her grip on his arm tightened. "First doesn't count, I need to be *only*. Promise me an exclusive. The one you gave me on that celebutard earned me brownie points for a month."

"Deal," said Aaron.

Her hand loosened, dropped off. She whispered, "Can't you at least give me a hint?"

"If you can find out more about any link between Book and Ax Dement—without arousing attention—I might end up with more than a hint."

"Book and Dement," she repeated, as if committing a phrase to memory. "We've got to be talking dope. Because Book's never met a drug he doesn't like and seeing as Dement's a waiter with nothing going on but spare time, he probably smokes, sniffs, shoots, whatever, just to keep from dying of boredom."

Aaron said nothing.

Merry smiled. "Oh, Denzel," she said, raising her voice, "you are nothing if not strong and silent."

Over in the corner, the servers quaked with confusion.

Moe ate raw vegetables, listened to police calls, watched the mouth of Swallowsong Lane.

It was eleven p.m. and he'd been there since nightfall, dressed for the long haul in a baggy sweatshirt and jeans, brown corduroy car coat at the ready if he needed to hide his gun.

The chance it would get that exciting was low; during the last three hours, only one vehicle had rolled toward the *No Outlet* sign. Pale blue Prius driven distractedly by a ponytailed, cell-phoning brunette in her forties. Moe had noticed the vehicle in the driveway of a neighboring property, so no link to the house at the top of the hill.

The calls on the police band were the usual: 415 disturbances, burglar alarms likely to be false, a few traffic stops that required further attention when license checks turned up wants and warrants.

A deep, throbbing rumble from the intersection made him switch off the radio. A black Dodge Ram truck rolled down from Swallowsong, barreled through the stop sign, sped past before Moe could run the tags or see who was inside.

But make, model, and color matched Ax Dement's drive.

Aggressive hunk of metal, strutted high on oversized, black-rimmed wheels. From the sound of the engine, lots of aftermarket beef. Not your typical Industry-brat ride, but in that family portrait Ax had been working the Rural Shitkicker bit.

The truck was long out of view but Moe could still hear it. His choice was follow or wait around on the off chance Mason Book would go tooling by, either alone or chauffeured by Rory Stoltz.

For all he knew, Book was in Ax's passenger seat right now, playing good ole boy. But if so, Moe didn't see it as a club prowl; the Ram would attract too much attention on the Westside.

Were Book and Ax slumming?

Looking for some unsuspecting female to gang?

No serious reason to believe that, but Moe turned the ignition key.

By the time he reached Sunset, traffic was sludged up, everyone too irate to let him in. He idled and cursed his indecision. Then a burst of horns and shouted curses directed him to the source of the jam: the black Ram was five yards up, perpendicular to the flow, blocking every eastbound lane.

Easy enough to reconstruct what had happened: The truck had bullied its way into the slow-moving stream, only to get stuck when the light turned red.

The light turned green.

All the vehicles east of the truck took off but the Ram didn't budge, leaving its western neighbors stranded.

More cell phone distraction?

No, too much time was passing for that.

No engine breakdown, the Ram was growling.

"Move it, asshole!"

"C'mon dickbrain!"

"Moooove!"

Burst of horns. Dumb move on Ax's part if Mason Book was a passenger.

Unless Book was too stoned to care.

Or he *liked* the attention.

The honks grew deafening. The Ram's brights flashed twice, talk about a screw-you move.

More noise. The Ram's driver's window rolled down and a thick, tattooed arm right-angled upward, flipped the world a giant bird.

"Asshole!"

"What wrong with you?"

A huge black guy in blue velvet sweats got out of an Infiniti and moved toward the truck. Moe unlatched his seat belt, had one hand on his 9mm, the other on his door handle when the Ram revved loud and peeled out.

The black guy gaped, then everyone started honking *him.* Scowling, he ambled back to his car, drove off. Within seconds, Sunset was moving again and the Ram was nowhere in sight.

It took a while for Moe to muscle himself

into the flood of happy travelers and by the time he'd reached twenty per, he spotted the truck. Nearly two blocks up but— elevated by the sprung chassis and big tires—an easy target.

He made a few lane changes, gained ground, got a block behind. Then three car lengths, where he stayed.

Tossing a carrot stick into his mouth, he chewed in rhythm with the pounding of his heart.

The truck stayed on the boulevard all the way through Hollywood and into Echo Park, driving through dark blocks of the gussied-up thrifts posing as antiques shops and the fly-by-night boutiques that signaled the district's flimsy gentrification. Laundromats, Latino bars, and liquor stores cast their votes for Old School. Off in the distance the grid-lit downtown skyline beckoned.

This far east, fewer cars traveled Sunset. Moe hung back. Lucky move, because the Ram veered without signaling and parked. Dousing his lights, Moe swung to the curb at the end of the preceding block.

Reaching for his binoculars, he framed the truck.

Hard to see much in the dark. Soviet-surplus infrared scopes like Aaron probably had would be nice . . .

The Ram sat there, same way it had when wreaking momentary havoc on the Strip.

Moe checked out the terrain. Quiet block, lots of shuttered windows, one functioning establishment marked by a smudge of neon at the far end. He refocused the binocs, made out the sign.

The T ll Tale in sputtering red, above a blue happy mask similarly malfunctioning.

Probably The Tall Tale. Poor bulb maintenance; your basic low-rent alky bar.

If Mason Book was a passenger in the truck, was he figuring he wouldn't be recognized here? Risky. So was the possibility of some juicehead taking a random swing.

Maybe whoever was in the truck had no intention of getting out and this was a dope pickup.

If the quarry did enter the place, could Moe chance going in? He thought about that for a while, decided he'd dressed perfectly for the part. What Aaron called Moe's 818 wardrobe would fit in a whole lot better than Aaron's overpriced Italian stuff . . .

But clothes only made the man to a point, his muscles and obvious health would stand out. He'd lay on some stoop and shuffle, hang his arms in a way that narrowed his shoulders, mumble when he spoke, like the bar wasn't his first stop of the night.

All that became hypothetical when two people exited the bar and walked toward the truck.

Big person, smaller person.

As they got closer, details blossomed. Small had long hair, unmistakable female curves. Big shuffled and slouched.

The two of them reached the truck and held a brief sidewalk conference with whoever was inside. Then they continued walking—in Moe's direction. Passed Moe and gave him a look.

Tight clothing for her, baggy for him. She swung an undersized purse, had a loose-hipped walk, kind of theatrical. The two of them stopped at a compact car three vehicles behind Moe. The man took a long time to get his keys out, dropped them, cursed loud enough for Moe to hear.

Finally, they were both in the car and the black truck's lights had switched on.

The car—a dark Corolla—pulled away first, driving with its own beams off for an entire block. The Ram pulled away, sped up until it was on the Corolla's butt, continued to follow closely.

Forgetting the lights and the way the Corolla weaved signaled an obvious DUI. Moe hoped no patrol cars were around. Hoped the idiot didn't hit someone and leave Moe feeling guilty for the rest of his life.

The truck and the car headed toward downtown but stopped short of the bright lights.

Out of Hollywood Division and into Rampart, where Central American gangs thrived and the potential for random bullets and other bad news was high.

The Corolla pulled into the parking lot of a place called the Eagle Motel. The Ram followed.

More faulty signage, this time a cracked

plastic panel featuring a poorly rendered, leering raptor, more buzzard than National Symbol. Making matters worse, the crack ran down the bird's beak, made the mascot look downright goofy. Smaller signs promised cable TV and movies on demand.

The layout was typical: a dozen rooms around a U-shaped parking lot. A dark-skinned clerk sat in a glaringly illuminated front office. Iron grating protected the door, but to Moe all that light made the clerk a sitting target.

Ax Dement got out of the Ram, but no one exited the passenger side.

Dement had the same badass-hick getup he'd displayed in the family photo: plaid Pendleton, jeans, motorcycle boots. Sleeves rolled to the elbows exposed chunky, inked-up forearms. Greasy hair was tied back in a ponytail; a full, unruly beard framed a nose that looked as if it had assaulted someone's fist.

Big guy, like his dad. Hitching the jeans, Dement Junior swaggered to the motel office, pushed a button, pulled open the iron grate, then the door, emerged within seconds swinging a key on a chain.

Quick transaction. A regular?

Ax Dement nodded at the Corolla, which Moe now had a fix on: mud-brown, mashed in several places, primered in patches. He wrote down the tags as Dement lit up a cigarette, made his way to a room on the northern arm of the U.

Most distant room of twelve, that corner of the lot swathed in darkness.

The Toyota's occupants got out.

The woman had teased-up dark hair and a coarse, blasé face. Midthirties, Anglo, five two in stiletto heels. White tank top, short red skirt; the purse was black patent leather. Gigantic red hoop earrings swung alongside a squarish face. Good overall figure, but a little thick and loose in places. Like someone who'd once been toned but had given up.

She ran a finger over her lips, fluffed her hair, gave a little hip wiggle that the guy with her didn't notice because he was fumbling with a cigarette pack.

He was older—forty, forty-five. Anglo, five ten or eleven, skinny except for a protruding gut. Bald on top, but the hair on the sides was long—streaming down to his shoulders. A bushy mustache bandi-toed a weak-chinned, unmemorable face.

A hugely oversized white tee tented over sag-jeans. Moe wondered if he wasn't the only one concealing firepower.

The man lit up, started walking toward the room Ax Dement had entered. The woman followed, teetering as the asphalt fought her heels. One time, she tripped and had to flail to maintain balance. Her companion never noticed.

Moe hurried out of the Crown Vic, stood as close to the room as he could without being spotted.

No knock; they walked right in. Quick flash of incandescence before the door shut.

Your basic hooker-pimp-john dope party?

Moe hazarded a jog over to the Ram.

No passenger. So Mason Book's plans for the evening didn't include this level of slumming. For all he knew, Book didn't even live at the house on Swallowsong, that was Dement Junior's place, just another Industry brat living off Daddy.

For all he knew, the skinny guy Aaron had seen leaving ColdSnake wasn't even Mason Book—no, that didn't make sense, Stoltz worked for Book, why would he be driving anyone else in the middle of the night?

For all he knew, Stoltz was on the job *tonight,* had come by to pick Book up right after Moe left the scene.

For all he knew, none of it related to Caitlin Frostig.

Returning to his car, he ran the Corolla's tags, expecting nothing.

Then the info flashed on the MDT screen and he was pierced by an icy-steel hit of adrenaline, that needle of excitement jabbing his brain.

A few more key-clicks and he was in heart-pumping cardiac marathon mode.

Wanting to *pounce.*

CHAPTER

20

Ax Dement left the motel first, after thirty-two minutes of party.

Moe, antsy the whole time, watched him go and decided to stay until the couple exited.

Hoping a couple would exit. Given what he'd learned. Talk about guilt . . . to his relief, the woman stepped out, tying her hair in a high ponytail. Heading straight for the motel's front office, she got buzzed in without ringing the bell. Once inside, she placed her hand on the clerk's shoulder. Smiled. Squatted and disappeared from view.

The lights went out for just under three minutes. The woman exited the office massaging the back of her neck, waited by the Corolla until her companion appeared.

He staggered to the car. She rubbed his bald head and the two of them got back in. The Corolla bumped out of the parking lot, turned right on Sunset.

Again, the idiot forgot to turn on his lights. This lapse extended for three and a half blocks.

The idiot had a name, courtesy Moe's mobile terminal.

Raymond Allison Wohr.

Street moniker: *Ramone W.* Every mope considered a nickname his birthright.

Male white, five eleven, one eighty, brown and brown. A DOB that made him thirty-seven, an address in La Puente that was probably outdated.

A little younger than Moe's guess, but no surprise given Wohr's history.

The MDT had spat out a twelve-page sheet, and that didn't include the sealed juvenile record. Nearly two decades of arrests, mostly dope. Lots of weed possessions, a few intents to sell the herb, pills, cocaine, a heroin charge that went nowhere. Wohr had served lots of county jail time awaiting trial, meaning he was no big-time player and no one cared enough to go his bail.

Despite that, his win-loss record wasn't bad, split nearly evenly between acquittals and convictions. The latter had sent him on periodic trips to various branches of the California penal system where Wohr had been judged a possible "affiliate" of the Aryan Brotherhood, but never a member. Meaning the gang didn't want him because he was too stupid, unpredictable, or lacked courage, but was willing to use him for low-level scut.

During Wohr's intermittent spells of freedom, he amassed traffic violations, resulting in a license suspension, still in effect.

The Corolla was registered to Arnold Bradley Wohr, two years older. Same address in La Puente, no criminal record.

The older, law-abiding brother, giving his clunker to Ray out of pity, family loyalty, whatever?

Too bad, Arnie, you've left your law-abiding self damn vulnerable.

Raymond Wohr's vehicular infractions included a couple of speeders, a trio of failures to make a full stop, some ticky-tacky license/reg stuff in La Puente that was probably a local uniform knowing Ramone was a mope and harassing the fool.

The kicker was four—count 'em!— driving without headlights and two DUIs, both of which Wohr had managed to beat.

As if not busy enough, Ramone W had also managed to rack up a slew of petty larcenies: the small-change shoplifting and sneak-thieveries that financed an impoverished druggie's chemistry experiments.

Now he was pimping shopworn street girls to Hollywood brats.

Moe calculated how much of Wohr's thirty-seven years had been spent behind bars, came up with just over fourteen, not counting juvey time. Your basic turnstile con, nothing particularly interesting until you got to Wohr's latest involvement with the criminal justice system.

Eighteen months ago, he'd been hauled in by Hollywood Homicide—by Petra Connor and Raul Biro, talk about your small cop-world—as a person of interest in the murder of a woman named Adella Bertha Villareal.

No charges had been filed against Wohr, and as far as Moe could tell the case remained open.

Adella Villareal's body had been found three months before Caitlin Frostig stepped into darkness and melted away.

There were limits to what the computer could teach him; the details he needed were in a blue-bound Hollywood murder book. He'd call Petra in the morning.

Now he followed Wohr's illegal wheels west on Sunset, but this time the Corolla bypassed the boulevard at Virgil, continued north to Franklin, turned left.

Back into Hollywood, the quieter, seamier east end of the district, where European tourists sometimes ended up on deserted, creepy side streets, hoping to spot someone like Mason Book but more likely encountering someone like Raymond Wohr.

Said felon pulled in front of a cheesy-looking apartment building on Taft and Franklin and let his hooker girlfriend off. She looked cross as she turned her back on Wohr. Entered the building as Moe jotted the address.

Wohr continued south on Taft, parked just above Hollywood Boulevard, slouched, head down, hands in pockets, straight to a bar not dissimilar from The T ll Tale.

Bob's Evening Lounge.

Cheap plywood door painted red, port-hole window.

A bit of nautical? Shades of Riptide?

Moe watched as Wohr paused to light up a cigarette. Tossing the match on the sidewalk, Ramone W flung the door open.

Two minutes later, Moe was inside, too, at the far end of a sticky, urethaned bar, nursing a Bud, staring down at souvenir drink coasters from long-dead Vegas casinos, trapped in the varnish like insects in amber.

His fellow drinkers were half a dozen rummies well into their cups. Seven, including Raymond Wohr, rubbing his hairless crown and tossing back double bourbons. A cop show played on a fuzzy TV. A grubby pay-to-play pool table topped with wrinkled felt had attracted no comers. Wohr chain-smoked and drank and tried to follow the show when he could keep his eyes open. On the screen, big-bosomed blondes intimidated bad guys who looked like waiters at the Ivy, everyone double-handing their guns in absurd poses, tossing around "perp" and "forensics."

Moe's beer tasted diluted and sour and he avoided it while sneaking quick looks at Ramone W. Up close, Wohr looked way older than thirty-seven, with silver streaking the long side hair, pitted, gravelly skin, a lumpy, rummy nose, kangaroo pouches beneath exhausted eyes.

It took fifteen minutes for the mope to finish drinking. In all that time, he'd talked to no one, no one had talked to him. Six doubles and to Moe's eye, Wohr had entered the bar intoxicated.

Still, he managed to stay on his feet, was able to open the door on his second try.

Moe tossed cash on the bar, was back on Taft in time to see Wohr enter the same ratty building as the woman in the white tank top.

Pimping his girlfriend. A man of sterling character.

He drove back to West L.A. Division, found the big D-room empty except for a night-shift detective named Edmund Stickley filling out paperwork. Lots of empty desks, but Stickley had chosen Moe's.

Moe had talked to him a few times; one of those older burnouts who liked catching cases at shift's end, passing everything along.

He said, "Reed? You're up past your bedtime."

"Nightlife ain't no good life," said Moe, "but it's high life."

"The lyric is 'my life,'" said Stickley. "Got something to do? I'll move."

"Don't bother, I just need a screen."

Stickley shifted to a neighboring desk anyway. Moe logged onto the reverse directory, plugged in the address of the apartment building on Taft, obtained eighteen landlines running to that address. Raymond Wohr's name wasn't among the registered users. Seven were female.

He began working his way through the list, found a match on his fourth try.

Alicia Constance Eiger, thirty-two, two-page biography emphasizing dope and prostitution.

Blond and brown in her most recent mug shot, nearly a year ago. Deep lines scored her face. The nightlife, indeed.

Moe Googled her name combined with murder victim *Adella Bertha Villareal,* pulled up zilch. Same for Villareal by herself. The media hadn't covered the crime and no one close to the victim had created a website.

The criminal data banks also came up empty, as did missing persons sites. No easy link to Caitlin, too bad.

Maybe because the cases weren't connected.

Nothing else to do before daybreak. Moe felt like jumping out of his skin but left the station and drove toward the 405 on-ramp. Changed his mind and stayed on Pico, going east, took Beverly Glen to Sunset and sped east.

Climbing toward Swallowsong Lane for the second time, he found his eyelids lowering. He tuned to a hard-rock radio station, cranked it loud.

None of that worked and he was considering pulling over for a catnap when high-intensity headlights snapped him alert.

Some idiot speeding toward him. Racing down the narrow street, passing within inches of the Crown Vic.

Moe strained to catch a glimpse of the fool.

Silver Porsche Cabriolet. Top up, driver's window open.

Aaron's face expressionless as he down-shifted for the next curve.

21

When Moe was six years old, a girl in his class whispered in his ear: "Your brother's a monkey."

Moe had just started first grade, didn't know if this was part of getting out of kindergarten. He ignored the girl and returned to his addition workbook.

The girl giggled. Later, out on the yard, she brought an older boy, probably a third-grader, to where Moses was bouncing a ball by himself, the way he liked to do.

"This is *my* brother," she said.

The big boy smirked.

Moe looked around for Aaron. None of the fifth-graders were on the yard.

Bounce bounce bounce.

The big boy punched air and moved closer. He and the girl laughed.

He said, "Your brother's a monkey *nigger*," and placed his hand on Moe's chest.

Moe lowered his head and charged, churning his arms like they were a machine. His hands turned into rocks and his legs were real fast-kicking robot legs that couldn't stop.

Suddenly the big boy was on the ground and Moe was sitting on top of him, and he still couldn't stop moving. Tasting blood but not feeling any hurt anywhere and red was shooting out of the big boy's nose along with snot and the big boy was screaming and crying.

Each time Moe's fist pounded into the boy's head and his body he made a hopeless noise, kind of like *Oh no.*

It took two teachers to pull Moe off. The big boy did nothing but cry.

In the principal's office, Moe got a bad feeling from Mr. Washington and refused to talk until Mommy showed up.

He whispered everything into her ear.

She listened and nodded and translated for the principal.

"That's certainly not good, Mrs. Reed. If it indeed happened that way."

"It happened that way, Mr. Washington. Moses never lies."

Washington, black as coal, broad as a garage door, said, "Indeed."

"Trust me, Mr. Washington. You'll never meet a more honest child."

The principal studied her, then Moe.

"Has he ever caused problems before, Mr. Washington?"

"This is first grade, Mrs. Reed. We've only been in session for two weeks."

"Call his preschool. Moses had an impeccable behavior record. For him to do something like this, there had to be a good reason."

"There's never a good reason for violence, Mrs. Reed."

"Ah," said Mom. "I wonder if the protesters in Selma, Alabama, feel differently. Not to mention residents of the Warsaw ghetto, the Navajo—"

"I don't believe I need a history lesson, Mrs. Reed."

"I'm sure you don't and I'm sorry for being presumptuous. However, if that kind of racist sentiment is common among your student body, it's no surprise there'd be some sort of—"

"Our student body is excellent, Mrs. Reed. Let's not get off target. Moses beat a boy bloody. Now, I'm sure you believe he's a good boy. But this isn't what you'd call a good start. Under no circumstances can any sort of physical acting-out be tolerated. No circumstances, whatsoever."

"Of course not, sir. And he will be duly punished, I can assure you."

Mommy never punishes me. Oh, no!

Moe tried to catch her eye but she kept looking at Mr. Washington like Moe wasn't in the room.

Mr. Washington said, "I suppose we can call this to a close with a warning. For Moses, and for your other son."

"What's Aaron done?"

"Nothing. Yet. I'm trying to ensure it stays that way. There'll be no personal vendettas, absolutely no attempt on anyone's part to get even."

"What about the other side?" said Mom. "Will they be warned as well?"

"Side?" said Mr. Washington. "That's confrontational terminology, Mrs. Reed."

"I didn't mean it that way, sir. I just wanted to make sure that no one aggresses against my boys."

"Your boys will not be aggressed against. What I need from you is an iron-cast assurance that they won't bother any-one else."

"They will not, I swear." Suddenly, Mommy was touching Moe, squeezing his hand like she did when holding him back from traffic. Maybe a little harder.

He looked at her. What was on her face had nothing to do with comfort or safety. Flat, like a mask. He shivered.

Mommy squeezed again.

Mr. Washington said, "Well, I sincerely hope you're right because here we are, just two weeks in, and already Moses is skating on thin ice." He shuffled some papers.

Mommy said, "Everything will be per-fect."

"Perfect?" Washington smiled. His desk clock ticked. "So as not to keep this exclu-sively negative, Mrs. Reed, I will tell you that Aaron is one of our top fifth-grade students as well as an excellent athlete. That would imply a certain degree of self-discipline."

"You bet," said Mommy. "Aaron's always been super-disciplined."

Washington lowered his eyes to Moe. "And this one?"

"This one as well, sir."

Washington picked up a pencil, studied the eraser.

Mommy said, "Both my boys are wonderful. They never give me a lick of trouble."

"It's good that you think so, Mrs. Reed. Have a nice day."

"You, too, Mr. Washington. Thank you for your flexibility."

The principal hoisted his enormity from a creaking chair, came over to Moe, cast a gigantic shadow. "Son, your mother says you're wonderful. Don't make her change her mind."

Moe mumbled.

"What's that, son? Speak up."

"Mom never lies."

"An honest family," said Washington, lowering a huge hand onto Moe's quaking shoulder.

◆

Clutching Moe's now sweaty fingers, Mommy led him—pulled him—through endless beige school corridors into abrupt, stunning sunlight, across the play yard and past the guard at the gate.

"Morning, Mr. Chávez."

"Morning." Chávez, always friendly, turned away.

Mommy pulled Moe harder.

He said, "Ow."

Silence.

She always talks. This is different. Oh, no!

When they were inside the van, she said, "Belt up, buster, we're going for a ride."

"Where?"

"Baskin-Robbins." Leaning over, she kissed the tip of his nose. "Even tough-guy heroes need Jamoca Almond Fudge."

By the time Aaron came home an hour later on the upper-grade bus, Moe and Mommy were waiting at the kitchen table with the ice cream and glasses of milk. Aaron breezed past them. The door to his bedroom slammed.

Mommy said, "Well, *that* was different," and went after him.

Moe heard loud voices ringing through the door. He sat there for a while, finally got up to listen.

"**. . . don't need his help!**"

"**. . . not the point, Aaron, it was a vile thing to say and he was trying to defend you—**"

"*. . . don't* need *his defending!*"

"**. . . what we call spur of the moment, darling. He didn't think, he just loves you, so he acted—**"

"*. . . loved me he'd mind his own* business*!*"

"**. . . think you're being a little harsh on—**"

"**. . . always embarrassing, he's so weird. Everyone calls him a retard because he stands around by himself and bounces that stupid ball and doesn't talk and I have to always stick up for him and say he's not a retard. Since he came to school it's been—**"

"**Well, I'd certainly hope you stick up for him. Retarded! That's horrid—**"

"**. . . acts so weird—whatever. Just tell him to stay out of my face. Okay?**"

Silence.

"Okay, Mom? He really needs to stay out of my face!"

"Aaron, I really don't understand this attitu—"

"He's making me look like a fag who needs to be protected! I can protect myself, okay? The only reason he's trying to be a big-shot hero is 'cause you're always talking about how they were heroes. But they weren't! Not both of them! My dad was a hero, Jack was just a stupid drunk who sat there while—"

Sharp report.

"Oh, God, I'm so sorry, honey. I didn't mean to hit you, I've never hit you, how did that happen!"

Silence.

"Aaron, honey, please. Talk to me, I don't know what got into me, please forgive me, please please—"

"He brings problems."

"Oh, Aaron—"

"Yeah, yeah, I forgive you."

Later, when Aaron came out of the room, saw that Moe had been listening, he sneered: "What do you want? *Hero.*"

"I . . . I . . ."

"I . . . I . . . I . . . I . . . blah blah blaaah."

Shoving Moe aside, Aaron continued to the kitchen. "Mmm, kinda hungry. Gonna get me some big-time *hero* ice cream."

It was that same smug, mocking tone Moe heard over the phone.

Eight a.m., still tired. The laughter in Aaron's voice when Moe said, "What?" caused Moe's hands to clench.

"I said nice to see you last night, however briefly. Thought you'd want to know that Rory Stoltz picked Mason Book up just after you left the first time."

Aaron had been able to watch him, unseen. He had been unaware of Aaron. Until hours later, the Porsche speeding by. Big Brother *wanting* Moe to know.

"You're sure it was Book?"

"No one but, Moses. I got a clear look through the passenger window. Older than he looks on screen. Haggard, like he's been through some rough times."

"Where'd Stoltz take him?"

"Nowhere in particular, they just drove."

"Where?"

"All the way to Ocean Front, I'm thinking *Yes! They're going to stop at Riptide.* But Stoltz turned the other way—north—got on PCH, kept in the slow lane and cruised under the speed limit. Now I'm thinking they're gonna head over to Lem Dement's place in Solar Canyon, maybe do a little early-morning praying. Negative, again. They made it as far as the Colony, turned around, went home. Ten minutes after Stoltz drops Book off, the gates open and he drives away himself."

"Moonlight cruise up the coast," said Moe. "Sounds kind of romantic."

"Yeah, I thought about that, maybe Book's got a secret life and his head's in Stoltz's lap. But anytime it was safe, I got close and they were just sitting there. Book looked like he was heading for a funeral. So if he did give the kid head, he did it at Olympic pace. I honestly don't think it happened, Moses. Stoltz is Book's gofer, Book's got insomnia, he makes a call, the kid's there to do his bidding. That's the whole point of walking-around guys. They make you feel important. My question is, what's Book losing sleep over?"

"Dope can do all sorts of things to your cycles."

"True. But what we've been guessing— guilt over Caitlin—could also explain it.

Not that I saw overt guilt. More like stupor. So how was your night?"

"Uneventful."

"Sorry you missed the action."

"Moonlight cruise?" said Moe. "Sounds like you didn't catch much, either."

A beat.

"Okay," said Aaron, "but at least we know for a fact that Book crashes in Dement's house. Whether or not Ax lives there remains to be seen."

No, it doesn't.

Moe said, "Something actually happens, feel free to call."

Before Aaron could answer, he clicked off, punched in a number at Hollywood Division.

22

Petra Connor was one of those women you could get distracted by, if she wasn't so smart and business-like that you forgot she was a girl.

Thin as a model, but none of that brain-dead dullness in her wide, dark eyes. Flawless ivory skin, the graceful moves of a dancer or a runner. Shiny black hair that she wore in a neat, functional cap.

The few times Moe had seen her, she wore black pantsuits, and this morning was no exception—something with a little stretch to it, tailored to hug her fatless frame while concealing the bulk of her weapon.

Her partner, Raul Biro, Moe had never met. Before leaving the station, he'd stopped in at Sturgis's office, inquired about the guy.

The Loo said, "Really bright, works like a dog, probably gonna be a star."

Moe didn't want to be paranoid, but he was still wondering what that meant as he drove to Hollywood Station.

When he met Biro, he was surprised. The guy looked like a kid. Though his hair was from another era—combed back and slicked at the sides, sprayed in place on top. Aztec features, the build of a light-weight wrestler. Aaron would've approved of Biro's smooth tan suit, white shirt, powder-blue tie.

All put-together, like he never expected to get his hands dirty.

Sturgis said he was a worker, go know.

The three of them sat around a table in a Hollywood interview room. After some small talk about Sturgis, Delaware, the marsh murders, Petra patted the blue folder to her left. Thin; not a good sign. "Adella Villareal, not one of our tri-umphs."

Biro clicked his tongue.

Moe said, "Maybe my dead end can intersect with yours."

Petra said, "That would be nice, let's do some show-and-tell."

Moe did the polite thing and talked first, summarizing his history with Caitlin, the links among Rory Stoltz, Mason Book, and Ax Dement, Dement's motel party with Raymond Wohr and Alicia Eiger.

No reason to mention Aaron's involve-ment.

In the retell, it sounded like an air sand-wich.

"Eiger's a new name for us so we asked Vice," said Petra. "They know her, your basic aging street girl. They didn't know her as shacking with Wohr and back when we questioned Wohr he claimed there was no woman in his life."

Biro said, "At least not a live one."

Moe said, "Villareal was his girlfriend?"

"If only it was that simple," said Petra. "No, that's doubtful—let's start at the beginning. Adella was hit on the back of the head, but not hard enough to kill her.

We figured that for a subduing blitz before she was strangled manually. She was fully clothed. No signs of sexual assault, no forensic evidence of any sort."

She flipped the murder book open, turned pages, slid the file over to Moe.

Five-by-seven shot of a really pretty Hispanic girl holding an infant wrapped in a blue blanket and flashing a megawatt smile.

Moe had checked out Adella Villareal's stats last night. Twenty-four years old at the time of her death, a DMV photo that showed her as dark-haired, decent looking but nothing like this.

Same girl, no question about it, but this portrait—maybe happiness—made her beauty-queen gorgeous, with long, lustrous hair curled at the ends, lightened to chestnut, streaked with honey. A fitted white blouse and brown slacks showed off nice curves.

Moe said, "When was this taken?"

Petra said, "Twenty-two months ago, Phoenix, her family's house. The baby was a month old, she flew home to show him off. Boy named Gabriel. Four months later, she was dead."

Biro frowned. "Night she was murdered,

she had the baby with her. He hasn't been seen since."

Moe said, "Oh, man."

Petra said, "If I was the praying type, I'd ask God to make it a kidnapping."

Biro said, "We looked into that, never got any sort of lead. No whacks with fake pregnancies, no other snatches or attempts."

Moe said, "Who's the dad?"

"Good question."

Petra said, "Adella grew up in a conservative family, Dad's an auto mechanic, Mom provides home health care for old people. I was also raised in Arizona, know her neighborhood. Solid working class, lots of religion. Adella was a decent student, high school cheerleader, until tenth grade when she started hanging with a different crowd, got into some dope trouble, ended up posing for the wrong kind of pictures. Her parents found out, there was a huge scene, Adella ran away to L.A."

"High school porn?" said Moe.

Biro said, "She got wangled into some nudies by a guy claiming to work for *Hustler.* What he called art shots—getting explicit with herself."

Petra said, "By today's standards no

huge freak, but by her parents' standards she was speeding in the fast lane to hell. After she left, there was a total break-down in communication—zero contact. Until one day the bell rings and Adella's standing there, with a one-month-old. Paternity never came up because Adella never volunteered and the family didn't want to pressure her, afraid she'd leave again, they'd never hear from her. Despite their treading on eggshells, she only stayed three days, Mom woke up, found her bed and the crib empty. She and Adella had just bought the crib—fun shopping trip. Poor woman was upset. Now she's shat-tered. Family gave us names of some tough kids Adella hung with in Phoenix, as well as the photographer. We worked them all, no dice. The Villareals are salt of the earth but the sad truth is they're clue-less about Adella's life for the last eight years."

Biro said, "She lived in a single on Gower, not a dump, but nothing fancy. Slept on a foldout couch with the kid next to her in a porta-crib, most of what was in there was baby-stuff. We found some pay stubs, traced back to a poker club in Gardena where she cocktail-waitressed for three years until a few months before the pregnancy. Wohr tended bar at the same place but only for a month before he got fired for not reporting his felony record. We got interested in him because surveillance cameras showed her walking with him to her car several times and another dealer remembers the two of them hanging out during smoke breaks. Wohr's sheet is thick, but there's no violence against women. But you know how it is. Guys get away with stuff, decide to kick it up a notch. We looked at him right away."

Petra said, "Once we found him. He'd been off parole for a while, last address was way out of date. One of our cruisers finally spotted him on the boulevard. He claimed to be living in La Puente but that turned out to be his brother's house, where he crashes from time to time. We never did put him at a local address."

Moe said, "Now he's got one."

"Pimping and living with a hooker," said Biro. "Interesting."

"Brother Arnold," said Moe. "The car Wohr's driving illegally is registered to him. Maybe somewhere down the line, we can leverage that."

Biro said, "You're figuring to lean on the reverend."

"He's a minister?"

"Runs a small neighborhood church, feeds the homeless, has a wife, two kids, all of them about as wholesome and straight as it gets."

Moe groaned.

Petra said, "But feel free to talk to him. To anyone. We've put this one in the fridge, welcome anything new."

"Does your gut say don't bother with the rev? With Wohr, period?"

"There's no evidence implicating Wohr, but our gut's not strong on this one."

"He have an alibi for the time frame of the murder?"

"That's part of the problem, we're not sure of the time frame. Adella's cell phone record breaks off thirty days before she was found, but she wasn't dead nearly that long, coroner estimates two, three days tops. She d.c.'d the account, switched to pay-as-you-gos."

"Hiding something?" said Moe.

Biro said, "If she was hooking, throw-aways would come in handy." Looking at his partner.

Petra said, "We did have one person—old woman living in the same building who thought she was hooking but she had nothing to back that up, just 'intuition.' No one else felt that way. In fact, every other neighbor we talked to said that one was loony. They liked Adella, said she was quiet, minded her own business, concentrated on the baby. Now that you've told us Wohr's pimping, it opens up possibilities. Adella did have money—nearly four thou in a WaMu account and she was long gone from the casino."

Biro said, "Problem is we've got nothing saying Wohr was pimping back then and I'm having trouble seeing him with someone like Adella on his payroll. We're talking a big step upward for Ramone W."

Moe said, "What about cell phone records from before she canceled the account?"

"Mundane stuff," said Petra. "Takeout, baby shops, Southwest Airlines to buy her ticket to Phoenix. She booked both ways, clearly had no intention of sticking around.

We got into her computer, and she didn't use it much. Some online ordering of clothes for her and the kid, some eBay purchases of kiddie books and toys."

Biro said, "When we questioned Wohr, he said Adella was a casual work buddy, he walked her to her car for her safety. He volunteered knowing she lived in Hollywood, but denied he lived here. Though he did admit to coming down on the bus, hanging around the boulevard. When we asked him why, he gave a dumb smile and said, 'To have fun.' All of us knew he was scoring, maybe selling, he really wasn't trying to hide what he was."

"Too far gone?" said Moe.

"Just his general demeanor. He came across more dumb-ass loser than conniving psychopath and that was verified by our Vice guys and a couple of uniforms who knew him."

Moe glanced at the photo.

Petra said, "Poor little thing. We found the baby's vaccination records in Adella's apartment. Western Pediatric, there was no regular pediatrician, Adella used the clinic. The nurses who remembered her said she was a happy attentive mom, showed up on time, into breast-feeding. One nurse did recall a comment Adella made about her boobs finally being put to proper use. Which led us to wonder if she was back to posing, stripping, whatever. Or had never stopped. We canvassed top-less clubs, photographers who do that kind of thing, never turned up a lead."

Moe flipped to the murder book's front-page summary. "Body in Griffith Park."

"Back of Fern Dell, near the stream."

Biro said, "Crawfish got interested."

Moe said, "That's pretty close to her apartment."

"Reasonably close," said Petra. "But the park wasn't the kill-spot, just the dump. Her place wasn't the crime scene, either, we still don't know where it happened. Once the coroner gave us that three-day frame, we had Wohr picked up again and talked to him. Guy was unfazed, said he'd been drinking on all three nights, pro-duced backup from other juiceheads at the bar. Bob's, where you just saw him, he's a regular. By itself, that's no alibi, the murder could've happened during the day. But nothing indicates guilt either."

"You felt strongly enough to question him twice."

Biro said, "He's all we had."

Petra said, "We figure whoever killed her picked her up somewhere, because her car was never moved from her parking slot at the apartment. The seat adjustment fit her height, there was no sign anyone but her had driven it. Maybe she *was* freelancing to pay the bills, ended up on a real bad date. If we could tie her to Wohr, or to any other pimp, we'd be dancing in the hallway, Moe."

"She did drugs in high school. What about later on?"

Biro said, "Nothing in her apartment and her blood was clean."

Moe turned back to the picture. "You're probably right about being a bad fit for Wohr. She had the looks to play in a bigger league. But that could've led to some high-rolling clients. Like a zillionaire director's kid."

Petra said, "Sure, but from what you saw last night, Ax Dement doesn't go high-end."

Biro said, "Maybe he's into variety. Male psychology, it's all about novelty."

Petra laughed. "As opposed to women who crave the same darn thing over and over?" She turned to Moe. "You're looking at Dement because he hangs around with Mason Book. And you're looking at Book because he's Caitlin's boyfriend's boss?"

Moe said, "And because Book's suicide attempt came only a week after Caitlin disappeared."

Biro said, "Crushing guilt in an addict movie star? Anything's possible, but those types self-destruct all the time. Just because they're stupid."

Metal in his voice.

Petra grinned. "My partner loves actors."

"What I love," said Biro, "is when I tell people I work Hollywood and they get after me for autographs."

" 'People,' as in cute girls," said Petra. "That's a problem, huh, pard?"

"The problem is, I got nothing to show 'em. Working in Hollywood doesn't mean you get *Hollywood.* It's Westside has all the fun."

Moe said, "Robert Blake was the Valley."

Biro ticked his fingers. "O.J., Hugh Grant, Heidi Fleiss, Mario Fortuno, Paris and Mischa and Lindsay and every other celebutard who DUIs for fun and profit."

Moe said, "Hey, a lot of that was the Strip, complain to the sheriffs. Phil Spector was out in Alta-freaking-*dena.*"

Petra mimed a pistol aim. "*Blam.* Talk about wall of sound."

All three detectives laughed. Better than thinking about whodunits with no serious leads.

Moe shut the murder book. "Thanks for your time, guys. For lack of anything else, I'm going to try to find out how a mope like Wohr connected with a trust-fund baby like Ax. Then maybe we can backtrack to Book and/or Stoltz, then to Caitlin. And Adella."

Biro said, "Maybe Ax gambles his daddy's money away, including at the poker palace."

Moe said, "Or he's into buying sex and loves to slum."

"Or Ax and Wohr hooked up at a post-Oscars party."

Weaker laughter; no one's heart was in it.

Petra said, "If you can wait around, we'll copy the whole book for you."

"That would be great."

Biro said, "You busy on the Westside?"

"Not too."

"It was like that last year for us. Months without a single murder, the *Times* wrote about it, hexed us. We started this year with that decapitation that linked to a serial case of Sturgis's. One week after that, two gang things go down, and they're still wide open."

Petra said, "Four kids gunned down in front of a party and no one saw a thing. We've got a pretty good idea who's behind it. Son of an allegedly reformed banger who scored a big city grant to keep guns out of the hands of people just like him and his offspring."

Moe said, "Meaning pretend to work it hard but don't do squat without the mayor's okay."

"Listen to him," said Biro. "So young, yet so cynical."

One of Sturgis's favorite lines. Moe's appreciation for the Loo's influence climbed a notch.

He said, "I'll go with you to the copy machine."

On the way over, Petra said, "Who's your partner on this?"

"No one."

CHAPTER

23

Aaron sat in the Opel, within eyeshot of Swallowsong Lane, listened to music on his iPod and fought the erosion of confidence.

Billing Mr. Dmitri for hours of surveillance was okay up to a point. He had to produce.

Moses being involved didn't help. Hand his brother a simple case, Aaron had no doubt Moe could close it. But a deep-freeze whodunit?

Maybe he was being too hard on bro, letting a lifetime of . . . relationship get in the way.

Blood ties be damned, he and Moses had turned into strangers.

Had they ever been anything else?

Complicated . . . well, they could always blame Mom.

One of a kind; thinking about her made him smile.

She never stopped smiling.

Except when she did.

Bagpipes and tears, so many men in blue, some of them are also crying.

Mom in black, veiled.

Big blue shapes looming over his four-year-old self, talking about Dad.

Off to one side, Jack sits there, crying harder than anyone.

All of a sudden, he's living in the house.

It had seemed like the very next damned day. Years later, when Aaron had acquired snoop skills, he went looking for the marriage certificate, found it easily enough in the County Archives.

Mom and Jack had tied the knot three months after the funeral. Civil ceremony, probably one of those deals where couples waited in line to get their ninety seconds of semi-attention from a half-asleep judge.

Despite that, he'd never think of it as anything but the next damned day. That was the
point. A four-year-old needed to construct
his own reality and hell if he hadn't *coped.*
Never opening a fresh mouth to Jack, even
when Jack nodded off in the middle of a
chess game or Monopoly or watching TV.

Never ratting Jack out when he picked
Aaron up from school, stinking of booze.

Poor little Aaron had a new daddy,
everything was going to be just fine. Meanwhile, poor little Aaron's waking up in the
middle of the night, sweaty and shivering,
seeing his real daddy's smiling face. Getting tossed up in the air by his real daddy,
tossing the football, man this feels so good,
feels so damned damned good.

Then: Real daddy lying in a pool of rich,
deep blood.

Smiling up at Aaron, despite the blood
and the pain. Mouthing *Good-bye, little
man.*

Aaron lived with the dream for years,
never told anyone about it because that
would be chickenshit.

New daddy.

New *baby.*

Pink and freckled as Jack, unable to do

nothing but squall and crap and suck on Mom's . . .

As Aaron grew older, he craved details about Dad. Mom had no problem pulling out the photo albums, talking about the love they shared, what a wonderful man, a handsome man, a smart man. Jack, sitting off by himself, watching the tube, able to hear but it didn't even bother him. What kind of man was *that*?

When Aaron was seven, he built up his courage, got Jack alone, asked Jack what had happened.

Jack avoided looking at him. "That's just a real sad story, son."

I'm not your son!

Jack reached for his glass of vodka. Or scotch. Or whatever was on sale at the liquor store.

Aaron walked away and Jack didn't follow. That decided it for Aaron.

He's a coward. Maybe that helped kill Dad.

Freeze him out.

Jack dealt with Aaron's rejection by being super-permissive, sometimes indulging Aaron behind Mom's back. That only decreased Aaron's respect for the intruder who slept with his mother.

No spine. The way he'd corroded his own liver was proof positive of that.

When Aaron was thirteen, Jack went *out* with no style.

Falling off a damned stool. No bagpipes.

Mom crying, but in a different way.

When Aaron had a year of patrol under his belt, he went looking for the original case file, finally found it at Parker Center, stashed like any other hopeless unsolved on a dusty metal rack.

Waiting until the records clerk left, he pounced, dry-mouthed, wet-eyed, heart churning like a drill-bit.

What he found was two pages of poorly punctuated cop-prose describing the basics of Patrolman Darius Fox's untimely demise, and an unsigned paragraph at the end blaming Dad and Jack for being careless.

Sitting on the cold, concrete floor of the records vault, crying silently and hoping to God no one walked in, Aaron pored over the arid memorial. Went over it again. Again.

The anonymous author of the blame-conclusion suggested that August 9, 1979, be used as a teaching tool but the case had never come up during Aaron's training.

Aaron nosed around the academy library in Elysian Park, finally unearthed a fifteen-year-old manual that included the case among several examples where "failure to observe procedure produced disastrous results."

Most of the blame visited on Dad, for letting his guard down.

But that was based on Jack's report that Dad had let his gun drop when the Cadillac's driver's window rolled down.

So where the hell were you?

Aaron returned to the vault, planning to photocopy the file, forced himself past emotion, tried to squeeze something evidentiary from Dad's behavior.

A seasoned cop relaxing meant he'd faced someone he didn't consider threatening.

Or knew.

Suddenly the file was nothing but paper and ink. He stuck it back and left without copying.

One day, he'd work the case. When he had enough money to kick back for an extended stretch of time, really concentrate.

He was doing great financially, each year better than the previous, his retirement fund was looking okay, and his equity in the house was growing. So maybe sooner rather than later.

How would Mom react?

How would Moe react?

Let the damned chips *fall*.

At twelve forty-six a.m. headlights slapped him alert.

White Jag with the top down driving down Swallowsong. Middle-aged couple, woman at the wheel, man looking grim. Six minutes later, a painfully slow-moving dark Range Rover rolled down and passed.

Two gay-looking guys, the passenger mussing the driver's hair, causing the SUV to swerve toward the Opel, then correct jerkily.

Hoots as the SUV rolled away. Must be nice to enjoy your own stupidity.

Aaron stretched as much as the Opel's seat would allow. His eyes felt like they'd

been rubbed with beach sand. He mois-
tened with the drops he carried in his Dopp
kit. Popped another can—Coke, not Jolt,
let's not push the endocrines too hard.

He'd taken two sips when the black Ram
pickup appeared.

Running the stop sign as usual. Aaron
was ready, spotted Mason Book slumped
in the passenger seat. That same zombie
stare he'd spied during the drive to the
Colony with Rory Stoltz.

Moments later Aaron was easing back
and forth in light west-moving Sunset traffic, playing the Opel like a trombone slide.
Sneaking in split-second stares that coa-
lesced into a single image, like pictures in
a flip book.

Ax Dement, wearing a black leather
jacket despite the heat, greasy hair tied
back in a tail, broke the speed limit by ten
mph as he puffed a doobie in plain sight.

Lynyrd Skynyrd thumping out the driver's window, all bass-enhanced.

Rich kid really piling on the outlaw thing.
Where was the Confederate flag and the
gun rack?

They were in Beverly Hills, now, a city

teeming with cops, but illegal smoke was still blowing out the truck's window. So Ax was a serious risk-taker. Maybe because Daddy's dough had buffered life's sharp edges. Or he was just too stupid to be afraid.

Aaron shifted to the right, hazarded another look at Mason Book.

The actor sat low, stared straight ahead, mouth small and tight.

Indulging in nothing but misery.

The Ram continued west.

All the way to the beach, and down the ramp to PCH, big surprise.

Here we go again. Mason Book craving ocean breeze, had found himself another chauffeur.

For all his outward depression, Book was the star, Ax just a pseudo-macho hanger-on who came panting like a puppy when Book commanded.

Ax had his foot to the pedal and keeping up with him worried Aaron; all he needed was some Highway Patrol hotshot pulling him over.

Black man at the beach.

As they neared the Colony, Aaron braced himself for a turnaround. But this time, the truck kept on going, picking up even more speed past the Pepperdine campus, where Caitlin had once studied and Rory still did. Where Malibu began turning rural.

Heading to Daddy's spread in Solar Canyon? Late-night mass at the family church?

But the Ram zipped right past Solar, Kanan Dume, Zuma, Broad Beach. Hooked a quick right that caused Aaron to kill the Opel's lights as he downshifted.

He watched from twenty yards back as the truck pulled off at the land-side entrance to Leo Carrillo State Beach.

About a mile before L.A. County gave way to Ventura, and some of California's prettiest sand and water.

On the land side, where the truck was, were trails leading to campground and wilderness hikes. A couple of years ago, a cougar had mauled a mountain biker to death not far from here.

Aaron rolled a little closer, trying to spot the truck's taillights. The angle of the dip into the lot and the surrounding brush hid the Ram. To Aaron's left, the poorly limned ocean was more sound than sight.

Steady whoosh of tide. In and out, like lazy sex.

Aaron had driven by this spot tons of times, on trips to Oxnard, Ventura, Ojai, Santa Barbara. But the last time he'd actually stopped at Carrillo was . . . his sophomore year in college, he'd taken a girl there to explore the tide pools, stretch out on clean white sand. Pretending to care about starfish and sea anemones in order to get some romance going. Hoping to catch a glimpse of dolphins, because chicks loved dolphins.

Toward sunset, he and . . . what was her name . . . had spotted a pod of Flippers and that had done the trick. Great session in the back of his car, what *was* her name . . . brunette, half black, half white like him, said she wanted to be a psychologist . . . Ronette . . . *Ronelle* DeFreeze, long, lithe body, green eyes, pretty head turned to one side as she . . .

Concentrate, Detective Fox.

He edged the Opel closer, got twenty

feet from the entrance to the park where a sliver of the lot was visible. The truck was parked fairly close to the highway, blocked by yellow gates that closed off the park after dark.

Impossible to see if it was occupied or not. *Gee thanks, starless night.*

That day with Ronelle, Aaron had parked just past the yellow gates. Concentrating, he dredged up memories. Ranger booth, list of regulations. Entry road shaded by trees.

Ax and Book were either sitting in the truck or had exited to proceed on foot. Either scenario was risky: a darkened vehicle illegally parked could easily attract attention from a patrolling park ranger. So would the marijuana reek sure to cling to the truck's interior.

But this was a guy who sped through B.H. toking up.

Maybe the boys had been here before, knew it was safe because ranger patrols were infrequent.

If budget cuts stuck a handful of Smokeys with covering miles of wilderness, that made sense.

What did that say about the safety of

camping—something Aaron had always considered a pathetic grab at phony machismo.

And this was Carrillo, he'd heard rumors about the place, the good old days of the Manson Family, other assorted whacks running cannibal parties under full moons. Human sacrifices, blood rites, not to mention your garden-variety sexual psychopath lurking behind every pine.

C'mon, Jimmy and Judy! Mom and Dad have found a super-neat place to set up our little Sterno stove and cook our wienies and our marshmallows . . .

Even if the rumors were tall tales, what was the pleasure in waking up at sunrise with achy muscles and a mouthful of dirt, some rabid raccoon or weasel or whatever farting on your head . . .

What were Mason Book and Ax Dement doing here at close to two a.m.?

One way to find out.

Nope, too risky.

Encountering the two of them would blow his cover and render him useless.

Moe would love that . . .

First Commandment of the job: Thou Shalt Not Fuck Up.

He settled down for another bout of inactivity.

Twenty-four minutes later, he saw two figures return to the truck—so they *had* taken a walk.

The Ram backed away from the yellow gates, swung onto PCH, hooked an illegally acute left turn that took it across the double-double. Starting up the Opel, Aaron checked for ongoing traffic, completed his own iffy turn, pushed the car up to seventy.

Moments later, with the Ram just starting to come into view, red lights flashed in his rearview.

Wonderful.

Before Aaron could respond, the CHP cruiser flashed its brights.

Patience, man, what's it been, a nanosecond?

Next the idiot would be bellowing over his loudspeaker. Aaron pulled over at the first hint of turnoff.

The cruiser glided to a stop twenty feet behind.

It took a long time—way longer than usual—for the Chippie to approach. Careful to keep his hands on the wheel, Aaron watched the patrolman head his way through the side mirror.

Young, just a kid. Big and pouty-mouthed and heavy.

Slow, deliberate John Wayne waddle, one hand resting near his gun.

Black man at the beach.

The CHP officer stopped five feet behind the Opel, just stood there.

No reason to be worried, Kiddie-cop. You've already taken your sweet time running the tags.

Following proper procedure.

Hefting his flashlight high, the way they teach you in every police academy, the Chippie advanced some more. Stopped again. Hand *on* his gun.

Aaron sat there.

Finally: "Step out of the car, sir."

Pasting his best guileless/harmless/aw-shucks look on his face, Aaron complied at exactly the pace he would've appreciated back in his uniform days.

Smiling, as the officer blinded him with his flashlight.

Keeping his mouth shut because anything he said would be wrong.

CHAPTER
24

The Reverend Arnold Wohr had business in the city, insisted meeting at the station would be no trouble at all.

Moe would've preferred to get a look at the La Puente house, maybe catch some sign Ramone W still bunked out there occasionally. But given the rev's easy cooperation, he was in no position to argue.

Ramone's respectable sib showed up ten minutes early. The senior brother by two years, Arnold looked a decade younger, a trim, balding man in an unstylish, spotless gray suit, white shirt, blue tie, brown shoes.

Moe searched for some family resem-
blance to Raymond Wohr, found it in
skimpy chin endowment.

Arnold's gaze was steady and clear, his
handshake cool and dry.

Moe thanked him for coming, asked
what kind of business he had in L.A.

"This business, Detective. I didn't want
my family involved."

"In what?"

"Anything to do with Ray. What's he
done?"

"Sounds like you're used to being called
by the police."

"The police, the parole office when Ray
was still on parole, the liquor store in my
neighborhood when there's a sudden cigarette shortfall just after Ray's been there
to purchase a stick of chewing gum. Luck-
ily, the owner's a member of my congre-
gation."

"You've been cleaning up after him for a
while."

"You can't pick your relatives, Detective, but you can try to help them."

Moe said, "Would you consider Ray
incorrigible?"

Arnold Wohr frowned. "If I didn't believe in change, I couldn't stand up every Sunday and preach it."

"I guess you hear all the time how different you and Ray are."

"Not really," said Arnold. "Few people see us together."

"Ray doesn't come by much."

"Ray was arrested when he was fourteen, Detective. For stealing peach brandy from a supermarket, then shoplifting sneakers from a Wal-Mart. He spent a few months at a youth camp. The day he was released, Mom and Dad threw him a welcome-back party. He repaid them by emptying Mom's purse in the middle of the night and sneaking out. We didn't hear from him until his next arrest, a year later, also for theft. That time he got sent to adult jail and never bothered to let us know he was out. Mom and Dad were solid working people, we had plenty of discussions trying to figure out what Ray was escaping from. My parents died wondering. After I got out of the military, my search for answers led me to the ministry."

"Wanting to understand Ray."

"Ray, people like him. You turn all

the facts over—the psychology, the sociology—but they don't explain it. So you look to a higher power."

"The devil made Ray do it."

The reverend's frown caused Moe to regret his flippancy.

He said, "Sir, I don't mean to make light of the situation—"

"It's all right, Detective. I know that faith-based notions of good and evil don't wash in today's society. But no one's given me a better explanation for my brother's behavior."

"You see him as evil."

Arnold's eyes rose quickly, dropped to below Moe's level. "I see Ray as misled. I'm not saying some unseen arm is guiding him—it's not a matter of a demon with a forked tail. More like Ray's negative energy overpowered the positive."

That sounded new-age. Or all faith simply boiled down to belief in the invisible.

Moe said, "Do you have any idea why I wanted to talk to you, Reverend?"

"I have an idea now," said Arnold Wohr. "When I asked for you downstairs, they informed me I'd be going to Homicide. I'm terrified."

But he'd wanted the interview away from his family even before that—expecting something bad. Arnold Wohr suspected there was more to his brother than dope and petty theft.

Time to soften him up.

Moe said, "Well, I don't mean to scare you, but we are investigating your brother's association with a homicide victim."

"Association? Is Ray a suspect?"

"Not yet."

"But he might be?"

"Would that surprise you, Reverend?"

"Ray's never been violent. Yes, of course it would surprise me."

Moe slid Adella Villareal's happy-face color photo from her murder book and showed it to Arnold. A tremor plinked the corners of the guy's eye sockets then slow-walked to his hairline. "*She's* dead? My God."

"You know her."

"I met her once. She was with her baby—in that same blue blanket. Dear Lord—what happened?"

Moe said, "Where and when did you meet her?"

"Ray brought her for Easter. Not last Easter—two Easters ago."

Barely a month before Adella's murder.

Moe said, "Easter dinner?"

Wohr nodded. "We'd stopped inviting him years ago because he never responded. So wouldn't you know when he's not invited, he pops in? Holding some flowers he'd obviously picked out of someone's yard."

"With this woman."

"That was the second surprise. Ray bringing anyone, he always came alone. The third was that she—what was her name . . . something Spanish—Elena? . . ."

"Adella Villareal."

"Yes, that's it, Adella. The third surprise was her not being the type of person you'd expect Ray to associate with."

"How so, Reverend?"

"She was well groomed, polite—a really nice young lady. Excellent manners—she insisted on helping us serve."

"Different from the other women in Ray's life."

Arnold sat back. "I've never met any

other women in Ray's life, Detective, it's just . . . it seemed as if she and Ray didn't fit. Not that Ray wasn't trying to be on his best behavior. When Ray shows up it's always for money. That day he didn't ask for any. Was dressed decently, collared shirt, clean jeans. I told myself maybe she's a good influence."

"You saw them as a couple."

"I didn't know what to think. But there he was, with her and baby. So yes, of course, I assumed. I remember thinking *Poor baby, if Ray's his dad.* Lord forgive me."

Moe produced a mug shot of Alicia Eiger.

Arnold said, "Who's that?"

"Another friend of your brother."

"This would be more what I'd expect."

"How did Ray introduce Adella to your family?"

"Just, 'Hi, we're here, this is Adella.' My wife ran off to set extra places. No point embarrassing the girl."

"You assumed Ray was the baby's father but at some point that changed?"

"There was nothing romantic going on. Ray and Adella hardly talked to each other—mostly she talked to my wife about the baby. Mostly, she focused on the baby."

"And Ray?"

"Not the least bit interested. When Adella got up to nurse him—he was a boy, cute little thing, lots of hair—Ray just kept shoveling food into his own mouth. The way he learned in prison." Hooking his arm and hunching.

"Protecting his food," said Moe.

"Exactly. Do you have children, Detective?"

"No, sir."

"In the early stages it's all about physical caretaking. Feeding, burping, changing, then more of the same. Adella seemed to relish that. She ate so little at the table that we prepared her a little care package." Frown. "Ray cleaned his plate then moved on to hers. Said something like 'She'll never get to it, no sense wasting good grub.'"

"When Ray and Adella did interact, how did he treat her?"

"You think he killed her."

"Reverend, where the case stands right now is Ray knew her and because of his criminal record, he needs to be looked at."

"He's never been violent."

"Sometimes people do things they never get arrested for."

Arnold didn't answer.

"Would it totally shock you if Ray did kill someone?"

Arnold Wohr's eyes trampolined. "You just said you have no evidence."

"That's true. I'm just asking."

"Detective, the idea that my brother . . . no, I really can't see it. Ray's never been violent. Never . . ."

"But . . ."

"But nothing."

"Sorry," said Moe. "I thought I heard a *but.*"

Arnold Wohr crossed his legs, tugged at a lapel. "If you had evidence, of course I'd . . . no, no, I just can't believe Ray would ever go that far. But if he did something like that, of course I'd want him put away where he could never hurt anyone else."

"Anyone else," Moe echoed. "Is there something you need to tell me about your brother?"

Arnold's eyes zipped to one side, like a shotgun slide. He stared at a spot on the wall. "I'm not sure what you're asking, Detective."

Sounded clear to me.

"Reverend, I could be totally off base here, but I've been picking up some serious concern on your part. Maybe because you know something about your brother that no one else does?"

Silence.

"Reverend, I understand about family loyalty, but protecting the innocent is what we're both about."

Arnold stared at him. "You look young but you've been doing this for a while, haven't you?"

You are my new best friend.

Moe smiled. "You look a lot younger than your brother."

"The virtues of clean living," said Arnold. Then he laughed. "My wife says that. I tell her it's more the absence of dirty living."

His attention shifted to the floor. "Yes, I do need to tell you." Deep breath. "What you picked up isn't concern about Ray being violent. Not in the strict sense of causing physical harm . . ."

Moe waited.

"I feel like Judas, Detective."

"Judas betrayed a savior. Doesn't sound as if your brother fits into that category."

"*The* savior," Arnold corrected. "Are you a religious man, Detective?"

"Depends what day you catch me."

"Fair enough . . . I know it's my moral obligation to be truthful. But this is . . . I guess if I could be sure it was relevant, but I can't."

"Ray's hurt someone in your family."

"No!"

Moe shifted closer, spread his shoulders, establishing dominance. "What, then, Reverend?"

Head shake.

"Reverend, there's no morality in delaying. This is a homicide case. Adella Villareal was strangled and dumped. Her baby hasn't been seen since."

Wohr's hands covered his face. "My God."

"I think we both know what God thinks about that—"

"Ray never hurt her," Arnold blurted. His hands dropped. "But he frightened her. My daughter. My younger daughter, Sarah.

She's thirteen, caught him watching her through a window."

"Her bedroom window?"

Nod. "The girls share a room. Eve was out with friends."

"Sarah caught Ray peeping."

"Dear Lord, yes."

"When did this happen, Reverend?"

"Six months ago. Ray was back to his usual—filthy T-shirt, baggy shorts, the rubber sandals. He *stank* of alcohol."

"Back to asking for money," said Moe.

"This time he had a story. He'd turned his life around, was now a 'great investment.' I gave him everything in my wallet—a hundred and ten dollars. He asked for more, I said no, he cursed and left."

"Is that when you gave him your car?"

"My car—oh, the Toyota. No, that was donated to the church last year. I thought my wife could use it so I paid the church full blue-book value. But it wasn't practical. I've got a second job, I install prefab cabinets and sometimes Francine and I need to deliver materials to a site. We purchased an old Suburban and gave the Toyota to Ray."

"Instead of money."

"I was short on cash, figured he'd sell it."

"You never signed over the pink slip."

"I didn't?"

"No, sir."

"Oh . . . did Ray do something with that car—hit someone while drunk?"

"No, Reverend. Back to your daughter. You helped your brother out and he repaid you by snooping on Sarah. Was that before he asked for a handout or later?"

Arnold's jaws clenched. "Sarah didn't tell me until several days later. She'd been looking upset and I finally got it out of her. I thought it was something about school, friends. I never expected to hear *that*."

"What did she say happened?"

"She was in her room, getting ready for bed, spotted movement from the window, caught a clear glimpse of Ray's face. Then he disappeared. She was sure it was Ray. That mustache of his is pretty distinctive. Fortunately, she's a modest girl, wears a long nightgown. But just the fact that he was out there . . . Sarah was more angry than scared."

"And you doubted it was a onetime thing."

"We talked about it as a family and my older daughter, Eve, said she'd always gotten a strange feeling from Ray. He never actually did anything but his presence made her feel uneasy. Eve's a bright, perceptive girl."

"Makes you wonder about a darker side to your brother."

"Was Adella . . . was there *that* kind of assault as well?"

Instead of answering, Moe said, "Is there anything else in Ray's history you want to tell me—sexually speaking? Like when you were growing up?"

"No, no, nothing that I know—will he be charged with snooping on Sarah?"

"Do you want him to be?"

"The reason I didn't report it in the first place was I didn't want to put Sarah through anything traumatic. And she insisted that's what *she* wanted. We talked about it as a family and came to a decision. Ray was to be barred from the house forever. It seemed the best solution. Now you're telling me Ray may have committed an act of perversion—"

"No, sir, I never said that."

"But you didn't deny it when I asked you if Adella was assaulted."

Moe took pity on the guy. "She wasn't, Reverend Wohr. And to be honest, I don't see how Ray can be charged for snooping."

"Too much time has passed?"

"Even if you'd reported him at the time, I doubt he would've been charged. Being spotted on the other side of a niece's window when she's fully clothed when he wasn't trespassing can be explained away easily. He was out there smoking, just happened to pass by." Looking straight at Wohr. "If he's never done anything along those lines before."

"He hasn't," said Wohr. "Not with my girls."

"Then no cop would've busted him, sir—not here or in La Puente."

But the sexual element was definitely worth looking into.

"Thank you," said Arnold. "For trying to make me feel better."

"I'm being honest, Reverend. I appreciate you coming all the way out here and doing the same."

Wohr squirmed. "There is one more

thing, Detective. Something Ray said the last time I saw him. Part of that speech about getting his life together. He could see I was skeptical, so he got specific, claimed he was representing people in entertainment."

"Representing how?"

"I asked him that but he just repeated himself. Representing. Like he was some sort of an agent. Then he brought up Adella, said 'Remember her? High-class, Arnie. She's what I'm talking about.' I said, 'Ray, if you need money, just come out and say so and stop spinning yarns.'"

Arnold shook his head. "I never talked to him like that, something must've come over me. He started using foul language. Jammed his palm right up in my face, said 'Fill the collection plate, Scrooge.' That irritated me, I smacked the bills into his hand hard. He made some blasphemous remark, how if the God squad behaved this way, God must be a loser. At that point, I knew he had to leave before I did something I'd regret. I was still smoldering when Sarah told me what happened. It was like lighting a match to my soul. I called my brother, left a message telling him to get help for his perverted impulses, told him I never wanted to see him again. And he's honored that request."

"Six months ago."

"Not to the day, Detective. Give or take."

Representing a dead woman.

"Anything else you want to tell me, Reverend?"

Arnold shook his head. "Where's Ray living?"

"I don't know, sir." No sense in a confrontation between the brothers at Alicia Eiger's crib.

"You don't have him in custody?"

"No, sir."

"So he really *isn't* a suspect."

"Not at this point."

"Okay," said Arnold Wohr, sounding more regretful than relieved.

"Something else on your mind, Reverend?"

"If you do put him in custody, Detective Reed, I'd like to know. So I could visit him. See how I could help."

Back at his desk, Moe distilled droplets of fact from his interview of Arnold Wohr.

Brother Ray's scumbag image had filled out nicely. No violence on his sheet, but the guy was sexually twisted enough to peep a thirteen-year-old.

The "entertainment" connection Ramone W had bragged about was another nice nugget, tying in to Ax Dement and the Eagle Motel. Sex, dope, or both. Probably both.

Was Wohr's Industry biz limited to a fringe hanger-on like Ax? Or had he actually networked with serious money types?

With unhealthy appetites.

If Wohr's reach did stretch to A-list dope fiends like Mason Book, this could get really interesting.

Mountains of money to indulge the *gimme gimme gimme.*

Ramone's boast of "representing" Adella might mean he really had pimped her. Or he was making himself more than he was.

She had accompanied him to Easter dinner.

With her baby.

Who Ramone showed no interest in.

The creepiest part was Ramone bragging about representing Adella long after her murder. No official violence in his sheet but he was callous enough to exploit her memory in order to cadge money out of his brother.

Arnold and his family had been confused about the relationship between his brother and the surprisingly polite "young lady."

Because citizens like Arnold and his family had no clue.

Moe thought about the rev's description of the interaction between Ramone and Adella. No affection, no conversation.

Scooping food off her plate when she went to feed the baby.

Why would Adella, a devoted mom, hang with him?

No reason but money.

The Easter visit had probably been Ramone's idea of a joke. Bringing high-priced flesh to his devout brother's house on a sacred day.

Callous *and* mean-spirited.

Toss in Ramone peeping his own niece during a visit to ask for yet more money, and you ended up with a really nasty picture.

Cold, uncaring, sexually impulsive.

Exactly the combo Delaware had listed during the marsh-murder investigation when describing the classic kink-wired, career-criminal psychopath.

Meaning Ramone was capable of *anything.*

Moe fetched himself coffee, drank amid the low buzz of the D-room, visualizing Technicolor flash-frames filled with mind-searing brutality.

Caitlin's pretty young face, contorted in agony.

Adella Villareal thinking she was a pro but getting the worst kind of surprise.

Two good-looking young women, as different from each other as any two people could be, united in death.

The baby.

Moe had to get air or he'd start hitting something.

Making his way past half a dozen other detectives, he hurried out to the hallway that led to Sturgis's closet-sized office. Race-walking past the Loo's closed door, he repeated the circuit a couple of times. Got dry-mouthed and itchy-eyed and bought a Coke from the machine before returning to his chair.

Phones continued to ring, men and women with intent expressions talked on the phone, clicked computer keys. Del Hardy caught Moe's eye and gave a little salute.

Moe half expected him to come over, ask how Aaron was doing.

Waving back, he returned to Adella's murder book, not expecting to find anything, just wanting to look as preoccupied as he felt.

His eyes kept returning to the photo.

Pretty dead girl caught smiling. All that joy because of a tiny blue-swaddled form.

Gabriel, a tiny bud of humanity, with an angel's name.

Four grand in Adella's bank, despite no job. Had the challenges of single motherhood led Adella to work for Ramone W?

Moe thought about how she'd dropped in on her folks with the baby, snuck out soon after without saying good-bye. Not unlike Ramone's unannounced drop-in at his brother's.

So maybe the visit had been *Adella's* idea.

A girl who liked to play games.

Was that why she refused to say who'd fathered the kid? Because Daddy was useless, so why get him involved?

Or just the opposite: Daddy was *real* useful because he was rich and famous, had paid Adella off not to go public.

Then why whore?

Because more was more?

Or whoring had conceived the baby— Moe shut the file to get the pictures out of his head, concentrated on setting up a logical sequence of events.

Adella parties with Rich Industry Guys, maybe at a gig set up by Ramone W. She gets pregnant, figures out which R.I.G. is the daddy, asks for money to keep her mouth shut. Gets some.

At the time of her murder, the baby was five months old and she'd died with 4K in her account. Less than a grand for each month of Gabriel's existence. Maybe it had taken a while to come to an agreement—two months, for argument's sake, making two and a half K per month. But that was left over after expenses, say two a month.

Leaving an estimated gross of 4.5K a month—round to 5. Sixty grand a year. To an Industry honcho, chump change. To someone like Adella, serious money.

Until she gets greedy. Asks for more.

Or maybe she'd accepted an initial low-ball offer because the joy of motherhood, hormones, whatever, had numbed her brain.

Or Rich Daddy had promised more somewhere down the line.

Either way, she realizes she's living in a crappy single, budgeting for Pampers and pablum, meanwhile Rich Daddy's living large.

House in the hills, private jets, VIP rooms on demand, premium tables at Koi, the Ivy, wherever those types stuffed their faces. Moe was certain Aaron could rattle off the names . . .

Deciding to cash in big-time, she leans on Rich Daddy.

Becomes a problem.

Call in Ramone W, or someone like him, a psychopathic lowlife capable of anything.

One question: Why wouldn't Rich Daddy keep her happy by upping the support?

Because he's a narcissistic asshole used to doing things his way, sees no reason why some vagina he pumped who should've taken precautions has the right to share The Lifestyle.

Why the hell hadn't she aborted in the *first* place? Because she'd set out to screw him—literally and financially—from the beginning.

She'll just keep asking, you'll never be free.

Better to eliminate the problem.

Two problems.

The pictures rushed back into Moe's head. Little blue-swaddled package, moldering somewhere. The rest of the world became background noise as he hunkered down trying to logic out how Caitlin Frostig fit into the picture.

Caitlin had worked at a bar where celebs had once hung out. Maybe that included Ax Dement and/or Mason Book.

Adella's pimp supplied sex and drugs to Ax Dement. Maybe also to Mason Book.

Maybe, maybe maybe . . . something missing . . .

Then it hit him. *Rory Stoltz* knew everyone: Caitlin, Book, and Dement.

Had the All-American boy—ambitious, maybe too ambitious—been sucked into something dark and nasty? Did his adoring mommy sense that about her only child? Did that explain her hostility when Moe cornered her at work?

Rory Stoltz, All-American Walking-Around Guy. Did his duties including passing cash to Adella? Or to a hired killer?

Worse?

If Rory was the glue connecting Adella to Caitlin, this stretched all the way to Mason Book.

How did Caitlin figure in?

Maybe Rory had told her too much and Caitlin, a moral girl, freaked out.

Now *she's* a problem.

Would Rory go along with offing his girlfriend?

Caitlin was dead and Rory was still working for Mason Book. The world he'd entered, women were to be used. Discarded when no longer useful.

Uh-oh, one little logical obstacle: At the time of Adella's murder Rory was waiting tables at Riptide, not working as Book's heel-and-fetch.

Moe thought about that, decided it wasn't an insurmountable problem. Just because Rory hadn't been *formally* hired didn't mean he wasn't bootlicking the actor. How many crimes had grown out of booze-soaked bar conversation? A whole bunch of wrong-time, wrong-place.

What if Book had sensed something weak-spined about Rory?

Hey, wanna help solve some problems, kid?

What if Rory had *earned* the P.A. job because he'd passed the amorality test?

Passing the test, but flunking life.

Moe logged online and looked up employment agencies in L.A. Narrowed the list to half a dozen that specialized in personal assistants, private chefs, chauffeurs, other industry-type jobs.

An hour later, he'd confirmed that Rory Stoltz had never registered with any of them.

Expanding the search to an additional six agencies, even though they didn't specialize in high-life gigs, brought the same answer. Same for the Pepperdine student employment office, where Moe's easy lie about being a lawyer whom Stoltz wanted to work for was believed, no questions asked.

New skill set, he'd never been a good bullshitter, Mom always kidded him about his face being a one-way mirror into his soul. Nothing like on-the-job training.

And maybe the same applied to Rory. Just another California kid hoping for a toehold in the industry, Master Stoltz had learned all *sorts* of new skills.

Stuff you couldn't put on a résumé.

No agency registration wasn't proof Rory had been hired because of a relationship begun at Riptide—Moe had yet to place Mason Book and Ax Dement at the bar—but it did add weight to the balance scale.

So let's assume, for the moment, that Rory had connected, early on, to Ax Dement and Book, and lost his moral footing quickly.

Either because he didn't have much to begin with, or celebrity, charisma, and wealth were a lot more seductive than cramming for exams and backseat tumbles with Caitlin.

This was a city—this was a *world*—where people got famous for showing up, where sex tapes were career-enhancing, nothing was beyond the pale.

Why not sell out your girlfriend if it meant Something Big?

Moe revisited the screenplay he'd outlined. Turned it over, again and again. Each time, it got uglier. Made more sense.

Now how to prove it?

Focus on the victim.

A film crew was actually shooting in Hollywood, jamming up La Brea between Melrose and Sunset, and the drive to Adella Villareal's last known residence on Gower took a smog-choked hour.

When Moe finally reached the address, he found it surprisingly uncrappy, a nice twenties-era, six-unit château-type with all sorts of fancy moldings and trim. Painted peach with a burbling fountain out front.

No answers at the three ground-floor units, but no big deal, Adella had lived on the second.

The tenant now residing in her single was a cute young Asian woman in a white coat. A Kaiser Hospital name tag said *Karen Chan, M.D., R-II, Medicine.* Chan looked around eighteen, despite eyes drooping with fatigue as she braced herself in the doorjamb and informed Moe the unit had been spotless when she'd moved in.

"But talk to Mrs. Newfield, next door. She knows about that girl, talked to me about it."

"What she say?"

"That my 'predecessor' was murdered and it was never solved. Like that was supposed to scare me. But the rent's great and with what they pay residents, no way I'm leaving. Then I found out the girl hadn't even been killed here, so what's the big deal?"

"Why would Mrs. Newfield try to scare you?"

"I'm not saying she did, it was more like sharing the anxiety. Like she's still freaked out. Anyway, I need to get some sleep. Going to be on call again before I know it."

Moe thanked her and continued up the corridor.

His knock was followed by a strained "Who is it?" through the door.

"Police."

"Who?"

"Police, ma'am."

"About what?"

"Adella Villareal."

Two beats. "Hold on."

The door cracked an inch. Dark eyes peered out behind a chain.

Moe parted his blazer, showed the badge on his shirt pocket.

"Hold on." Silver-nailed fingers fumbled with the chain. The door swung open quickly, as if destined for that position. The woman who stared at Moe was his height and broad-hipped. Seventy, seventy-five, with shoe-polish black hair cut in a page-boy. Gray-shadowed brown eyes were a pretty good match to her nail polish. Thickly powdered skin was the color and consistency of wet tissue paper. She wore a pearl-gray kimono printed with mauve fish. Diamond-colored gems strung around a scrawny neck were too huge to be real.

"Detective Reed, ma'am."

"*You're* new."

Did he look that green? "Pardon?"

"The first time the cops sent a woman. I was in the hospital with gallstones, my husband talked to her. Totally useless, what with his memory. Leonard said she was pretty, kept going on about it, trying to get my goat. He succeeded. I burned his dinner for a week. She came back and talked to me—the female. Didn't seem interested in what I had to say."

Moe smiled.

"I'd have thought," said the woman, "that she'd be interested, seeing as Leonard's memory is useless."

"Did you call to let her know you were available?"

"That's my responsibility? You've got to be kidding."

"True," said Moe. "Well, I'm here, ma'am."

"A new one," said woman, looking him up and down. "They're growing 'em young nowadays."

"I'm interested in anything you have to say, ma'am. May I come in?"

"I'm Ida Newfield. Sure, why not—uh-oh, hold on, wait wait wait. Show me that badge again, along with some printed I.D. You look like a cop, but a girl can't be too careful."

After thirty seconds of squinty-eyed, bifocaled scrutiny, Ida Newfield let him into her living room.

He'd expected musty, overstuffed clutter, found very little of anything.

Gray felt walls, matching carpet, one low-slung charcoal leather couch, a chrome-and-glass coffee table, a single black lacquer chest with no handles.

All the warmth of an airport terminal. Like Aaron's place.

Ida Newfield announced, "Sleek, isn't it? I'm an interior decorator, did houses you can't even imagine." Drawing a remote-control module from a kimono pocket, she clicked. A grinding noise accompanied the ascent of a forty-inch flat-screen TV from a slot in the top of the black chest.

"Nice," said Moe.

"It's all about negative space," said New-field, pushing another button and causing the TV to descend. "Know what that means?"

"Stuff you don't see?"

"All the stuff that *surrounds* the stuff you *do* see," she corrected. "Meaning sanity, because space feeds the soul. *She* didn't get that." Hooking a thumb at the wall shared with the unit next door. "Not she, the *doctor.* She, the *other* one. The one you're here about. She was clean enough, but *stuff* was everywhere—baby clothes, cribs, her pullout bed, bottles, food. Ugh." Head shake. "Have you heard George Carlin on stuff? First you acquire stuff, then you need stuff to take care of your stuff and places to *store* your stuff. Man was a genius. I almost did his house, years ago."

Moe said, "So you knew Adella Vil-lareal."

"Not in the sense of friendship. But I sure know what she did."

"What did she do?"

"As if you don't know."

Moe waited.

"You don't?" said Ida Newfield. "Oh, come on. She had sex for money. I'm a feminist and that offends me deeply."

"How do you know she—"

"Because she went out late dressed like a tart. Because she offered to pay me to take care of her baby when she had to 'work' suddenly. Always at night. I've raised my own two, the last thing I want to do is burp and change pooey diapers. No, sirree."

"How often did she go out dressed like a tart?"

"I wasn't out in the hall keeping count. I saw her that way by accident—let's say six times, does that work for you? What a getup, you'd think men would tire of the old clichés and show some imagination."

"What kind of getup?"

"Tart-couture. She tried to hide it under her coat but I knew what was going on. Fishnets, skintight micro-dress that she's falling out of, five-inch spikes, tiny little purse for her condoms. A lot different than what she pretended."

"Pretended what?"

"That she was just a nice young

mommy." Ida Newfield clucked her tongue.
"A nice mommy should live with a daddy.
Or at least, another mommy, I don't judge.
But raising a kid all alone? Oh, sure, *that*
works. Even Leonard was somewhat helpful, back in the back-then. Maybe if she'd
had help, that baby wouldn't have squalled
so much."

. Another hoarse laugh, this one bereft
of glee. "*He* offered to babysit for her.
Leonard, I mean."

"Doing a good deed," said Moe.

"Oh, sure, I married a saint. Not that
he'd ever follow through. No memory. He
was just in one of his moods. 'Why didn't
you offer *my* services, honeybunch? In
exchange for *her* services.' I punched his
arm. He loves that."

"Where is your husband?"

"Hillside Memorial," she said, without
blinking. "He passed two months ago."

"Sorry—"

"He was ninety-three. I was his young
chick. So who killed her?"

"That's what we're trying to figure out,
Mrs. Newfield. Do you have any idea who
did babysit for her?"

"Different people."

"You saw them."

"Coming in and out."

"How many different people?"

"At least two—no, three. There could've been more, I saw three. Like I said, it's not as if I was spying. If I just happened to notice something, I noticed."

"Such as?"

"Such as people going in and staying there while she went out all tarted up."

"Can you describe these people?"

"I didn't get a close look. A couple of times it was a man and two women, one looked like she'd been around the block— probably helping out a fellow tart. For all I know, the younger one was, too. The man was just a bum—I've seen him around the neighborhood, near the bars."

Moe showed her Raymond Wohr's photo.

She said, "You bet. Is he the one killed her?" Even voice, but her hands were quivering.

"There's no evidence of that, ma'am."

"You're just carrying his picture around for fun."

"I'm carrying pictures of various people Ms. Villareal knew. Such as this woman."

Alicia Eiger's mug shot elicited another "Yup, that's the older one. That's a police photo, right?"

Moe nodded.

Ida Newfield said, "Maybe I can be a detective, too. I read that on the back of a matchbook. Show me the younger one and we'll go three for three."

"That's all I've got. Can you describe the younger woman?"

"Typical."

"How so?"

"California," said Newfield. "The whole blondey-blond thing. Not overtly tartish, but who knows? Maybe she fulfills stupid men's fantasies—deflowering the inno-cent."

"How young was she?"

"Young. Like a college student. Not that she went to college."

"Why not?"

"If she did, why would she be associat-ing with lowlifes?"

"Could I show you a picture at the sta-tion, ma'am?"

"You're kidding," said Ida Newfield. "Like

I'm going to leave the comfort of my home and go traipsing all the way to Wilcox Street?"

Hollywood Station was a few blocks away. What he needed to show her was at West L.A. He thought of something. "Do you have a computer, ma'am?"

"Why?"

"I could have the picture sent right now."

"Just like that?"

"Just like that."

"I'm impressed," said Ida Newfield. Then she cracked up. "You mean the police department has finally replaced horse and buggies with *motor* cars? Of *course* I have a computer."

Clicking her remote, she brought the flat-screen back up, pressed more buttons. A Windows log-in filled the screen.

"The hardware's down below, the TV's the monitor. I've got a cordless Wi-Fi keyboard and mouse if I need it, but this little thing usually does the trick. And you'll notice I don't need to open the cabinet. Which I designed thirty-five years ago, Knoll was going to manufacture it but the timing wasn't right. All the *stuff* stays out of sight because the system responds to an infrared signal."

Have you met my brother? "I'm impressed," said Moe.

"Negative space, young man. The less we have, the richer we are."

She mixed herself a Gibson, dropped in two extra pearl onions while Moe cell-phoned the West L.A. D-room. He talked to Delano Hardy and explained what he needed.

Hardy said, "Love to help you, but I'm too old for that techno-babble. How about Burns?"

Gary Burns, a thirty-five-year-old D-2 and devoted gamer, listened and said, "Sure, if the scanner's working. Where's the file?"

Several moments passed, during which Ida Newfield sipped her drink and talked about houses she'd decorated "back in the back-then." Suddenly the TV went from blue to polychrome as Caitlin Frostig's clean, wholesome, now grotesquely enlarged visage filled the screen.

Wrought monstrously happy. The horror

of her death hit Moe, maybe for the first *real* time since he'd caught the case.

Ida Newfield said, "That's her. Leonard thought she was cute. I thought she was bland. So she's a hooker, too?"

"No, ma'am," said Moe, "just a girl who got involved with too much stuff."

26

The woman was typical.

Another leggy, tan, bleach-blond soldier in the army of those who lunched but didn't eat much.

By Aaron's estimate, well-to-do X-ray types made up a third of the crowd at the Cross Creek shopping center in the heart of Malibu.

This one wore her texturized ash-and-gold just over the shoulders, with feather bangs. A youthful look she could still pull off, at least from a distance. If she'd been tucked, her surgeon deserved a medal for subtle.

Aaron approved of her style—long-sleeved, sage-green polo shirt, probably from Ron Herman or Fred Segal, low-slung velvet pants the color of good bourbon, chocolate-brown designer sneakers—Gucci, he was pretty sure. Diamond studs sparked her ears. Not showy but big enough to get the message across: *Someone cares about me.*

The black BMW X5 SUV that she drove poorly while yakking on her cell phone filled out the picture. Only her walk differentiated her from the loose-limbed, confident Battalion of the Privileged: She held her head kind of low, moved on the slowish side, stopped several times mid-stride, looking blank, before resuming the inevitable trudge to the Starbucks.

Typical to the casual observer, but Aaron was watching on a whole different level.

He'd been following Gemma Dement for over two hours by the time she entered the coffee chapel. Found a spot for himself at an outdoor table of an oh-so-cute vegan café just across the narrow lane that ran through the oh-so-cute boutiques.

Lunch would be noodles with fake

shrimp. Good chopstick skills helped him blend in.

The Starbucks was jammed. Fifteen minutes later, she was still in there.

No sweat, he was fully awake, into the hunt. Finally.

He'd been in Malibu all morning, after alarming himself up at five thirty feeling like someone had dumped a bucket of turd in his mouth. Forcing himself to work out extra-hard, then assaulting his body with a cool shower.

Shocking himself alert so he could be back at Leo Carrillo early. Trying not to think about last night's traffic ticket, the damned Chippie.

Idiot wanted to stick him with three separate violations. Added to the speeder he'd gotten a few months ago, that could put his license in jeopardy. Unmoved by Aaron's P.I. credentials or the Xerox of the nice letter his captain had written him when he left the department, the stubborn bastard's only concession was knocking it down to two.

Sign here, sir. Have a good evening, sir. Drive carefully, sir.

Driving like a brain-dead geezer, he still

reached the state park by seven a.m. On the beach side, the tide was moderate and gentle. No surfers, the only vehicle in sight a Winnebago pulled to the side so its tourist inhabitants could snap cell phone pix of water and sky.

The yellow gates were open. Over in the land-side parking lot, the ranger's booth was empty. Aaron began scouring the area from where the truck had parked to the beginning of the entry trail for a roach, a plastic bag, anything interesting. He'd covered the asphalt and was moving toward the neighboring brush when an open-sided parks department jeep cruised in and parked next to his Porsche.

The driver was a young woman with short brown hair, wearing the ranger uniform. Small girl, athletic body, pixie face. She appraised Aaron with sharp little cop eyes and got out.

He'd made sure to dress beachy without sinking into tacky: white silk aloha shirt printed with discreet, teal-blue palm trees from a boutique Bologna designer, cream linen pants, Italian glove-leather sandals, no socks. Today's watch was a chrome TAG Heuer that said *I don't need to flaunt.* He'd splashed on Givenchy men's cologne and that was still working.

The lady-ranger said, "Morning, sir. Looking for something?" *L. Martin.*

"I am, but I doubt I'll find it." Rolling his wrist. "Lost my other watch on Sunday, I was here with my kids, took a walk. Wasn't until I was all the way back to Beverly Hills before I noticed it was gone." He grimaced. "Band must've broke."

Mention of the high-priced city arched the ranger's eyebrows.

Is this guy for real? Some sort of celebrity? Too small for a basketball player . . . an actor?

She eyed the TAG. "At least you've got another one."

"The one that fell off was just a cheapie digital. But my kids gave it to me for Father's Day, the whole sentimental-value thing."

"Bummer," she said. "You think it fell off here?"

"I'm starting here. We only made maybe half a mile before the kids ran out of steam—do you have a lost and found?"

"We do, but there are no watches in there. T-shirts, towels, hats—you tell me

you attended the Better Than Ezra con-
cert tour, I can help you."

Aaron grinned. "You wouldn't happen to
have a Smokey Robinson tee?"

The ranger grinned back. "No such
luck—you know him?"

"Smokey? No, I just love his music."

"Oh." Clear disappointment. She pointed
toward the path leading into the park. "Best
thing is retrace your steps. Good luck.
Maybe the Force will be with you today."

"From your mouth to God's ears."

Perhaps the Deity liked cute females in
snug uniforms, because it only took a few
minutes for Aaron to find the spot.

Two clear sets of shoe prints veered
off the road into a thicket of eucalyptus
and lower shrubs, well before the camp-
grounds. A section of broken branches had
cued him in. Once he got past the trees,
the ground grew smooth and the roaches
were obvious. Two little nubby brown paper
things, easy to miss if you weren't looking.

Aaron stooped, didn't touch a thing, as
he took in the area. Small clearing, backed
by stubbier, denser trees, tangles of spiky
plants.

Smooth-soled footwear had left deep impressions. A heavyweight. From the shape of the heel, maybe some kind of boot.

Longer, shallower impressions bore a tire-tread pattern.

Your basic Tijuana huarache sandal; maybe Mason Book wasn't into fashion footwear. Or the guy was rich enough not to care.

No sign of disturbance of the soil indicating a burial. But fifteen months had passed since Caitlin's disappearance, so that meant nothing.

Close to the path for a burial site. Though he supposed a couple of arrogant, entitled killers might be that reckless.

He gloved up, collected the doobie-butts, dropped them in a plastic ziplock. Something near a rock caught his eye. Five burned paper matches. A foot from those, a one-inch square plastic bag.

Empty, but he was able to make out a couple of tiny granules trapped in a corner. Brownish. Maybe Mexican tar.

He sniffed. Sometimes H gave off weird smells—a vinegar-and-cat-piss cocktail. This stuff was odorless. Maybe good H.

Bagging the Baggie, he looked around for anything else interesting.

Off to his left, maybe ten yards away, the trees ruffled and a dark shape protested his presence with a high-pitched squawk.

Shooting upward, a missile-shaped creature cleared the tree canopy. Aaron made out the wide, fringed wings of the hawk as it soared out of view.

He thought of Mr. Dmitri. Little birdie, indeed.

Stopping at the Hows Market at PCH and Trancas, he bought a bagel and a quart of milk, ate and drank in the parking lot while watching construction workers drive in and out in trucks. A couple of maids in uniforms entered on foot, probably from the big houses that lined Broad Beach.

A few of the hard-hats checked out the C4S. Aaron, concealed by tinted windows, chewed on his breakfast and wondered why Ax Dement and Mason Book had driven all the way to western Malibu in order to smoke up.

Had to be something about that particular spot.

Lacking authority, he couldn't very well return with a shovel.

Even for Moe to return, there'd have to be probable cause.

State park, Coastal Commission, he could just picture the scene. Probably end up like that TV show a few years back, some talk-show dude opening Al Capone's vault, building the suspense up for weeks, then the damned thing turns out empty.

A paunchy guy with a tool belt came close to the Porsche and attempted to look through the passenger window.

Aaron slid the window down, guy nearly fell over.

"Morning."

"Yeah, hey—cool wheels. Do the X-17 upgrade on it?"

"Nah," said Aaron. "Paid fifteen grand less and got it up to 415."

"Awesome . . . have a nice day, man."

"You, too."

Aaron had chosen his own wheels for today because a black man at the beach needed to look as rich as possible. Plus he missed the car's fantastic handling. Not to mention the general aura of cool that engulfed him when he got behind the wheel.

Keeping the top up, though, because this day at the beach was a job, like any other.

As he nourished himself, he made calls to people who owed him favors.

Remembering the diminishing pattern of phone calls between Mason Book and CAA, he started with a talent agent at a competing outfit whose divorce had gone smoother because of what Aaron had learned about the guy's much younger not-so-loving wife.

The guy said, "I've got a meeting in five. Why're you asking about Mason?" Dropping the star's name in that casual way that said *I play in that league.* Even though the guy's client list topped out at soap opera fill-ins.

Aaron said, "Nothing juicy and this needs to be confidential because we all know what happens when things aren't confidential."

Confident the guy would remember his ex's proclivity for being shat on by Japanese businessmen. Reduced alimony and full custody of the Lhasa apso was one thing, being suckered so everyone knew it was another.

"Of course." Pompous, as if there'd never been any question about being discreet. "So what do you want to know?"

"Is Mason still hot?"

"Hot?"

"In demand."

"Maybe not as much as he used to be, but a helluva lot of people would still be happy to work with him. Once they know he's okay."

"Okay, as in . . ."

"You're the private eye. You're telling me you don't know?"

"I need specifics, Ken."

"Word has it there isn't a drug Mason's met that he didn't date."

"That serious, huh?"

"His last shoot took way longer than usual. Because of looong naps. Coke and weed don't do that. Catch my drift?"

"Heroin."

"They say it has that effect."

"Does he shoot or smoke?"

"How would I know—smoke, I'd bet. Can't afford any needle marks."

Aaron said, "But the picture did get finished."

"*Loose Change for Danny*? Hell, yeah, made a nice profit. Maybe."

"Maybe?"

The agent laughed. "Depends on who the accountants are. I did a project with Pam DeMoyne—from *Shadows of Our Days*? She was amazing, I'm talking on a level with Streep and Mirren. But the suits sent it straight to video anyway—I'll send you a DVD. It's really great, historical story about Shakespeare's secret gay life, Pam was Anne Hathaway, she was—"

"The accountants," Aaron prompted.

"Right," said Ken. "The accountants. I got Pam a twenty-five percentage of net, which is amazing, even if it is net, at that level you should see some payout. Never saw a dime of royalties. We do an audit, there's a three-hundred-thousand 'distribution fee.' I say what's that, they hem and haw, finally they tell me it's the price of driving the film from the production office in Westwood to the editor in Burbank."

"High-priced taxi. I'll take the gig."

"Oh, yeah. So did Book's last picture make money? Probably, because he's got clout, they might be afraid to pull bullshit like that."

"But maybe diminishing clout."

"He hasn't worked in what . . . a year and a half, two, three? Are you snooping around because something nasty's gonna pop, Aaron? Like he's over the edge and the studio's gonna be suing him for breach?"

"Nothing like that, Ken. Now tell me about Ax Dement."

"Who?"

"Lem's oldest son. I hear he hangs out with Book."

"News to me," said Ken. "I've got no time for hangers-on."

"Would you work with Lem?"

"You mean because he's a fascist and a racist and a fundamentalist hypocrite? Not my idea of integrity, Aaron."

Aaron said, "What if the accounting was good?"

Ken laughed. "In that case, sure. But don't tell my mother."

Aaron's second call was to Liana Parlat.

"How about another trip to Riptide, same fee structure."

She said, "Sure. Maybe I'll run into Dr.

Rau again. But could it be in a couple of nights?"

"Busy?"

"Cartoon audition. I need to sound like an obnoxious twelve-year-old."

"Not much of a stretch," said Aaron.

Liana laughed and whined nasally: "Thanks. Dad."

"You never called Rau, huh?"

"Not because I'm scared, Aaron. Because I've been working."

"Another brat voice?"

"One of those classy animations under consideration at one of the so-called edgy networks. Disgusting family, even more disgusting flatulent dog."

"Gas noise is part of your repertoire?"

"Actually, I'm under consideration for Sinead, the twelve-year-old daughter." Putting on a high, reedy voice: "'Oh man, Daddy-person, when you said this was a *field* trip, I didn't know we'd actually be out in the field listening to the growls and howls of Gyro's *bowels.*'"

"Here I come, Mr. Oscar."

"Beats honest labor, Mr. Fox. As does lancing for you. What's the drill for my second visit?"

"Just sit around, soak up more atmosphere. If the topic ever comes up naturally, work Ax Dement into the conversation."

"The son but not Lem?" she said. "You've got something concrete?"

"Not even close, Lee. The case is arctic but I'm sifting dirt wherever I can." Smiling at his choice of words; the clearing at Carrillo was still on his mind.

She said, "It would sure be nice to dig up some downright filth related to that abusive asshole." Resuming the kiddie voice: "'Gee, sure, Mr. Fox-person. That would be a *real* field trip!'"

By ten a.m., Aaron had completed his fourth sally up and down the poorly paved, tree-lined highway that snaked past Len Dement's Solar Canyon spread, ten miles above PCH.

Each cycle raised the risk of being spotted. He tried to buffer the threat by stretching the time between passes, driving a good fifteen miles past the watch-zone before coming back down.

If nothing happened soon, it was back to the city with plastic bags and question marks.

Barely half a mile past the property, the real estate switched to public domain: undeveloped state conservancy land along an increasingly rutted road. Sloping granite on one side, shallow canyons on the other. Aaron eased the Porsche around curves, enjoying the way the four-wheel drive embraced the asphalt.

Small birds flittered above the brush, unaware or uncaring about hawks—man, there were a lot of winged creatures out here—gliding, scoping out the buffet. Swooping.

Google Earth had defined Dement's sixty-plus acres with an aerial shot. Only one access, a single-lane entry road from the roadside gate connecting to a few acres of flat pad. The big rectangle right of center had to be the main house. Farther back, to the left, several smaller outbuildings sprouted like buds. No sign of any church under construction, but maybe the picture was old.

Twenty Solar Canyon, a cinch to find. The gate was mesh, manually operated, nearly flush with the road. Barbed-wire fencing stretched from the posts a good five hundred feet in either direction.

No mailbox, no address numerals, no fake-o cowboy brand over the gate, like some of the other places he'd spotted driving up.

On the other hand, no snarling dogs or *No Trespassing* warnings, any other go-away.

On his third pass, he hazarded a stop, looked for a well-concealed security camera, failed to find one. So either high-tech developments had gotten past him, or Dement didn't bother to keep watch.

Figuring a camera would be too conspicuous?

The guy had tons of dough but chose to live away from the Industry hubbub of Beverly Hills, Brentwood, the Colony, Broad Beach.

A place meant to be *ignored.*

Beginning his fifth pass, Aaron was ready to call it quits when a black X5 crested the road above the gate and rolled down erratically.

He zoomed past, parked precariously on the narrow highway, just out of view of the SUV, ran down to where he could see and not *be* seen.

The X5 was idling, its driver's door open.

A slim, fair-haired woman was unlocking the gate with a key. Once she'd pushed the heavy metal frame wide, she returned to the SUV, drove out a few yards, got out again, relocked the gate.

Aaron's long-range lens captured the whole tedious routine. Maybe Lem Dement didn't want people coming and going that easily. By the time the X5 was gone, Aaron was inspecting digital images, include a nice close-up of the woman's face.

But no need to guess; he'd memorized every face in the Malibu paper's family portrait of the Dement clan.

Gemma Dement hadn't changed a bit.

Seven-hundred-dollar Fendi shades hid Mrs. Lem Dement's eyes. The rest of her face was blank.

Coming straight at him—had he gotten that rusty?

Bracing himself for a confrontation, Aaron chopsticked a phony shrimp, pretended to savor. As she got closer, he opened the book he'd brought for cover. Paperback biography of George Washington Carver. Looking intellectual never hurt, especially intellectually black.

Gemma Dement kept coming. Even with

sunglasses on, he sensed she was staring at him.

Big mess, where had he screwed up?
The designer jeans boutique? The organic
market? The bikini shop?

Two hours of stalking while the woman
looked but never bought. She'd seemed
preoccupied but obviously, she'd figured it
out.

Okay, Plan B: If she hassled him, he'd
fake surprise, work the charm, hoping
she'd feel foolish and walk away.

If she persisted—got nasty or downright paranoid—he'd find a way to let her
know he'd found her attractive but was no
weirdo.

What was the worst she could do, call
for one of those brain-dead security types
in charge of policing the shopping center?
By the time they arrived, he'd be gone.

What did he look like, ma'am?
They all look the same.

Now she was ten feet away.

She stopped, did that absent-eyed
thing. Stood right in the middle of the narrow street. No cars gliding past, but still, a
woman could get pulverized that way.

Good-looking woman; finding her attractive wasn't a lie. Back at the bikini shop, he'd pretended to be interested in the surf-wear place next door, had gotten close enough to her to eye some details.

She'd tried on several swimsuits, frowned a lot, always dissatisfied. But not because she couldn't pull off skimpy. Under her clothes was a tight body. Lines on her face, but so what?

Fifties, but secure? Despite what Liana claimed about her being pounded regularly by Lem?

Aaron hadn't spotted any bruises or other telltale marks, but cotton and velvet were hiding most of her flesh.

She resumed walking, beelined for his table. Shit.

He put his nose in the book, faking concentration. Gemma Dement got close enough for him to smell her perfume.

Something light, grassy.

Aaron braced himself.

She glided by, entered the vegan joint.

He wiped sweat from his hairline, returned to his food. Hazarded an over-the-shoulder peek inside the restaurant.

No other customers at the order-counter.

Skinny woman, but nice ass, that bit of extra cheek that gilded the lily. Looked natural, maybe no lipo.

Five minutes later, she was outside, carrying a plate of something green and beige.

Two other tables were positioned to the north of Aaron's, both empty.

She chose the nearer one. Chose the seat closest to his.

Fluffing her hair and straightening her back, she sat like a charm school grad, shoulders square, platinum butt barely touching the cushion. Inspecting her mushroom/sprout/tofu whatever, she unwrapped her own chopsticks.

Stared in Aaron's direction until he was forced to look up.

Smiled.

Said, "Yum."

He finished a couple of pages on peanut technology, went inside and ordered iced tea. All the place served was hot and green but he cajoled the counter kid for a cup of ice, tossed in some sugar because the brew tasted like liquefied lawn trimmings.

When he got back to his table, Gemma Dement was still there, maybe even a little closer. Eating daintily and reading her own book. Something by Anna Quindlen.

Didn't Quindlen write about abused women and the like?

This time it was Aaron who tried to get eye contact going.

She didn't bite. Began humming. Closed her book, dropped it into her bag, picked up her plate, and placed it on Aaron's table.

Toed the purse over to a chair directly across from Aaron and sat down.

"Good afternoon." Throaty voice, maybe a smoker. But no smell of smoke, just that fresh, clean fragrance.

Aaron didn't have to fake surprise. "Afternoon."

She nodded, as if he'd said something predictable. Her eyes were aqua-blue, same color as the sea this morning.

Gemma Dement said, "Of course, it could've been *Good morning.*"

"Pardon?"

"Proper fit is such a hassle. But you know that by now."

Aaron stared.

Her smile was crooked, oddly girlish. "We didn't exchange greetings an hour ago. When I was agonizing over bikinis and you were watching me struggle."

Aaron didn't answer.

Gemma Dement clasped her hands prayerfully and leaned closer. "Please don't tell me I imagined you watching. You brightened my day."

"I did?" said Aaron, amazed at how he'd morphed into an aw-shucks geek. *Gee, Mrs. Robinson.*

"You certainly did. Mr. . . . Reader." Reaching across the table, she touched his book. Short nails, no polish. Clean hands. Had Aaron imagined the tremor that passed through them quickly?

He said, "Light reading." Felt a welcome rise of internal warmth as her fingers quivered again. Her weakness fed his strength. Time to *work* the woman.

She said, "Doesn't look light to me."

"It is compared with what I usually have to deal with."

Another skewed smile, this one hard to characterize. Aaron thought he spotted a dark splotch of skin peeking above the hem of her T-shirt, frosted by a granular patch of cover-up. Texture was the give-away, the color was perfect, blended expertly with her golden skin.

Long years of practice hiding bruises?

She said, "Now I'm supposed to ask what you usually have to deal with."

"Not unless you care."

She laughed. "Has to be something boring—are you a professor?"

Aaron said, "Attorney. Legal briefs."

"Ah," she said, sitting back. "One of those."

Aaron spread his arms. "Here come the lawyer jokes."

"Don't know any lawyer jokes. I'm not much for jokes period." She turned serious, as if illustrating. "So tell me, Mr. Lawyer Who's Also a Recreational Reader, why have you been watching me for the last hour?"

At least he'd gotten away with half the surveillance.

"Because you're gorgeous," he said.

Her face went blank. That same glazed expression as when she stopped mid-stride and spaced out.

Aaron said, "You stood out."

Did her eyes just get wet? She'd swiped them too quickly for Aaron to be sure.

"Please forgive me if I freaked you out. I thought of approaching you, then I saw your ring." Eyeing her four-carat diamond.

She said, "Oh, that," twisted the gem out of sight. Her other hand rose. She smoothed down hair.

Pulling out his little alligator card case, Aaron slid out the topmost rectangle, pre-positioned like a magician's trick deck.

High-quality paper, pale blue, embossed navy lettering proclaiming the credentials of *Arthur A. Volpe, Attorney at Law.* The Kansas City address terminated at a mail-drop, the phone fed to the sad bachelor pad of Arthur A. Wimmer, a distant cousin of Mom's. Arthur was a problem drinker who claimed to be a chemist but couldn't hold down a steady job. Aaron's yearly retainer went toward answering the line in a business-like voice and saying the right things. Decent dough for maybe an hour all year.

Gemma Dement scanned the card quickly, gave it back. "Lawyer on vacation."

"Long-overdue vacation."

She pouted. "All by your lonesome?"

"Aptly put," he said. "L.A.'s a tough place when you don't know anyone."

"Volpe," she said. "You're Italian?"

Aaron searched her face for irony. Saw dead-serious curiosity.

"Mom's side is from Milan." Picking the city, the way he usually did when questioned, because it was the hub of fashion.

"Like that character on that show—*Homicide.*"

"Lieutenant Giardello," said Aaron. "He was half Sicilian, that's the south. Milan is up north."

"Well," she said, "sorry for not knowing Italian geography. I like that show. Lots of guilt and atonement. Don't you think that makes for a good story?"

"Absolutely," said Aaron. "Nothing like guilt as a motivator."

Spinning the line off lightly. Gemma Dement's blue eyes clouded. She forked her food, didn't eat. "Volpe. What does that mean?"

"It's Italian for 'fox.'"

"Do you go there regularly? The Old Country, I mean."

"Never been there. My Italian cousins keep telling me I need to go. Eventually, I'll get around to it."

"Too much lawyer work."

"Way too much. I do real estate litigation and there's never a shortage."

"Meanwhile, you come to Malibu and watch much older women agonize over bikinis."

"Slightly older women."

"Liar," she said, cheerfully.

"May I ask your name?"

Eyeblink. "Gloria. Like in the song . . . well, Mr. Volpe the lonely, busy attorney. You did make my day. By noticing."

"Gloria," said Aaron, "you are extremely easy to notice."

Pulling the line off with utter sincerity because he meant it. Up close, the tight and lean was even more impressive, the total package enhanced by generous breasts too soft and bouncy not to be real. Those lovely little bumps of unfettered nipple. He imagined her dressing quickly but expertly in a mansion ranch house, green acres vivid through a crystalline window. Nothing to do today but try on bikinis.

Eyes the color of the ocean as the sun kissed it.

The dark patch right beneath the hem of her shirt, oddly appealing. Aaron wanted to help her. Knew he couldn't, she was nothing more than . . . a potential data bank.

Rich, good-looking woman who paid for her humongous diamond and the rest of her lifestyle with pain.

Guilt and atonement.

She'd given him something to work with.

He said, "Going back to the whole guilt thing, I guess the difference between good people and bad is the level of atonement."

She said, "Speaking of which."

"Pardon?"

"You could atone for your sin."

"What sin is that?"

"Standing there watching while I went through those bikinis. What if I *was* the type to get freaked out?"

"I really am sorry. It was just . . ."

"Just what?"

"What I said before. You're an extremely—"

She silenced him with a finger over his lips. Her skin was warm, slightly dank, maybe even a little greasy. As if she'd used

lotion recently. Or was secreting something.

Aaron could feel little bubbles of his
own sweat popping in his hair.

Gemma Dement shifted closer. Her
hand lowered to his. She rubbed the space
between his thumb and forefinger. Pretty
blatant, out in public like this.

People walked by, no one seemed to
notice.

No one recognizing her. A woman
ignored.

Aaron's lips were dry. He restrained
himself from licking.

Gemma Dement's eyelids lowered. Big,
curling lashes. Another flash of Pacific.
Twelve cylinders of perfume.

"Your sin," she said, "was watching me
but not following through."

He followed in the Porsche as her X5 drove
out of the Cross Creek lot, turned right at
the light, continued north on PCH.

She drove faster and better than she
had on the ride from home. No absent-
minded sways, no cell phone distraction.

Aaron kept to the speed limit, he couldn't
afford to do otherwise.

As if sensing it, Gemma Dement slowed down so he could stay with her.

Like a dance.

Like a woman fixing herself to your rhythm. Putting you back inside when you popped out.

Where was she taking him? Back to the ranch? Lem out of town on some shoot, the kids in school, whatever staff was around that discreet?

A woman that blatant, he could see why she got beat up.

No, scratch that, there was never an excuse.

Still . . .

What was he getting himself into?

Just south of Point Dume—well before Solar Canyon—she stuck an arm out of the driver's window, jabbed three times to the left.

Aaron pulled into the center island behind her, hoping no Chippie would happen by. The X5 waited for traffic to pass then swooped up a steep blacktop driveway.

At the top was a series of white, clapboard bungalows. A sign on a post read *Surf 'n Sea Beach Hotel.*

Daily and Weekly Rates, Premium Cable, the AAA seal of approval.

Hotel, my ass, this was your basic fifties-era motel.

Not the first time the job had taken him to a drive-in tryst. Only this time, he'd be more than a guy with a camera.

Rigors of the job; little Moe had no idea.

When the coast was clear, he turned.

She'd waited fifteen feet in, half hidden by a cloud of bougainvillea. Her arm shot out again. Aaron was supposed to hook a right. He complied, found several parking spaces shaded by a gigantic coral tree. Messy thing, the Porsche was sure to get dirty, but he could see why she'd picked the spot.

Out of visual range of the northernmost bungalow that served as the motel's front office.

As he pulled in, Gemma Dement cruised past. Five minutes later, she was walking toward him, looking grave, Fendi lenses flashing coppery light. On the surface, all business, but her body language disputed that: swinging a key on a dolphin-shaped holder in wide, playful arcs. Like a kid ready for an adventure.

◆

Once they were inside the small, dim, mildewed room, she drew the drapes, tugged several times to make sure no sliver of daylight intruded.

One step short of total darkness. Aaron's pupils dilated as he strained to follow her movements. She moved easily, familiar with the layout.

What the hell have I gotten into?

As he stood there, she got into that humming thing again. Powered up the twelve-inch flat-screen sitting atop a tilting bureau. Punched a code without consulting the guide.

Home away from home.

The station she selected was all music. So-called smooth jazz, heavy on repetition and low on imagination.

Lots of brush-percussion. Lots of lazy saxophone.

Oh, Lord, a porno soundtrack.

He still hadn't budged from just inside the door when she marched to the bed, folded back a corner of the comforter, ordered, "Get naked and comfy. I'll be back in a jif."

She took her purse into the bathroom. Aaron listened for telltale sounds, anything weird. Heard nothing.

Okay, this was the choice point: make his escape and possibly miss the chance for a serious lead, or go with it.

Seconds later, he was under the covers, clothes folded neatly over a chair, wallet, watch, cell phone safe at the bottom.

He watched numbers shift on the cheap digital clock next to the TV.

"A jif" stretched another four minutes, during which he fantasized about terrible things.

She's got a gun.

A razor.

I'm an idiot.

The bathroom door opened and she was at the side of the bed, standing lean and unclad, brown-pelted crotch inches from his nose, ready for inspection.

Not a young woman's body, but beautiful. That long-waisted configuration he liked, but still plenty of leg. That nice belly curve women developed when they didn't get crazy about starvation. Those child-bearing hips defined by angular bones.

Generous breasts, no false advertising by the T-shirt. A little droopy but for some reason that appealed to him. She'd pulled her hair into a ponytail. The diamond ring was nowhere to be seen. That last fact—and her ass—got him instantly hard.

As she bent at the waist and leaned over him, he smelled her breath, astringent with alcohol. Gin, the junipers were in bloom. She'd fortified herself with a bathroom belt.

He touched her. Mixed business with pleasure and looked for bruises.

None but the single camouflaged patch. How many internal wounds, he had no idea.

Gemma Dement got in bed and his nose filled with booze and perfume. Clapping one hand on his head, she fed him her left nipple.

"Suck it hard but don't bite it. Keep your eyes closed. I really am much older."

Aaron wondered how he'd itemize this on his next bill to Mr. Dmitri.

He went into it expecting craziness—manic sex, followed by tears, guilt, some sort of histrionics.

Sobbing discussion of guilt and atonement.

She worked him like a pro, athletic, silent, not even breathing hard. Positioned herself serially, as if playing for an unseen camera.

While she was in the bathroom, he'd gone over every damned inch of the room to make sure there wasn't any camera.

They stayed in a lock until she eased away yet again. Did something with her legs that looked unlikely, managed to guide him in.

"Comfortable?"

"Oh . . . yeah."

Obliging, considerate, business-like. Going along with anything he wanted, then rewriting the script without warning as she assumed a new pose.

This was choreography and she was in charge.

That should've bothered Aaron. He enjoyed himself, anyway, had to work at holding out, wanting to keep this level of pleasure for as long as he could.

She knew he was ready before he did, said, "Come in my pussy, it's safe. Or anywhere else, it's your choice."

The detachment in her voice caused him momentary self-doubt, an instant of diminished blood supply.

She did something with her hand and her mouth and he was back in the saddle.

"Anytime, Artie," she said. "You've already rocked *my* world."

Afterward, she said, "Please stay in bed," and went to dress in the bathroom. When she emerged, her hair was loose and she looked as if she'd just taken a pleasant nature walk.

As she moved to the door, Aaron said, "*You're* leaving?"

"You're the one on vacation. Regards to Kansas City."

They got some crazier little women in Malibu.

Aaron sprang out of bed, hurried to her side. "Stay. You're beautiful."

Looking down, she laughed. Took hold of him, gave a playful tug. "You're a healthy boy, my lawyer. Sorry, bye."

"You're leaving me here to atone all by myself."

Anger tightened her face. She stepped away from him.

Disgusted.

Aaron said, "What did I say?"

Her face churned, turned ugly. Got pretty again. Spit flew with each word: "Atonement is for assholes who actually sin. Let me out of here."

Moe sat at Liz's computer searching for Web images of Adella Villareal with either Ax Dement or Mason Book.

Book was everywhere, lanky and blond and handsome and heavy-lidded.

Dement Junior showed up a handful of times, always as a second-row leech, almost always unidentified.

Adella was nowhere.

Being strangled, with who-knows-what done to your baby, didn't merit attention unless someone wrote a movie about it.

He thought about Caitlin babysitting for Adella. Set up by Rory? Or had Adella come into Riptide, chatted with the friendly college girl? Why would Caitlin, going to school, already with a job, have taken on an additional gig all the way in Hollywood?

Maybe Adella had charmed her. Or Caitlin had been introduced to Adella by someone more high-status than Rory, like Mason Book.

He had two points of entry: Rory or Raymond Wohr. The kid could refuse to talk to him—with that mother of his, a likely response. The last thing Moe needed was Rory going the lawyer route. Maybe a high-powered lawyer hired by Mason Book . . . Wohr was definitely a better bet. He'd find some way to brace the lowlife.

Liz awoke and called him into the bedroom. Later, they showered together, she left for the lab, and Moe dressed for the job. Glad she wasn't there to see today's work clothes.

Driving to Hollywood, he phoned Petra Connor to inform her he'd be working her turf.

She said, "Have fun. We've been to Vice, seeing if we missed anything. No one has information about Adella selling her body. Wohr and Eiger are low-level hustlers with no showbiz connections anyone's aware of."

Moe said, "Wohr's twisted," and recounted his talk with the Reverend Arnold.

Petra said, "His own niece. What a dirtbag."

"What I keep thinking about is he showed no feelings for the baby, basically ignored it."

"And who doesn't like babies."

"Exactly. In my mind, he's shaping up as all kinds of bad."

"Makes sense," she said. "You're on him today?"

"Soon as I get to his crib. I'm at La Brea and Santa Monica."

"Welcome to Hollyweird."

He parked six blocks from the apartment on Taft, psyched himself up to shuffle slow, look glassy-eyed.

Dressing for the job meant forgoing shaving, a gray watchcap pulled low on his head, a T-shirt rescued from the bottom of his laundry hamper, his grungiest jeans and crappiest sneakers, under a stale-smelling, previously worn green hoodie he'd just bought from a street vendor at Hollywood and Highland for nine bucks.

He'd checked the garment carefully, couldn't shake the feeling some sort of microscopic vermin had set up house in polyester.

Street cred came with a price.

If he was even pulling it off.

No one paid him attention as he rounded Hollywood Boulevard, so maybe he was.

Slouching, sucking in his cheeks and jamming one hand deep into a jeans pocket as if he had a stash buried down there, he half stumbled up Raymond Wohr and Alicia Eiger's block.

One apartment building after another, a few half decent. Theirs wasn't, with cracked stucco, sagging gutters, a brown lawn. Up above Franklin, the housing got a little nicer. Better to avoid that and not chance alarming some nervous citizen. He turned west on Franklin, covered a couple

of blocks, reversed himself, lit up a cigarette that never touched his lips. Repeated
the whole damn drill several times.

The aimless routine of a lonely, addled
loser.

Lots of cars, few people; L.A.'s motto.

On his fourth circuit, he encountered a
tough-looking, crew-cut, multipierced girl
walking an off-leash white pit bull that
looked to be ninety pounds of muscle.

Huge, big-toothed critter. The dog spotted him, padded forward. Moe's gun was
tucked in the small of his back, he hoped
to God it wouldn't come to that.

The dog reached him. Sniffed his
shoes. Licked his hand.

Inhaling, Moe petted an iron-ingot neck.

The girl said, "Iggy likes you, man. You're
cool."

Street cred, indeed.

On his seventh trip down Taft, he spotted
Ramone W and Alicia Eiger arguing on
the sidewalk. Too far to hear what they
were saying, but the body language was
clear.

Both of them in sweatshirts and jeans,
no makeup for her, her hair was as ragged

as Ramone's side fringe. She wore unfash-
ionable horn-rimmed eyeglasses. The two
of them could've been any pair of shopworn street people.

She was doing most of the talking,
Ramone just stood there looking miser-
able.

Letting Eiger yap, staring over her head,
not even faking paying attention. She
finally figured out she was being shined
on, poked his chest until she got eye contact. More monologue. Again, Ramone
zoned out.

Eiger poked him again, started waving
her hands, trying to stir up a response.

He nodded stupidly.

Eiger wasn't satisfied, stepped up closer,
embarked on another tirade.

A Mohawked kid walking by turned to
stare and she switched her ire to him. The
kid held out his hands peacefully, hurried
off. Eiger resumed her rant. This time
Ramone tried to shush her with a finger
over his lips.

She hauled off and hit him hard, across
the face.

Ramone staggered back, rubbed the
offended spot. Moe's hand snaked around

to his gun, expecting the return blow, a full-out brawl.

Stepping into the middle of it would be a disaster for the case, but letting a psychopath maul a woman in public was out of the question.

Alicia Eiger didn't seem worried. She clapped her hands on her hips, dared Ramone to retort.

Stupid woman. Cemeteries were full of them.

Moe inched forward so he'd have enough time to be effective. As far as he could tell, neither of them noticed him.

Raymond's shoulders tightened up. Eiger taunted him. Flipped him off. Ramone shrugged, sagged, turned his back on her and walked south, toward Hollywood Boulevard.

She mouthed a word. Moe read her lips.

Stupid.

Maybe he should talk to this charmer. But while he was considering his options, Eiger stomped back inside her building.

'Scuse me, ma'am, LAPD Homicide. Why is Ramone stupid?

Moe shuffled past the shabby building.

Ramone was out of sight, probably drown-
ing his sorrow at Bob's or some similar
dive.

Moe considered checking out the bar.
Was he good enough to nurse a beer on a
neighboring stool, get the guy talking?

What chance was there Ramone would
admit to being a total pussy?

Speaking of which.

Witnessing the encounter had shaken
up Moe's preconceptions. He'd been
thinking of Ramone as a murderous thug
but the mope had just come across scary
as milk.

He walked back to his car. Encountered
a few other dog-walkers, including an old,
bent woman with a tiny, fluffy white mutt
who snarled viciously as Moe passed.

She said, "Good boy, Champ. He's a
bum."

When he returned to his desk at West
L.A., Aaron was sitting in his chair, playing
a BlackBerry. At the sight of Moe, his
brother sprang up. "I may have something
for you."

"May," said Moe.

"Where can we talk?"

That assumed a lot; Moe's instinct was to say so. But something in Aaron's demeanor stopped him: no wise-ass glint in his eyes, that intense *purpose* on his face—the same look Aaron had worn back when he was throwing long passes or adjusting his batting stance. Completing the pass, more often than not. Great RBI.

Moe said, "Let's go."

Once they were in a windowless room and Aaron had checked for hidden mikes, he said, "I may have found Caitlin's burial spot."

Still totally unaware of Adella Villareal, Raymond Wohr, Alicia Eiger. Moe indulged himself in brief self-satisfaction, saying "Tell me about it" as he sat back.

Aaron described Mason Book and Ax Dement's drive to Leo Carrillo, the clearing where they'd smoked up and sniffed heroin.

"You know for sure it was heroin." Getting picky about a probably irrelevant detail because between this and Eiger chewing Ramone a second asshole, his head was swimming with uncertainty.

"Did a presumptive test." Now Aaron's know-it-all grin was back. "Home chemistry set, Moses. I can't promise you the place is the tomb—the ground wasn't disturbed. But it's been a long time, stuff grows. And before you ask, sure, it's possible the two of them just love getting high at the beach. But it's a helluva ride from the Hollywood Hills just for that. Why not enjoy their dope behind gates up on Swallowsong? I think the spot has psychological significance and they were engaging in some sort of ritual."

"Returning to the scene of the crime."

Aaron crossed his legs, smoothed a lapel, stared at Moe, trying to figure out if he was being put on.

For some reason, Moe felt like a pain in the ass. "It happens with psych crimes, right? Reliving the thrill."

Aaron relaxed. "It does . . . look, I know this isn't hard evidence, Moses, but it was all I could do not to go back with a shovel myself. I meant what I said about not getting in your way. A cadaver dog could answer the question pretty easily."

"I'm not hearing enough justification to

call in the K-9s. Especially in a public park—in Malibu. Coastal Commission would probably get involved."

Listen to me: like every other regulation-spouting suit.

"Okay," said Aaron. "I just want you to know whatever I learn."

His brother's glum expression threw Moe. Self-doubt had never seemed part of Aaron's repertoire.

"I'm not saying it's not interesting, Aaron, it is. Especially with Malibu coming up over and over. Everything about Caitlin seems to hover around the coastline."

Except her babysitting gig in Hollywood.

Aaron brightened. "My thought exactly. Caitlin and Rory go to school at Pepperdine, work in Santa Monica, Lem Dement's ranch is in Solar Canyon. And now I've seen Mason Book take two nighttime trips to PCH."

"Restless sleeper," said Moe.

"Guilt can do that to you. Though it doesn't look like Mr. Book's remorse extends to self-mutilation."

"What do you mean?"

"Just before you arrived I was clearing

a text message." Tapping the BlackBerry. "One of my sources heard a rumor there were no cut marks on Book's arms, or anywhere else on his body during his supposed suicide stay at Cedars. No sign, period, that he'd placed his life in danger."

"Who's the source?"

"Sorry," said Aaron. "And given all the hubbub over at the U. about patient confidentiality, you don't want to know."

Good point. Moe said, "Reliable source?"

"Very."

"Someone who works at Cedars?"

Aaron smiled. "Someone who's connected to someone who knows someone who works at Cedars. But before you dismiss it, I will tell you we're talking an embittered Industry person being edged out of a job on the way to career oblivion." Quoting Merry Ginzburg word for word. "Strong motivation to help clear the case."

"Why?"

"I promised a scoop once the dust settles."

"Once, not if," said Moe. "Nothing like optimism."

"Only way to live, bro—sorry." Aaron

adjusted his jacket. Today's was smooth silk the color of dark chocolate, a hue black men pulled off better than anyone. Moe was thankful he'd stopped at his locker and changed out of his bum clothes. Tossing the green hoodie into the trash because he couldn't shake the feeling it was *alive.*

He said, "If Book didn't try to off himself, why was he hospitalized? And why announce he's a suicide?"

"Good questions, Moses."

"Exhaustion," said Moe. "Isn't that how celebs spin when they check in for detox?"

"No detox here," said Aaron. "No drugs of any sort—that's what tipped off my source's source. It was like the guy was using the place for a hotel."

Moe said, "Maybe no prescription drugs, but he had friends bring in recreational chemicals—maybe suicide was a cover for something worse career-wise. Like a total mental meltdown. If Book fell apart totally, his handlers wouldn't want it publicized. Better to cover with a half-truth."

Aaron's eyes widened. "I like that. Going off the deep end, total blithering lunatic . . . people shy away from crazy, but depression, suicide—climbing back up from adversity—that's the cover of *People.* That's Oprah being your new best friend—yeah, that makes sense, Moses."

Moe said, "And the fact Book never made it to *Oprah* or *People* could mean he's still nuts—the problem didn't go away. It also syncs with his not making a movie in three years. Hearing voices, seeing little green men, would make it hard to follow the script. But one thing bothers me. They treat psychotics with drugs, right? Is your source's source certain there were no meds at all?"

"That's what I'm told," said Aaron, careful to avoid any hint of Merry's gender.

"Then maybe we're wrong."

"Or maybe Book found himself a shrink who doesn't use drugs. I like the total-whack angle because it makes him capable of some real bad behavior. As in picking up a starstruck girl like Caitlin at Riptide, bringing her over to his place to party, once he gets her under control, he goes all Lecter."

"Has his way with her in the Hollywood Hills," said Moe, "and buries the body forty miles away to be safe."

"With Ax Dement's help, because Ax is Book's primary walking-around guy, could very well have been part of the kill. I say that because choosing Malibu points to Ax's involvement, Moses. He's been brought up there. Hell, maybe *he* was the one chose the burial spot because he knows the area, nice and close to Daddy's ranch."

Moe said, "And Book, weird as ever, returns to the scene to get high, relive the experience. Chauffeured by Ax—who could also be getting off on the whole thing."

Aaron said, "Rory Stoltz chauffeured Book to Malibu the first time. Even though Book chickened out and they turned back at the Colony, Rory could've been in on the kill, as well. The three of them meeting up in that damned bar."

Moe said, "Book's nuts but he can still feel guilt. That's why he checked into Cedars a week after Caitlin went missing. Freaked out over what he'd done."

Aaron leaned over, clapped him on the back. "This is good, Moses. I know it's all theory, but it *feels* right."

Moe went silent, thinking about his

options. Show his hand to his brother? Or keep working Aaron as an outside guy.

Aaron was smart, would eventually figure it out.

Aaron would be smarter if he was informed.

"What, Moses?"

"There's more."

For the first time in his life, Moe realized something about Aaron.

His brother could be an excellent listener.

Aaron didn't move a muscle as he took in the facts. Adella Villareal, Baby Gabriel, Ax Dement's Eagle Motel tryst with Raymond Wohr and Alicia Eiger. Wohr's peep of his own niece. Caitlin Frostig babysitting for Adella.

The only thing he didn't tell Aaron was Wohr's passivity in the face of Eiger's verbal abuse, which had shaken up Moe's notion of him as a dominant psycho killer.

Because he was still trying to figure out what that meant.

When he finished, Aaron said, "Whoa." Genuinely knocked over by everything Moe had uncovered. Not a trace of *now you choose to tell me?* "So now we've got a link between two dead women . . . oh, man . . . okay, my op's over to Riptide. How do you feel about getting me a jpg of Adella?"

"Could be too risky."

"My person knows how to be subtle."

Moe knew his brother could get pictures of Adella with or without his help. He said, "Let's go back to my desk, I'll get you a scan."

"Thanks. Now it's my turn for something additional. Nothing I was holding back, I just didn't get to it after we started brainstorming about Book. This morning, I spent some time with Gemma Dement. Ax's mommy." Keeping his voice even, but he shifted uncomfortably.

It was unlike his brother to fidget.

Moe smiled. "Good-looking woman."

"For her age."

"The two of you discuss politics?"

"We discussed peanuts—forget all that,

the point is the woman's seriously Weird. Obsessed with guilt and atonement. Quote unquote. Normally, I might attribute that to some sort of religious conviction— her and Lem finding God together." *Though she doesn't put much stock in the Seventh Commandment.* "But if baby boy Ax was involved in murder, she might be tormented by the knowledge."

Moe said, "Living with a big, dark secret—did she come across guilty herself, or just talk about it philosophically?"

Aaron shook his head. "There was emotion there, but hard to pinpoint what it was."

"What does that mean?"

"What it means is she wasn't bent over with guilt or grief or anything like that, but she brought up the phrase out of context. Guilt and atonement. The last time she got into it, it made her really angry. Unpredictably angry."

"But nothing about any murder."

Aaron hesitated. "It wasn't that kind of conversation."

"Still, sounds like you got to know her pretty well."

"Well enough to know she's a seriously messed-up lady, Moses. Who Lem is still beating on. I saw a bruise."

Bet you did.

Moe said, "Getting pounded could mess you up."

"I think this was more. I'm no shrink, it's just an aura she gave off. Something dark and deep and troubling."

"That's the second time you mentioned that."

"Mentioned what?"

"Not being a shrink," said Moe. "Seeing the direction this is taking, maybe we should talk to someone who is."

Aaron went off to a corner of the D-room and called whoever he was sending over to Riptide. A woman, Moe figured, from the way his brother loosened up and put on the charming smile for an unseen audience. Seconds later, Aaron gave the thumbs-up, they scanned Adella Villareal's photo and sent it to lp-vox36 at a Hotmail account.

Moe called Dr. Alex Delaware, connected to the psychologist's answering service.

"Is this an emergency, sir?" said the operator.

"Not a medical emergency, ma'am. I'm an LAPD detective."

"A new one?"

Moe stiffened. "Pardon?"

"The doctor always gets called by Detective Sturgis. Is it that kind of thing—murder?"

"Yes, ma'am."

"Hold on."

Seconds later, Delaware came on the line. Without getting into details, Moe asked if he and Aaron could come by to discuss a case. Not sure what Delaware's financial arrangement was with the department. Not knowing what he'd say if Delaware brought that up.

"I'm out the door, Moe, court appearance in Beverly Hills. But even if I'm called to testify, I should be free by four, so let's aim for a quarter to five. My place would be best. I need to check in with my dog."

Driving above the converted bridle path that wound above Beverly Glen, finally sighting the crisp, white contours of Delaware's house high up, nestled among pines and redwoods and sycamores, Aaron thought: *This is the endpoint of the dream, beyond cool, look at this, dead-silent when you needed to meditate on something, talk about green—and that sky, you'd never know it's L.A. and only a short drive to Westwood Village, down-town Beverly Hills, the Strip, anywhere you want to go, really. Guy probably sees hawks all the time. Wonder if his drive is a ragtop, have to be, how could you fully enjoy this with metal over your head, and this place, whoa, bigger than it seemed at first glance—full two stories, interesting angles, obviously custom architecture, nice the way they positioned it on the lot, not intrusive, fits great into the landscape, talk about contemporary-cool, the inte-rior's probably just as fresh and clean, maybe bamboo floors, vaulted ceilings, all that nice natural lighting, maybe even a home theater . . . nope, it's an old Seville. Nice shape, though . . . maybe there's a convertible in the garage . . . great land-scaping . . .*

One day . . .

Moe thought: *Nice house.*

◆

Dr. Alex Delaware thought: *Both of them, sitting on my couch, looking uncomfortable.*

Like patients.

Like a married couple barely clinging to civility.

He'd worked with the brothers on the marsh murders, had sensed a complicated relationship.

You didn't need to be a psychologist to figure that out.

Alex had been on the stand for nearly an hour in Beverly Hills, avoiding unsubtle pressure from a predatory divorce lawyer to say something stupid for the record. Arriving back home twenty minutes before Reed and Fox showed up, he'd taken Blanche outside for a garden bathroom break, refreshed her water, gave her the attention she craved. Robin was out on a wood-buying trip in Ojai, due back around eight. No time to get out of his court clothes—charcoal pin-striped suit, yellow shirt, maroon tie—but he'd peeled off his jacket, rolled his sleeves to the elbows, fortified himself with black coffee by the time the doorbell rang.

Now the little blond French bulldog sat

in his lap and smiled at the detectives, turning on all that feminine charisma.

Aaron Fox smiled back.

Moe Reed, all business, said, "Thanks for meeting with us, Doc."

"No prob. What's up?"

"It's kind of involved."

"By the time I hear about it, it usually is."

Reed did most of the talking and Fox seemed okay with that, though Alex did catch him fighting the urge to interrupt. Each time, the older brother sat back with a resigned look and drummed his fingers on his knees. Birth order was a potent factor.

When the summation ended, Alex said, "I see what you mean. What do you think I can do for you?"

Moe Reed said, "First off, what can you tell us about Mason Book's mental status?"

Delaware shook his head, loosened his tie, rubbed behind the dog's bat-ears. "Diagnosis at a distance is a loser's game, guys. If you're asking could Book be psychotic and not be treated with drugs while hospitalized, it's theoretically possible."

"But not likely?"

"First-line treatment for schizophrenia is medication. It works well for many patients, but not all. If Book hasn't responded in the past—or if he still has an addiction problem—I can see a careful psychiatrist stepping back and observing. Any idea who his primary doc was?"

Head shakes.

"If you find out, let me know."

Aaron Fox clicked his BlackBerry.

Reed said, "What does that mean, stepping back? They put him in a hospital bed and just watched him?"

"Admitted for observation," said Alex. "When in doubt, do no harm."

"On the VIP ward?"

"Better yet."

Fox said, "He's definitely still doping, Doc. Like I said, I found weed and Mexican brown at Carrillo."

"He's doping," said Alex, "or his pal is."

"Book and Ax Dement drove out there together, Doc. You think a dope fiend could just sit by and watch his compadre get high?"

"Granted, it's unlikely. So let's stick with the drug thing for a moment. Maybe Book was hospitalized for detox."

"For just a week?"

"A week would be inadequate, but what if he changed his mind before he cleaned up and walked out? There was no involuntary hold. He wasn't even in the psych ward. Which tells us something."

Reed said, "He's crazy, he'd have to go in the psych ward?"

Alex thought. "Generally, but celebrity bends rules."

Reed said, "Everywhere those people sleep becomes a five-star hotel. Book wants to leave Cedars, who's going to argue with him?"

Alex said, "Are you certain he received no medication the entire stay?"

Reed looked at Fox. Fox said, "We're not sure of anything, the information comes from a secondary source."

"More like tertiary," said his brother.

Fox didn't argue.

Alex said, "Someone told someone who told someone." He sat back in his battered leather desk chair. The surface of the desk was clear.

The whole office was pin-neat. Aaron approved. He said, "The source is generally reliable but, sure, we'd prefer photos and a YouTube video."

We. Making it sound like they were a team, but from their body language Alex wasn't convinced.

He ran his hand through dark curls and looked off to the right, focusing on a George Bellows boxing lithograph good at stimulating his thoughts. His eyes were gray-aqua, clear, piercing, active, almost alarming in their intensity.

The little bulldog yawned, flews fluttering, closed her eyes, went to sleep. "Sorry I can't be specific, guys. Book could be psychotic, phobic, drug-impaired, clinically depressed, choose your diagnosis. Or he was hospitalized for something nonpsychiatric."

"Something physical?" said Reed. "Then why couch it as a suicide attempt?"

Fox said, "Exactly."

"Or," said Alex, "it could be a mixture of the two. If the pictures I've seen are accurate, he's a really skinny guy."

The brothers stared at him.

Reed said, "Some kind of eating disorder?"

"In Book's profession, it's an occupational hazard. And not limited to women. But still identified with women. Being tagged anorexic or bulimic could be more damaging to a male actor's career than a suicide attempt. Ignorant folk might consider self-starvation too feminine for a leading man."

Fox said, "Suicide, on the other hand, can be thought of as chic."

"Unfortunately, in some circles, there is a certain romanticism attached to it. People love the whole notion of a tortured soul, especially when it comes to the arts. The final act of *Romeo and Juliet* doesn't feature two kids wasting away or jamming their fingers down their throats."

Reed said, "Guy gets into some kind of medical situation, checks in for nutrition and fluids, leaves when he's no longer in danger. That would explain no meds."

"It would, but I'm just guessing," said Alex. "And I'm not sure Book's mental status is all that relevant to your case."

"The whole guilt thing isn't relevant?" said Moe Reed. "Checking in one week after Caitlin disappears?"

"But also several *months* after Adella Villareal's murder. If you're tying the two cases together, it's hard to see a pattern."

"You don't think they're connected?"

"They might be if both women encountered the same bad guy. What I don't see is Caitlin being murdered because she babysat for Adella. Too much time lapse between the disappearances."

Fox said, "We've got a disappeared baby, too. And no one knows who the father is."

Reed said, "If Mason Book's the daddy, there'd be all sorts of motive to get rid of Adella as well as the kid. It could also explain the time lapse, Doc. What if Adella leaned too hard on Book and Book got Ax Dement to take care of the problem, maybe with the help of his favorite lowlife, Ramone W—who'd probably introduced Adella to Book in the first place because he was pimping her. Later, when Rory Stoltz started gofering for Book, he learned something and blabbed to Caitlin. She was a straight-arrow, had known Adella, babysat for her, freaked out, threatened to go to the cops. So they offed her, too. Whether or not Rory was directly involved in it, he figured out what happened to his girlfriend but can't say a thing. Too damn scared the same thing will happen to him. That would explain his mother being so protective."

"Or," said Fox, "Rory's also a sociopath and that's why Book hired him, and he just doesn't care. In either case, no baby means no paternity test."

The brothers had edged closer together on the couch, seemed more of a unit. They both studied Alex.

He concentrated on the lines and empty space that spelled out Bellows's ringside exuberance. "It's possible. And if you ever do gain access to Book and he is impaired, he might fold easily. But right now, he's an unlikely point of entry and guessing about why he was hospitalized isn't useful. You've got nothing to tie him to any of your victims and he lives a cosseted life with Lem Dement's son in a house owned by Lem Dement. Who you *know* is connected to Ramone W."

Fox said, "You're saying we should concentrate on Ax."

"What you described, Aaron—holding up traffic, then peeling out and flipping off the crowd—paints an interesting picture. Blithe, reckless, hostile."

"Stone sociopath," said Reed.

"If you can nail him for acts of cruelty, I'll take that bet. And growing up with a father who abuses his mother could sure feed sexual violence."

"Believing that's how a real man treats women."

"Precisely."

Fox said, "Mom gets pounded but sticks around and likes to talk about guilt and atonement, maybe because she raised a really bad boy."

Alex said, "What was the emotional temperature of that talk?"

"What do you mean?"

"Did she seem remorseful? Angry? Or was she mouthing words as if they were scripted."

Fox thought. "Maybe all of the above. The sense I got was a really screwed-up head."

Reed observed his brother, as if expecting more.

Fox shrugged. "That's it."

Reed said, "How does the religious

aspect fit in, Doc? Ax's daddy gets big-
rich off what's basically a splatter flick
camouflaged as a hymn, now he's building a church on the family compound."
Before Alex could answer, he turned to
his brother. "For all we know, they've got
a damn cult blossoming there and Mason
Book got sucked into it. Actors are ripe for
that, right? Always into the Next Big
Thing."

Fox nodded.

Reed said, "Guy's an anorexic,
addicted zombie with no will—hell, maybe
they were programming him in the hospital and *that's* why he got admitted. Or
someone else was *de*programming him,
whatever. Any way you can find out who
his doc was?"

Fox smiled. "Going through alternative
channels? I'm sure gonna try—forget you
heard that." To Delaware: "Is this session
confidential, like therapy?"

Delaware laughed. "I'll have to study
that."

Reed said, "What about the religious
aspect, Doc?"

"Moe, a wise man once said, 'Religion's

a good thing for good people and a bad thing for bad people.'"

"Meaning anything's possible with this bunch . . . okay, so we concentrate on Ax."

"Not necessarily," said Alex. "Same as with Book, there's not enough evidence and Daddy's dough makes him a big fish. Rory Stoltz is a minnow but that protective mother and theoretical access to Book and Dement's legal resources cools him as an entry point. Also, he may be totally innocent."

"Why theoretical?"

"Big fish eat little fish. They'd sacrifice him if it suited their purposes. On the other hand, you do have someone you could leverage, because he's likely to get into trouble and has really poor judgment."

"Ramone W," said Reed.

"A loser with impulse-control problems," said Fox.

Alex said, "And no gates to hide behind."

"I started watching him," said Moe Reed, "and Petra Connor got a rookie in plainclothes to take over when I'm not there. Problem is, Doc, what I saw today surprised me big-time." He described the sidewalk encounter with Alicia Eiger.

"She smacked him upside the head and he just stood there and took it. And here I was thinking he's capable of mindless brutality."

Fox said, "Maybe he was too stoned to react."

"Still," said Reed, "what kind of tough guy lets himself get smacked down in public by a woman? That doesn't smell of contract killer."

Alex said, "Ramone got caught peeping his niece but it's likely that wasn't the only time he'd tried it. How old is he?"

"Thirty-seven."

"Interesting. Voyeurs generally start young and some progress to sexual violence. The fact that he's still watching implies a certain passivity."

Reed said, "What does that say about his ability to get bloody and homicidal?"

"Maybe nothing," said Alex. "Wars are planned by generals but carried out by foot soldiers."

"Following orders," said Fox. "Sure, why not, think Manson Family—think any whack-group—hell, *that* fits with a bizarro cult thing. We need dogs out in Carrillo, Moses."

Reed didn't appear to have heard. "Fine, I'll keep on Wohr. Anything else, Doc?"

Delaware said, "Sounds like you're doing all the right things."

Fox said, "And *that* sounds like therapy."

Liana Parlat adjusted the washcloth draped over Steve Rau's right nipple.

Terry cloth was a lot easier on her cheek than Steve's steel-wool chest hair.

He said, "You okay?"

"Mmm." She laced her arm over his barrel torso.

"If you're not, I could shave it."

"And subject me to stubble?" Liana traced his jawline with a fingertip. Felt stirring under the bedcovers. Saw visual proof.

"Oh, my, Stephen."

"It's been a long time, Laura. I probably forgot stuff I never knew."

The use of her fake name bothered her. For the first time. She said, "Fishing for a compliment? Fine: You're a stud."

That lowered the flag to half-mast. "Oh, no," she giggled. "Sorry."

A sensitive one. But so sweet. He'd entered Riptide half an hour after she'd been sitting at the bar. Accomplishing nothing because the place was nearly empty and the few rummies in sight were well on their way to stupor. The barkeep wasn't the guy she'd seen the first time—Gus. The taut woman with some sort of southern accent projected the couldn't-care-less attitude of a temp, had trouble locating lime juice.

When Liana asked how long she'd been working there, she squinted as if faced with a calculus problem. "Um, four days. Tonight's my last."

"Don't like it?"

"Dead. No tips." She turned her back on Liana, checked her cell phone, let a filmy used beer mug sit on the bar.

A Diet Coke and two sips of a gimlet later, Liana was feeling low. She hated serving Aaron an empty plate.

Receiving Adella Villareal's photo had put it on a personal level.

Happy, beautiful girl. Baby in a blue blanket.

That flashed Liana back to the October of her senior year in high school.

Backseat oops that led to the bump. More family turmoil than if Liana had died, Mom closing up like a scared anemone, Dad even worse, shutting her out completely the entire pregnancy. Their relationship had never been the same; her feeling she'd failed him, his never saying the opposite, made her hate him.

Her brother and sister treated her like a freak.

Especially when she was forced to drop out of school because the rules said girls like her were a Serious Bad Influence.

Morning sickness and depression ravaged her body and her self-esteem. At four months and two days into the ordeal, cramps seized her and made her feel like a rotary razor was churning up her insides. Five hours after the pain started, she was spewing a bloody mass into a toilet at a truck stop.

Relieved.

Crushed by guilt.

Even though she'd done nothing to bring on the miscarriage. Or had she? All those prayers, wishes, bad thoughts. Maybe she hadn't eaten right. Dehydrated herself?

Or the stress her family had put her through had killed what had grown inside of her.

She got her GED, left home, found a waitress job.

Three years later, at the age of twenty-one, not really sure why, she had her tubes tied.

Adella Villareal had *produced* life. Only to have it taken from her.

Someone had to pay.

She was constructing revenge scenarios, knuckles white around her gimlet glass, when Steve entered the bar. She pretended not to notice when he looked at her. Continued the act as he ordered a beer and headed over.

Dressed casually this time. Dark green polo and khakis, nice match for his fair coloring. But still wearing clunky brown wingtips that went with a suit. The boy needed help.

Big smile. He waved like a tourist. She looked his way.

"Laura." He took the adjacent stool, spilling significant beer in the process. "Oops."

Smooth. Oddly, she found that endearing.

"Hi, Steve."

"So . . . how've you been?"

"Fine. You?"

"Just great—working—is it okay?"

"Is what okay?"

"My sitting here."

"Fine with me." That sounded cold and he winced. Impulsively, Liana served up a nice, warm smile. Sat up straighter and made sure the pink satin blouse stretched over all the right places. Soft-but-strong pink, worked great with her black pencil skirt. Her hair was brushed out and gleaming, Michal Negrin jewelry glinted in all the right places, she knew she smelled great.

Steve smelled a little musky—like Interested Guy. Probably hadn't renewed his antiperspirant after getting home from work.

Oddly, that didn't offend her.

"What've you been up to, Dr. Rau?"

"Nothing interesting," he said, but her open face and her wide eyes and the fact that he was a guy led him to embark on a five-minute discourse on South American economics trajectories as they related to oil futures. Then another five psychoanalyzing Hugo Chávez.

Liana faked interest as she thought of the folded color photo inside her purse. She'd taken pains to fold in a way that didn't cut into Adella Villareal's face. Or Baby Gabriel in his blue blanket.

Aaron hadn't volunteered the infant's name, had been perplexed when she'd called him an hour later to ask.

She said, "Humor me."

"Okay, Lee. Gabriel."

"Little angel."

By the time Steve Rau's second beer arrived—inadequately filled by Snooty Ms. Dixie, but he didn't complain—he and Liana had been small-talking for twenty minutes.

Stupid stuff that neither of them cared about. He was as nervous as a high school boy on a first date. Did boys today even get nervous?

Oddly . . .

When he made a move at touching her hand, then pulled back, she made serious eye contact and smiled, gave him psychic space for a second attempt.

Instead, he said, "Laura, is there any possible way you'd consider going out with me?"

Liana said, "I would."

"Really?"

"How about now?"

They walked north on Ocean toward Ivy at the Shore as Steve cell-phoned the restaurant and asked if a table was available.

"It can get jammed, all those movie types," he told her, while on hold. As if she'd never been there.

She'd her arm laced through his. The boy was built solid. Sweating, though the night was cool.

"Yup," he said, "I'm still here—okay, great, thanks, see you right away."

They got seated inside, at a table next to a noisy party of rich kids, a placement Liana knew was D list. Steve hadn't a clue, was thrilled to get in.

They both ordered Sapphire Martinis and as usual, Liana nursed the booze. So did Steve. Explaining, "I'm not a major-league drinker."

She ordered the soft-shell crabs that were always on "special." He had a steak.

As they ate, they small-talked some more while Liana figured out a way to bring up Adella Villareal.

Tough, because it meant a confession of her own.

The proper moment never came up. They split key lime pie. Drank decaf. Steve left a generous tip and they stepped out to a briny night. Most of the lookie-loos hovering around Colorado Boulevard were gone, a few nocturnal cyclists wheeled by on Ocean Front. Several of the homeless psychotics Santa Monica welcomed with open arms prowled the sidewalks.

Steve put his arm around her shoulder as they headed back toward Riptide, where they'd both parked. Instinctive protective-ness, no weasely attempt to cop a feel.

For some reason, this felt like the senior year she'd never had.

They walked in silence. Steve had a bounce in his step, but not the triumphant stride of a player who'd closed the deal. Just being with her made him happy and she knew she should cut it off, return to the bar, try to do *something* for Aaron.

She offered Steve a cheek to peck, changed her mind at the last minute and aimed her lips at his. Parted them and gave him some tongue.

He broke away, gasping. "Wow."

Soft eyes. You couldn't fake that.

Liana said, "Let's go do something."

Working hard to erase Adella Villareal's face from her head.

The baby.

Her baby.

Aaron Fox's polished, almost too-handsome face. Now, there *was* a player.

When Steve said, "Pardon?" she said, "Let's hang out a bit more. Unless you're tired."

"No, no—um, at the risk of being . . . my place isn't that far. You could follow me. If you're comfortable, with that, I mean . . . or sure, we could find somewhere to hear live music—"

Liana said, "Which car is yours?"

He pointed. "That VW." White Passat.

She said, "I'll follow you."

"Isn't that far" turned out to be a high-rise on the south side of the Wilshire Corridor, a few blocks east of Westwood.

L.A.'s highest-end condo row. Nice crib for a Ph.D. working on grant money. True, Steve's building was comparatively plain, when appraised alongside its neighbors— simple, beige, sparingly landscaped. One of the earlier structures, starting to show its age. But still, serious money.

Full-service, with a uniformed doorman out front.

The guy said, "Evening, Dr. Rau."

"Hey, Enrico. This is my friend Laura."

"Ma'am." Enrico tipped his hat, hurried to open the door. "Ma'am."

As they entered a small, mirrored lobby, Liana was wondering if she'd stay Laura.

Twelve floors to the building. The elevator was déclassé gilded mirror and flocked wallpaper. Kind of an old-person smell.

Steve's one-bedroom unit was four stories below the penthouse, with a nice view
of city lights. The furnishings, also geriatric:
fussy, quilted floral couches in unfashion-
able colors with all sorts of buttons, pecan-
wood furniture, brown shag carpeting, a
shade of green on the walls Liana hadn't
seen since the seventies.

Avocado appliances in a kitchen.

Time warp—a time before Steve's.
Some kind of inheritance? Even so, why
not update?

Maybe inertia—or being stingy—had
led the ex-wife to split. But, no, he'd tipped
thirty percent.

He said, "This is it . . . ta-dah . . . want
some water? I'm a little parched myself."

"No, thanks."

"Another decaf? Anything."

"I'm fine."

He filled himself a glass from the tap.
"Oh, sorry—please sit, make yourself
comfortable."

Liana perched on a sofa. Stuffed as
firm as a surfer in a wet suit.

**Why am I in this guy's place? He just
happens to show up at the bar? Okay,
he's a regular, he didn't stalk me. But**

that could be even scarier; a regular at a place where two women disap- peared, and for all I know, I've walked right into his—

Aaron's voice overtook her own: *Stupid, Lee, not what I pay you for. Run like hell . . .*

Steve Rau rinsed his glass, walked toward her, stopped a couple of feet away. "Ultrachic décor, right?"

"It's . . . nice and domestic."

He laughed. "Full disclosure: My parents own it. Five years ago they moved to a retirement community outside Las Vegas and what started out as house-sitting ended up quasi-permanent. I say quasi, because they keep threatening to come back."

Liana said, "The boomerang genera- tion."

"That's good—I think I'll steal it for a paper."

"Be my guest."

"Anyway, I'm not allowed to change a thing, just in case. Except the books— they took all their paperbacks and Dad's medical stuff, so at least I've got that."

He pointed to a case full of drab text- books. Econ, poli sci, business, math, com-

puter programming, human-factors psychology.

Exactly what you'd expect for what he
claimed to be. And he'd used his real
name—the doorman's greeting was proof
of that.

Doctor Rau.

And Gus the bartender had confirmed
the ex-wife thing.

So far, on the level. Unlike someone
else we know.

Liana said, "If my parents left me anything, I'd be thrilled." She sashayed to a
large, single-pane window. "Look at that
view."

"I love it, but I should still get my own
place." His voice was low, throaty, warm
against her ear. He'd moved behind her
silently.

She turned, faced him.

He said, "Oh, man, you are so incredibly beautiful."

Oh, man?

Oddly enough . . . she kissed him.

He was putty.

The first time was on one of his parents'
floral couches. Scratchy polyester itched

Liana like crazy but for the ninety seconds the whole thing took, she was okay.

The second time was in his bed. A whole lot better, in all regards.

He drifted into REM sleep, eyes shifting beneath the lids, back and forth like windshield wipers.

Liana extricated herself, sat up, waited, making sure he was out.

His mouth dropped open. He began snoring. She slipped into her panties, left the bedroom, explored his living room.

Frozen dinners in his freezer, three bottles of Heineken in the fridge, along with an old pizza and a single orange growing penicillin. The avocado oven looked to be rarely, if ever, used. A microwave sitting on the counter smelled of oregano, tomato paste, and stale cheese.

She examined some of his textbooks. In many, he'd printed neat notations.

Does this connect to Ecuador?

Corr, caus, both? Orthogonal? Reg.analysis worthwhile? Prob no.

Hedge fund manip of unreg fuel funds relev to short-term per/barrel? Saudi p.f.?

A small desk in the corner comprised his study. In the drawers were bank receipts and credit card bills that confirmed his identity and said he was frugal. And doing all right: a hundred nine thousand bucks in a money market account. He paid his credit card debt in a timely fashion.

The bottom drawer was filled with notebooks featuring the same academic printing. Also, a letter from his boss, a Dr. Hauer, praising Steve's presentation at "the World Affairs Council meeting."

Nothing false, nothing kinky, nothing remotely evil.

She headed back to the bedroom.

Steve met her in the doorway, wearing a blue bathrobe, looking groggy. *Big* guy.

"You okay?"

"A little restless," she said.

"I'd give you a tour, but there's nothing to see."

"I was enjoying the view."

"Let's enjoy it some more."

"I'd better get going."

His face sagged. "You're sure?"

She nodded.

"Okay . . . I was hoping you'd . . . I

understand, it's up to you. But don't take that as apathy, Laura. I . . . this was . . . I'm so glad we met up again."

Cupping her chin, he pushed hair away from her face, kissed her eyelids. She was naked above the waist but his hands didn't explore.

She rested her head on his chest. This time the pelt didn't bother her. His heart was racing.

"I'm glad, too, Steve. But I really need to be getting home."

"Where's home?"

Liana hesitated. He laughed. "Talk about premature interrogation. I don't even know your last name."

Now what . . .

Her silence must've stretched longer than it felt, because Steve sighed. His shrug was heavy with defeat. "I'm sure you've got a good reason to guard your privacy . . . is there any way we could do this again? Not come here, I mean. Just go out—hang out, like you said?"

Liana's mind raced.

His face fell. Backing away into the bedroom, he searched the floor for his clothes. Remembered he'd left them in the living room and passed Liana and retrieved them. "Whatever you're feeling, Laura, for me it was . . . sorry. I'll walk you down to your car."

Liana stood there.

He dressed quickly and awkwardly. Turning his back, as if struck with sudden modesty. "Laura, if I said something that bothered you . . . my ex said I was always saying things that upset her, claimed I was pushing her buttons. But God help me, I had no idea, and I guess I'm still clueless."

Liana looked away from him, into the bedroom. Jumbled sheets. The smell of sex lingered. The washcloth he'd fetched to protect her from "my steel wool" had fallen to the carpet. His idea. Not wanting to bruise her.

"Laura . . ."

Hearing the fake name made her feel cheap.

She said, "Let's sit down."

31

Delaware's recommendation made sense to Aaron: Keep a close eye on Raymond Wohr, use the pimp to leverage up.

But that put everything in Moe's lap and left him with nothing to do and when Mr. Dmitri called to ask how things were going, he had to fake.

The Russian wasn't fooled, telling him, "If something ever happens, tell me. Maitland is not looking happy."

Click.

Aaron drove to the German, retrieved the Opel, called Merry Ginzburg for the third time, wanting her to press for more on Mason Book's hospitalization. Still no answer.

Next stop: someone who'd definitely cooperate.

Manuel Lujon's father and grandfather were skilled gardeners who'd kept up some of the grandest estates in San Marino. Manuel's three older brothers had contin- ued the family tradition, moving Lujon Land- scaping to the Westside where they tended ego-scorecard properties in Holmby Hills and Beverly Park.

Manuel, twenty-five, bright, with no affec- tion for mulch, had gotten a B.A. in screen- writing from the U. that hadn't landed him anywhere near the Industry. His day job was working in a used-book store on Pico near Overland. Aaron called on him when he needed a certain type of camouflage.

Asking Manuel to just *be,* not do—the kid was too honest to be an actor. Unlike Liana, who could deceive like a pro.

She also hadn't returned his call, had probably learned nothing during her sec- ond trip to Riptide.

His day for being shut out by women. He could always call Mom.

That made him laugh out loud, but the sound felt contrived.

Like I'm an actor.

The next line, delivered in Moe's voice: You're *not?*

When Aaron arrived at Once Again Books, Manuel was selling a stack of bruised Elmore Leonards to a stout, bearded guy in an aloha shirt, who'd brought his own plastic covers and took a long time to slip them on. After that, Manuel attended to a kid who paid with crumpled bills and rolls of coins for a Robert Crumb.

No other customers; Aaron drifted forward from the tumbledown plywood stacks. Manuel placed a bookmark in his own reading material. *Gravity's Rainbow* by Pynchon.

Manuel said, "*Amigo!* Whad chaykin! Ronn por de border!"

"How much to borrow one of your brothers' trucks?"

"You jest."

"I jest not."

"How would I know? And frankly, I'm injured. Usually, you want my thespian skills, not hardware."

If you only knew.

Aaron said, "I need both."

"Me in the truck?"

"Exactly."

"Ah," said Manuel. "Where de azalea go, Meester Patron? Onder de weelow or behind de—"

"Could you call now and ask them?" said Aaron. "I'll pay seriously." He looked around the empty store. "How soon can you abandon this hub of commerce?"

"To go where?"

"Hollywood Hills."

"To do what?"

"Sit around looking Mexican."

Manuel laughed. "Dude, you don't even try to be politically correct."

"Neither does the world," said Aaron. "That's why I need you." Touching his own face.

"There are black folk in the hills, Aaron."

"I loiter too long, there'll be one less."

"Same for me," said Manuel.

"The truck'll buy you time. Make sure there's lots of gear in the bed."

"Churning up sod," said Manuel. "Another invisible man. Should we toss in a few bags of manure for authenticity? On the other hand, who needs that shit?"

When they both stopped laughing, Manuel said, "What's the pay scale?"

"The usual."

"Thirty-five an hour."

"The usual's twenty-five."

"Maybe the usual should change, *amigo.*"

"Thirty," said Aaron, touching the Pynchon. "But don't bring that."

"You don't like literature?"

"Today *you* don't."

"Jus' a iggorant cholo churning chayote for chump change."

One of the trucks was working on Hillcrest Drive in Beverly Hills and just finishing up. For an additional hundred bucks, eldest brother Albert Lujon ordered his men to transfer the keys to Manuel and return home on the bus.

Clear family hierarchy, thought Aaron. Must be nice . . .

He checked his phone. The only thing he'd received were prerecorded scam texts for cheap phone service and Internet hookup. When the case was over, he'd have to switch his cell number yet again.

When.

If ever.

By three p.m., Manuel, wearing grubby work clothes, nails dirtied by scraping soil, was stationed in the perfect watch-spot Aaron had found after cruising the neighborhood: a construction zone half a block north of Swallowsong, no one working today.

The project was a sharp-edged contempo house, months away from landscaping. Lawn and parkway had turned to weed-strewn meadow. When Manuel began mowing, a woman walking by muttered, "Finally."

Talking to the air, not to the man pushing the machine.

When she was gone, Manuel phoned Aaron. "I really should be getting thirty-five."

"Why?"

"I could develop an allergy."

"To grass?"

"To being a nonentity."

◆

Aaron drove around the Hollywood Hills, passing Manuel's truck time after time, liking the ruse he'd set up but knowing it had to end by sunset. Manuel was raking lawn trimmings into neat little piles. Maybe that deserved thirty-five.

At four p.m., Aaron took a break for coffee and a sandwich at Mel's Diner on Sunset, finding an empty booth flanked by retarded rock-star wannabes whose dialogue consisted of belches and grunts.

All keyed up for no reason, he left most of his food on the table, was returning to the Opel when his cell beeped. Moe.

"Hey."

"Anything on your end?"

Aaron said, "Don't have much of an end, Moses."

"You're not improvising?"

"Make a suggestion, Moses."

Silence.

Moe said, "You learn something, tell me right away," and hung up.

Does he expect me to learn something? If so, first compliment his brother had ever tossed his way.

He headed back into the hills, ready for yet another circuit, maybe this time he'd actually hazard a pass by the house with the fancy gates.

Before he arrived, Manuel called in. "Got something maybe interesting. Jaguar XJ, long wheelbase, gunmetal gray, lady at the wheel. She went up Swallowsong and something about her intrigued me so I followed and guess where she went? I'm a natural, you need to start thinking about forty an hour—"

"You left your post?"

"You want to bitch, go ahead, but it worked out. I carried a rake and an airgun up the street just in time to see her drive through those crazy gates. No one called La Migra, okay? She definitely went in and she definitely came out. Total time in there twenty-eight minutes. Nice-looking lady."

"Blonde? Brunette?"

"Gray," said Manuel. "But nice—like she kept it that way on purpose. When she came out she looked grim. Like whatever had gone on during those twenty-eight minutes hadn't been fun."

"Did you get the plates?"

"I'll give you a two-dollar discount, settle for thirty-eight if I get dibs on the dirty details for a screenplay. Stuff I've been working on doesn't work. Too much Pynchon and DeLillo, not enough *Story of O.*"

"The plates," said Aaron.

"So it's a deal? Excellent. Got a pen?"

Aaron used a pay-as-you-go cell to contact his DMV source.

Ka-ching, Mr. Dmitri.

The tags matched a one-year-old Jaguar registered to Arlene Frieda Solomon, forty-one years old, brown and green, five two, one twenty. Home address on McCarty Drive in Beverly Hills.

Nice neighborhood, just south of Wilshire, pretty, well kept, two-story houses running three million plus.

Arlene Solomon had let her hair go gray since her license renewal two years ago. Her DMV photo showed a thin-faced, big-eyed brunette.

Real serious—almost mournful. DMV hassles could do that to you, but still, this one seemed downright morose.

Aaron BlackBerried onto the net. *Arlene Frieda Solomon* evoked over a hundred hits.

Psychiatrist Arlene Solomon cited the rise in eating disorders among

younger and younger children as evidence of pressure by . . .

Arlene Solomon, M.D., a Beverly Hills psychiatrist specializing in anorexia-bulimia, says . . .

A panel of experts at the Oak Center in Beverly Hills, chaired by Dr. Arlene Solomon, an expert in . . .

He logged off, phoned Alex Delaware.

The psychologist said, "I've heard of her, but don't know her personally."

"What've you heard?"

"Smart, well trained, knowledgeable. She used to run the eating disorders clinic at the U., may still be doing that."

"Dedicated, too," said Aaron. "Nice office on Bedford Drive, but she makes house calls."

"Her type of patients sometimes need that, Aaron."

"And patients like Mason Book get all kinds of special privileges."

"Hard to say, unless we know how she deals with everyone else."

Doctors. Always protecting each other.

Aaron said, "Your guess was spot-on, Doc."

Now maybe, you'll give me another.

Delaware said, "Sometimes you get lucky."

"Anything else you can tell me?"

Several beats. "Nothing comes to mind."

Aaron said, "Well, at least we know why Book was hospitalized."

"Probably."

"What do you mean?" said Aaron.

"An eating disorder doesn't eliminate all sorts of other issues. Book's nutritional status might be okay, but he still could've come in for depression, anxiety, even suicide."

"Rumor based on truth . . . I guess starving yourself could be thought of as slow suicide, right?"

Delaware said, "It could. And you guys might end up where you started."

"Meaning?"

"Guilt."

Aaron called Dr. Arlene Solomon's office, got a frosty, male answering service operator.

An unfriendly gatekeeper hadn't hurt

business. The psychiatrist was booked
solid, not taking new patients.

Calling himself Clarence Howard, one
of his fake I.D.'s, Aaron put a couple of
strategic catches in his voice and spun a
tragic tale of a teenage daughter out of
control and veering toward premature
demise.

The operator said, "It's not up to me,
sir."

"My daughter is really sick and everyone says Dr. Solomon's the best."

"I'll relay your message to the doctor."

Click.

Aaron sat back in the Opel's driver's
seat, watched the sky darken over canyons
and peaks, the fanciful roofs of distant
mansions nailed up in a city with no rules.
Manuel had just driven off in the company
truck. No one but Dr. Solomon had entered
or left the house on Swallowsong.

He was parked atop one of the highest
streets in the neighborhood, in front of
another construction project. Half the lots
up here were in various stages of demoli-
tion and rebuilding. High-priced dustbowl.
Did anyone in L.A. ever simply *enjoy*?

Wanting to soak in some quiet, he'd put his cell on vibrate. He'd just popped a can of Red Bull when it began bouncing on the passenger seat.

Merry Ginzburg. Finally.

"Long time, Ms. G."

"If you keep calling me, darling, I'm going to start feeling popular again."

"Busy day?"

"Meetings," she said. "Then meetings about meetings. An unnamed local station might want me to highlight Industry dirt for their late-news broadcast. Not exactly Carbon Beach and Bentleys, but beggars can't be yadda yadda yadda. Anyway, I may have found out why you-know-who went to you-know-where."

"It's a secure line," said Aaron.

"Okay, then: My source's source talked to another source who had a source, so this could end up as one of those games of telephone, but like I said, beggars. What it comes down to is that Mr. Book no longer eats."

"Really," said Aaron.

"Anorexia's no longer a girl thing, Denzel. 'Specially in the Industry—all that pressure to be hollow-cheeked. But given someone of Book's status going cachectic, we're talking Big-Time Dirt."

"Ca-what?"

"Morbidly malnourished, darling. It's a medical term. After I heard about poor Mason, I spent some time exploring the topic. Couldn't find any cyberlink between him and no-cal dieting, but I did enlarge my vocabulary. *Cachectic.* Nice, no? All sharp-edged, one of those onomato-whatever. Anyway, poor Mason was probably admitted to Cedars for intravenous sushi and Kobe beef. That would explain no meds, right? Maybe *cachectic* people can't handle chemicals. I've started making calls, still trying to find out who his doc is, once I do, I'll find a way to worm my way—"

"Don't," said Aaron. "Please."

"Don't what?"

"Don't take it any further, Mer."

Long silence.

"Mr. Fox, Mr. Foxy-Fox. Why am I feeling you already know all of this and for some God-knows reason have allowed me to prattle like a meth-addled starlet trying to gain access to Spielberg's boot-tips?"

"I haven't," said Aaron, lying smoothly. "It's serious info that I appreciate more than you can imagine. Which is exactly why I need you to keep a lid on."

"Book not eating relates to *murder*?"

"I can't say more, Merry—please don't jump to any conclusions."

"Without info, my dear, Merry's naturally creative mind jumps to all kinds of places."

"I understand, but at this point, poking around further could jeopardize the investigation."

Merry let loose with a throaty guffaw that rang in Aaron's ear and caused him to move the phone away. The same almost masculine laughter he'd heard when they slept together. Post-orgasmic glee, as if he'd just fucked a longshoreman. She was good enough, technically, but that laugh was *wrong.*

He said, "What's funny, Mer?"

"The way you just got all stuffy, darling. 'Jeopardize the investigation.' Right out of a two-bit teleplay."

"But it's true nonetheless. I need you to be discreet."

"Are we planning on solving this little mystery by the sixth commercial break, Denz? 'Cause if not, I can't see giving up a succulent morsel of dirt that could be peddled to any number of tabloids for considerably more dough than I'd earn in months at a shitty little local station—"

"Let it ride," said Aaron. "When the time's right, I'll clue you in big-time. Enough dirt for an entire show."

"So you say."

"Have I ever failed you, Mer?"

"Of course you have, darling."

"When?"

"You're a man," she said. "You don't need to *do* anything to fail me, you just need to *exist*. But fine, I'll keep Book's problems under the radar. But not forever."

"Thanks, Mer. Maybe after this is over we can have dinner. No business, just fun."

Silence.

She said, "You, my love, are a total bastard."

Aaron lacked the energy—and the facts—to argue.

32

Petra said, "We've got a problem. Instead of just watching Wohr, the rookie I put on him busted him last night, didn't hold up the paper long enough to keep him in our lockup. Early-morning bus took him to County."

Moe said, "I'll call over there."

"I already did. They can't find him."

"Released by accident?"

"Doubtful," she said. "I'm sure you've dealt with the system over there. Or lack of. All that overcrowding, guys sitting around, takes days to find 'em. I'm really sorry, Moe."

Moe had never dealt with County. Petra wasn't much older than he was, but she was a vet. He said, "We'll work it out. What did Wohr get busted for?"

"Soliciting a prostitute. *Underage* prostitute, so it couldn't be just a citation. Ramone comes into lockup tagged as a pedo, doesn't get segregated, you know what could happen."

"Oh, man."

"I know, I know. If this screws up your case, I couldn't feel worse. Unfortunately, sorry don't pay the bills."

"Hey, it happens." Keeping his true feelings inside. *It wouldn't have happened with West L.A. working the case. Me and Sturgis.*

No logic to that chauvinism. No comfort in it, either.

Petra said, "In the rookie's defense, I'm not sure a more experienced cop would've done different. The prostie turned out to be seventeen, but I've seen her mug and she looks twelve."

"Playing kiddie," said Moe. "Where'd it happen?"

"Not far from Ramone's crib—alley off Western, near a chicken joint that's a known perv hangout. Rookie says Ramone never went home at all yesterday. Eiger being such a battle-ax probably scared him away."

"Not so scared he didn't prowl for youngblood."

"Or being humiliated made him want to dominate someone," she said. "They ducked into the alley, by the time the rookie got there, hooker's head was you-know-where. Meaning an overt act, kind of hard to ignore."

"The girl's in custody?"

"Nope, she ran off. But Ramone gave up her I.D. right away—he's a regular, but claimed she was legal. Delena Guzman, street name Delishus. Salvadoran, but so far no link to M-13 or any of the other monster gangs. Still, right now I wouldn't want to be Ramone."

Moe said, "First his niece, now this. Delaware was right about him being chronically twisted."

"Delaware's in on this one?"

"We just consulted him. All the psych overtones, I figured why not."

"He's a smart guy," said Petra. "Anything profound?"

"He thinks Mason Book could be anorexic."

"Really," said Petra. "Yeah, Book is kind of skeletal . . . so what does that mean?"

"It could explain Book going into the hospital and claiming suicide."

"Tragic figure as opposed to pathetic X-ray."

She'd decoded the psych angle right away. "I'll keep bugging County to locate Ramone. I've already called one of the sheriff jail captains, asked for our boy to get put on High Power or the psych ward. Guy said he'd try but their computer system's acting up, it's all they can do to keep tabs on gangbangers."

"What's the captain's name?"

"Rojas. Sure, go ahead, add your name to the petition."

Moe said, "Citizens to Keep Ramone W Safe."

Petra said, "Only for as long as we can use him. After that, he's chum for the sharks."

Captain Rojas was smooth-sounding, outwardly cooperative, more like a politician than a cop. Moe wondered if he was being shined on.

He hung up, blocked out noise from the D-room, considered his options.

At this point, not too many.

No way to get to any of the principals and now even Ray Wohr was out of reach.

Delaware's advice reverbed: Find a weak point and start wedging.

Ramone W was locked up and unavailable, but the woman who'd bitch-slapped him in public view was free and clear.

This time he parked close to the apartment building on Taft. Back to his blazer and khakis, white shirt and tie. Not pretending to be anything other than what he was as he marched up to the front door.

Unlocked, no security provisions of any sort.

That fit the urine-bitter corridor carpeted in wrinkled gray felt, the dirt-colored hallways livened by graffiti, the poorly fitted black plywood doors, some of them a good inch above the floor, souvenirs of once-thicker flooring. Missing bulbs overhead creating artificial evening. The tilting stairway banister looked as if it wouldn't stand up to a nudge.

One thing you could say for the place: quiet. Maybe all the night-prowlers were catching up on their Z's.

White metal mailboxes just inside the entrance hung askew, as if they'd been wrenched in rage. Dented, too. Definite anger-management issues.

Eight units on each of two floors. Half the boxes were unlabeled, the others were identified by any number of methods: pencil, ballpoint, plastic tape, stick-on letters.

A. Eiger had been scrawled in what looked like brown eye shadow over the slot labeled 7. Meaning, she was the one who paid the rent, not Ramone W.

Her bod gets peddled in cheap motels, she's got to freebie the clerk for a discounted rate, she's stuck with the bills. Meanwhile, Ramone chases youngblood. Maybe that's what had set her off.

Unit Seven was ground-floor rear, to the right of an unlocked back door that opened to a fetid alley lined with trash cans and sporting a luxuriant crop of weeds.

Moe stepped out, scanned; no one

lurking around. He returned to the hallway, rapped Alicia Eiger's door.

Prepared to answer her dope-addled
Yeah with *Police.* God knew what that
would unleash from the denizens of this
dump.

No response, mumbled or otherwise.
He tried again. Put his ear to the door.
Heard nothing. Then a low hum—some
kind of electrical device?

A sudden tickling sensation in his ear
made him jerk away with the same instinctive repugnance that had led him to toss
the secondhand hoodie teeming with imaginary vermin.

This time the bugs were real.

Little black flies, circling and swooping,
letting out whiny, buzzing noises.

Lots of flies. Streaming through the gap
between door and carpet.

Moe had seen the same kind of insect,
hovering at the sparkling glass doors
leading to the administrative offices of the
county coroner.

All of Mission Road's wet-work took
place on the other side of a clean, pretty
mini-plaza, but that didn't stop blowflies

from expressing their enthusiasm anywhere they saw fit.

One of the little shitheads zoomed up
suddenly and buzzed Moe's chin. He
slapped it away, edged back some more.
Removed his gun from his holster.

Stared at the doorknob.

Milo Sturgis always carried a pair of
surgical gloves in his jacket. Moe had
resolved to do the same, but had failed to
follow through.

No gloves in his car, either. No reason,
this was just going to be an interview.
Assuming Alicia Eiger was home.

Moe bet she was.

Using a corner of his blazer, he took
hold of the doorknob. Turned.

The door swung open easily. As if he'd
been expected.

Some welcome.

No attempt to conceal.

Just the opposite: an ad for dead.

Alicia Eiger was splayed on the floor of
a rancid kitchenette, facedown, an oversized T-shirt, once yellow, now tie-dyed
crimson, yanked above her waist.

Chunky legs were parted in unmistakable display. No panties. No obvious splotches of semen. But plenty of body fluids: a torrent had issued from the woman's deactivated bladder and bowels.

Varicose veins on the backs of her calves. Add some blue to the red.

A once feisty woman, reduced to this.

Moe worked with death, but he really hadn't seen that many intact corpses. This corpse made his gut lurch. He slow-breathed himself steady, took in the scene. Realized he'd left the door to the corridor wide open, backed up, covered his hand with his sleeve and shut it.

Just me and her.

Keeping safe distance, he used his eyes like wide-angle cameras.

No sign of forced entry. No disruption at all to the shabby, barely furnished apartment.

Tiny place; a lav off to the side and the dinky kitchenette—front room combo was the totality of Eiger's—and Ray Wohr's—home-sweet-home.

No big puzzle about COD. A wood-handled knife was buried in the left side of her back. Moe counted at least ten more stab wounds ripping the T-shirt, but all that blood could be concealing others.

A front view would have to wait until the coroner's team arrived.

Oh, yeah, they couldn't arrive unless someone informed them.

After he finished with that, he reached Petra at her desk.

She said, "You found him?"

He said, "My turn to deliver bad news."

A coroner's investigator named Maidie Johansen said, "Fools rush in, kids. Unfortunately, I'm one of those angels who fears to tread."

Petra said, "Aw c'mon, Maidie, make a guess."

Johansen was around sixty, a sturdy woman with indoor skin, curly gray hair, and wide brown eyes behind wire-rimmed specs. She reminded Moe of a fifth-grade teacher whose name he couldn't remember. A woman who hadn't liked him. Despite that, he'd ground away, pulled an A-minus both semesters.

Alicia Eiger's horn-rimmed specs had been revealed by the body-turn. Frames bent and twisted under her weight, but both lenses intact. No entry wounds in her chest or abdomen. Her entire front was unmarked, freakishly so when contrasted with the chopping block that had once been her back. The knife long enough to pierce vital organs but too short to come out the other end.

Fifteen wounds, by Maidie Johansen's count. She said, "One thing I will go out on a limb about: This was done with mucho force."

Pointing to the warped blade, tagged and bagged. What looked to be a kitchen utensil, the wood now glazed an unpleasant copper. Surprisingly, Eiger's knives were a set, cheap and white-handled. Either the murder weapon was the lone mismatch or someone had come prepared for butchery.

A killer Alicia Eiger had been comfortable turning her back on.

Maidie Johansen said, "Someone sure didn't like this poor girl." Sighing. "At least there are no pockets to go through."

Petra said, "TOD?"

"Not a clue."

"Jeez, Maidie, you've been doing this long enough to educate your guesses."

Johansen drew herself up. "Child, you saying I'm a crone?"

"I'm saying give us a guess, off the record. The way the bodies are stacked over at your place, who knows how long it'll be before she gets a prelim, let alone autopsied."

"You're one of my favorites, Detective Connor, but no dice."

Moe said, "I saw her yesterday afternoon, so that narrows down the time frame."

"Then that's my guess: no earlier than yesterday afternoon."

Petra said, "Those flies—"

"Can sniff out a DB within seconds," said Johansen. "This being interior space might theoretically slow them down but you've got a nearby door to an alley full of crap, a gap under the door. Word goes out in the fly community, it's 'Let's hurry over and make maggots.'"

"Don't see any maggots on her."

"They take time to hatch, Petra. Could be eggs in her nostrils or her ears, her anus or vagina. Or they're already crawling around inside. That's the point: It can't be pinned down easily. And don't go asking me about algor, rigor, livor, any of that good stuff. Dr. Srinivasan just gave us a lecture and guess what? All those calcs based on ninety-eight point six being normal body temp are off because the true normal is probably closer to ninety-seven, all the old thermometers are basically screwed up. And don't go telling me a degree and a half cooling per hour's gonna be definitive. Dr. Srinivasan gave us a lecture *last* week saying there's all kinds of new data that can screw up *that* calc." She ticked her fingers. "Body fat, ambient room temp, humidity, seasonal variation of temp-humidity, how deep in the liver you probe."

Moe said, "She's not fat, the weather's temperate, there's no Santa Ana winds, and it hasn't rained in weeks. And I'll bet you're pretty consistent when you jab the liver."

"Flattery is for chumps," said Johansen. She grimaced and stretched. That reminded Moe of Sturgis. This thick, surly woman could be Ann to the Loo's Andy.

Petra said, "So much for talking for the victim."

Johansen said, "Now it's guilt."

"Guilt's a great motivator, Maidie."

Moe wondered if Petra was thinking about Mason Book. He sure was.

Johansen said, "So is covering one's butt, Petra." She stared down at the body. "If you absotively need something for a kick-start, I'd bet on within eight hours, give or take. Try to pin that on me, I'll plead Alzheimer's."

Squarely within the time frame Raymond Wohr had been under surveillance. Damn.

Petra said, "How much give, how much take?"

Johansen shook her head. "Kids today." She adjusted her glasses. "You want quotable quotes, my pretties, talk to someone who went to med school. Speaking of which, can we take her now?"

The rookie's name was Jennifer Kennedy.

Petra had never mentioned gender. Why should she?

Kennedy was ruddy and round-faced, not bad looking in a farm-girl way, with cornflower eyes and pasta-colored hair cut short and peaked on top—almost a faux-hawk. Three holes in one ear, two in the other. Moe wouldn't be surprised if her uniform hid some tats.

Sitting in a plastic chair in a Hollywood interview room, she worked hard at not showing anxiety.

Failing. The blue eyes gave it away. Despite the fact that Petra and Moe were proceeding gently.

Like Petra had said before they entered the room: no sense adding to the kid's stress.

The kid; Kennedy's stats put her at four years older than Moe. She'd worked as a secretary for a medical insurance company for eight years before entering the academy sixteen months ago.

Those same organizational skills led to precision: a carefully logged surveillance of Raymond Wohr, down to the minute.

No chance Wohr had been in his apartment from six p.m., when Kennedy had started watching him, until three a.m. when she'd busted him.

The only window of opportunity for him to stab Alicia Eiger, the two-hour lapse between the end of Moe's watch and the start of hers.

Ramone would've had time to backtrack to his crib, confront Eiger about the bitch-slap, wreak vengeance, clean up, and reemerge on the street to drink and lurk and troll for an underage hooker. Ditch bloody clothes.

But lack of violence in Ramone's past and the passive way he'd tolerated Eiger's abuse, combined with Maidie Johansen's educated time-of-death guess, made Moe wonder.

He said, "Tell us about the bust."

Kennedy said, "Did I screw that up?"

"Wohr's a bad guy, he was having sex with a minor, you did the right thing."

As if Moe had failed to comfort her, Kennedy looked at Petra.

"You had no choice, Jennifer. Wohr being in lockup is fine, we'll have access to him."

Once we find him.

"Okay," said Kennedy. "So what happened was obviously I was watching him and mostly it was a lot of nothing. Drinking, walking around, finding another bar, walking some more."

Moe said, "Did he call anyone?"

"He could've, inside one of the bars, but not out on the street. Finally, he walked to Western, there were a bunch of girls working the chicken place, at first I wasn't sure if they actually were girls."

Petra said, "Sometimes they're not."

"The girl he went to," said Kennedy, "it was obvious they had a prior relationship.

Or whatever you want to call it. From how fast it was, there was no discussion, they just ducked into the alley. By the time I get a look, he's with his back against a wall and she's on her knees. She looked eleven, who knew?"

"She was a minor, Jennifer."

Kennedy frowned. "Seventeen years, eight months. When I busted him, he went down easy, no resistance. Didn't react when I found that weed I logged. She ran but I made the decision to concentrate on him. She was so young looking. I wanted it to *end.*"

They let Kennedy go and stayed in the room.

Moe said, "Solo officer in plainclothes tells him to assume the position, he doesn't fight."

Petra said, "Female officer, no less." She grinned. "I'm allowed to say that. Yeah, he's pretty darn passive, but even passive guys blow fuses."

"I'm not feeling it," said Moe. "That murder was brutal and someone took the time to pose her sexually, maybe to throw us off."

"My instinct, too, Moe. Your question about calling someone—you think he set Eiger up with someone nasty enough to do it?"

"I'm sure going to find out if he's got a phone account. If not, we'll see if there's pay phones in any of those bars."

Petra nodded. "One good thing about passive: We get him in a room, he could be workable."

"I'm looking forward to it." He thanked her, left Hollywood Station and drove to West L.A.

Thinking: I'm developing instincts.

Two hours later, he was still at his desk, going over Caitlin Frostig's file for the thousandth time. Raymond Wohr had no account at any phone company. Tracking pay phones in bars would take hours, but he had no choice.

Petra had just called, still wrestling with County Jail bureaucracy; no one in the custodial megalith had a clue as to Ramone W's whereabouts. For all Moe knew, the mope had paid for his perv tag already—sliced, diced, stashed behind some jail boiler.

Eiger getting murdered so brutally after her tirade made Moe wonder if the motive wasn't revenge but someone shutting her up about something important.

As in two dead girls.

And a baby.

During her rant, Eiger had seemed to be exhorting Ramone. Trying to goad him to do something. Giving up and calling him *stupid* before whomping him upside the head. Had she known that he was in possession of explosive information, got frustrated because he wouldn't exploit the knowledge?

Explosive as in the paternity of Baby Gabriel? Something *Caitlin* might've learned getting close enough to Adella to sit for the infant?

Rich-guy paternity as in Mason Book?

If Ramone W knew or even suspected that, he sure hadn't profited. Living in that dump, pimping Eiger to Ax Dement and the motel clerk.

Too passive to exploit? But Eiger isn't, she nags him, he puts her off because he's too dumb, or too scared to figure out an angle?

Eiger, tired of being a commodity, loses

patience, braces Ramone on the street, slaps him down.

Now she's dead.

If there was a link there, Moe figured it could've gone two ways.

Option A: Ramone finally gives in, makes a blackmail call, flubs, and turns Eiger into a victim. Narrowly misses getting killed himself. Remains in jeopardy.

Option B: Furious at Eiger for humiliating him, but a sneak, not an action guy, Ramone makes a call that tags her as dangerous. Turns Eiger into a victim. Is *still* in jeopardy.

Oh, yeah, the third option, C: None of the above.

Moe's hands clenched. His jaw hurt. He'd been grinding his teeth without realizing it.

Damn jail . . . scumbag *had* to show up, eventually. Moe was pretty sure he could crack the idiot open like a peanut.

When, not if. He had to believe in something.

Sitting in the dark, above Swallowsong Lane, Aaron checked his expense log.

He knew it by heart but nothing else to

do, now that his sandwich was gone and he'd taken a couple of whizz-breaks in the bushes.

The glamorous side of private detecting. People like Mr. Dmitri didn't have a clue.

Aaron cheered himself with mental calculations of the final bill he'd present the Russian. Maybe his last bill to the Russian if he had nothing to show.

Liana still hadn't called. Where the hell *was* she?

The chance that she might be in danger plagued him personally and professionally. He'd never had a better op than Liana and a part of him—some part he couldn't really label—felt deeply about her.

Nothing he could do now, so he shoved his worries into a filing cabinet at the back of his head.

The key was to keep everything compartmentalized.

Where are you, Lee? He assured himself yet again that she was smart. He'd briefed her fully on this one. *Urged* her to be careful.

It was just after one a.m. During the

past five hours, six cars had driven up Swallowsong: Three vehicles ferried neighbors home and one of them, an old Mercedes diesel sedan, reemerged thirty minutes later with an elderly man behind the wheel and a woman of matching vintage prattling in the passenger seat.

Tux, gown, some kind of party, everyone in a good mood.

Probably one of those perfect couples, together for forty years.

Must be nice . . .

At ten thirteen p.m. Rory Stoltz chauffeured Mason Book home in his Hyundai, stayed with the actor for a mere twelve minutes before speeding down the hill.

Probably not an errand, the kid hadn't reappeared.

Shortly after eleven p.m., Ax Dement, solo in his pickup, did his customary run of the stop sign and zoomed up the hill. His stay was also brief—twenty-four minutes. Just long enough to smoke up or sniff or drink and savor the high.

Aaron caught a glimpse of Dement Junior's squat, bearded face as the truck sped away. Ax didn't look high, quite the contrary.

Preoccupied.

One fifteen.

Convinced Mason Book wouldn't be receiving any more visitors, Aaron left the Opel and began the silent hike up Swallowsong.

From his easy lope, no outward sign of the tension—the frustration—that seized every cell of his body. He realized his heart was pounding and he took some time to deep-breathe it slower.

Later, looking back, he'd marvel at his own daring. Or stupidity, depending on how you looked at it.

Right now, standing outside the Baroque gates of the house Mason Book rented from Lemuel Dement, noticing how many foothold opportunities the complex ironwork provided, tired of being stymied by the layout of the property—the curving drive and Italian cypresses that blocked any view of what lay beyond—he said, "What the hell."

Whispering out loud. Feeling his lips move but inaudible above the distant buzz of traffic from the Strip. Leaves rustling in a warm, sweet Hollywood Hills breeze.

Making sure his Glock was buttoned down firmly in its nylon holster, running a lint-remover over his black nylon jacket to remove errant hairs, he gloved up, looked around. Breathed in deeply and placed two hands on the upper-left quadrant of the gate, nudged a toe into a convenient circle of space afforded by an iron curlicue.

Exhaled and hoisted himself up.

34

Standing on Lem Dement's private property—a black man in dark clothes and gloves, packing a gun—triggered a rush of what-ifs in Aaron's head.

There could be motion detectors. A guard dog.

A *herd* of guard dogs.

Maybe even a bodyguard or a rent-a-cop. Or two. Though in all the time he'd watched the house, he'd never spotted any muscle coming in or out.

Unless Ax Dement counted for that.

Less threatening employees could be a problem, too. Maids, butlers, houseboys, whatever. Not spotting any of those meant little if live-in help rarely left the premises.

With a big enough property—your own private town—there'd be no reason to leave. Especially with a gofer like Stoltz as the outside guy.

Black man in the Hills.

Nothing Aaron hadn't considered before vaulting the gate. Lord knew, he'd mulled this move in his head a million times.

Risks he'd *chosen* to disregard because two girls were dead and so was a baby and he was fed up with being hampered by rules and regs and whatnot bullshit. By the wet-blanket voice-in-his-head that passed itself off as Common Sense.

He was an *Un*common Man, not some damned civil *servant.*

Groupthink; he'd tasted that thin soup for ten years, spit it out in favor of a gourmet broth seasoned by Personal Initiative and Free Enterprise.

Let Moe and people like Moe deal with wants, warrants, orders from downtown, cover-your-ass freeze-tag. Hurdle after hurdle imposed by a brain-dead system.

Aaron hadn't heard from his brother since the meeting with Delaware.

Someone else who wasn't returning his calls.

Here we go: Intrepid Masai warrior faces the the abyss.

He smiled at the self-inflation. But there was truth to it. Two girls were dead. A baby, for God's sake, and he'd accomplished zero and Mr. Dmitri demanded results. Rules and regs were *not* going to cut it.

He'd quit the damned system because he was tired of being penned up like some pet pony.

Fearless black stallion stands tall among the dray horses. Snorts and bucks as he races for freedom.

No guard dog yet.

Not smart, Detective Fox.

Better to be a living fool than a dead cog. His life—the life he'd made for himself—was all about tough choices and living with the consequences.

The consequences had been sweet. Three hundred K a year, the Porsche, the private haberdashery, the women—he deserved a vacation once the case was buttoned up.

Once, not if.

Black man in the Hills.

Maybe moments away from the biggest disaster of his life.

He remained still for a long time, standing to the right side of the curving drive, concealed by columnar cypress shadows. Took a step forward. Waited some more.

No stampeding rottweilers, no concealed sensors that he could spot. Those suckers were easy to hide, he'd installed more than his share of them.

Twenty more steps brought no view of the house, just rough, winding concrete beneath his feet. Same for fifty. A hundred. Tree after tree forming opaque green-black walls. The property was vast.

Still no canine growl. No alarms, no warnings canned or live. No padded rent-a-cop footsteps.

Aaron kept going, hand on his Glock. Damned drive was what—half a mile long?

Italian cypresses said it was probably one of those Tuscan villas, maybe an eight-figure teardown-buildup, Lem Dement all flush from his biblical splatter flick.

Or maybe what lay up ahead was one of the old original Italianate mansions that had studded the Hollywood Hills during the Golden Age that Aaron had read about.

He liked that notion, kept most of his head focused on the job but allowed a small corner to be decorated by fantasy.

Big-snouted chromed monsters—Duesenbergs and Packards and Rolls Phantoms—tooling up this very drive on a warm night like this one. Liveried chauffeurs, laughing passengers. Bud-vases, champagne buckets in the trunk—the boot.

Gleaming chariots cruising up silently, dropping off the likes of Harlow and Gable and Cooper and Hedy Lamarr in the porte cochere of a fifty-room wedding-cake mansion. The entire place alive with golden light and witty chatter.

Slim stylish people in gowns and evening jackets talking in that clipped, self-satisfied almost English accent, highball glasses lofted gracefully by manicured hands.

A life filled with one cocktail party after another—in the mansion's great hall, a grand piano—Gershwin himself plinking the keys.

Billiards, brandy, cigars for the men.

Bird-chatter giggles and frothy girl-drinks for the women.

Everyone loving their life . . . as he trudged, ever watchful for threat, Aaron imagined the mansion's interior. Soaring arched windows offering heart-stopping views. The city spread in repose, a woman of leisure.

From that to Mason Book and Ax Dement in Hyundais and pickups, buying sex at the Eagle Motel. Smoking up and sniffing H in a damned state park.

Guilt and atonement. That crazy woman . . .

Aaron stopped, listened. Just the traffic buzz, a little louder now.

No parties tonight.

Not the type anyone enjoyed.

He completed another forty yards before the drive finally straightened and the cypresses ended and he was facing a wide, unadorned circular driveway of the same ugly concrete.

No vehicles in sight.

Nothing remotely Tuscan.

Nothing remotely Golden *Age*.

The house was one-story, free-form, a

long, low knife fashioned of iron girders and glass.

Glass-on-glass, no apparent seams. Wedge-like—a spaceship, perched on the edge of a cliff, pointy snout extending well over the precipice.

Prepared to launch.

Below oblique steel struts fastening the structure to the cliff, miles of light. Free fall into oblivion. Staring at it made Aaron feel dizzy and he looked away to clear his head.

Not a trace of green anywhere around the house. A cold, deliberate structure.

Nowhere to hide once he set out across the motor court.

All that glass. Lights on in room after transparent room.

White, wide rooms, the kind of low, black leather furniture Aaron liked.

So cold; maybe it was time to reconsider his décor.

Empty.

Then it wasn't.

Mason Book, wearing a too-large black robe, face gaunt, yellow hair wild, appeared around a white wall and walked—more like

hobbled—toward the front of the house—
right into the wedge that hovered above
empty space.

The actor stood there, staring straight
ahead.

Protected by darkness, Aaron jogged
forward, positioned himself ten feet from
the house, with a side view of the knife-
point.

He peered under the building. Just
enough backyard for a bright blue infinity
pool.

Still no dogs, no alarms and all those
interior lights put Mason Book on full
display—like one of those performance art
pieces.

Book had no clue someone could be
watching. Let's hear it for false confidence. Too many years being buffered
from reality.

He stumbled, barely caught his balance. His robe fell open.

Lousy skinny body. The actor sat down
with apparent pain. Continued staring out
at what had to be black, blank space.

Like a kid ready for takeoff.

Aaron edged closer.

Sad kid, weeping.

35

Moe was driving home, talking to Liz on his cell, when Call Interruption beeped.

He said, "Can you hold for a sec, honey?"

Liz laughed. "Something tells me you won't be dropping by after all."

If it's a lead, from your mouth to God's ears. He said, "Nah, it's probably something stupid."

It wasn't.

Raymond "Ramone W" Wohr sat in yellow psych-ward pajamas in one of the therapy rooms used by the jail shrinks.

A little nicer than the usual County interview space, but not by much.

Moe and Petra gave Wohr the uphol-stered chair they'd jammed in a corner, pulled up the pair of plastic seats, and faced their quarry.

Wohr was one of those long-legged types who shrank when seated. A rash had broken out on his bald head. The side fringes hung greasy and limp. In less than a day, jail pallor had set in. Moe wondered if it was some sort of fear reaction, not absence of sunlight.

Or the overhead fluorescence wasn't being kind to Ramone's seamed, sagging, bleary-eyed, gap-toothed, addict face. The huge mustache was ragged, more gray than brown. His hands shook. A gray-blue tat ran up his neck. Crude blue band fash-ioned of circles and squares and X's. Like a tie gone awry.

It was just after one a.m. and Petra's tenth call of the evening had finally annoyed the sheriff's jailers sufficiently for them to really dig through their paperwork.

Ramone had been booked nearly twenty-four hours ago, shoved right into the general population. News of his pedo bust had arrived before him and though Wohr's cellmates were nonviolent types, a flurry of less-than-veiled threats from a couple of hypermuscular gangbangers in the adjoining cell had caused Wohr to whine, bitch, and moan. Finally the mope had attracted the attention of a jailer who *really* didn't want to have to deal with *another* in-house death-stomp.

The problem was where to put Wohr. High Power and the psych ward were full up and the felony charge didn't qualify him for trustee status. Finally, he was stashed in temporary quarters: a tiny reading room in a far corner of the jail's inmate library, where he was tossed a blanket and told to go to sleep.

The space was vacant because furniture could be used as weaponry. Jailers doing pass-bys woke him up every few hours with flashlight glare and foot nudges. Your basic solitary confinement and Ramone W was an empty-eyed wraith by the time a psych bed emptied after an agitated bipolar rapist stroked out.

The transfer had taken place twelve hours ago, but the paperwork lagged.

"Anyway, we've got him," Petra told Moe.

"Meanwhile, I've got Vice guys looking for Delishus. Where are you?"

"Turning right around and heading for the freeway." After hours of futile traces on bar pay phones, he ached for sleep. "I can be there in twenty."

"I'll meet you in front." A beat. "This is your baby, I'm just there for backup."

He couldn't figure out if she'd said that out of good manners, or relief.

Raymond Wohr said, "I still don't get why I got busted." Not even convincing himself.

Moe said, "No one told you the charges?"

"Yeah, but . . ."

"You molested a minor, Ramone."

Wohr didn't answer.

"Pedo is serious stuff, Ramone."

Wohr scratched an eyelid.

"You made our job easy," said Moe. "Put on quite a show for Officer Kennedy."

"Aw, man." As if he was the aggrieved party.

Moe said, "Aw, man, what?"

"She said she was twenty."

"Who did?"

"Deli- whatever she calls herself."

"Too bad she looks ten."

"Not to me," said Wohr. "It's a case of . . . how you see things."

"You wear glasses, Ramone?"

"Huh?"

Moe repeated the question.

"No."

"To you she looked twenty. To everyone else, she looks ten. She's a minor and you got caught with your dick in her mouth."

Wohr's scratching hand lowered to the crook of his arm. Old tracks, but no fresh punctures. Along with the bag of weed, granules of what was sure to be cocaine had been scraped from a pocket of his jeans. Along with a pay-as-you-go cell Petra had already submitted for analysis.

Moe smiled at Wohr. Wohr sat there. Not a trace of emotion and so far the mope hadn't even come close to asking for a lawyer. That could be a problem with these idiots: not enough anxiety.

Moe put forth a lie: "Delishus informs us the two of you have a long-standing relationship. Real long-standing, and that you know darn well how old she is."

Liking the sound of his treachery. *Instinct.*

Wohr said, "Aw, man—sir. I didn't mean nothing crazy. Just tryin' to get off."

"Basic human need."

"Exactly, sir."

"We understand human need, Ramone. Unfortunately, the system doesn't. Courts are coming down real hard on child molesters. I mean, we're talking some serious time."

"I din't *molest* no one. She got paid."

"Your basic business transaction."

"Exactly."

"How many other look-like-twentys you generally do business with?"

Silence.

"Maybe you don't go that far with all of them," said Moe. "Maybe sometimes you're happy just looking at 'em."

One of Wohr's droopy eyelids twitched. He stopped scratching, placed his palms on his lap.

"I guess that could be thought of as good manners, Ramone. Just peeping through windows, handling your own business, no one gets hurt."

Silence.

"Plus, it's free. So how come this time you paid?"

Wohr closed his eyes and hunched.

"Had a bad day, Ramone?"

"Nah."

"Want something to drink, Ramone?"

"Nah."

"Sure? Your lips are looking dry."

"A Coke?" As if snagging the drink was a pipe dream. Petra was up before Moe could ask her.

During her absence, Moe scrawled useless notes in his pad. Ramone reacted by closing his eyes and pretending to doze. Beneath the guy's eyelids, though, was a buzz of frantic activity.

Like the blowflies celebrating what had once been Alicia Eiger.

Petra returned with a tall paper cup of something brown. Wohr gulped all of it, pressed the flat of one hand under his rib cage. Belched and smiled at Petra. "'Scuse me, ma'am."

She said, "Hey, enjoy. While you can."

Putting emphasis on the last word, Moe figured it was a prompt. He said, "Enjoy *any* little thing, you're going away for a real long time."

"Aw, man . . . I din't do nothing bad."

Moe shrugged, wrote some more. "What can I say, Ramone?"

Petra took the cue and starting checking her cell phone.

Being with two bored detectives made Raymond Wohr fidget. "So what you're saying is, if I give you something, it could help me, right?"

"I didn't hear us say anything like that, Ramone."

"You're here."

"Just clearing paper, pal." Moe continued to write.

"Sir," said Wohr.

"Uh-huh."

"What if I *do* give you something?"

Moe's heart thumped. He looked up from his notes. "Like what?"

"Names, places, sir. Big deals all around Hollywood, sir. I got a good memory."

"Drug deals?"

"Man, I've seen stuff. I know who. I know what. I could clear half your cases."

Moe turned to Petra. "That's pretty generous."

She said, "Sure is."

"Gimme pen and paper," said Wohr. "Hope you got time because I'll write you a book."

"Sounds like a bestseller," said Moe.

"More than we could ever hope for," said Petra.

Both of them using a mocking tone. Wohr had instincts. "Something wrong with that?"

Moe said, "What's wrong with that is we're not dope cops."

"Uh-uh, no way, I can't give you sex stuff," said Wohr, lying effortlessly. "Don't know about that, not my thing."

"Don't want to rat out other pedos?"

"I'm not a—I don't *know* that stuff, sir. Like you said before, it's human need, I mind my own business."

"Sticking mostly to peeping, huh?"

Head shake. "I'm not saying that, either. I just don't *know* that stuff."

"So the way you look at it," said Moe, "it's all victimless—a business transaction, who cares how a guy gets off." He slapped his forehead. "Oh, yeah, judges and *juries* care. But guess what? I don't. And neither does Detective Connor."

Moe leaned in close, fighting to keep

his nostrils open after a cloud of Wohr's reek blew his way. The stink of jail and fear and poor personal habits.

"We're not sex cops, either, Ramone."

Wohr's eyes swung wide to the left. "What are you?"

"We're murder cops."

Wohr's head snapped up and back as he tried to retreat as far as possible from Moe. The way they'd tucked his chair into the corner meant he wasn't going anywhere.

"Aw, man."

"You keep saying that, Ramone. Like it's some prayer, going to get you redeemed."

Wohr lowered his head to his lap, clasped both hands behind his own neck. "No, no, that I *really* don't do."

Moe waited.

Wohr looked up.

"Hear that, Detective Connor?"

Petra slipped her cell into her purse. "Uh-uh, sorry, what?"

"Mr. Wohr says he *really* doesn't do murder."

Ramone said, "Nope, man—sir—ma'am. Someone told you that, they're lying."

"Who would tell us that?"

Eye-dance. "No one."

"*Why* would anyone tell us that, Ramone?"

"No reason—they wouldn't."

"They, meaning . . ."

"No one." Wohr folded scrawny arms across his chest.

Moe turned to Petra. "Remember what they taught us about guys who like little girls? It's all about power and control. And we know the same thing goes for murder. Especially sicko murder." Back to Wohr: "No bigger power-trip than being in charge when the lights go out."

Ramone's hands shot out palms-forward. "No way, no, no, no."

Moe sighed.

Petra's knowing smile was perfect: *You believe this guy?*

Ramone W scratched his head, then his arms, rocked a bit. "Aw, man. Gimme paper and a pen, I'll write you a book on dope— you can trade it to the dope cops, you give 'em something, they give you something, everyone walks away happy."

Petra said, "You've got an interesting view of police work."

"Hey—ma'am, everything gets traded."

"Guess that's true," said Moe. "Including human life."

When Wohr didn't answer, he went on: "Everything's got a price. Every*one.* Some lives are expensive, some lives are cheap. Cheap lives get traded away easy so expensive lives can continue. Experienced individual such as yourself knows which is which."

"Aw, man, I don't know *nothing* about *that,* you want *that* there's all sorts of guys right *here* who can tell you good stuff, just walk over to general pop and say tell me about *that.* Not me, sir, no way, no."

Long speech. It took Wohr's breath away and he sat back, trying to regain wind.

Moe said, "Expensive lives, cheap lives." A beat. "Guess Adella Villareal's life was pretty cheap."

Wohr sat there. Not moving, not blinking. None of the eye-calisthenics Moe had expected.

Could I be that wrong?

"That name's not familiar to you, Ramone?"

Wohr let out a long, raspy sigh. Now his

eyes were bobbling, like floats on a trout line. Scratching hard enough to raise welts on his arms. He forced the eyes still, but the resulting stare—scared, frozen—was the biggest giveaway of all.

Yes!

Moe said, "Adella and Gabriel. Tiny little baby. A tiny life means super-cheap in your world?"

Wohr buried his face in his hands. Rocked some more.

"Cheap lives," said Moe. "We know a lot."

Wohr's fingers spread, revealing runny eyes. "That was *not* me, sir."

"That?"

"What happened."

"What *happened*? Like we're talking about a something, not a someone? A *what,* not a *who*? This is a mommy and a baby we're discussing, Ramone. Human beings. They got murdered and we know who did it and we know you're involved."

Wohr's eyes rounded and for a bizarre instant, terror made the old dope fiend look young, almost child-like—still vulnerable to surprise. A second later, the old weariness/wariness returned and the guy was squinting—first at Moe, then Petra. Figuring the odds.

Moe said, "You can help yourself, Ramone."

"How much can I help myself?"

"What do you mean?"

Sly smile. "Business transaction. What's the deal?"

"I'm not going to lie to you, friend, 'cause that would be wasting everyone's time. And you've been around long enough to know reality. Anything official is up to the D.A. But we're murder cops, the D.A. listens to us."

"Misdemeanor," said Wohr. "No jail time?"

"On what?"

"Delishus."

Meaning he wasn't worried about his involvement in murder. Or was the mope that clever?

Moe said, "Detective Connor?"

Petra said, "Theoretically, if two murders get cleared, I can't see any problem with that."

Moe said, "Clearing *three* murders would be even better."

"No doubt," said Petra.

"Three?" said Ramone. Confusion clouded the mope's face.

Uh-oh.

Moe made the plunge. "Caitlin Frostig."

"Who?" Not a hint of evasiveness in the squinty eyes. Real confusion.

"Caitlin Frostig," said Moe. "Adella's babysitter. Pretty blond girl."

Wohr said, "Oh, her."

"You know her."

"I seen her once, maybe twice. She also got killed?"

"Is that a real question, Ramone?"

"Yes, sir, yes, yes, yes, sir—I met her once. Coming to pick up Addie, like you said, Addie's going out, that girl's there with the baby. One, two times is all—yeah, it was two. That's it, sir. She got dead, I don't know about it."

"But you do know about a dead mommy. And a dead baby," said Moe, remembering the Reverend Wohr's account of his brother's cold attitude toward the infant. "Little, tiny baby with a name. Gabriel. Like the angel. Now he *is* a little angel, Ramone."

Wohr didn't respond.

"Dead baby, dead mommy, dead

babysitter, Ramone. Quite a scoreboard for a guy who doesn't *know* about stuff like that."

Wohr's bony butt levitated out of the chair and for a second Moe thought he'd need to restrain the idiot. But Wohr sank down heavily, hugged himself, shook his head. Tugged at his cheeks.

"You're in it for triple murder, Ramone."

"Oh, Jesus God."

"Maybe you're not that bad of a person," said Moe. "Maybe it really bothers you."

"Aw, man—you should—in here." Slapping his forehead. "Bad pictures, sir. Even though I never actually *seen* nothing."

"Pictures of what?"

"You know."

"Tell me, Ramone."

"Dead people. I worked hard at turning them off. The pictures."

"Trying to switch the channel."

"Yeah, yeah."

"Did getting *paid* to forget help, Ramone?"

"Huh?"

"One of your transactions," said Moe. "Keep your mouth shut for the opportunity to keep pimping to rich folk."

Stolid silence, but no denial.

Moe went on, "You might've cleared your own head but the law doesn't see it that way, Ramone. You're in the middle of it. It won't be any big stretch making this a three-strikes deal, Ramone. But even without that, we're talking . . ." To Petra: "Like forever?"

She said, "I'd guess forever plus a hundred years or so." She edged closer to Wohr. "Poor little Gabriel. Talk about a tiny skeleton, like a toy, at first you don't even think it's real."

"You found him?" Wohr blurted.

"Any reason we shouldn't?"

"No, no, no. I just . . ."

Moe hardened his voice. Crowded Wohr. Got closer to Petra, in the process. Her girl-scent helped take the edge off Wohr's stench. "You just what, Ramone?"

"I never heard he got found."

"But you heard he got killed."

Silence.

"Here's the deal, Ramone: Some people don't like surprises, but we do. Helps relieve the boredom. We've got all sorts of surprises about things you can't even imagine."

Wohr's eyes passed from Moe to Petra, back to Moe. The guy's body was slumped and shaky and pathetic, but the eyes belonged to a stronger, shrewder man.

All the dope he'd pumped, all the booze he'd soaked up, his IQ could be down to double digits and he'd still retain a certain type of cunning.

He said, "You know what you know, but I don't know nothing."

Moe sensed it: The danger point, any minute the mope could clam, ask for a lawyer.

Time to take another plunge. "Well, then, Ramone, we'll share—so everyone will know everything. You got paid off to keep quiet about the murders, but it was only a small-time payment. You never cashed in like you could've."

Wohr's eyes froze but he couldn't plug up the sweat glands slicking his face and neck.

Petra's perfume no longer masking the stink.

Wohr's mustache trembled.

Moe said, "Maybe you didn't cash in because you were scared. Maybe you're basically a small-time guy, happy with small-time compensation—happy to keep peddling skin to rich folk. Maybe making nice to rich folk lets you pretend your own life is expensive, not cheap like Adella and Gabriel and Caitlin."

Wohr shook his head.

"Thing is, Ramone, that flesh you kept peddling was Alicia's and she had enough, wanted you to cash in big. She was tired of partying in shitty motels like the Eagle because you were too scared to make demands. She got frustrated. Downright pissed-off frustrated. To the point where she bitch-slapped you on the street, front of the whole neighborhood."

"No one saw nothing," Wohr snapped.

Moe smiled. "You think?"

Realizing his error, Wohr shook his head hard enough to fling sweat. Droplets landed on Moe's khakis. Petra's black pants, too. Neither cop moved to wipe it off.

Wohr said, "What I'm sayin', Alicia wouldn't do that, she never hit me."

"Then how do you think we know about it, Ramone? I was there." Letting that sink in. Describing Eiger's and Wohr's clothes made Wohr shake like he'd detoxed too fast.

Moe said, "She called you stupid, disrespected you, then hauled off and bitch-slapped you." Moe rattled off the address on Taft. "I saw it, Ramone. Not a love pat, a real hard smack, you could hear it up the block. And what do you do? You just slink off like some beat-down dog, go get juiced up at Bob's, then you buy some dope from another mope over near Cherokee, then you wander around Hollywood all day and into the night, walking and drinking and smoking, like some useless, abused mutt. And *then,* because you *still* can't get rid of the anger at being disrespected but you can't stand up to Alicia, you go looking for someone you *can* control. Because Delishus looks ten and reminds you of all those little girls you peep when they don't know you're lurking outside their bedroom windows."

"I don't do that—"

"Your niece Sarah says you do."

Ramone's mouth dropped open.

Moe smiled. "It's your day for surprises, my friend. Just like you were surprised to find Officer Kennedy right there when Delishus's head was where it shouldn't."

"Aw . . . no." Moan of despair, not denial.

Placing both hands on Wohr's shoulders, Moe exerted pressure. "We know *everything.* And you still don't have the smarts to stop playing with us in order to better your situation."

Wohr lowered his chin to his chest. Sniffled.

Moe gave an eye-signal to Petra.

She said, "I, for one, am feeling sorry for you, Ramone, because you're not a violent person. But who I'm really feeling sorry for is Alicia. Poor girl was getting smart, all she wanted to do was stop selling her body. How long has she been on you to make some serious dough from those murdering bastards?"

Head shake.

"How long, Ramone?" she said, gently. "Probably right from the beginning, right? Because Alicia saw an easy big payoff— I mean, we're talking multiple murder, rich folk, kind of a no-brainer."

"Too scary," muttered Wohr.

"To pressure the rich folk?"

Nod.

"Unfortunately, Alicia didn't see it that way," said Petra. "Maybe because you were still selling her to the people who did those murders."

"Alicia doesn't get it," said Wohr.

Present tense dictated the next move.

Moe released Wohr's shoulders from his grip, drew two Polaroids out of a blazer pocket.

Alicia Eiger's multi-stabbed back, and a full-frontal close-up of her gray, lifeless face.

"Ramone, Alicia is never going to get anything anymore."

Wohr stared. Began shaking violently. "Oh, Jesus God." Lurching forward, he retched. Both detectives scooted back. Nothing but stink emerged from his gaping mouth. "Oh, Jesus, oh Jesus God Jesus."

Feeling masterfully cruel—enjoying the feeling—Moe said, "Oh, yeah, four murders. Add a dead girlfriend to the score-card. And you set her up."

Wohr's legs shot back, hit the legs of his chair. "No way, no, no, no—"

Moe and Petra moved back in. Inches

away, totally in the mope's face. Moe held the Polaroids in one hand, used the other to take hold of Wohr's jaw and rotate Wohr back toward the images.

Expecting Wohr to shut his eyes. But Wohr punished himself and looked.

Some capacity for guilt?

Moe said, "Hitting her back wouldn't have been nice, but it sure would've beat making that call, Ramone."

Wohr murmured unintelligibly. Moe released the pressure on the guy's jaws. Wohr rubbed his mandible. "You didn't have to hurt me."

"You don't need me to get hurt, Ramone. You're hurting yourself just fine. Maybe, like Detective Connor said, you're not a bad person, but you sure are a *weak* person. Always taking the easy way out. But funny thing, that always seems to put you in a hard place, doesn't it?"

Slow nod.

"We've got your throwaway cell, Ramone. We know about the call you made to set up Alicia."

Hoping hoping hoping.

Wohr licked his lips. Blinked hard.

Victory!

"That's accessory to Murder One, Ramone. Now we're giving you the chance to help yourself, friend. But you've just *got* to stop lying—to yourself. *We* already know the truth."

Wohr groaned. Knuckled an eye.

"Maybe you never intended to get Alicia killed, maybe you just thought they'd scare her. But that's not how a jury's going to think."

"She hit me," said Wohr. "Again. I got tired of it."

"There you go," said Petra. "Mitigating circumstances." More like motive and evidence of premeditation. "If we had a history of domestic violence calls to your crib, that might help you. Without that, who's going to believe a big strong man was afraid of a small woman?"

Wohr said, "You don't know Alicia. She's fierce."

"Was fierce," said Moe, waving the Polaroids. "Even if we believe you, who cares? We're not who you're going to have to convince."

Wohr didn't answer.

Moe checked his watch. Stood and did a Milo stretch. In addition to looking relaxed, it felt good after all those hours sitting.

Petra got up, too.

Moe's yawn was genuine. He pocketed the photos. "We gave you a chance to better your situation and once again, you made the wrong choice. Hope you enjoy incarceration, Ramone, because that's all you've got ahead of you."

Petra opened the door, called for a jailer.

Raymond Wohr said, "Gimme a pen and paper. I'll write you a different book."

When the detectives agreed, the fool started crying.

Dr. Steve Rau said, "A private eye."

"I *work* for a private eye, Steve. I'm an actress by training."

"Obviously a good one."

More stunned than angry. But no one liked being lied to. His wife had made a fool of him, Liana had no way of knowing if this was turning into bad déjà vu.

She'd positioned herself close to the door, just in case.

After the night they'd spent together, kind of a cart-after-the-horses thing.

Steve said, "Liana . . ." As if trying on

her real name for size. "So that first time was an assignment?"

"My boss and I are looking into Caitlin Frostig, that girl who disappeared." Making herself sound more important than she was.

Performer's reflex, because life was an audition.

"And I brought her up before you asked," said Steve. "You must've thought that was a strange . . . I also told you about a couple who disappeared, talk about purveyor of good cheer. Later— when I got home that night—I did a little computer research. Turns out the couple was running from the law and got caught." Smile. "But you probably know that."

"I do."

"I felt like an idiot," he said. "Meeting you and bringing up people vanishing. No reason you'd ever call me, you probably thought I was bizarre . . . so you were back there tonight to work?"

"That was the plan, Steve. It kind of got sidetracked."

"Pardon?"

"This," she said. "Everything that's happened tonight. That had nothing to do with work."

Though if you happen to have info I can use, I won't complain.

"Oh," he said. "Well, I was *thrilled* to see *you.* Liana." Tasting her name. "I like that better than Laura—not that Laura's not a fine . . . you really are Liana?"

"Want to see a birth certificate?"

"Sorry."

"I should be, Steve. You have every right not to trust me."

"Since that first time, I've been hanging out at Riptide more regularly than before, hoping to see you again. I pretty much gave up. I did have to do some traveling—delivering papers. Have you been back before tonight?"

"No," she said.

"So this is almost . . . karma . . . though I guess it really isn't that remarkable, just simple probability. I'm there high-frequency, so anytime you drop in, there's a good chance we'll meet."

Liana smiled. "Sounds like another learned paper."

He slumped. "Mr. Smooth."

"You're a good guy. Stop being so hard on yourself."

She got up, sat beside him on his parents' fusty old sofa. He reached for her hand, hesitated. She made the move, squeezed his fingers.

"Liana, tonight, seeing you again—it was as . . . life was finally working out. If that's coming on too strong, I don't care. Nor do I care what brought you there in the first place."

"You're not coming on too strong."

"Really?"

"Really."

"So we can keep seeing each other? That's what I care about—I don't see why it should interfere with your assignment—is that what you call it?"

"It's just a job, Steve."

"Sounds like an interesting job."

"Not usually."

He played with her fingers. "Undercover operative. Your mission should you choose to accept it." Slowly spreading grin. "Do you get to wear costumes?"

What do you think this *is?*

Liana said, "The truth is, Steve, I do it because I can't do what I really want."

Putting herself out there.

"Acting's a tough thing," he said. "I admire your perseverance."

"The only acting I've done for years is voice-overs. For cartoons."

"Really? Can I hear a few?"

"Some other time." She kissed him. It made *her* feel better.

They sat there for a while, holding hands.

He said, "There's no way you could stay the night?"

"I have an audition tomorrow."

"Private eye or voice-over?"

"The latter," she said. "Goofy squirrel." She rattled off a line of stupid rodent dialogue.

He cracked up. "How about this: I'll set the alarm and we'll both get up early."

"Not tonight, Steve." She reached for her bag, pulled out her genuine business card. "Here's my number. I promise it's real."

He studied it. "You're in the Valley."

"Does that disqualify me?"

"Hey," he said, "Sherman Oaks born

and bred until Mom and Dad decided to socially climb. When can I see you again? Give me a time or I won't be able to concentrate."

"If work doesn't get in the way, how about tomorrow, say eight?"

"I've got meetings till eight. Nine, okay? I'll make a reservation—you like Italian?"

"Who doesn't?"

"Excellent. Il Travino, not far from you in Tarzana."

"Looking forward to it."

The next kiss was his move. Longer and softer. For a beaten-down quasi-nerd, his technique was getting good. That second time, in bed, he'd made her feel things she hadn't felt for a long time. Even that bear-pelt was something she could get used to.

He said, "Now I feel great—let me walk you down."

"Steve, at the risk of being totally tacky, I'm going to do something totally work-related right now." She drew out the photo of Adella Villareal and her blue-blanketed baby. "This is another girl related to the case. They found her strangled in Griffith Park."

Steve winced. Nodded. "I've definitely seen her at Riptide. Several times. Never at the bar, always in a corner table, back in the VIP area. Years ago, when the celebs were still—this is *that* kind of case?"

"Could be," said Liana.

"She had a baby? I wouldn't have thought so."

"Why not?"

"She seemed more of a party girl . . . I guess anyone can be a parent. The baby's okay?"

"No one's seen the baby since his mama got killed."

"Oh, my God. Okay, okay, let me remember what I can . . . I never saw her with Caitlin. She was always in the back room. Dolled up, laughing. The reason I remember her is because she was extremely . . . she was a good-looking girl."

"Sexy," said Liana.

"In a flashy way. Maybe overdressed . . . you've been to Riptide, it's casual. And she was never alone—this could get interesting for you and your boss, Liana. Because she was always with the same people."

He told her who.

She took hold of his face and kissed him hard.

"What'd I do to deserve that?"

"Delivered good news, sweetie. Smooch the messenger. Maybe I will stay the night. But first I need to text my boss."

37

If Mason Book had chosen to press his face against a cold glass pane of the house, he might've caught a glimpse of Aaron Fox watching him.

The actor sat in a square black leather chair, robe flapped open on an emaciated body. Sobbing.

Guy looked way older than on screen, not just because of no makeup and heartless lighting. His cheekbones jutted in a way that couldn't be healthy. Vertical creases scored his face, hair well overdue for a color-rinse was showing some gray among the blond.

Thirty-three and starting to look like a withered old man.

Career transition, friend. Time to move on to character roles.

As a matter of fact, I've got a screenplay for you, but you're not going to dig the ending.

Aaron tried to figure a way to gain entry without setting off something he couldn't control.

He'd come with a host of little helpers, each in a designated pocket of his black, waterproof Swiss cargo pants: flashless pen camera, his cell phone for photo backup, mini infrared binoculars, similarly undersized tape recorder outfitted with one of Mr. Dmitri's speakers.

Plastic wrist ties, in the event it came to that.

Ditto the Filipino fighting knife.

One of the pockets twitched. His cell phone vibing.

Could he chance taking it out and allowing the screen to create illumination?

As spaced out as Book appeared, too risky.

Plus, whoever was calling, it couldn't be more important than what was happening right now. He no longer needed to hear *about* things; time to make things *happen.*

Reminding himself to maintain a strict dual focus—observe Book while looking out for the return of Ax Dement or any unwelcome visitor—he sidled along the glass.

There were seams, but so tight that even this close they were tough to make out.

The entire house was constructed of huge glass panels, some of them had to be doors. But which ones?

He hazarded another few feet closer to the hovering nose of the house. Hearing one of his rubber soles let off a tiny rubbery squeak and stopping short.

Mason Book sat there.

Now Aaron was close enough to see blotches and zits marring the actor's once boyish face. Book's nose was a sharp, bony protuberance. Matched the angle of the house's snout.

As if the actor was a toy—an action figure—manufactured to fit the structure.

Book sat there, continued to suffer.

Stardom, indeed.

Suddenly he was up, standing, shaking, robe wide open.

Turning and facing the exact spot where Aaron crouched.

Hair shooting all over the place, eyes glazed, all skin and ribs, like a turkey carcass.

Looking straight *at* Aaron but not *seeing* him.

The actor belted his robe, headed for the rear of the house, passed through room after room.

The structure was a voyeur's dream. Ramone W would love it.

Maybe Ramone had been here.

Who *knew* what kind of ugly went on here?

Book stopped in a cold, bright kitchen. Black cabinets, limestone floors, two Wolf ranges, two fridges, both Traulsens, one steel-fronted, one a glass see-through.

When remodeling, Aaron had priced the brand. Opted to supercharge his Porsche and buy five Antonelli suits instead.

Book stood in front of the steel fridge. Did nothing for a long time, finally opened the door. On his second try, straining both no-muscle arms.

Breathing hard; Aaron could see the rapid rise and fall of his robe.

Something wrong with his heart due to all the starvation?

Book took something out of the fridge. Soda can—no, same size but the cover was white, lots of small print. Larger red letters.

Book held the can straight out in front, as if it were dangerous. Carrying it that way, he trudged back to the front of the house.

Sank into the same square chair, almost tripping over his own feet in the process, nearly losing hold of the can.

Panting, openmouthed, he held the can to his cheek. Stretched his arms out again and studied the white cylinder.

Offering Aaron a closer view of the red lettering. Aaron whipped out the mini-binocs.

ISO-CAL INTENSIVE
Balanced Protein Nutritional Supplement

Book's prescription snack, probably brought by that house-calling anorexia doctor.

The actor put the can on the floor, cried some more.

All weepy because he couldn't bring himself to take in calories?

Aaron was in no mood to be understanding. Rich man's pathology; no eating disorders in the Sudan.

Book retrieved the can, labored to pop the top, finally succeeded. Bent his elbow and brought the can closer to his lips.

Stopped. Stood. Upended the can and poured thick white liquid onto the floor.

Standing there until the can was empty, he placed it gingerly in the middle of the mess he'd created.

Slipping out of his robe, he strode, naked, with sudden purpose, toward the glass wall where Aaron was stationed.

Straight *at* Aaron.

Aaron hustled backward, was ten feet away when Book used both hands to push at the glass.

The wall swung open.

Mason Book stepped out into the night, skeletal, goose-bumped, bleached-out hair feathery in the breeze.

Off in some other galaxy, the actor made his way toward the structure's proboscis. His progress was painfully slow, his body recalcitrant.

Finally, he got to the snout, slipped under it.

Aaron moved in closer. Book continued toward the cliff-edge. The actor's eyes widened as they filled with the heat and light and color of the city.

Book pressed his hands together. Rocked on his heels. Shrunken genitals dangled. The guy's limbs were sticks, his back flecked by scatters of rosy rash.

Book kept his hands pressed together. Rocked some more.

Some sort of prayer ritual?

Book bent his knees, moved forward so his feet curled over the cliff-edge.

Spread his arms wide.

Oh, shit!

Aaron became a bullet.

Screaming bullet. Hoping his voice would freeze the idiot.

Just the opposite.

Book turned, saw Aaron. Smiled.

Bent his legs again and took off in flight.

38

Skin and bones helped.

But even a flimsy hundred-twenty-pound sack of dehydrated sinew could wrench your arms out of their sockets when you were flat on your belly in the dirt, all scuffed up and scraped from the slide, fighting to hold on.

Gripping the damned thing by its ankles as it dangled toward oblivion, and gravity kept kicking your ass.

Book wasn't resisting.

But he wasn't helping, either.

Idiot just hung there, silent, limp. Deadweight. A weird kind of patience—like he was just waiting for Aaron to let go of his ankles so he could do his thing.

Not so easy, you sick, pathetic, murderous bastard.

Having another set of hands on board would've fixed the situation in seconds. Moe's power-lifter guns . . .

Aaron said, "Hang . . . in there, buddy."

Book giggled.

"'S funny?"

"Hang in there," said Book, in that easily recognizable, reedy but charming voice. "I'm hanging."

Every syllable caused the idiot's body to jerk. Each twitch ratcheted up the agony in Aaron's shoulders, the searing strain in his abdomen, back, and hips.

Thank God the fool was a self-starver . . . Aaron felt his grip loosen, braced his toes in the dirt. Pulled up again on Book.

Again, Book slid up toward him, only to slip back as Aaron's muscles failed to stand up to the increased pressure. This time, the downward jolt nearly caused him to lose his hold. The pain in his shoulders was unbearable.

Sucking in breath, concentrating,

focusing, thinking of dead people, a dead baby, how this asshole wasn't going to weasel out so easily, he said, "Press your hands against the side of the mountain, buddy. So that you're not just hanging there loose."

"It's not a mountain," said Book. "It's a hill."

"Whatever."

Book giggled again. Like this was just another role. Asshole.

"*Do* it—brace yourself."

"Why?"

"I . . ." gritting his teeth, "said so."

Book didn't respond.

"Do it." Aaron's jaws clenched tighter. His hands felt ready to detach from his wrists. A few more seconds of this and . . . *"Do it!"*

"Okay, okay." Whining, like the spoiled brat he was.

"Both hands. Press . . . hard."

Book obeyed. Aaron's relief was immediate. Sucking in oxygen, he bore down, inhaled again and prayed and released his left hand and shimmied it up Book's scrawny calf. Getting a grip on bone and not much more.

He dug his fingernails into Book's flesh. It had to hurt. Book didn't even murmur.

Aaron let go of his right hand, dug that into Book's other calf.

"I'm going to count to three. On three, push back. Hard."

"Huh?"

"Like you're trying to flip yourself up."

"Wh—"

Aaron concentrated on reserving breath. Delivered his rapid speech: "Do it or I'll tell everyone about the baby and the world will find out you were no noble suicide."

Silence.

"*Do* it."

No answer.

"Baby Gabriel. *People* magazine, *Us,* the *Enquirer*—"

"Okay, okay," said Book, with a catch in his throat.

"On three. You push back." Shutting out the pain, as he marshaled his strength, Aaron felt his own legs flutter. Muscle strain? No, the damned cell was *vibing* again.

You've reached Fox Investigations. Mr. Fox is currently out of the office

and quite possibly about to screw up royally . . .

"Ready, Mason?"

"You know my name."

Imbecile.

"Of course I do. Ready?"

"Yes, sir."

"On three. Push hard."

"Yes, sir."

Here goes: Action. Camera. "One. Two. *Three.*"

Book's push was wimpy and Aaron's grip on the legs slipped, but he managed to pull Book up high enough to claw under the idiot's rib cage, continued yanking, mindlessly groping—tugging the guy upward.

Book's body flopped like that of a fought-out fish, Aaron got hold of Book's long, wild hair, yanked violently.

He dragged the bastard well clear of the cliff, dropped him harder than necessary, flat on his back. Fought for breath.

Mason Book, wearing a beard of grit and blood, looked up at Aaron with what seemed like wonderment.

Aaron stood over him, gasping, feeling

his heart in his throat about to rip loose and fly out of his mouth like some bloody bird. His clothes were torn, his body felt as if it had done a full-day shift in a cement mixer. Blood all over his palms, knees, cheeks, elbows. Maybe mixed with Book's. He hoped the bastard wasn't infected with anything.

Book smiled. "I know you."

"That so."

"Black Angel."

39

When Liana's third text to Aaron went unanswered, she was comfortable switching her cell off and retiring to bed with Steve.

If Mr. Fox is free to party, I'm off shift.

The chest-hair washcloth was back in place, she was wearing one of Steve's T-shirts, he was in p.j. bottoms, and both of them were trying to sleep.

The towel bounced as Steve made a *Huh-huh* sound that rumbled through torso and terry cloth.

"Are you laughing, young man?"

"Uh-uh."

"What's funny?"

"Imagining."

"What?"

"Not important."

"Hey, big guy, it's all about communication."

"It's kind of juvenile."

"Always happy to get in touch with my inner child." She nudged his ribs.

"Okay, okay." Now he sounded fully awake. "I was thinking about detective work. One thing I'm not bad at is research. Give me a topic, I burrow like a mole. I was imagining you and me—like Nick and Nora Charles. Some fantasy, huh?"

My aspirations, sir, are more along the line of this thing we have going, whatever it is, lasting long enough for me to find out if you're really as sweet and kind and understanding as you seem to be. If you are, I can do some expert patchwork on your self-esteem, which is really the only thing missing from the picture—and who knows, maybe you wouldn't be as nice if you got too puffed up. So I'd need to be careful about not overdoing it, turning you into the typical arrogant man. But I'll bet I could do it just right. Then I could remodel

*this place—meet your parents and con-
vince them it's in everyone's best interests, believe me, honey, I could get them
to like me, show them I'm the perfect girl
for their boy, look how much you smile
nowadays. As opposed to when that
grasping bitch was on the scene. My fantasy, Steve-o, involves you and me living
up here on the Wilshire Corridor, both our
cars in the garage, the doormen greeting
me by name, carrying my packages. Getting you to chill more, take some fun vaca-
tions, I'll show you how to live. Including*
that. *Lots* of that. *Between RAND and my
voice-overs, we'd do just fine in the
money department. I'd sell my condo, add
to the kitty, I'm talking a full loving partner-
ship, not some kept-woman situation. And
your parents would like me so much,
they'd kick in some dough for the . . .*

Steve whispered, "You asleep, Liana?"

She said, "You're right. That's some fantasy."

Raymond Wohr's signed statement was less than Moe had hoped for but still enough to justify waking up Deputy D.A. John Nguyen.

Nguyen had worked on the marsh murders, had raised all sorts of cautious lawyer objections during that investigation.

This time, he said, "I like it."

Moe said, "We need Wohr out of County and back to Hollywood lockup. Sooner the better."

"I'll get that started."

◆

Moe reentered the interview room, gave Petra the thumbs-up. She smiled.

Ramone W was drinking coffee and eating his third donut, powdered sugar bearding his grizzled face. He said, "What?"

The detectives ignored the question and took him through the statement a second time. No change in demeanor or narrative, as he continued to deny any direct role in the murder of Adella Villareal or her baby. But he did admit setting up what he continued to insist was just another sexual transaction.

Phoning Adella on short notice and telling her he'd lined up a monster gig, whole different class of john, the guy wanted her now.

She'd been wary: *"How come?"*

"I showed him your picture." A lie, but so what? This could work in her favor, how was he to know it wouldn't?

Another "relationship" begun at Riptide. Adella had lucked into Riptide after he, Ramone, had taken her and Alicia there for drinks to celebrate Adella's birthday. No one noticing Alicia, but Adella, all dolled up, that tiny black dress, a whole different story.

The night of the transaction, he said, "Client likes your picture."

"You showed him my picture?" she said. "Like some ad on Craigslist?"

"What's the diff, monster client, Addie."

"Right. The last 'monster' you set me up with was that four-hundred-pound slob who cried when I asked him for an extra hundred."

"Forget hundred, Addie. This is three thousand big ones."

No answer.

"You still there, Addie?"

"Three thousand," she said.

"At *least.* Asshole's good for a whole lot more, trust me."

"Three thousand," she repeated. "What do I need to do for three thousand?"

"Nothing special," said Ramone.

"Spell it out."

"Round the world, no anal."

"Three thousand . . . shit, I don't have a babysitter."

"Not to worry, me and Alicia'll take care of the kid. In fact, bring the kid, that way minute it's over, he's back with you."

"Leave Gabriel with you? You couldn't

change a diaper if someone wrote you instructions."

"Me and *Alicia.* Alicia has two kids."

"I never seen them."

"Two," said Ramone.

"Where are they?"

Who the hell knows? Ramone said, "All grown up."

"I don't know, Ramone, Gabriel's been cranky. I think he's teething or something."

"Alicia can handle it. Three big ones, Addie, who knows how big the tip'll go."

"I'm not splitting the tip."

"Aw, man . . ."

"Nope," she said. "No way. It's like a restaurant, the server gets the tip."

"That sucks donkey," said Ramone, "but fine. Be at the Hyatt, the one on the Strip. Here's the room number. He'll let you in."

"Three thousand," she said. "For sure no anal? Since giving birth I've got some tearing."

"Front door only, Addie."

"Three biggies for normal."

"Soft john, he usually don't pay for it but I showed him your picture and he's hot for you."

"Hot? He's whack?"

"No, no, he's ripe, that's all I mean. Even with that, you take too long, he's gonna change his mind. Bring the baby, Alicia'll meet you in the hall near the room—bring bottles, diapers, whatever."

"How about four?" she said.

"Hold on." Standing in Alicia's apartment by himself, he covered the phone with one hand and faked out consulting the client. "He says three and a half but you got to get there soon. You in?"

"Yeah," she said.

"Now I can tell you who the john is." Whispering a name.

She said, "No way!"

"Yes way. Is Ramone the man or is he the man?"

"Jesus—okay, yeah, yeah, I'll wear my good undies."

Wohr finished his donut. "That's it. Same as I told you the first time."

Moe Reed said, "You had no idea what was going to happen?"

"Nope."

"What'd you do with the baby?"

"Addie had the baby when she went in. I wasn't there."

"And neither was Alicia."

"Nope."

"So bringing the baby was the client's idea."

"The plan was for Alicia to be in the hall but she had to go to the bathroom, so she missed meeting Addie."

"Sure," said Moe. "*That* happened."

Long silence.

Petra said, "There were two plans. The one you told her and the one you carried out."

"I wasn't even there."

"And neither was Alicia. Alicia never even came along."

Silence.

Moe said, "That whole bullshit about Alicia was to get the baby there."

No answer.

"Maybe Adella even said she'd call a babysitter and you said don't bother, we'll handle it."

"Uh-uh," said Wohr. "That never came up."

"Maybe Adella said she'd call Caitlin Frostig."

"Nope, don't know her."

"You met her twice."

"That's not knowing."

"Caitlin had nothing to do with this."

"I don't know her, I made a call, that's it."

"And drove to the Hyatt."

"No!" Ramone blurted. "I never went."

"That's a new twist."

"It's true."

Moe resisted the urge to throttle the guy. "Don't insult us, Ramone. We see lips flapping but we don't hear the truth and the truth's the only thing going to set you free."

"I told you the truth."

"You told us a *story*. The truth is the *baby*. The whole *point* was the baby. Otherwise you wouldn't have told Adella to *bring* the baby."

Wohr looked at the floor.

Petra said, "Sending a baby to a gig. That's one sick deal."

"Aw, man . . ."

Moe raised his voice. "Tell us about the baby."

"I don't know nothing about no baby."

"Not any baby, Ramone. Baby Gabriel, Adella's baby Gabriel, the cute little baby you had Adella take to the Hyatt." Waving the signed statement. "By your own admission, Ramone."

Wohr hugged himself, slouched lower. "I made a call, that's *it.*"

Moe placed a thumb on Wohr's collarbone. Found a pressure point. Pushed. Wohr whimpered.

Moe said, "The point was Adella bringing the baby."

"I guess."

"You guess."

"I did what I was told."

"For a thousand bucks."

Silence.

Moe said, "You didn't wonder why someone would slip you a grand just to make a call?"

"Addie worked for me."

"We know you bragged about that—representing her, you were Mr. Hollywood. But it's not like she was in your stable. Because you don't *have* a stable, Ramone."

"I got her other gigs. Rock guys, like at the Whiskey."

"Great," said Petra. "You're a heavy pimp. Doesn't that come with responsibility? You make a call, never see her again, you're not trying to find out what happened?"

"I figured she went back," said Wohr.

"Back where?"

"Arizona," said Wohr. "To see her family. She did that before, didn't tell me or nothing."

"You set her up on a high-priced date, make sure she brings the baby," said Petra. "Then she drops out of sight, you're not the least bit curious."

"All I did was make a *call.*"

"Thousand-dollar call," said Moe. "Go to the Hyatt on the Strip, here's the room number, you're free and clear. She gets her pretty self murdered and dumped in Griffith Park and you don't know about it?"

Silence.

"You expect us to believe you thought she made a family visit, meanwhile everyone knows she got killed and no one's seen the baby?"

Moe pushed down a bit more. Wohr whimpered. "You're good at making calls, Ramone. You're a frickin' phone-call *specialist.*"

"Huh?"

"We got the trace an hour ago, Ramone." No longer needing to lie. "Ratting out Alicia, because she was making noise, getting on your case for not cashing in on the *first* call."

Wohr hung his head.

"After how she disrespected you, can't say I blame you," said Moe.

Petra said, "Me neither. I did that to my man, I can't even imagine."

Wohr's face tilted up.

Petra said, "My man and me, no one raises a hand to anyone."

Moe said, "Doing it right on the street. And it's not like you hit her back. You stayed cool, I respect that—Detective Connor respects that."

Petra said, "That's a whole lot of patience."

"You walked away," said Moe. "That was manly. Then you made one of your famous calls. What's the harm in that—there's facts, you state them to someone, how they handle it isn't your business. Problem is, they handled it by carving her up, Ramone, I'm talking taco meat. You want to see those pictures again?"

"No!" Wohr's hands wrapped around the back of his head. He bent low. "Aw, man."

"Horrible scene," said Moe. "Even for

detectives like us who see murder all the time. But that's not your business, you just made a call, how they chose to handle it was their decision. And that'll help you, Ramone. That's bound to help you, people understanding the difference between making a call and doing a fifteen-wound knife-murder."

"I didn't *know.*"

"Didn't know what?"

"Nothing."

"What would happen after you made the call?"

"Yeah."

"You make calls, that's what you do," said Petra. "You're the phone man, king of the phone lines."

Wohr kept his face hidden. She reached into her pocket, drew out her own phone, and Moe waited for some dramatic flourish. Instead, she read a text message. Mouthed, *John's here.*

Moe sat back down, positioned his knees an inch from Wohr's. Tolerated the stench of the guy's breath, the sour despair emanating from Wohr's pores. "Notice, Ramone, that we're telling you about Alicia, not asking. 'Cause we don't need you."

Wohr looked up again. "Yeah," he said. "Yeah, what?"

"She *hit* me, I called." Touching his cheek. "She hadda know that *wasn't* gonna work out."

"Good man," said Moe. "Being straight is what's going to help you. Now pick up that pencil and give us all the details you left out the first time."

Wohr complied. When he was through, Moe pulled him to his feet and cuffed him, recited the charges, read him his rights.

Wohr said, "Murder? For using the phone?"

Moe and Petra walked him to the door. Deputy D.A. John Nguyen was outside, talking to a jailer, holding papers. He looked at Wohr. "This is him?" As if disappointed.

Petra said, "This here's the Emperor of the Phone." Laughing. Moe thought she looked really pretty, fresh and confident and calm, not a wrinkle in her pantsuit.

His own head was filled with bad music: a little bit of melody but too many missing notes.

Aaron was the shepherd, Mason Book, the sheep.

The actor stood naked and skeletal in the front room of the rocket-ship house as Aaron dressed him in the discarded robe. Docile as a pet. Spills from the protein drink Book had dumped left creamy, clotted stains on the black chair and the smooth stone floors. Aaron was careful not to step in the stuff as he steered Book to a nearby sofa, then realized that position offered a great city-lights view.

Suicide view; no sense reminding him

of what he'd missed. Taking Book by the elbow, he guided the actor into an adjoining space, smaller, set up with red suede chairs, a black desk with a gray tweed swivel seat and black-lacquered bookcases, mostly empty but for a handful of DVDs on one shelf.

Recent movies, all crap, probably freebies from the studios or the Academy. None of Book's films on display.

He put the actor in the swivel seat, aimed it at a red wall, slipped a hand into a pocket of his cargo pants, and activated the mini-recorder. Nice and silent; it always paid to have good gear.

"Tell me what happened, Mason."

"When?"

"The night Adella Villareal got murdered."

Book licked his lips. "I didn't see that."

So much for the power of guilt. *Here we go with the mind-games.* "Tell me what you did see, Mason." Smiling reassuringly at the actor, as he tried to forget the pain that continued to course through his body. Fingers of fatigue scratching through the adrenaline rush.

Telling himself this would work out, had to work out, Book was a whack, could be opened. Hopefully no one would show up at the wrong moment.

Book sat there. Aaron's hand glided over his nylon holster. "Mason, it's time to be true to yourself."

Book said, "I saw everything but not that."

"Not what?"

"Killing her."

"So you know she was killed."

Book's cadaverous face tilted up. Pale hair swooshed as Book spread his arms in a *Who-me?* gesture. Appealing boyish, despite the self-inflicted ravages.

With enough makeup, the right camera angle, the guy might be able to pull off one of his charming roles.

"I'm your angel, Mason. You need to tell me everything."

Book sniffled, let loose more eye-water.

Self-pitying bastard. Aaron felt like smacking him.

Book turned away and dry-heaved. The actor's rib cage expanded like bellows as cloudy amber liquid dribbled out of his mouth, flowed over his chin, plinked the floor.

Meltdown on its way. Damn. Where is Delaware when you need him?

Aaron said, "Tell me what you know, Mason. You'll feel a lot better."

Book retched again. Breathed loud and raspy, lost control and got sucked into a coughing fit. Aaron slapped his back until the paroxysm stopped. Book took to comfort like a wounded puppy, pressing his head against Aaron's thigh. Grasping Aaron's sleeve with a filthy-nailed hand.

Was he like *that*?

Aaron patted Book's hand. Book pressed closer. "You're here for me."

"Of course I am, Mason. But I need to know everything."

He peeled Book's hand from his arm, pulled up a red chair and faced the actor. Scooting forward until his knees were an inch from the actor's bony bumps. Memories of drab, departmental interview rooms. This place was pretty but no less oppressive.

"Go ahead, Mason."

"He said it was just a meeting with her."

"He, being?"

"A friend. I didn't even know her."

"What's this friend's name, Mason?"

"His real name's Ahab."

"But everyone calls him Ax."

"Ax. Yeah—you know him?"

Jackpot! Aaron could almost feel the recorder whirring in glee.

"We angels know all sorts of things."

"He's not famous," said Book. "He wants to be, but he's not."

"One of those," said Aaron. "Bet you know a lot of them."

"Oh, yeah . . . ," said Book. "I thought he'd protect me. He's fat-strong. Eats what he wants."

"Lucky him . . . so Ax said he was meeting with Adella."

"He said a girl from that place."

"What place?"

"This place we used to go to."

"A club?"

"More like a bar," said Book.

"A bar where you and Ax went to drink and hang out?"

Book's eyes fixed on Aaron. "You look like Denzel."

"People say that."

"Denzel could play an angel," said Book. "He's a really talented guy."

"Yes, he is," said Aaron. "This place where you and Ax went, it has a name."

"Riptide."

"Adella hung out there, too."

"I don't know her name," said Book. "I never was with her there."

"Ax was."

"I never saw that."

"But he told you."

"Yeah."

"The night it happened, Mason, what kind of meeting did Ax say it was?"

"You know."

"I don't unless you tell me, Mason."

"To party. All of us."

Aaron said, "You and Ax were going to do a threesome with Adella."

"I didn't know her name. He said a real piece of ass he knew from Riptide, she was wild."

"Perfect for a threesome."

"It never happened," said Book. As if he still regretted that.

"What did happen, Mason?"

"We went to a hotel."

"Which one?"

"The Hyatt."

"Which Hyatt?" said Aaron, certain he knew the answer.

Book said, "Sunset."

Five-minute drive from Swallowsong. "Next to the Comedy Store."

"Yeah."

"The party was at the hotel."

"When we got there, Ax said no, let's do it different, out in the open."

"Outdoor party."

"Sounded good to me," said Book. "Ax went in and came out with her." Book shivered. "You know about the baby, right?"

Aaron's heart pinged with joy. He kept his face grave. "Like I said, Mason, I know all kinds of things. So Adella came out of the hotel with Ax and the baby."

Nod.

"Where were you?"

"In the truck."

"Where was the truck?"

"Parking lot of the hotel."

"Ax wasn't afraid of leaving someone famous like you in a truck in a hotel parking lot?"

"He told me to lay down in the back. We do that."

"When?"

"When we don't want me to be seen."

And you just obeyed because you're a brain-damaged fool.

Book said, "It was all wrapped up. Blue blanket. Guess it was a boy."

"She goes to a party with a baby."

"Pretty weird," Book agreed. "She got in the back of the truck. I sat up and she was real happy."

"Why?"

"Because she saw it was me."

No brag, just stating the facts.

"You were the reason she was there."

"Yup."

"She thought she was hooking up for a date with just you."

"Ax likes that," said Book. "I meet girls, he meets girls."

"Girls Ax couldn't meet on his own."

Book smiled. "He's a little fat."

"So he uses you as a lure."

"Yup."

"He did that with Adella."

Book said, "Because he wanted to kill her."

Aaron's airway constricted. He forced himself to breathe easy. "He told you that."

"I figured it out. When she didn't come out."

"I thought she did come out of the hotel."

"She came out of there," said Book. "But not the park."

"The park," said Aaron. "Let's back up for a minute, Mason. You picked up Adella at the Hyatt, where you thought the date was going to be. But Ax wanted to party outdoors so you drove to a park."

"Yup."

Killed where she was dumped? Moe had said no. "Griffith Park."

"Not that park," said Book. "One near the beach. She said it was too far. I paid her some money and she was okay. Even with the baby in front and crying a little."

"The baby was in front of the truck?"

"In a baby seat," said Book.

"Ax brought a baby seat."

"He told her don't worry, we got a baby seat. Said he was a daddy himself. He had other stuff, too."

"Like what?"

"Diapers, bottles."

"Did you find that weird?"

Book blinked. "I guess. I wasn't thinking about babies."

"*Is* Ax a daddy?"

"No," said Book. "He murdered her, so I guess lying was no big deal."

First time the idiot had expressed anything resembling insight. Maybe his head was clearing. Aaron preferred him zoned out and blabbing, decided to keep the questions minimally threatening. "I think I've got the scene, Mason. You and Adella are in the backseat of the truck, the baby's in front, in a baby seat, everyone's chilled out."

"Not her," said Book. "She was a little . . . like nervous. I gave her more money."

"How much?"

"I don't know . . . maybe five thousand?"

"Five thousand dollars?"

"Maybe two. Three, six, I don't know, it was a bunch of hundreds, I get them in stacks for allowance."

"You get cash delivered."

"By Myron," said Book. "He's my business manager. Sometimes Ax goes to the ATM."

"Ax has your PIN number."

"I don't like to go places."

"Okay," said Aaron. "Back to that night. Which park at what beach?" Knowing the answer.

"Way out," said Book. "Past where his dad lives, his dad's got a big place somewhere."

"You've been to his dad's place?"

"Nope, it's on the land side. I like the beach side."

"This way-out beach—"

"Leo Carrillo," said Book. "He was an actor."

"Who was?"

"Leo Carrillo."

"That so."

"Yup." A trace of smugness had oozed into the actor's voice. Guy was a shriveled wreck, but he could still one-up an outsider. "He played Mexicans in cowboy movies. They named a beach after him."

Aaron said, "I know Carrillo. Pretty place."

"Real pretty," Book agreed. "The park's on the land side but the water's right across the highway, you can hear it. I like that sound, maybe I'll move to the Colony or something, so I can sleep."

"Did Adella think she was going to Ax's dad's place?"

Book gaped. "You really know stuff."

Aaron smiled. "Then when Ax passed the turnoff for his dad's place . . ."

"She said, 'Hey, where we going.'"

"And Ax said . . ."

"Nothing. He just kept driving. It wasn't that far after."

"Then what, Mason?"

Book licked his lips. Rotated his head, like some yoga exercise. Creaked audibly.

"Ax pulls in front of some gates, gets out of the truck, she's saying 'What the fuck?' He opens the door, pulls her out. Real hard."

Book's eyes closed. "I hate guns."

"Ax had a gun."

"When he brings it I always say put that away."

"What happened next?"

"The baby cried. Ax put the gun in her back and told her to walk."

"Into the park."

"Yup. She said 'Fuck you!' and started to cuss him out. Ax twisted her arm real hard and real quick and she started screaming.

The baby was *really* screaming. I put my hands over my ears."

Demonstrating.

Gently, Aaron lowered Book's hands. "Then what did Ax do?"

"Hit her in back of the head with the gun and when she fell he put his hands around her neck." Another lip-lick. "Cars were driving by on PCH. It was weird."

"Too dark for them to see anything, but you could see it."

"I didn't look. The baby was crying. Ax finished with her, put her back in the truck. Next to me. It smelled."

"What did?"

"She shit herself. The baby's *really* crying."

"Must've been scary for you, seeing as you didn't expect anything but a three-way party."

Book went silent.

"Your feelings are important, Mason. To me."

"I was . . . it was like . . . I was pretty wasted."

"On what?"

"A little blow, a little ice. To get up."

"Up from what?"

"Xanax. Restoril, Valium, Ambien . . . stuff."

Unwilling to admit to sniffing heroin. Aaron had seen that before. Upscale junkies 'fessing to everything *but* H.

Book said, "We did some E, too. It wasn't making me happy."

"Because you'd just seen Ax murder Adella."

"My whole head was . . . I was surprised."

"By what happened."

"She was so pretty," said Book. "I was surprised at how she got to smelling real bad. After that . . ."

"After that, what, Mason?"

"We-ell . . . my head got real noisy. I stopped sleeping. Stopped eating, too."

"Because you felt bad about what happened."

"I went to the hospital," said Book. "I wasn't sick but my doctor said go."

"Because you weren't eating and sleeping."

"They wanted to feed me in the veins," said Book. "I said no, not there yet."

"Not ready to be fed."

Book's arms shot out. Begging to be touched.

Aaron sat there. "Feeling guilty's what *good* people do, Mason."

"She came to meet *me.* She wanted to be *famous.*"

"What happened after Ax put Adella back in the truck?"

Book's arms dropped. "He said, 'We got to dump her somewhere.'"

"That's when you went to Griffith Park."

"Really long drive," said Book. "It smelled gross and the baby was screaming. Ax told it to shutthefuckup but that didn't help so he played Pink Floyd really loud."

"What happened at Griffith Park?"

"We took her into where it was dark and put her on the ground."

"You and Ax."

"He didn't want to carry her by himself, get her stuff all over him, so he took the feet, I took the hands. She kind of swung." Book stared at Aaron. "He spread her legs, said that makes it look like Ted Bundy. That was bad, huh? Helping him."

"You're doing the right thing right now,

by talking, Mason. What happened to the baby?"

"Ax drove me home."

Aaron repeated the question.

"The baby was in the truck."

"Ax took it somewhere."

No answer.

"What did Ax do with the baby, Mason?"

"We didn't talk about it."

Now Aaron did grace the fool with an angel's touch. Standing and resting his palms on Book's fragile shoulders. "You're doing great, Mason, but we need to take it all the way. What did Ax do with the baby?"

"Don't know, we don't talk about it."

"To set things straight, Mason, guilt's not enough. You need atonement."

"Guilt and atonement," said Book. "Sounds like a movie."

"A good one, Mason. You could star."

Book's laugh was nasal, eerie. Wriggling free from Aaron's touch, he pincergrasped the front of his own neck, pulling a pale flap of skin forward. "Not a star. Not there yet."

"Not where?"

Book's eyes clamped shut. Still holding on to the neck flesh, he twisted.

Aaron pried the fingers loose. Book's neck remained pallid. Guy's body was so starved, he couldn't even bring blood to the surface.

"Mason, there's another girl. Caitlin."

"Who?" said Book.

"Blond, twenty, worked at Riptide."

Book's brow creased. Twenty seconds of what looked like sincere contemplation.

Head shake.

"Caitlin Frostig," said Aaron. "Rory's girl-friend."

"Rory. He's my P.A."

"Gofers for you."

"Yeah."

"He have your PIN number, too?"

"No, he uses the petty cash."

"For what?"

"Buying what I need."

"That include blow and ice and stuff?"

Book frowned. "He shouldn't be in trouble."

"Why not?"

"He's a good P.A."

"There when you need him."

"Yup."

"Caitlin Frostig was his girlfriend."

No answer.

Aaron said, "Long blond hair, twenty, went to school with Rory—"

Book said, "The hostess."

"You know her."

"Cute," said Book. "I like girls to be blond and tall."

"Ever party with her?"

"She wouldn't want it."

"How do you know?"

"She liked Rory. Rory said they're in love."

"I'm sure you've partied with lots of girls who have boyfriends."

"Yeah," said Book, "but you can tell which ones are going to step out."

"Rory ever talk about Caitlin?"

"Just that."

"Good P.A., huh?"

"His dream is to agent. I said I'd help him when he's ready."

"When will that be?"

"When he finishes school. He wants to finish school."

Aaron sat back down. "Mason, is there anything you want to tell me about Caitlin Frostig?"

"Like what?" The guy was an actor, but Aaron was sure he wasn't performing. Visions of Mr. Dmitri's scowling face filled his head.

"Like anything, Mason."

"We-ell," said Book. "She was like that David Lee Roth song—'California Girls.' But not ripe to party."

"Why not?"

"You can just tell."

"Bet you can, Mason—okay, I need to get you out of here. In case Ax comes back."

"He's at his dad's. I sent him there. Sent everyone away."

"Who's everyone?"

"Rory. Kimora."

"Who's Kimora?"

"She cleans."

Wanting to be alone for his final swan dive.

Aaron said, "I still want you out of here. Let's get some clothes on."

In the huge, slovenly dressing room of a huge, slovenly bedroom topped by a vaulted skylight, Aaron found silk jockey shorts from a Savile Row shop, size 29

Rock & Republic jeans, a black Gucci sweatshirt, thousand-dollar alligator loafers. Book dropped his robe without embarrassment, stood there again, rubber-limbed, as Aaron dressed him. The jeans were too big; Aaron cinched a python-skin belt around the actor's waist.

"Looking sharp, Mason."

Book laughed.

"What's the code to open the gate?"

"Don't know . . . Kimora does it."

"Where can I find it?"

"In the kitchen."

"Show me."

A card next to the kitchen phone listed a series of gate controls and various service numbers. Aaron chose an option that would hold the gate open indefinitely. If anyone asked, he'd claim he found it that way, no trespassing had taken place.

That failed to explain why he'd made his way up the drive, just happened to be there when Book nearly plunged to his death. But this was about murder and he'd saved a life and he figured he was pretty safe.

"Okay, pal, let's boogie."

Book didn't budge. Fool was staring at

the chrome Traulsen from which he'd taken the can of supplement.

Then it came to Aaron: attempted last meal. Book had seen himself as a prisoner. Still couldn't bring himself to go out with a full stomach.

"Want anything before we go, Mason? A snack? Maybe something to drink?"

Book stepped back from the fridge while shaking his head slowly.

"Your angel thinks you should eat something, Mason."

"Uh-uh," said Book. "Not there yet."

"Not *where,* Mason?"

The actor repeated the pincer-grasp of neck-skin. "Too fat."

CHAPTER

42

Talk about the money shot.

Aaron framed it mentally like the prize photo it was, even as he experienced it.

Mason Book shuffling down Swallowsong Lane, arm in arm with an "unnamed companion." Not a paparazzo in sight.

How much could I sell this to the tabs for?

Book stumbled.

"Easy, Mason."

Unnamed *black* companion. No doubt they'd assume he was a bodyguard, maybe with an ominous past.

Aaron could live with that.

◆

Book didn't fuss as Aaron put him in the Opel's passenger seat.

Muttering, "Nice wheels. They driving this in Heaven?" and promptly falling asleep.

Aaron poked him to make sure he wasn't faking, then belted him in. Fishing out the plastic wrist ties, he used three: linking both of Book's hands together, then tying the right loop to the lap belt. No big deal freeing the belt, but in the actor's current mental and physical state, the setup was as good as a steel cage.

Now, where to take him?

Slipping the key into the ignition, Aaron remembered the three missed calls, checked his cell.

A trio of texts from Liana—one text, actually, repeated three times. *relbl source: riptide adlla w dmnts never bk*

Now he knew where he had to take his new pal.

Moe got the call as he and Petra were finishing coffee and eggs at a Denny's near Hollywood Station. Raymond Wohr was stashed in a solitary cell having downed a repast of donuts and Hershey bars and Mountain Dew.

Aaron said, "Working late, Moses. I figured I'd get your machine."

"Busy night."

"It's going to get busier. I've got someone you'll want to meet."

"Who's that?"

Aaron told him.

Moe said, "Did you do something illegal that's going to screw us over?"

"Me? I've been an angel."

Moe and Petra showed up at Aaron's office thirty-five minutes later. Mason Book was still totally out of it, napping peacefully under a down-filled Frette duvet, in the guest room that rarely saw action. The plastic ties remained in place, the right one now circling a stout, brass bedpost.

The actor had snoozed through everything, not even stirring when Aaron slung him over his shoulder and hauled him up the stairs. Book had stayed so inert that Aaron checked his breathing a couple of times. Nice and steady, good strong pulse. The second time Aaron poked him, Book's eyes opened and he smiled like a happy kid and went under again.

Some of that was probably post-adrenaline letdown, but Aaron figured a blood test would reveal all sorts of interesting biochemistry. No doubt some defense attorney would pounce on that and try to invalidate the tape. Now transferred to one of Aaron's computers and copied to a disk locked in Aaron's business safe.

Book had to be kept under wraps until his body fluids turned pristine. Aaron had a medical contact he could rely on—an internist he'd helped through a cancerous divorce. Guy kept offering him free check-ups but Aaron didn't believe in doctors unless you were sick. Or needed them for extracurricular work.

Meanwhile, Book had to stay *here.*

Which is exactly what he told Moe and Petra when they started jawing about taking the actor into custody.

Surprisingly, Moe said, "I see your point. But unless we file on him and lock him up, it looks a whole lot like kidnapping."

"Why? He's my guest," said Aaron. "You had no idea I even had him."

"A guest gets cuffed to the bed?"

"You never saw that."

Neither detective spoke.

Aaron said, "I saved his life, guys. It's only logical he'd be depending on me and that will turn out useful for you."

Petra said, "Hey, bring a girl over and call it a party."

"There you go."

Moe scowled. "A party is what Adella was promised. You believe Book about not knowing she was being set up?"

"I do."

"What about Book's claim of not knowing what happened to the baby?"

"On some level, he knows Ax killed the baby—that's part of the self-loathing. But right now he can't—won't admit it. Which is exactly why he needs to be kept under wraps. Give him time to stew, I work on him, he opens up more."

"Or just the opposite," said Moe. "What if his head clears and he shuts up? Or worse, he goes into some sort of medical crisis."

"I'll have a doctor check him."

Moe pondered. "I don't know . . ."

Aaron said, "You heard that tape. Without me, Book would be strawberry jam at the bottom of a canyon. I just handed you a bonanza."

The detectives exchanged looks.

"What am I missing, guys?"

Moe said, "We've got our own bonanza."

Aaron took in the details of Raymond Wohr's admission to setting up Adella with Zen-serenity. Same for the news of Alicia Eiger's murder, the cell phone trace verifying Wohr's call to Ax Dement three hours prior to the stabbing.

When it was over, he said, "That fits perfectly with my info, guys: Adella knew Ax from Riptide, but not Book. She was Ax's problem because Ax was the baby's daddy. Meaning Book's being straight about just being bait. This is all coming together— eyewitness testimony on Ax for Adella, and logic telling us he's the prime suspect for Alicia."

Petra said, "The way this bastard dispatches women, I'm wondering what else he's done. Book's pretty sure he's at Daddy's ranch right now?"

"You're wondering what else could be dug up there," said Aaron. "Like baby bones."

"The thought occurred to me."

Moe rubbed a massive bicep.

Aaron's arms still throbbed. *Where were you when I needed you, bro?*

He said, "Same old story: Girl gets pregnant from the wrong guy, tries to capitalize, oversteps. In terms of burial site for the baby, that could be. Leo Carrillo, where Ax and Book drove out to get high. Like it was some shrine."

Moe said, "Why a shrine for Book, if he's clean?"

"Don't know—so maybe Book does know more about the baby. Either way, I'd get a K-9 out there."

"Another day at the beach," said Petra. To Moe: "Whether or not Ax is at Daddy's, there's probable cause to go in."

Moe nodded.

Aaron said, "One more thing: What does Wohr say about Caitlin?"

"Seen her once or twice."

"On the level?"

"We think so."

"So Caitlin's a whole other story." *So*

what the hell have I gotten myself into. Good morning, Mr. Dmitri . . .

Petra said, "Not necessarily. Ax could've killed Caitlin just because that's what he does. He didn't need Book so he didn't tell Book about it."

Aaron said, "Not wanting Book to know too much because he's mentally unstable. Yeah, I like that."

Moe said, "For all we know, Ax is biding his time before getting rid of Book. A suicidal, self-starving dope-head? Who's going to be suspicious if he *does* turn into strawberry jam?"

Aaron said, "Guy's feather-light, I could've tossed him myself."

Moe said, "The motive for Caitlin could be a lust thing, or the same as Adella. She knew too much. Because of her relationship with Adella. Or Rory Stoltz flapped his gums and confided in her, she got horrified, threatened to go to the cops. Instead of shielding her, Rory told Book. Or went straight to Ax and warned him."

"Selling out his girlfriend?" said Petra. "Cold."

Aaron said, "I'm certain Rory scores dope for Book so he's clearly not the All-

American kid his mama thinks he is. Little prick wants to parlay his P.A. job into a big-time Industry gig, it pays to prioritize."

Petra said, "Utter corruption, perfect tutorial for the Industry."

Aaron said, "Meaning, Caitlin's bones could be buried on that ranch. All the more reason to go in."

Moe said, "Book's medical condition still bugs me."

"You want him, he's yours. But that means publicity, lawyers, stuff you won't be able to control. Keep him here and I'll get a doctor and someone rock-solid reliable to watch him."

Imagining Liana's face when she learned her new assignment. Female and gorgeous should make the actor feel right at home. Hell, Liana could wear a blond wig. "By the time we get back here, Book'll be gelling his hair and eating steak."

"Get back from where?" said Moe.

"Our little party."

"Our?"

"What can I say, Moses? I'm into plural pronouns." Aaron thought he saw Petra smile. But now she was looking detached and he couldn't read her at all. "Moses,

I'm not asking you for an explicit expression of appreciation. But I did get you pure gold, why would you want to cut me off?"

Now Petra definitely *was* smiling. Moving to hide it behind a slim, white hand.

Moe's eyebrows rose. He said, "What do you think, partner?"

She said, "Doesn't bother me, but you're the primary."

Moe ran a finger inside his shirt collar. Massaged his arm again, as if soothing an ache, and faced Aaron. "Thank you. *Bro.*"

43

The party started at four a.m.

Bring your own Kevlar vest; no RSVP required.

The open layout of the Dement spread dictated a cover-of-darkness soiree. Gray night, rather than black, courtesy of a skimpy frosting of stars and a filmy half-moon.

LAPD Detectives Moses Reed, Petra Connor, and Raul Biro rode in unmarked sedans. Deputy D.A. John Nguyen sat in the back of Petra's car, LAPD Detective (ret.) Aaron Fox accompanied his brother.

Ahead of them, six officers borrowed

from the twelve-person Fugitive Warrant Squad rumbled along in a reconditioned military Humvee, experts in the art of surprise.

Bringing up the rear, fifteen sheriff's deputies, including two lieutenants and a captain. All those khaki uniforms because Malibu was sheriff's turf.

All that khaki brass because now that the deal was set, everyone wanted to rub up against celebrity.

Celebrity had almost screwed the deal, sheriff's honchos arguing for a "comprehensive interdepartmental planning session," "strategic delays," the need to be careful with this "high-profile family."

That translated to a butt-covering snail-trail pushing the raid well past daybreak, initiating entry to the property with a phone call from the gate, offering the Dements or one of their employees a chance to drive down from the ranch and spring the padlock.

John Nguyen said, "Oh, sure, and let's have O.J. supervise the search."

Nguyen's boss made a call and restored logic.

As a face-saving gesture, the sheriff's

captain, a man named Carl Neihrold, got to cut the lock.

That took a while because the bolt was heavy-duty and Neihrold had been desk-jobbing for years, hadn't used cutters since his rookie year doing dope raids.

Several grunts later, the steel gave way and the gate swung open.

"Forward," said the chief fugitive cop, a man named Juan Silva. "Headlights off, five miles per."

Sounding confident, but no one knew what lay ahead.

The entry road was over half a mile of dirt meandering through high grass, the occasional oversized clump of rosemary, thatches of poppies, wind-dwarfed sycamores, drought-loving California oaks.

No sign of guard dogs, no alarm bells.

Fifty yards from the road's upsweep to a broad plateau, Aaron noticed tiny blinking lights in the boughs of a large oak. Short-lived, then gone. As if stars had plunged to earth and died on contact.

Seconds later: more pinpoint strobes, this time from a nondescript clump of sage.

"See that, Moses?"

"What?"

"Infrared cameras—they're all over the place."

Moe radioed Juan Silva. Silva said, "We saw it, were just gonna call you. We're putting on helmets. Tell everyone we could encounter some preparedness. And let's lower it to a crawl—two m.p.h. No action whatsoever until I say okay."

The Hummer came to a stop at the mouth of a broad plateau, leaving just enough room for Moe to inch his Crown Vic in.

Beyond an open wooden arch was empty dirt turned silver-gray.

According to the county assessor, Lem Dement's spread was sixty-three acres but from what Moe could see only three or four of that was flat, the rest a repeating pattern of overlapping hilltops that bled into darkness.

Just left of the entry to the plateau, maybe twenty yards back, was a corral. What used to be a corral—two sides of collapsed fencing shouted *nonfunctional.* So did the absence of horseshit perfume.

Moe lowered his window another

couple of inches. The place smelled of *nothing.*

As the Humvee sat there, Moe's attention shifted to right of the arch—deeper in than the corral.

The nearest structure was a substantial house—the large rectangle that had showed up on Aaron's Google Earth aerial. Farther back sat several smaller outbuildings—shacks or cabins peppering the base of the foothills. Moe counted four but darkness could be concealing others. A field the size of a baseball diamond separated the house from its satellites. Three oaks sprouted haphazardly in the dirt, twisted branches and sere foliage cookie-cutting chunks out of the sky.

No sign of any church, no construction vehicles. But the dirt patch on the aerial map was obvious: off to the far right, thirty or so paces from the main house.

Big stretch of dirt ringed by taut string on wooden stakes.

Preliminary layout for some sort of project, but no groundbreaking.

That said nothing about hand-digs.

As the Hummer continued to idle, Moe wondered about engine noise. But no lights had gone on in the house or the outbuildings.

That could mean anything.

Weird place to raise your family—talk about isolation. And nothing Hollywood about it. Lem Dement had squirreled away a fortune from his alleged faith flick but you'd never know it from his homestead.

The main house was generous enough, but not fancy. Low-slung, log-sided, with a swooping roof hosting a satellite dish that listed sharply and a full-length covered porch furnished with a few folding chairs.

The property had once been a summer camp. This had probably been the administration building/dining hall.

Hundred bottles of beer . . . no short-sheeting tonight.

Several cars were parked in front, but the Hummer blocked them from Moe's view.

Aaron whispered, "Not exactly Hearst Castle. More like your basic shitkicker hunting lodge."

That filled Moe's head with pictures. Heads over mantels. Trophies no decent person would want to look at. He kept silent.

Half a minute passed before Juan Silva

radioed, "We're going to park up by that horse corral, but you guys stay in place." As he spoke, the Humvee rolled to one of the battered fences, came to a halt, switched off its engine.

Now Moe could see the entire front of the house and there, parked dead-center, was a prize: Ahab "Ax" Dement's black Ram truck, a likely source of forensic treasure.

Eight other vehicles were lined up, perfectly parallel to one another. As if precision mattered to someone.

Aaron identified the black X5 as Gemma Dement's ride. The others conformed to the reg info Moe had obtained: Lem Dement's Mercedes coupe with *LEMDEM* plates, the director's Escalade truck tagged *LDTOO,* three baby Benzes that were the designated wheels for son number two/Ax look-alike Japhet, and teens Mary Giles and Paul Miki. Last and quite least, an old Jensen Interceptor on four flat tires, some serious dents highlighted by heavenly glow.

Time chugged along as the fugitive guys sat and planned in their armored vehicle.

Dark windows everywhere, still not a peep. Did the infrareds feed somewhere useless? Was Dement security—whatever that meant—falling down on the job?

Was the entire family peacefully beddy-bye and about to have the worst nightmare of their collective lives?

Juan Silva radioed, "I'm getting out to check."

Moe watched the tall helmeted figure glide silently around to the back of the log house. Silva emerged moments later and got back in the Humvee.

"There's another porch out back and we've got two back doors, nothing serious, crappy locks. I saw kids sleeping in the back, so that's a complication. Any idea who or what's in those cabins out back?"

Moe said, "No."

"Well, I saw three kids in one room with bunks, two more in singles. That leaves two more kids plus the parents, and the house is several rooms deep, so they could be anywhere. We're going to want max manpower to ensure quick control. That means us six leading and the rest of you uniforms as backup. Okay, Captain Neihrold?"

Neihrold said, "Sure."

Silva said, "I know we never found any records of live-in staff, but it's logical there'd be some with a place this big. Maybe they're unregistered, that could be who's in those cabins. At this distance, we'll consider them medium-risk, so you detectives can keep a watch. Should be boring unless someone's got long-range military hardware."

Moe said, "Don't see any missile launchers."

"It's what you don't see that can bite you, Detective."

Aaron mouthed, *Funny guy.*

Silva said, "Use those trees for cover, keep your eyes and your radios open. We're hoping for a smooth one, but once we start popping the tab on this can it could get interesting."

One by one the raid vehicles rolled up to the plateau, parked near the corral, disgorged their occupants.

Another brief, whispered meeting among Silva and Neihrold and Moe.

At four seventeen a.m., Silva gave the thumbs-up and led his squad to the big

house. Helmeted figures fanned out, surrounding the structure. Sheriff's deputies
stood just behind. Moe and Petra and
Raul hustled for the trio of oaks.

John Nguyen remained in Petra's car,
happy to be there, because he hadn't
gone to law school to play G.I. Joe.

Aaron got out of the Crown Vic and
joined his brother behind a tree.

Moe looked at him. Shook his head.

Resignation, not debate.

The go signal.

Simultaneous battering of the front door
and the pair at the rear of the big house.

Splintering wood, shattered glass, the
usual bellowed warnings.

Light on in front.

No reaction from the cabins out back.
Moe's attention—everyone's attention—
shifted to the action.

The first fruits of the raid appeared within
seconds: Ax Dement, ponytailed, bare-
chested, pajama bottoms fastened under
a pendulous gut, was hustled outside by
the two biggest fugitive cops. Cuffed at the
back, head down, eyes barely open, shuffling as the helmets dragged him forward.

Next: brother Japhet, in shorts and a T-shirt marked *Occidental College.* Cuffed and bewildered and tripping several times as sheriff's deputies led him to one of their cruisers.

No longer a look-alike: he'd lost about thirty pounds, shaved his beard, trimmed his hair to a neat, blond brush cut.

Not a bad-looking kid—more Gemma than Lem, thought Aaron. He watched for her to appear. Felt bad for her. Beaten for years, a murderous psychopath for a kid.

What would she say if she saw Aaron tonight?

Flattering himself that she'd care.

Sheriff's deputies brought out three more people—the youngest Dement kids. One broke down and cried and a khaki lifted the child into his arms and kept going.

Next, two teens—Mary Giles in a pink bathrobe. Tall, slim, with long dark hair and her mother's angular good looks. Unrestrained but for hands on both arms. Suddenly she fought to break free.

"Why the fuck are you doing this! Why the fuck are you doing this!"

Screaming loud enough for anyone in the cabins to hear.

No reaction from the cabins. The outbuildings were vacant or they housed illegal alien workers, too terrified to show
their faces. Either way, good. This would
go down easy.

As his sister was led away, two other
deputies appeared with the last Dement
offspring, seventeen-year-old Paul Miki.
Baggy T-shirt, saggy shorts. Surfer-do, zit-
face, gawky as a heron.

Stunned and passive.

But for Ax Dement, stashed in the rear
cage of the Hummer to await interrogation, all the Dement children were hustled
off the property.

Juan Silva came out of the house, spotted Moe, jogged over. "We got some
weed, some weapons—three revolvers,
two rifles. Also a knife collection, all from
Ax's room. That's what was in plain sight,
feel free to search to your heart's content.
Where do you want your suspect going?"

"Keep him here for the time being," said
Moe. "What about the parents?"

"Master bedroom was empty, bed
made. I asked the daughter where they
were, but she got obscene. Do they have
another residence?"

"Not that we've found," said Moe. "They used to live in the Hollywood Hills, but someone's renting the place."

Silva's eyes wandered. Bored, now that his job was done. "Maybe they went on vacation." Eyeing the Humvee. "Okay to transfer Porky to your vehicle?"

Raul Biro said, "Want to use mine? It's got a cage."

Moe said, "Sounds good . . . guess we'd better clear those." Pointing to the cabins. "After that I'm calling in the coroner's guys and a couple of K-9s."

Silva said, "Sounds like a plan."

Removing his helmet, he ran a hand over short black hair. All confidence and poise, another mission accomplished.

That changed seconds later, when gunshots cracked the night.

44

Three firecracker snaps.

Seconds of dead air.

Three more shots.

By the time Juan Silva, the three Homicide D's, and four other fugitive cops assumed new positions closer to the cabins, lights had gone on in two front windows of the centermost outbuilding.

Everyone thinking the same thing: *Weird. Why advertise?*

Nothing but yellow light could be seen behind lace curtains.

Snick snick snick, as pistols and rifles put the windows in their sights.

Aaron Fox hung back a few feet. Close enough to see and hear, but well away from anyone's nervous trigger finger.

The target was slope-roofed and log-sided, with a full-length covered porch. Mini-me of the main house.

Silva handed his rifle to one of his squad members, cupped his hands. *"Police, come out now! Walk backward with your hands on your head now! You are surrounded now! Come out now!"*

Nothing.

Silva repeated the warning, motioned two of his men to circle to the back of the cabin.

Before they got going, a woman's voice said, "I'm safe . . . thank you. Come in. Please."

"You come out, ma'am."

"I . . . can't   move . . . too   scared. Please."

Juan Silva re-conferred with his men. "Go back there and see if you can breach safely. If it's righteous, exit out the front."

Gemma Dement sat on a peach-colored rocking chair next to a molded plastic bed shaped like a race car. She wore a heavy, oversized plaid shirt and pink sweatpants. The bed sported realistic-looking plastic tires, headlights, bumpers. The automotive theme extended to a thick wildly colored comforter printed with Ferraris and Lamborghinis and other shovel-nosed monsters. Matching throw pillows, lots of them. From the height and bulk of the comforter, additional bedding below.

Lots of cold nights in the Malibu hills; no sign of heating in the cabin.

Gemma's pale hair was loose, frizzed by the distant ocean. The peach of the chair was good for her complexion. She'd pleaded with Silva, then used smiles and eye-flutters, claiming she'd wet herself, was still too scared to move. No obvious sign of bladder problems on her sweatpants but no one was asking her to budge.

Petra said, "Raul, please get a camera."

Biro left.

Gemma Dement's mouth puckered. "I was so scared," she recited, woodenly. "He tried to hit me. Again."

To her right lay a small, square, chrome handgun, its magazine now in the custody of Moses Reed.

To her left was Lem Dement. Flat on his back, one meaty leg bent, the other straight. A monumental hillock of belly aimed at the ceiling. A gelatinous face grizzled with white stubble dipped past the neckline of his T-shirt.

Dement's mouth had flopped open. A dental appliance—a partial upper bridge—dangled from slack lips. His hands were thick, hirsute, outstretched. The left palm was pierced by a ruby-fringed hole.

The shirt was a *Saul to Paul* souvenir, once white, now pretty much scarlet. The blood deepened in hue when viewed on the absorbent brown velour of Dement's white-piped sweatpants. The director's blue-veined feet remained encased in black suede slippers with little gold wolves on the toes.

Two feet from Dement's head sat a gray hat, grubby, battered, studded with bass lures.

Aaron thought: *No water in sight, who's he been trying to kid?*

For no particular reason, he began counting bulletholes.

In addition to the defensive wound in Dement's hand, he spotted two in the right upper thigh, two in the torso, one of which looked like a nice clean heart-shot.

Messy one in the groin. All kinds of leakage pooling on the pine-plank floor.

Three shell casings in plain sight, the others had probably rolled under furniture or were embedded in the wall—oh yeah, there was one behind the bed, five feet above the comforter.

Six shots, six hits.

No scorch or powder rings around any of the wounds that Aaron could see, but too much blood to be sure.

Gemma Dement said, "I'm starting to breathe again." She demonstrated.

A muffled sound came from under the race-car comforter. Movement jostled a Ferrari. Fabric rolled.

Gemma snapped, "Quiet, you!"

Petra and Juan Silva took hold of her arms, stood her up, guided her away from the bed.

Moe Reed lifted the covers. A child—a boy—a toddler—button-nosed, chubby-cheeked, ruddy-bronze with black hair, huddled on a urine-soaked sheet, teeth chattering.

He wore blue p.j.'s with built-in feet. Diapers bulked the rear flap. To Moe's eye, he looked to be two or so.

Gemma Dement's eyes said the child was shit on satin.

Aaron thought: She's been with him longer than his mother ever was and hates him. Feeling his gut tighten, he stepped forward so Gemma could see him.

She mouthed *Oh,* but didn't utter the word. Softened her features. Mechanically—weirdly—she smiled.

Aaron said, "Guilt and atonement."

Expecting some sort of explosive reaction.

Gemma Dement winked. Nothing sexual. Sly and all-knowing. Smug.

Enjoying a private joke that Aaron didn't want to understand.

He watched Moe pick up the little boy. The kid clung to Moe like one of those orphaned monkeys at the zoo who'll love anything warm.

His brother looked uncomfortable with the contact and Aaron suppressed a smile. Smiling right now, all this blood and death and misery, would brand him as an asshole.

As if something had passed from the

boy's body through Moe's, Moe suddenly cradled the kid tenderly, tousled his hair. "Gabriel?"

Gemma Dement laughed.

Petra said, "Something funny, ma'am?"

"He's not *Gab*-riel, he's *Adra*-el." Another wink—comical and all the creepier for that.

"Adrael who, ma'am?"

"Oh, please," said Gemma Dement, as if the question was beyond absurd. "Study your scriptures. Study your *Jew* scriptures because *those* people *know*."

The boy burrowed his face deeper, not minding the roughness of the Kevlar.

He's been with her longer than his mother but he knows . . .

Gemma Dement's shoulders stiffened as Petra and the fugitive cop tightened their grip.

Moe said, "Mrs. Dement—"

"I've got nothing to worry about. But *you* do." Cocking her head at the child. "You're touching him and he's a messenger of trouble."

The kid couldn't see her, but maybe he'd sensed the contempt; he began to whimper, tiny frame bouncing against Moe's massive chest.

Moe patted his back. "It's okay, little buddy. Get her out of here."

Petra and the fugitive cop eased Gemma toward the door. Gemma didn't resist, but she strained to keep her eyes fixed on the tiny body.

No interest in the other body. Blood spreading, slowly, steadily. Cops having to shift their position to keep out of the expanding pool.

Aaron thought: *Obsessed with the kid. It's all about the kid . . .*

The boy began crying.

"Silence, you!" Sparkling white teeth didn't prettify Gemma Dement's snarl.

Suddenly she fought to break free, was held fast. Spit flew. Some of it landed on the fugitive cop's vest. He remained impassive.

The boy was sobbing, gulping air, and Moe was comforting him.

As Gemma Dement was dragged through the door, she said, "Curse you, Adrael."

Not screaming. Chanting—in*cant*ing. In

a flat, detached, crazily *rhythmic* voice that mocked music.

As metallic as the gun on the floor.

"Curse *be* you, curse *be* you, curse *be* you, Ad*r*ael. *Blessed* damned *blessed* damned *angel* of *death.*"

CHAPTER

45

Good news, bad news.

Which way the joke went depended on your perspective.

Good news for Gemma Dement and bad news for the D.A.'s office was her having the money to hire Maureen Wolkowicz, arguably the most effective, ruthless, amoral defense attorney west of the Mississippi.

Wolkowicz lost no time sealing her client's trap shut, bringing in a score of hired-gun shrinks, and holding a well-attended press conference during which she announced that the death of Lem

Dement had resulted from "the clearest case of self-defense in the face of chronic, brutal, repeated domestic violence I've ever seen."

What that had to do with the murder of Adella Villareal and the abduction—and the year and a half of emotional abuse of baby Gabriel Villareal—Wolkowicz didn't say.

John Nguyen vowed to work the baby angle. If he didn't get dumped from the case.

For four days he'd been waiting to hear if his boss would take over. That would mean Nguyen still doing all the work, the boss singing the courtroom arias and garnering the glory.

John was a far better prosecutor than the boss, an elected blowhard who, according to courtroom wags, couldn't convict a fart out of a bean dinner.

It was all about the odds.

Likely conviction, it's mine.

Another O.J./Robert Blake/Phil Spector, it's yours.

Bad news for Gemma Dement and good news for public safety was that, unbeknownst to her or to Maureen Wolkowicz,

Ahab "Ax" Dement despised his mother beyond her wildest imagination—hated both of his parents, really—and was ready to spill his guts even before the no-death-penalty deal was inked.

Surprising fellow, Ax. Despite the greasy hair, the blunt face, the matted beard—the image of backwoods vulgarian that he'd calculated for years—the eldest Dement spawn was an intelligent, articulate young man who'd earned honors in English and chemistry at Harvard-Westlake and spent a year at Stanford as a foreign relations major before dropping out to pursue a music career that never took off.

"In place of fame, he settled for the side effects," said Aaron, watching through the glass as Moe and John Nguyen and Ax and Ax's lawyer, an aptly named sharpie named Charles Toothy, danced around fine points of law.

Dr. Alex Delaware nodded. The psychologist was here at Moe's request, to offer his impression of the accused double murderer. Delaware had also agreed to evaluate Gabriel Villareal and to oversee the child's psychosocial progress after he left for Arizona to live with his maternal grandparents. He'd just arrived from a visit at Western Pediatric Hospital where Gabriel was under observation. Answered Aaron's inquiry with, "As well as can be expected."

Aaron returned his attention to the interview.

Charles Toothy, wearing a bad suit but a good shirt and tie, said, "Then it's agreed."

"If," said John Nguyen.

"If will be *when,"* said Toothy. "To keep things crisp and accurate, rather than go over the details orally and possibly miss something, my client has prepared a written statement and would like to read it for the record."

Removing papers from his briefcase. The statement was a well-rehearsed collaboration between client and mouthpiece.

Moe said, "He can read what he wants, but he also needs to answer any questions we have."

"Any questions," said Toothy, "that I don't object to."

Nguyen said, "If you object too much, no deal."

Toothy stroked his Hermès tie. "I'm sure there'll be no problem."

"Remains to be seen."

Ax Dement cleared his throat. "May I please start? I'd like to get this over with."

My name is Ahab Petrarch Dement. I'm known by my friends as Ax. I'm a musician, specifically a rock guitarist and electric bassist. My primary residence is at 20 Solar Canyon, Malibu, California 90265.

Approximately three years ago, I became acquainted with a woman named Adella Villareal, through a mutual acquaintance named Raymond Wohr. Mr. Wohr was employed as a bartender and, apparently, Ms. Villareal had worked as a cocktail waitress at a poker club in Gardena, California. I say apparently because I do not have firsthand knowledge of those facts and rely upon the report of Raymond Wohr.

I met Mr. Wohr through my interest in illicit drugs, specifically methamphetamine, cocaine, marijuana, hashish, and prescription tranquilizers, all of which Mr. Wohr sold at various times. I believe I first met Mr. Wohr outside a club called Bang Hole, in East Hollywood, a now defunct place of business. But I am not certain of that, as much of my memory of that time period has been erased by drug abuse.

At some point, Mr. Wohr informed me that he also had access to professional prostitutes and would be happy to set up dates between myself and professional prostitutes. I was not an habitual user of prostitutes but I did occasionally indulge in their services and I agreed.

Subsequently, Mr. Wohr did introduce me to several prostitutes, including a woman he was living with named Alicia Eiger. I cannot recall the exact number of dates with her or with any other women arranged by Mr. Wohr but there were several. Well into my relationship with Mr. Wohr, he informed me that he now had "higher-quality goods" but that such goods would "cost a shit-load more." I expressed interest and a few days later, Mr. Wohr introduced me to Adella Villareal, who was noticeably younger, more attractive, and, according to Mr. Wohr, "major-league fresh."

Over an approximate one-month period, I participated in three dates with Ms. Villareal and found myself extremely attracted to her. For that reason, rather than limit my contacts with her to her apartment, where one date took place, or to the Millennium Biltmore Hotel in Los Angeles, where the other two dates took place, on her birthday, I met her at a bar on

Ocean Avenue in Santa Monica that I'd frequented in the past. The name of that establishment is Riptide.

During her second visit to Riptide, Ms. Villareal, officially my date, met and became interested in another man. That individual was my father, Lemuel Dement, a film director. This surprised and chagrined me greatly because of my attraction to Ms. Villareal. However, since the man who supplanted me was my father, I found myself confused and unsure of how to respond. Lemuel Dement, taking advantage of my confusion, offered me ten thousand dollars to "feel better" about the situation, with the contingency that I'd harbor no ill will to him or to Adella Villareal and simply "go with the flow."

I accepted the money, though my inner emotions were not at peace with this arrangement. Sometimes, in fact, I felt as if I was going crazy. My drug use increased.

Adding to my discomfort was that shortly after beginning a relationship with Lem Dement, Adella Villareal became pregnant with his child. Neither Ms. Villareal nor Lem Dement seemed unhappy with that turn of events. In fact, both seemed quite pleased and my father, especially when he was intoxicated, began dropping hints of "life change," which I took to mean that he planned on leaving my mother, Gemma Dement, and marrying Adella Villareal.

This caused me considerable emotional pain and plunged me deeper into a morass of violent and aggressive thoughts. My use of illicit drugs increased further, as did my patronage of professional prostitutes. Often those activities were combined and both Raymond Wohr and Alicia Eiger were participants.

Approximately twenty-four months ago, Adella Villareal gave birth to a baby boy that she and Lem Dement named Gabriel. I am of the opinion that it was Lem Dement who actually chose the name because, while intoxicated, he confided to me that the child was "my little angel—looks like an angel, acts like an angel, he deserves an angel name." I took that to mean that Lem Dement was contrasting the baby's sweet disposition to my personality and to my behavior, neither of which could be considered angelic. I was emotionally injured by the comparison, and angry.

Despite Lem Dement's talk about a new life, he did not leave my mother and marry Ms. Villareal. However, he did send Ms. Villareal money for child support in the sum of three thousand dollars a month. Those payments were made in cash and Lem Dement offered me a thousand dollars a month to deliver the cash to Adella Villareal at various restaurants and bars in the Hollywood area. In restrospect, I believe this to have been motivated by cruelty on my father's part, but when someone is in the middle of something they sometimes cannot understand the full implication of what is happening to them. At that point in my life I was severely depressed, angry, confused, and otherwise rootless and I was willing to do anything to earn my father's approval. Plus, the money my father paid me was useful in purchasing illicit drugs, which I was using regularly.

I made four deliveries of three thousand dollars to Adella Villareal, all of which she accepted without comment. When I brought the fifth delivery to Ms Villareal, her demeanor was different. On that occasion, she expressed frustration with the inadequacy of the payment as well as with my father who, apparently, had stopped returning her calls. I say apparently because once Ms. Villareal supplanted me with my father, my father and I never talked about the details of his relationship with Ms. Villareal, only that she was "hot in bed." On the night that I delivered the fifth payment, Ms. Villareal threatened to "go public" with the fact that Lem Dement was the father of her child and to "bust open that hypocritical Bible-spouting cult you call a family." Those may not be exact quotes, but they are close.

I did not respond to Ms. Villareal's tirade, nor did I report it to my father. I did, however, report it to my mother, Gemma Dement, a woman with a history of mental illness and alcohol abuse, possibly due to domestic violence abuse heaped on her by my father throughout the course of their marriage. My mother has also reported being allegedly abused by several men she knew prior to marrying my father. I say allegedly because my knowledge of those events is limited to what my mother has told me while she is intoxicated.

My mother reacted calmly to my informing her of Adella Villareal's threats. I was surprised, even shocked, at how calm she was. She told me that she was aware of the situation, had been for months, and had been "figuring out what to do about it. Now I know."

The next day my mother met me for lunch at The Mesa Rock Café in Agoura Hills, California, and laid out her plan. I was to abduct Adella Villareal as well as her baby and bring them to our family home in Solar Canyon, Malibu. The timing of the abduction was to be during a period when my father was traveling on business. I was to "do whatever it takes" to get Ms. Villareal and her baby under "total control" including violence, physical restraint, "even damn tranquilizer darts if you need them." Once Ms. Villareal was in my mother's custody, she was to be bound and deprived of food, water, and sleep and subjected to what my mother called "reeducation," until she agreed to give up custody of her baby to my mother and to leave our family alone. My mother would offer Ms. Villareal ten thousand dollars "for her trouble" once she moved to a state other than California.

I expressed to my mother my opinion that ten thousand dollars would not be sufficient.

My mother smiled and said, "Well, then she's dug her own grave." I took that to mean that Ms. Villareal's death was not something that would displease my mother. I was motivated to make my mother happy, something I hadn't done in years. Additionally, my mother offered me the sum of fifty thousand dollars to carry out her plan, as well as my own house in the state of Oregon, a state where I have long expressed an interest in living because I love nature and wish to get away from urban living.

It was under those circumstances that I followed my mother's instructions, using Raymond Wohr to set up a fictitious date between Ms. Villareal and a celebrity individual whose identity would attract Ms. Villareal. The celebrity I chose was Mr. Mason Book, the well-known actor, because Mr. Book rents a house from my father, a situation brought about through my association with Mr. Book for several years.

Mr. Book had no prior knowledge of my plan, nor did he engage in any criminal activity. Nor had he any prior contact with Adella Villareal.

I met Adella Villareal in a rented room at the Hyatt Hotel on Sunset Boulevard, in Hollywood, and informed her that while Mason Book had changed his mind, my father wanted to see her tonight because he'd decided to leave my mother and marry her. My instructions were to bring Ms. Villareal to be with my father at the family residence in Solar Canyon, a place Ms. Villareal had expressed interest in visiting but had never seen. I lied and told Ms. Villareal that my mother and my siblings were away on vacation and that she'd be alone with my father. I also instructed her to bring her baby, because my father was going to proclaim the baby as his legitimate son and would have a lawyer present to sign papers.

Ms. Villareal was initially suspicious and taken aback by my presence. However, since I'd previously played a role in bringing her monthly cash payments from my father, she eventually believed me and accompanied me to my truck.

I drove Ms. Villareal and her baby to Malibu but instead of heading to Solar Canyon, I continued several miles north to Leo Carrillo State Beach, a place I'd enjoyed going as a child and as a teenager, walking alone among the trees when I was depressed, or hiding out among the trees while I used illicit drugs. My intention was to physically subdue Ms. Villareal before she met my mother, so that my mother would be able to assume the total control she requested. Because of that, I came prepared with a .38-caliber pistol and plastic handcuffs purchased over the Internet from a company called Submission.net.

I stopped the truck just outside the gates to the Leo Carrillo State Beach parking lot, a relatively open spot that seemed safe for what I was going to do because I believed this was going to be a brief process.

It was not.

Ms. Villareal grew extremely angry at my attempt to get her to leave the truck and walk with me to a dark, secluded spot. My intention at that point was to get her alone so I could cuff her hands. When she resisted, I showed her my gun. I was surprised at her lack of concern for my gun and at her attempting to attack me physically.

It was that surprise that led me to panic and hit her in the back of her head with the gun and, then, to put my hands around her neck. My intention in doing so was only to subdue her but somehow I strangled her and she stopped breathing.

Once I saw what I had done, I panicked and put her back in my truck and drove her far from Malibu, to Griffith Park. I chose Griffith Park because it, too, represented a pleasant memory from my childhood, from when my parents and my siblings would take trips to the zoo and to the carousel and to the Gene Autry Museum where all sorts of entertainment industry and musical memorabilia are displayed.

I left Ms. Villareal's body in the Fern Dell area of Griffith Park and drove the baby back to my mother, who was waiting for me five miles up the road from the family residence. My mother was happy to see me and told me I'd done well. She said she was renaming the baby Adrael, apparently one of the names used by the Angel of Death. I say apparently, because I am not religious and have, in fact, grown to hate religion due to understanding my parents and their use of religion to corrupt themselves and others.

Though my mother describes Adrael as evil and a source of evil, she has cared for his physical needs ever since, including giving him a car-shaped bed outgrown by my youngest brother. However, I am concerned about what she might do to him eventually, and that fact has caused me great anxiety and increased my mental instability and illicit drug use.

For nearly a year and a half, Adella Villareal's death remained unsolved and I believed I'd gotten away with this crime and worked hard at forgetting what I did. Several months later, I was contacted by Raymond Wohr who began by asking why he hadn't heard from me in a while. I replied that I'd been busy. He then said, "Not too busy to take care of Adella and her kid, huh?" At that point I realized I had a problem and I went to my mother. After reviewing the facts, my mother said Mr. Wohr had nothing on me other than the fact that I'd picked up Ms. Villareal at the hotel. My mother went on to say that Ms. Villareal was "just a skank-whore and those types get killed all the time," and that Mr. Wohr was "just a skank-pimp. Try paying him off and if that doesn't work, we'll find a solution."

I arranged to pay Mr. Wohr a lump sum of five thousand dollars in exchange for his silence. I also agreed to resume employing the services of professional prostitutes arranged by Mr. Wohr, most frequently Alicia Eiger, and to pay double for those services.

This arrangement seemed to be working until

three days ago when Raymond Wohr phoned me, saying Alicia Eiger was frustrated at not getting more money from me and was threatening to go public about her suspicions regarding Adella Villareal's murder. Mr. Wohr also said that baby-killing would be seen as a terrible crime. Even though he, personally, couldn't "give a shit about any rugrat."

I told Mr. Wohr that he needed to keep Ms. Eiger calm. He replied that he couldn't, she was "nuts, totally whack," to the point of screaming at him and hitting him in the face, in broad daylight on their street of residence, Taft Avenue.

At that point, I phoned Alicia Eiger and informed her that Raymond Wohr had told me of her frustration and that I wanted to make everything good. As such, I'd be coming by with another two thousand dollars in cash. She said two wasn't enough, she wanted ten. We negotiated and agreed on seven thousand five hundred dollars. I set up an appointment that day to deliver the money, stopping along the way at the Bed Bath & Beyond at the Beverly Center and purchasing a medium-sized kitchen knife I could conceal in a jacket pocket.

I drove to Hollywood and parked several blocks from Alicia Eiger's apartment on Taft. Alicia Eiger welcomed me into her apartment. She looked confident. We made small talk for a while, then she demanded the money. I said sure, reached into my pocket, spun her around and overpowered her and stabbed her repeatedly in the back. I chose the back because I did not want to see her face while I ended her life. Contrary to what others may think, I am not a monster, nor am I a sadist who enjoys seeing people suffer or die.

I am the victim of years of physical and emotional neglect and abuse but I know that I have taken lives and must pay for that. My hope is that I receive the proper care so that my personality flaws mend and I can learn to become a productive member of society.

Sincerely,
Ahab P. Dement

Ax cleared his throat and put the papers down.

Charles Toothy said, "That's pretty comprehensive, can't imagine there'd be too many questions."

Moe said, "When your father returned home, how'd he react to the baby being there?"

Ax said, "I can't answer that from personal observation as I was living elsewhere. What my mother *told* me is that he was shocked. Her exact words were something like 'Daddy just about shit solid gold adobes.' She swears when she's drunk and mostly she's drunk when she calls me."

"She called you to report on your father's return."

"Yes, sir."

"He was shocked."

"He demanded to know how the baby had gotten there. My mother told me she didn't come right out and say but she did imply that we'd never be seeing Adella again and that if my father made a fuss, the entire family could end up in jail. Or worse, in hell."

"And . . ."

"And nothing."

"Your father just went along with it."

"He did."

"He didn't try to beat her up?"

"That was before," said Ax. "Before she got a gun. The last time he beat her up, my mother bought a gun and it stopped."

"He'd stopped beating her completely."

"Yes, sir."

"For how long?"

"Hmm . . . maybe a year. But . . ."

"But what?"

"She squeezes her own arm, sir. To bring up bruises. I don't know why, it's just something she does."

"I see," said Moe.

"I *don't* see," said Ax. "Maybe where you'll send me, I'll get some insight."

"How about giving me some insight about Caitlin Frostig."

"Who?"

Moe repeated the name.

Ax Dement said, "Nope, never heard of her. Wish I did."

"Why?"

"I want to change. Being helpful is part of that."

On a beautiful sunny Monday, Moe Reed and Aaron Fox drove north on Pacific Coast Highway. Aaron was at the wheel of his Porsche. Both brothers wore sunglasses and short-sleeved shirts, Aaron's a three-hundred-dollar white Malo, Moe's a navy no-name polo.

At first glance, they were a pair of good-looking young men, out for a day of fun.

The Porsche had a tiny, barely functional backseat if they needed it.

They parked in the visitors' lot of Pepperdine University, presented a warrant to the administration office, went to find Rory Stoltz.

Confronting the boy as he left a business management seminar, they escorted him away from his classmates onto the vast, perfectly green meadow of lawn that separated the campus from PCH.

Rory's blond hair was gelled and side-parted neatly, not spiked, the way he wore it when working for Mason Book. His shirt was an impeccable pale green button-down, perfectly pressed by his mother. Same for straight-leg khakis.

Tall, lean, tan. Aaron thought: Ralph Lauren ad in the flesh.

Except for the face, which was ready to crumble. "You can't—"

"We just did," said Moe.

Rory's face turned stupid-stoic, an obstinate kid digging himself deeper. He began picking at blades of grass.

"Here's what we know," said Moe. "You do regular dope pickups for Mason Book and Ax Dement."

Well-groomed fingers crushed grass, turned green at the tips. The kid had a *manicure,* for God's sake.

Not as good as mine, thought Aaron.

Moe said, "You've also been observed faking a dope pickup."

The kid hung his head. His hands fluttered.

Moe said, "Not only do you pimp drugs for Book and Ax, but you rip them off when they ask for prescription dope. You put together your own stash at a discount price beforehand and quote them a higher price. They give you money and send you to score, you drive around for a while, do nothing, come back and hand over the goods, telling them you had to work hard to find it, and pocket the profit. Sometimes Mason Book tips you extra for your effort."

Aaron said, "Those kinds of smarts, who needs a class in business management? How long did you think you could keep that up without someone finding out?"

"We found out really easily," said Moe. "You were *observed.* And guess what, we just tossed your bedroom and found all that Xanax and Ritalin and Valium you've been stockpiling. We're figuring you buy wholesale from your fellow students."

Rory shook his head.

"College is going to love you for setting

off a big-time scandal. Forget your degree, we've got enough to put you away for years."

The boy looked up.

"Years," Moe repeated.

"I never bought, people gave me extra and I saved it."

"Don't insult our intelligence, Rory."

Silence.

"The thing is," Moe went on, "we might not care about any of this."

"Huh—pardon?"

"Your buddy Ax has been arrested for murder. He's desperate to save his own skin, can't talk fast enough. Meaning any-one even remotely associated with him is going to get sucked into some serious ugly. We're assuming you don't want to be one of those people."

"Murder? I—I—didn't . . ."

Moe placed his hand on Rory's shoul-der, felt the boy's muscles shrink in fear.

Useful move, it was going to become part of his repertoire.

"Rory, you need to tell us about Caitlin. Now. Even if you killed her. 'Cause we'll find out and make it even worse for you."

"Kill her—no, no way I—" Gaping. "No, I never did that. I swear, no, never—"

The inevitable tears.

"Then what happened to her, Rory?"

More head shakes.

"Save your own ass, Rory." Moe smiled. "Who knows? Maybe one day you *will* be a big-time agent." To Aaron: "He could do it, right?"

Aaron said, "He's already got the moral qualifications."

Rory's tan had splotched with pink. Blue eyes were filmed by shock and salt water. "Oh, God . . ."

Moe bore down. "What happened to Caitlin, Rory?"

A beat. Two.

Three. "I promised."

"Now you're breaking your promise."

Rory looked past—through them—at the highway. Blue infinity.

All that pretty paint and chrome speeding to pretty places. The ocean a soft teal blanket, ruffled by an unseen hand.

"You can't quote me," he said.

Entitled little prick.

Moe said, "We can do anything we damn

well please. Speak before I throw your ass in jail."

"Okay, okay," said Rory. "But you need to understand: I did my best. No matter what you say."

The Convent of Santa Barbara is a one-hundred-fifty-year-old masterpiece of Baroque and Moorish revival, weathered brick walls adorned with arches and pillars, central courtyards jeweled by voluptuous gardens. Long designated a national landmark, the convent is central-casting-perfect for the role of Sacred Refuge.

The Sisters of Gethsemane Convent is a tract home on Santa Barbara's east side, set on an undistinguished, poorly paved street in one of the city's vulnerable working-class neighborhoods.

Just another stucco bungalow, hastily nailed up to accommodate returning World War II veterans.

The seven nuns who live at Gethsemane are immigrants from Central America and when they are not tending to sick children or Alzheimer's patients or homeless people, they answer to a Superior General in El Salvador who ignores them. The oldest nun, Sister Lourdes Echevarria, has lived half of her eighty-five years at the convent.

The tiny lot upon which the bungalow sits is one of many parcels of real estate amassed by the Catholic Church; its value has appreciated many times over since purchase in 1938. Six months ago, the bishop of Santa Barbara, ensconced in a lovely mansion in a more fashionable section of town, served an eviction order to the nuns. The house was to be sold to help pay a nearly billion-dollar settlement to victims of sexual predator priests. The order would be broken up, the nuns "redistributed" at the archdiocese's discretion.

Among themselves, the nuns discussed the injustice of having to give up their home to atone for the grievous sins of the priests. Publicly, they clung to their vows of obedience and awaited their fate.

Many of them cried when certain no one was listening.

Someone listened. Took the initiative to call a reporter at the *Santa Barbara News-Press.*

The resulting front-page story fomented local, then statewide outrage against the archdiocese. Evictions plans were halted, though on a temporary basis.

The Sisters of Gethsemane continue their good works and try not to think about the future.

The nuns wear white blouses and dark skirts and white flat shoes or sneakers. The three oldest cover their hair with blue kerchiefs. The bungalow is barely fourteen hundred square feet, partitioned into tiny rooms. The nuns own nothing and seven of them manage to sleep comfortably in bunk beds in two bedrooms.

A third bedroom at the rear is maintained for guests the nuns call "sojourners."

For sixteen months, a young woman with clipped dark hair, a soft voice, and willing hands has been the sojourner of residence. She calls herself Catherine and the nuns have never questioned whether or not that is her real name.

Catherine knocked on the door of the convent and asked if she could stay a few days. She insisted on pitching in with household chores, doing more than her share—doing the work of three, by Sister Lourdes's estimate. Days stretched to weeks, which stretched to months. Catherine asked if she could help outside the house as well, and she began accompanying Sister Maria-Guadalupe and Sister Maria-Anastasia as they made the rounds of a board-and-care home for severely retarded adults.

Catherine loves cleaning and feeding and singing to the patients. She changes their diapers without complaint.

The nuns love Catherine. All of them suspect it is she who phoned the reporter. The topic is never brought up because suspicion, accusation, and recrimination have no place in their world.

Of late, Catherine has put aside her young-person jeans and tops and has worn the white blouse and dark skirt favored by the nuns.

Alone in her bedroom, after a long day,

she sometimes looks out the window at the vegetable garden that takes up most of the convent's backyard, marvels at tomatoes, eggplant, artichokes, grapevines. Cries.

Mostly, she is at peace.

Aaron and Moe watched her take out the garbage. Wheeling the third of two plastic bins to the curb, then stopping to look up at the sky.

Different hair, same face.

Not wanting to frighten her, they approached smiling.

She said, "You're here."

Not a blink of surprise.

They'd warned Rory not to broadcast their arrival. The kid had defied them.

Gold stars for loyalty. Love.

Doing "the right thing," again.

Moe introduced himself and Caitlin pretended to listen. He was willing to bet Rory's call had included their names and a detailed physical description.

Despite that, she hadn't rabbited.

"Pleased to meet you, Detective Reed." Turning to Aaron.

He said, "Aaron Fox, Caitlin."

"Pleased to meet you, as well, Mr. Fox."

Pretty girl, clear-eyed, apple-cheeked. Same age as Rory, but she seemed more . . . adult.

Moe said, "We're not here to cause you problems. We know what your father did to you." The plural pronoun came easy.

"That's in the past," said Caitlin Frostig.

"It is, but it's still a crime."

"I know, Detective Reed."

"If you want to press charges—"

"I don't."

"You're sure of that."

"I am, Detective Reed. I've thought about it a lot and I don't."

"We respect that, Caitlin. And we know how hard it would be. But what if your coming forward prevents the same thing from happening to another girl?"

"He'd never do that," said Caitlin.

"How can you be sure?"

"Because I know." Grazing one of the trash cans with her fingers. She studied the sky some more. Took in the cracked stucco front of the bungalow. Tomato plants trimmed the front of the little house,

used as ornamental shrubs. Cherry tomatoes. Caitlin Frostig walked away and Moe
was sure he'd lost her.

Picking a handful of tomatoes, she
returned to the brothers. "Hungry?"

Moe quelled reflexive denial, took the
four little red orbs she was offering.
Popped one in his mouth. "Delicious."

"Mr. Fox?"

"Thank you . . . really tasty, Caitlin."

She said, "In terms of other girls, what
happened between my father and myself
was what psychologists call a situation-
specific dynamic. My mother died when I
was young. My father had no one and I
became a substitute. I'm not saying it was
right. But it won't happen to anyone else."

Pronounced   with   clarity.   Clinical
detachment. Either she'd dealt with it and
was ready to move on. Or the healing
hadn't even begun.

Moe said, "I'm so sorry for what you
went through."

"Thank you . . . will it be necessary to
tell him where I am?"

"Not if you don't want him to know."

"I don't."

"Then our lips are sealed."

"Thank you so much." Moving forward as if to kiss Moe's cheek, she stopped herself. "Would you like more tomatoes? They've grown like crazy, I'll get you a bag, take some for the road."

Nice way to say please leave.

Moe said, "We'd like that."

48

During the ride back to L.A. the brothers ate tomatoes and listened to music and didn't talk much.

Well before the transition to the 405 South, Moe said, "If you don't mind, stay on the 101 and take Laurel."

Aaron said, "Making a detour to Swallowsong?"

"Drop me at Liz's. She lives on Fuller near Melrose."

"No prob."

Midway down the canyon: "Moses, we did okay."

"It worked out."

"This was beyond whodunit," said Aaron.

Moe said, "Way beyond . . . Mom called yesterday night. I assume she called you, too."

"Oh, yeah."

Moe allowed himself a smile. "Kosher sausages are so yesterday. Welcome to organic, grass-fed bison. Ever have that?"

"Nope. She bought half an animal."

"Buffalo Mom."

Aaron said, "An eight-thousand-dollar barbecue grill. You *believe* that?"

Moe thought: *Actually, sounds like something you'd like. Oh, yeah, you never cook.* "Can you see her wearing one of those aprons, breathing in all that smoke?"

Aaron laughed. "Not easily . . . I thought I'd go. Make her feel good."

Moe said, "No sense not going."

"See you there, then."

"Yeah."

Aaron glanced at his brother. Moe was back to his serious self.

He could live with that. The two of them existed in a seismic world. Too much movement could crack the surface.

At Sunset, Moe said, "I appreciate it. Going out of your way and dropping me off."

"Who says it's out of my way?"

"It's not?"

"Who knows?" said Aaron, smiling. "Another big-time whodunit."

"Either way, thanks," said Moe. "Bro."

Moments later, Aaron watched as a beautiful black woman came out of her condo and greeted his brother with the warmest smile he'd ever seen. Cries of delight, big hug, a lingering kiss that would have embarrassed Moe if Aaron had stuck around to see all of it.

49

The air was warm but Aaron put up the top on the Porsche for the climb back up Laurel.

Wanting quiet as he phoned Merry Ginzburg and told her what she needed to know about Mason Book.

Parceling out appetizers, what amounted to a picayune scandal. The red meat, she *didn't* need to know.

With Ax Dement maintaining his loyalty, Book's name would never appear on any court papers. Wouldn't be associated in any way with drug use, suicide, the murder of the woman he'd helped lure to her death.

Aaron had spent some time with Book, was convinced Book really had been an unwitting dupe. Was certain the hourly fee for babysitting the actor wasn't influencing his opinion.

Liana agreed. Book didn't impress her. The man in *her* life was some number-crunching Ph.D. Aaron would have to check out.

Even the little he gave Merry was enough to rejuvenate her career. Maybe put some big bucks in Aaron's pocket if he played it right.

She said, "So I was right. He starves himself."

"Almost died, Mer."

"Thank you, Denzel."

"Don't I always come through?"

Sigh. "You do."

"Let's have dinner."

"A pity meal?" she said. "That's sweet, but no thanks."

"A good meal," said Aaron. "No business."

"That's impossible, my dear. For both of us."

"You never know."

"True," said Merry. "Older I get, the less I *get.*"

Mr. Dmitri said, "How much do I owe you?"

"I have to add it up."

Dmitri returned to his Russian newspaper. The factory was buzzing. On the way to the boss's office, Aaron had made sure to pass Maitland Frostig's cubicle. Frostig was away from his station.

Dmitri looked up, as if surprised Aaron was still there. "Thank you, Mr. Fox. I will call you when the next problem arises."

"I'm looking forward to it, sir." Aaron sat there.

Dmitri put the paper down. "What, Mr. Fox?"

"Sir, this may be presumptuous, but I'm getting the feeling that what I learned about Caitlin doesn't surprise you."

Dmitri smiled.

"I also noticed that Mr. Frostig wasn't at his desk."

"Probably in the bathroom," said Dmitri. "Tomorrow there will be another explanation for his absence."

"Sir—"

Dmitri laughed. "I am not Russian Mafia, Mr. Fox. Maitland's work product has been poor. He will be terminated." Chuckle. "His position at the *company* will be terminated. What happens to him is no longer any concern of mine. Did I ever tell you what my wife does?"

"She's a psychiatrist."

"Regina is excellent psychiatrist. In Moscow she was head of hospital that specializes in sexual deviancy. Before they imprisoned her for not poisoning dissidents. She is woman of great insight."

"I see."

Dmitri fingered his mega-Rubik's. "I see numbers, she sees people. I am proud of her."

"You should be."

Dmitri's eyes twinkled. "I'm thinking, Mr. Fox, I should be proud of you, too."

ABOUT THE AUTHOR

JONATHAN KELLERMAN is one of the world's most popular authors. He has brought his expertise as a clinical psychologist to thirty bestselling crime novels, including the Alex Delaware series, *The Butcher's Theater, Billy Straight, The Conspiracy Club,* and *Twisted.* With his wife, the novelist Faye Kellerman, he co-authored the bestsellers *Double Homicide* and *Capital Crimes.* He is the author of numerous essays, short stories, scientific articles, two children's books, and three volumes of psychology, including *Savage Spawn: Reflections on Violent Children,* as well as the lavishly illustrated *With Strings Attached: The Art and Beauty of Vintage Guitars.* He has won the Goldwyn, Edgar, and

Anthony awards, and has been nominated for a Shamus Award. Jonathan and Faye Kellerman live in California and New Mexico. Their four children include the novelist Jesse Kellerman.

www.jonathankellerman.com